By Todd McCaffrey
Published by Ballantine Books

DRAGONSBLOOD

DRAGONHEART

DRAGONGIRL

By Anne McCaffrey and Todd McCaffrey

DRAGON'S KIN

DRAGON'S FIRE

DRAGON HARPER

DRAGON'S TIME

SKY DRAGONS

SKY DRAGONS

SKY DRAGONS

ANNE McCAFFREY

and

TODD McCAFFREY

BALLANTINE BOOKS • NEW YORK

Copyright © 2012 by Anne McCaffrey and Todd McCaffrey

Published in the United States by Del Rey,
an imprint of The Random House Publishing Group,
a division of Random House, Inc., New York.

DEL REY is a registered trademark and
the Del Rey colophon is a trademark of Random House, Inc.

Library of Congress Cataloging-in-Publication Data
McCaffrey, Anne.
Sky dragons / Anne McCaffrey and Todd McCaffrey.
p. cm.
ISBN 978-0-345-50091-5 (alk. paper)—ISBN 978-0-345-53350-0 (eBook)
I. McCaffrey, Todd. II. Title.
PS3563.A255S58 2012
813'.54—dc23   2012010070

Printed in the United States of America on acid-free paper

www.delreybooks.com

2 4 6 8 9 7 5 3 1

First Edition

For Janis Ian

ACKNOWLEDGMENTS

Usually, I insist upon putting the acknowledgments at the end of the book. My thinking is that, like the credits of a film, they belong at the end—they're like taking a bow at the end of a play or other performance, where those who have made it all possible are singled out and honored.

Sadly, the circumstances of this book are not "usual."

To some of you—and I'm so sorry!—this news will come as a shock. After we had finished this book but before it was copyedited, my mother, Anne McCaffrey, passed away. She was eighty-five, she died "in the arms of a handsome man" (her son-in-law, Geoffrey), she died at home, quickly.

So, firstly, let me acknowledge Anne McCaffrey for her brilliant work as author, mother, cook, equestrian, friend to famous singers, astronauts, and everyone in between.

Speaking on her behalf as well as my own, I would also like to thank our editor at Del Rey, Shelly Shapiro, for all her brilliant efforts over too many decades to count, in keeping the Dragonriders of Pern® alive. She followed gamely in the footsteps of Betty Ballantine and Judy-Lynn Del Rey and never stopped challenging us to create the best possible books we could.

Additionally, Martha Trachtenberg has followed up with the copyediting for too many years to count—keeping our numbers accurate, asking great questions, offering brilliant suggestions.

I'd also like to thank Judith Welsh of Transworld Publishers—our U.K. publisher—for all her support in this and all the other books we've published together.

Diana Tyler, Mum's literary agent, was a bastion of support

through this very difficult time, as was my agent, Donald Maass. Thank you both.

Anne McCaffrey's long years and peaceful passing would not have been possible without the loving care and support of her daughter—my sister—Georgeanne "Gigi" Kennedy. She's been a brick throughout everything and continues so, even now.

And, again speaking on Mum's behalf, we would like to thank you all, for journeying with us to that amazing place that is Pern.

CONTENTS

▸ BOOK ONE ◂

Sky Weyr

ONE
▼▼▼▼▼▼▼▼▼▼▼▼

A Dark Dream
in Blue

This was not how it happened.

For one, the two moons were not in the sky: Belior and Timor had set long ago and it was early morning. But here, now, in her dream, the moons bathed the plain with their eerie light and awkward double shadows.

In her dream she could see under the ground. She could see tunnels and hives, teeming with life as the six-legged, slithering tunnel snakes dug their way to their prize—the dragon eggs nestled on the surface in sand-filled beds that were not nearly as safe as their guardians had believed. The dragon eggs that were the hope of Pern.

She wanted to shout, to scream a warning, but she was ghostlike, standing horrified sentinel over her sleeping form.

Above in the night sky, the Red Star pulsed malignantly far beyond the two pale moons. When the Red Star drew closer, Thread would fall.

Thread. Voracious, all-consuming. A touch of it burnt through flesh and clothing, even tough dragon-hide. It could drain a lush valley of all life in a day. Unchecked, it would consume all life on Pern. It drowned in water, froze on ice—and perished by flaming dragon's breath.

Without the dragons these eggs held, there would be too few dragons left to protect the world from Thread.

Even in her dream, Xhinna felt her blue dragon, Tazith, stir and try to follow her feelings. She turned to where he lay sprawled nearby and smiled. She was the first woman to ride blue in all memory, and as she looked at him, her heart swelled with love and pride.

Brown dragons and bronzes always chose male riders, just as the gold queen dragons chose female riders. According to Tradition, the blues and greens were also ridden only by males. But times had changed.

A sickness had risen, a sickness that killed dragons. They had fallen by the hundreds even as the first Fall of Thread in the new Third Pass required dragons to fly and flame to save Pern. It was only through the genius of Lorana that a cure had been found, created in an unprecedented cross-time collaboration with the original colonists. The price of Lorana's success had been her own queen dragon.

When a dragon died . . . "It is like having your soul ripped apart." The thought was so terrible that Xhinna whimpered. She turned in surprise to see her sleeping self whimper and then—

She was awake, shivering.

"Are you okay?" Taria asked sleepily. "You were having a nightmare."

"I'm okay," Xhinna said.

Taria wrapped her arms around her and pulled her close. "You're freezing."

"Just a bad dream."

In the morning the eggs were gone. Their shattered remains had been dumped in the sea, empty. Only twenty-three of the two hundred and fifty-three eggs had hatched; the rest had been ruptured, their contents devoured by tunnel snakes burrowing up from the ground.

This never would have happened in the high rocky Weyrs where the dragons usually lived, but here, on the uncharted plains of the Eastern Isle, the ground was too soft, the way too easy, and the tunnel snakes were too greedy.

The sun warmed her as she scanned the now-empty plain, but Xhinna shivered as she saw once again, in her memory, cluster after cluster of lifeless, dead eggs, their vitals destroyed by the voracious tunnel snakes. She remembered the desperate fight, the cries, the screams of agony, and the few—very, very few—triumphs in this one-sided disaster.

She turned as a baby dragonet gave a plaintive cry that was instantly answered by a consoling voice. Qinth, the only green to hatch, had been severely mauled by the tunnel snakes before it was freed by Jeriz—J'riz, now that he'd Impressed the grievously wounded dragon.

"It's okay, shh, little one, you'll do fine!" blond-haired Bekka said soothingly to both dragon and rider. She was small and young for a healer, but she made up for lack of stature and age with a fierce determination and a stubborn resolve never to lose a ward. Her mother was a midwife; her father had been a dragonrider, until the dragon sickness had taken his blue Serth.

If they were here, now, because of Lorana, then it was J'riz's father, Tenniz, who had set her on the way. Tenniz was one of the rare traders born with the gift of the Sight—the strange gift that gave glimpses of the future. With his Sight, Tenniz had recognized Lorana, had helped set her on the path that had led her and all the other Turns into the past and to the eastern of the two Great Isles—low-lying masses that had remained untouched by humans for hundreds of Turns.

J'riz did not have the gift of the Sight—that had gone to his younger sister, Jirana. Ten Turns was unusually young for Sight to manifest, but this adult responsibility did not prevent Jirana from being an extremely outgoing and passionate child. Xhinna loved both of them like a big sister, and the terrible plight of J'riz's green dragonet, Qinth, tore at her heart.

Despite Bekka's cheerful manner, Xhinna could think of no other dragon so horribly injured that had survived. She feared that J'riz might be a dragonrider for less than a sevenday.

If only the tunnel snakes had not attacked! Why had Tenniz, with his Sight, sent Lorana and the others here if not to find a way to repopulate the Weyrs of Pern?

Instead—now—Xhinna found herself wandering around a too-large camp wondering when and how she and the others would return to the present Third Pass and back to the losing battle against Thread.

"We haven't got enough food," Taria said to Xhinna later that morning, raising her voice to be heard over the creeling weyrlings.

"We'll send a party to round up some of the herdbeasts," Xhinna said. The assault of the tunnel snakes and the rampage by the Mrreows had broken the fencing around the camp's herdbeasts and those that hadn't been killed had run off.

"Who?" Taria asked, looking around. It took Xhinna a moment for the significance of the question to sink through—of all the dragons in the camp, only her Tazith and Taria's Coranth were old enough to fly.

"We should have kept more people behind for guard," Xhinna muttered to herself. She knew that Weyrleader T'mar had planned to send a group back to them as soon as the dragonriders had settled once more in Telgar Weyr. No one had expected the strange knot that had sprung up *between*, trapping both the returning Eastern Weyr dragonriders and the lost, presumed dead, dragonriders led by the old Weyrleader, D'gan.

The knot had been broken, but only after Weyrwoman Fiona had jumped off her queen, Talenth, into the nothingness of *between* in order to send Talenth back to Lorana. It had been Lorana who had figured out how to break the jam and free the trapped dragonriders—old and new—but in the ensuing events, no one had thought to reinforce those who remained behind with Xhinna.

She shrugged. "I guess it's up to you and me."

"If we had J'per or J'keran—" Taria began hopefully.

"We don't," Xhinna cut her off in irritation. J'per and J'keran were experienced brown riders who'd gone back with Fiona and Lorana to Telgar Weyr in the present Turn. Xhinna frowned as she realized that after living for three Turns on the Eastern Island, they had nearly caught up to the present time. "So we do what's needed." She managed a smile for her friend. "As always."

Taria heaved an aggrieved sigh, but said nothing else, instead turning toward her green.

"At least Tazith and Coranth are small enough that we can get low to the ground," Xhinna said, making a herding gesture with one arm.

"K'dan," Xhinna called before mounting her blue, "we're going to see about finding some food."

The harper nodded, seeming at a loss for words as he looked around the camp. Xhinna guessed at the worries in his mind, saw the way he pulled little Tiona and Kimar toward him while at the same time consoling his bronze Lurenth.

It took them the better part of an hour to round up a measly half-dozen herdbeasts. They had scarcely got them back into the half-repaired corral before K'dan and R'ney started the butchering necessary to feed the ravenous weyrlings. A line formed of anxious riders, eagerly looking for anything to carry back to their dragonets.

As soon as there was a free moment, Xhinna approached K'dan. "We're going to need you to take charge of the weyrlings."

"Weyrlingmaster, dragonrider, father, harper," K'dan said with a grin. "I think I'm being underworked."

Xhinna smiled at the first expression of humor the older man had shown all day.

"I could take a skiff out fishing," Colfet offered. The white-haired seaman had wandered the camp in the aftermath of the tunnel snake and Mrreow attack, offering what help he could where he could. He knew nothing of dragons and less of weyrlings, but he was an inveterate scrounger and he had the knack for organizing that Xhinna adored in anyone. His age alone was a source of comfort to the many younger, disconcerted new dragonriders—so many of them had just recently been orphaned, and all of them, save for J'riz and K'dan, had until the previous day never even imagined being at a Hatching, let alone Impressing a dragon.

Xhinna felt bad for all the others who had been here the day before—hundreds, for they needed at least as many Candidates as there were dragon eggs waiting to hatch. So many had come, eager for the chance to Impress a dragon, expecting to see the largest hatching on Pern—only to be so tragically disappointed.

Fiona had been right to insist that they be returned to their homes immediately. If it hadn't been for the Weyrwoman's foresight, the camp would have had more hungry, confused faces in it at the moment.

Not that Xhinna wouldn't have welcomed at least a few extra faces, Fiona's first amongst all of them.

As the problems of setting up a camp and recovering from the disaster of the day before settled upon Xhinna's shoulders, she had only greater respect for the heavy burdens that Fiona had borne uncomplainingly, despite being thrust so young into the role of Weyrwoman.

Somehow, lunch was arranged, and the camp's pavilion was restored to its position of prominence. It would have to be moved, though—the very next day, Xhinna swore. The beached ships that for three Turns had served as onshore homes had seemed such a good idea, but now they seemed ominous and foreboding—traps for people, and targets for both ravenous tunnel snakes and Mrreows.

"We need to get out of here," Xhinna said in a quiet conversation with Taria and K'dan over lunch. She made a face as she glanced around the too-large camp. "This place is too exposed. The tunnel snakes will come back, as will the Mrreows."

"The weyrlings can't fly for a month," K'dan reminded her.

Xhinna sighed. "Couldn't we have Tazith and Coranth carry them?"

Taria gave her a skeptical look, but K'dan nodded, a grin spreading across his face. His smile faded almost as quickly as it had appeared. "And when the others come back? How will they find us?"

"And we're not going to be so few when they return," Taria added. "So we'll want to find a place large enough for us all and close to food."

Xhinna mulled their words over, then said, "We could go back to the rocky promontory. I can't imagine Fiona sending more than a wing."

A wing, roughly thirty dragons, would be more than enough support for the young weyrlings. The rocky promontory was the place where the draognriders had first come when they'd arrived at Eastern Isle. But it had proved too confined for all the dragons and so they'd moved to their present location on the plains. Now, the promontory's isolated location would provide a safeguard against tunnel snakes and Mrreows both.

It was hard for Xhinna, after living three Turns back in time on this Eastern Isle, to imagine the huge, lofty, rocky Weyrs where dragons usually lived. She could easily picture a wing of dragons, even a Flight—three wings organized into a group large enough to handle a single Fall of Thread—but the full Weyr with its bustling weyrfolk, dragonets, halls, kitchen, and incessant activity seemed a distant, near-dreaming memory.

Life at what they'd come to call Eastern Weyr had been more demanding on the dragons and riders than was normal. Not only had the dragons of Eastern Weyr needed to train and learn to fight Thread, but they'd also been needed to hunt for food, build lodgings, find firewood, and do all the myriad other things that the weyrfolk did at a regular Weyr. There wasn't a dragon or rider at Eastern Weyr who didn't have a deep and abiding respect for ordinary weyrfolk.

"I imagine you're right," K'dan said. "Although it'll be T'mar who does the choosing."

Weyrleader T'mar had the responsibility for the disposition of dragons and their riders while Weyrwoman Fiona dealt with the day-to-day operations of the Weyr and its weyrfolk.

"We'll have to leave Qinth behind," Bekka said as Xhinna came back for her last journey to bring the weyrlings to the rocky promontory. She'd chosen that location as their new camp—the same one that had been rejected as being too small and too exposed when they'd first settled on the Eastern Isle. With just the two grown dragons and twenty-three weyrlings, it seemed spacious. "She's too fragile yet to move."

Xhinna swore; she should have thought of that. Bekka smiled at her, shaking her head. "You're doing fine. K'dan, Colfet, and I will stay with her and J'riz. We'll see how she's doing in the morning. Then we can see about rigging a wagon or something to move her."

"She'll still be here in the morning?" Xhinna asked, pitching her voice for Bekka's ears alone.

"We'll do our best," the young healer told her earnestly.

The night on the promontory was colder than Xhinna had feared. She, Taria, and R'ney kept watch in rotation. Xhinna jumped at every untoward sound. When the sun finally broke through the cloud layer at dawn, her eyes had dark circles under them from fatigue.

"I'm going to check on the others," she said as soon as she was certain that Taria was awake. She jumped up on Tazith, and in a moment she was fighting off the bracing cold of *between*—and then, just as quickly, she emerged in the air over their old camp.

The fire had gone out. There was no sign of K'dan, J'riz, Bekka, and Colfet. They were gone.

Desperation mounting, she had Tazith fly in a widening circle. She checked every one of their old ship-dwellings; Tazith called for Pinorth, for Lurenth, for Qinth, but got no response. Xhinna directed Tazith to fly out to the sea, where she searched for a sail but found none. Finally, in response to Coranth's increasingly nervous queries, she returned to the cold stone promontory.

K'dan had insisted that she take the twins with her and now, as she burst out over the small camp, she saw the two of them looking up, scanning the skies wildly, and her heart sank.

What do I tell them? she asked herself forlornly. What do I say to Fiona?

She thought of her friend, of her incandescent cheer, and decided that she'd do what Fiona would do in the same situation—she'd lie for all she was worth.

"Your father has gone on," Xhinna told Tiona when she asked. "He said that you'll get to stay with us for a while until he's ready."

"Okay," Tiona said easily enough. The little toddler was very much her mother's daughter: Fiona would likely have said the same, and just as easily.

Even though he had his mother's blond hair and sea-green eyes, in temperament Kimar was more like his father. The toddler was quiet, preferring to watch and absorb. As he grew older he had begun to spend more time caring for his twin, keeping her from the worst of her own excesses. Tiona accepted this as just another part of the world she lived in, neither fighting nor accepting too much her brother's restraining behaviors. Both were just coming up to the third Turn of their young lives. Because they had grown up in the constant company of adults, they were more mature than their age suggested, seeming more a steady three or a young four.

Kimar gave Xhinna a probing look, then turned to Tiona and hit her, hard.

"Kimar!" Taria exclaimed. "Why did you do that?"

Kimar shrugged just as Tiona went for his hair. Before another blow could be exchanged, Xhinna grabbed him and pulled him away from his furious sister, who had begun to growl in near-perfect imitation of a Mrreow.

No, it *was* a Mrreow. The tawny long-furred thing came charging straight for Tiona only to find itself blocked by Taria's swinging leg and pummeled by the fist of her free hand.

R'ney came charging in with a poker from the fire, and the Mrreow, deprived of easy prey, veered off and loped away.

As Xhinna's breathing returned to normal and she saw that no one was harmed, she wondered why it was that the normally peaceful Kimar had chosen exactly that moment to hit his sister. Had he somehow known of or sensed the Mrreow's impending assault? Certainly, if the toddlers hadn't been so firmly in adult arms, one—or even both—of them would have fallen to the Mrreow's claws or fangs.

"We're getting out of here," Xhinna announced. She turned to R'ney. "Organize the weyrlings, get the dragonets in the center of a circle with their riders facing out. Build up the fire, start plenty of pokers heating up."

The ex-smithcrafter nodded and turned back to the other weyrlings who'd only now had time to realize their peril.

"Taria, can you and Coranth fly guard?" Xhinna asked.

"Yes," Taria said instantly, handing Tiona to Xhinna and turning toward her dragon. Then she paused to call over her shoulder, "What about you?"

"I'm going to take these two—" Xhinna jounced the toddlers in her arms. "—and scout us a new home."

Taria waved and was aloft on Coranth before Xhinna had reached Tazith.

Can you carry us all? Xhinna asked, as she hoisted first Tiona and then Kimar up onto the blue's neck. She couldn't have managed that if Tazith had even been a small brown, but the blue was of a size that, on tiptoe and with a bounce, she could just reach his neck.

Certainly, Tazith replied and again Xhinna marveled at just how right his voice was to her, how perfect his blue hide was, how marvelous his whirling eyes were, how steady he made her feel. She might be a girl, but she was built to ride Tazith just as he had been born to carry her. Deftly she tied the twins one in front of the other on the narrowest part of Tazith's neck.

The blue lifted them effortlessly and, at Xhinna's direction, started south toward the end of the western half of the great island. The twins, lulled by the steady beat of Tazith's wings, were soon asleep, leaving Xhinna to scan for likely places without distraction.

She found nothing worthy of note. She hadn't expected to: Lorana and Kindan—before he'd Impressed and become K'dan—had scoured the whole island.

She came to the great sea-filled rift that separated the two islands—Eastern Isle and Western Isle. Why had Fiona warned them to stay away from the western one? Was that strange note that had been found mysteriously at Eastern Weyr because Fiona somehow knew that they would need to use the Western Isle now?

How had she known? Xhinna wondered. Clearly it was a Fiona from a different time and that could only mean from the future because if it had come from Fiona in the past she would have known and told them. Had that future come? Was Fiona on the western island already?

Coranth is worried about us, Tazith relayed.

We're coming back, Xhinna said. She shook the two toddlers back out of their drowsiness long enough to tell them that they would be going *between* back to the camp so that they wouldn't wake, terrified, in the cold darknes that was *between*. Kimar nodded sleepily and closed his eyes once more; Tiona perked up and took several deep breaths in anticipation.

"Can we do that again?" she asked when they'd returned from *between* and spiraled down to the camp.

"We'll see," Xhinna temporized, her eyes on the distant horizon. She had Tazith check his Turn as she peered into the distance. Something was falling, streaming down—

"Thread!"

TWO
▼▼▼▼▼▼▼▼▼▼▼▼

Flight to the Past

Taria looked up as she heard Xhinna's shout.

"Thread?" R'ney repeated in surprise.

"We've got to get out of here," Xhinna said, as she came running toward them. Two dragons alone with no firestone were no match for a Fall of Thread, which was normally met by no less than ninety well-trained fighting dragons.

"Where?" Taria asked.

"Are you sure it's Thread?" R'ney asked.

"Sure enough that we've got to leave."

"Very well," R'ney said, glancing nervously around the small camp. "I trust you to be right, blue rider."

"Where?" Taria repeated.

"When," Xhinna corrected her with a shake of her head. "How many hatchlings can Coranth carry?"

"Two or three."

"Make it two—can you carry the riders, as well?"

"Yes," Taria said. Turning to R'ney, she added, "Can you help us rig the slings again?"

Tazith carried three dragonets and their riders, Coranth two. They were airborne before Xhinna had an answer to the question of *where*.

Tazith, go here, she said, picturing a night sky over the channel between the Eastern and Western Isles. She examined the image carefully to be certain that it was three Turns in the past, carefully placing the stars to their positions back in time.

I can go there, Tazith told her, and in an instant, they were *between*. Five coughs later, a blue and a green hovered, motionless, over the Big Channel.

There, Xhinna said, directing Tazith toward a spot on the Western Isle midway up the length of the channel. The Eastern Isle had proved unusable; at least there was a chance that the Western Isle was more viable. *Land there.*

They unloaded their passengers and returned *between* for the next load.

On their fourth journey, they had only three hatchlings to carry back—which was just as well, as both Xhinna and Taria were bone-weary, though both dragons insisted they still had energy to spare.

After settling his Rowerth into the sling carried by Tazith, R'ney handed Tiona and Kimar up to Xhinna and then climbed on himself. The sound of Thread hissing could be heard nearby. A Mrreow suddenly burst from the undergrowth, driven by fear, and charged toward them.

Now! Xhinna cried to her blue. Tazith strained to get airborne. Behind them, she heard Taria cry out and Coranth bellow in pain. And then they were airborne and *between*.

Coranth bellowed again when they broke out in the starlit sky above the Big Channel.

Tazith landed first, and Xhinna wasted no time in directing the unloading. Coranth landed with another pained cry just behind them, and Xhinna raced to the green's side.

"A Mrreow got her!" Taria cried, tears streaming down her face.

The Mrreow had managed to dig its claws into one of Coranth's hind legs just after she'd jumped into the air. The cuts were deep and long.

Xhinna looked around for an aid kit, but realized that they'd had no time to organize their supplies.

"Get a blanket," she snapped to the person nearest her. "We'll use it to bind her wounds."

It was the best they could do. With Coranth's wounds bound up, the green's keening ceased and she fell into an uneasy sleep. Xhinna fought hard against the fatigue of so many quick jumps *between* time.

"I'll take watch," R'ney offered. "You rest—you look as green as Coranth."

Xhinna didn't have the energy to argue, merely nodding and trudging over to the twins. She lay down beside them and let their comforting presence warm her. A moment later, Taria joined them. Xhinna pulled Taria's head against her shoulder, and soon they were all asleep.

Xhinna woke at dawn to the sound of the twins giggling. She opened her eyes blearily, and then jumped bolt upright.

"You were supposed to wake me!" she called to R'ney. The brown rider had bags under his eyes, but he was busily making faces for the amusement of the twins.

"We're hungry," Tiona said, looking up at Xhinna. Xhinna noted that the toddler used "we" when she wanted to emphasize something, as if adding her brother would lend weight to her point.

"There's food in the trees, probably," R'ney said, casting his gaze over the taller trees that grew up beyond the lower brush. "I think I recognize that one from Eastern."

"You were supposed to be resting," Xhinna snapped irritably. She glanced down. Taria was still fast asleep. She debated waking her, but decided against it. Tazith was sleeping with Coranth, curled around her protectively. The green seemed comfortable; waking her rider might wake her.

Xhinna made her decision, telling R'ney, "You stay here, I'll scout."

R'ney nodded, turning back to the twins and starting to lead them on a circuit around their makeshift camp. With a smile for his skillful handling of the children, she started off toward the distant treeline.

The brush was not much different than back on the Eastern Isle, Xhinna noted as she walked through it, her eyes scanning for signs of tunnel snakes or Mrreows. She saw what might have been a tunnel snake hole, but it could also have been the dwelling of any one of Pern's other subterranean beasts. Still, she gave it a wide berth; they had too few supplies and fit riders for her to risk injury.

Xhinna grinned when she spotted a grove of the large-leafed trees that bore the hard nutfruit. It took some ingenuity for her to climb high enough to reach the large nuts and deft work with her belt knife to cut them down, but after a few minutes, she had two ready to bring back to the camp.

"Nutfruit!" cried Taria, who had been woken by the giggling of the twins, as she spotted Xhinna returning. "Where did you find them?"

Xhinna pointed, and soon a large party set out to fetch more. The leafy outer covering of the nutfruit could be hacked away to reveal a hard-shelled nut. Inside, there was a thin, milky-white liquid—it could be drunk alone, but it was better when infused with mint or some of the other edible leaves they'd found on the Great Isle. The white flesh could be scraped off and eaten. It had a taste all its own.

"This isn't a good place to stay," R'ney remarked quietly to her when his next circuit brought him close by.

Xhinna nodded. "When everyone's fed, we'll start scouting."

"We?" R'ney asked, glancing pointedly at Coranth.

"We," Xhinna repeated, indicating the whole group. "We need meat for the hatchlings. We'll have to send out a hunting party and a fishing party, while I scout for a better camp."

R'ney nodded, but then his eyes cut toward Coranth. "And when we have to move?"

Xhinna sighed and shook her head. "I don't know. Coranth will need more than a month to heal." She pursed her lips. "Maybe Tazith can help her into the air."

"Maybe," R'ney said dubiously. "But you'd have to carry all the others."

"Tazith is strong for his size," Xhinna declared staunchly. She couldn't help but turn toward the sturdy blue, who craned his neck up and lowered his head to peer at her, his multifaceted eyes whirling green with pride and confidence in his rider.

In that moment, with her dragon gazing at her with such adoration, Xhinna realized that everyone in the camp was looking to her. She was responsible for all six of the newest queens on Pern, more precious than anything, and fifteen bronzes who were just as valuable. And Fiona's children. As well as R'ney's brown Rowerth and J'riz's ailing green Qinth—along with K'dan and all the others who had so mysteriously disappeared. The weight of their loss bore heavily on her. And now, because of Coranth's injury, she was also responsible for Taria's green.

Xhinna straightened her shoulders as she nodded to R'ney. She thought she understood now how Fiona had felt when she'd gone to Igen Weyr. The weight of responsibility seemed both to crush her and buoy her up. She could not fail.

"We're three Turns back in time," she said. "We're safe from Thread. We can find a camp, find food, settle in, and let these weyrlings grow until help comes." She nodded firmly toward R'ney. "And, if need be, we can survive until we return with all our dragons fully grown and ready to fight Thread."

To keep the twins out of mischief, Xhinna brought them with her when she went scouting. Once aloft, she set a course northward along the coastline. She wanted to find something like a Weyr, a safe rocky place up high where neither Mrreows nor tunnel snakes could threaten them. She searched in vain for over an hour. Tiona had fallen asleep only to be pinched awake by her brother and was now presently bawling quietly to herself. Xhinna tried to ignore both children as she strained to scan the land below.

"Those trees are funny," Tiona said suddenly, pointing. "They're upside down."

"Broom trees," Xhinna said, following an imaginary line from Tiona's finger to its distant target. Silently, she asked Tazith to change direction. The blue complied with alacrity, spinning on a wing tip in a maneuver that still thrilled Xhinna and drew excited shrieks from the twins. "They grow larger at the top, like they were an upside-down broom."

"There are more branches at the top than the bottom," Tiona agreed.

"You could almost sleep in them," Kimar said in awe as they drew nearer to the trees.

"I've never seen them so close together," Xhinna said.

"Could Tazith sleep there?" Tiona wondered. "It looks itchy."

"Let's see," Xhinna said, the beginnings of a mad plan forming in her mind. She urged Tazith closer and the four of them inspected the forest. The broom trees, growing in a ring near the top of one of the taller hills in the area, were so close together that they formed a near-level canopy tens of meters above the forest floor.

How about it, Tazith? Xhinna asked her blue. In response, Tazith descended and lightly touched down on one of the sturdier trees.

"Xhinna," Kimar asked, "could we live here?"

"Let's see," Xhinna said, throwing one leg over Tazith's neck and carefully climbing down. She had a moment's fright as her foot almost slipped off the first branch, but soon, as she learned to choose her position carefully, she found herself at relative ease traversing the dense tops of the broom trees.

The leaves were thick and prickly, but not so much that they hurt. She heard a noise above her and saw Tiona scampering down Tazith's side.

"Careful!" Xhinna called, reaching out to guide the girl's foot onto a thicker cluster of leaves. Kimar followed after, and only on Xhinna's invitation.

"This is nice," Tiona said, as she spread herself out over a thicker cluster of leaves, then, "Ouch!" as one of the pricklers stuck her cheek.

"Careful," Kimar said in an imitation of Xhinna's voice. Tiona gave him an irritated look, but Kimar ignored her, asking Xhinna, "Can we climb down?"

"Let's see," Xhinna said, looking for a way through the thick leaves. It was Tiona who found it, quickly bored with pretending to sleep and idly examining the canopy for an opening. In an instant she was through, calling, "Race you to the bottom!"

"Tiona!" Xhinna called. "Come back here this instant!"

The toddler's head popped up through the canopy, her sea-green eyes wary.

"What would I tell your mother if something happened to you?"

"I'll be fine," Tiona said.

"I'd like to see you a bit older before you break your first bone," Xhinna told her.

"What's a bone?" Kimar asked.

Xhinna touched his forearm and, pressing down lightly, traced the bone. "That is a bone."

"They break?" Tiona asked, surprised at the notion and idly tracing the line of the forearm she was using to hold on to the top of the canopy.

"They do, indeed, break," Xhinna assured her gravely. "And they take months to heal."

"Months?" Kimar asked, his blue eyes wide.

"Months," Xhinna repeated. "In a cast, something that keeps the bone still so that you can't move."

"Can't move?" Tiona said, aghast. She examined her arm with more respect and slowly climbed back up to the canopy. "I'll stay here."

"You can follow me, if you're careful," Xhinna said.

"What if *you* break something?" Kimar asked.

"Well, I'd better make sure that doesn't happen."

Pretending to have more confidence than she felt, Xhinna cautiously picked her way through the canopy. Beneath it, she discovered a thick network of branches. It took concentration to negotiate her path through them, and after a while, she found herself at an impasse. With a sigh, she climbed back up toward the canopy, shooing Tiona ahead of her.

Tazith, keep an eye on Kimar, Xhinna thought to her dragon.

Always, the blue dragon replied laconically.

"There's a thin tree here!" Tiona said as they moved upward. "It's got a branch right here!"

Before Xhinna could say anything, she heard a grunt, and the toddler said, "Oh, these branches are *much* easier!"

Xhinna saw Tiona scamper on down beside her and wave from the other tree.

"I can go all the way down," the little girl exclaimed.

"Wait!" Xhinna called. "Let me get over there, too."

"Aw!" But Tiona waited for Xhinna to make her way across. The branch that Tiona had used was pretty thin for the adult dragonrider, but Xhinna managed and soon was among thicker branches. She glanced down and saw that Tiona was right: they could go nearly all the way down to the ground.

With Tiona still in the lead, the two went down to the lowest branch on the tree. Xhinna was relieved to see that there was a good half-dragonlength between it and the ground—high enough that she was certain neither a Mrreow nor a tunnel snake could negotiate the gap—not that Xhinna had ever heard of a tunnel snake climbing aboveground.

"Okay, time to go back up," Xhinna said. Tiona groaned in protest, so Xhinna added teasingly, "Race you to the top!"

Tiona, as Xhinna had planned, won easily and was peering down at Xhinna as she broke through the canopy. Kimar was sitting nearby, cross-legged, staring into the distance.

"I kept watch," he told them. "I think I saw some wherries."

"Wherries!" Xhinna said. They hadn't seen the avians on Eastern Isle. If they could be caught, they'd make good eating, particularly for the growing weyrlings. And their fat could be rendered into oil to soothe patchy dragon skin.

Tazith was stretched out in a circle on a thick part of the canopy. He looked comfortable enough. Xhinna scanned the treetops for other sites that might hold a dragon. She stopped when her count reached thirty—more than enough for the twenty-two of them.

Tazith, love, Xhinna thought softly to her blue, *it's time to go. We need to get back.*

With a tree-shaking yawn and stretch, the blue got carefully back on his feet.

If we could find a place near the edge, I could just glide, he told her.

First, let's get everyone here, then we can look.

▼ ▼ ▼

"You want us to live in the trees?" Taria asked when Xhinna explained her plan to the others.

"It's comfy!" Tiona said.

"And it's nice," Kimar added, then frowned. "Except for the pricklers."

"It's high off the ground, safe from tunnel snakes and Mrreows," Xhinna said. "If it doesn't work out, we can find another place."

"How are we going to get Coranth there?"

"Tazith can lift her and then she can go *between*," Xhinna said. "Up in the trees she'll find it easier to rest her leg— she can stretch it out without bumping into anything."

"What about when it rains?" Taria asked.

"By then we can probably make places for the dragons below the treetops and the leaves above will keep us dry," Xhinna said after a moment's thought. "We'll leave as soon as the hunting parties return."

"What about fire?" Taria asked. "I can't see making one up in the trees."

"No," Xhinna agreed, temporarily stumped. "We can build a fire someplace on the ground. We can abandon it at night if we can't protect it."

Taria grinned at her friend. "It sounds like you've thought of everything, Weyrwoman."

"Weyrwoman?"

"You're making a weyr and you're a woman," Tiona said reasonably. "And you're in charge, like my mother."

Taria smiled at her partner. Xhinna shook her head diffidently.

"It's either that or Weyrlingmaster," Taria warned her.

"No, that's K'dan's job," Xhinna said promptly.

Taria's face drained of color at the mention of K'dan. She moved closer to Xhinna and spoke into her ear, "What about the Thread? Did it get him and the others?"

Xhinna moved back and smiled at her. "I don't think so. In fact, I've an idea where to find them."

"You do?" Taria asked, surprised. "Where?"

"When," Xhinna corrected.

It took most of the day to move the hatchlings and their riders, two at a time, up to what R'ney instantly dubbed, "Sky Weyr."

After a lot of fussing, the new riders settled down with their dragonets who were, as usual, hungry. Leaving Taria to care for Coranth, Xhinna collected R'ney and Jepara.

"We're hunting wherries," she told them.

R'ney insisted on bringing one of the nets they'd used as a make-shift carrier for the hatchlings, while Jepara produced a bow with a half-full quiver.

"I helped K'dan with the hunting," she explained as she mounted Tazith. Xhinna vaguely remembered the younger woman as someone who'd returned from one of their wild Searches for Candidates rather than those who'd stayed in their holds waiting for the summons. She smiled fondly back in the direction of their camp. "Sarurth tells me that she's hungry—I never even expected to Impress—let alone a queen!"

R'ney snorted in agreement as he took a seat behind her.

"I understand completely," Xhinna said, mounting and telling Tazith to fly.

I see wherries, Tazith said in a little while, backwinging to slow down.

"What's your plan?" Jepara asked.

"Why not circle wide, drop us farther on, and have your blue herd them toward us?" R'ney suggested.

"No, toward me," Jepara said. "You stay with Xhinna and throw that net of yours if you think it'll help."

"Better," Xhinna said before R'ney could respond, "we put you in position, Jepara, and when you start shooting, any wherries that fly from your arrows will be caught in R'ney's net."

"So we'll get at least three," Jepara said smugly.

"Three?" R'ney asked.

"Yes," Jepara said, "you'll get one and I'll get two."

R'ney drew a quick breath to retort, but let it out slowly when Xhinna reached back to give his knee a reassuring pat.

"Don't shoot until you're sure of your footing," she warned as they dropped Jepara down among a group of broom trees.

"Of course," Jepara said, waving them off.

"She's going to get herself hurt with that attitude," R'ney said as he shook out the net.

"She might," Xhinna said. "Better now than later, though."

R'ney considered her response for a long moment before saying, "I suppose you're right."

"Taria and I have been handling the young for the better part of four Turns now," Xhinna said. "I hope we've learned a little in that time."

She turned her attention to Jepara, a small figure in the distance.

All right, Tazith, Xhinna said, urging her blue into a breathtaking dive. The dragon added a bellow of his own, and in a moment a flock of startled wherries flew into the air.

Keep it up, Xhinna said, as Tazith darted from side to side to keep the wherries moving in a straight line.

This is fun!

Yes, it is, Xhinna agreed with a broad smile. She patted her blue even as she urged him on and felt the strength of his muscles as he increased his speed, darting from one side to another, always herding the wherries until—

"There!" R'ney called when he spotted the first arrow. It went wide, but one of the wherries saw it and turned in midair. With a whoop, R'ney threw his net, careful to wrap the trailing rope several times around the riding harness while letting it slide through his wher-hide gloves.

"Got it!" he called, as Tazith turned in the air to accommodate the sudden weight of the trapped wherry. R'ney pulled on the slip knot to close the net and then hung on tightly as the wherry tried in vain to fly clear.

Xhinna glanced around urgently. "Where's Jepara?"

"Just get me to the ground and go find her," R'ney said.

Xhinna complied and was airborne again in moments, her eyes searching the broom trees for the young queen rider.

Suddenly Tazith scooped air, turned in one quick move, and stopped abruptly, throwing Xhinna forward on her fighting straps.

"Three!" Jepara cried up at them, holding up three fingers on one hand. "I'm going to need some help, though."

At Xhinna's urging, Tazith found a spot where he could let her alight and she moved carefully over two treetops to join Jepara.

"Well done," Xhinna said as she picked out the forms of three wherry carcasses lying in the nearby trees.

"We'll need the rope to get them out," Jepara told her. She glanced toward the blue dragon. "Where's the smith?"

"R'ney," Xhinna said, emphasizing the honorific contraction, "is dealing with his catch."

"I'll bet he'll be green with envy at my catch," Jepara crowed.

"And, gold rider, if he is, you'll be certain to ease his shame," Xhinna said abruptly.

"That's right," Jepara said. Her look was challenging. "I *am* a queen rider, and that means *you* answer to *me*, doesn't it? So why are we taking orders from you, a mere girl who rides a blue?"

"Because my blue is the only dragon who can fly right now," Xhinna said. "And because it's wise for youngsters to listen to their elders so that they might, one day, become elders themselves."

Jepara's eyes flashed in rebellion for a moment, but Xhinna met them unflinchingly. A moment later, Jepara said, "Sarurth's hungry— we need to get back."

"We'll get back when we've got this straight between us," Xhinna said, not moving.

"My *queen* is hungry, blue rider. Will you let her starve?"

"No," Xhinna said. "Will you?"

Jepara's jaw dropped in amazement.

Xhinna had heard only good things about Pellar and Halla from K'dan and C'tov so she couldn't quite understand why their daughter would be such a wherry-faced brat. But with that thought came the answer: It was *because* her parents had such a reputation. She could do no wrong because *they* could do no wrong. Xhinna guessed that, devoted though they might be, Pellar and Halla had so many duties running Fire Hold—where they mined the precious firestone—that they'd lost track of this child, assuming that she could easily adapt to their unconventional ways.

"Impressing a queen is a great honor," Xhinna said softly. "Impressing any dragon is equally a great honor—" She turned wistfully toward Tazith, assuring him that she would not have any other than him no matter what. "—but with honor comes responsibility."

She saw Jepara flinch.

"So, gold rider of a hungry *queen*," she continued, "what are you going to do? Are you going to learn manners and have your hatchling fed, or are you going to put on airs?"

"I'm sorry," Jepara said, lowering her eyes to the ground. "It's just that—"

"I know."

"How can *you* know?" Jepara shrieked. "You've been in the Weyr your whole life! You know everything about dragons, and you act like you ride a queen yourself."

Xhinna turned back to face her and shook her head. "I was an orphan. When I came to Fort Weyr, the headwoman took a disliking to me because I like girls more than boys. I had to keep quiet, keep out of sight, got the worst jobs, and had no one to —" She found the word hard to say, even now. "—no one to love me, even when I felt like I would die."

Jepara's eyes widened.

"And then I tried to Impress the queen, only she went to Fiona, so I hated her, too," Xhinna said. Her lips turned upward slightly as she added, "Until I got to know her and realized that she accepts me for what I do." Xhinna shook her head and corrected herself: "No, she loves me because she sees something more in me than I can."

"She loves you?"

"Like a sister," Xhinna said. She smiled. "You haven't seen enough of our Weyrwoman; she uses friends like blankets and she gives off love like others give off heat." She paused for a moment, then added, "When she left for Igen Weyr, I thought she was dead. And when she returned, I swore that I'd never lose her again. And now she's back in Telgar; I've lost her, and so have her children."

Her jaw set in grim determination as she swore, "But as long as they have me, Tiona and Kimar will have parents. And if something happens to me, then Taria will care for them. Because that's what we do, as weyrfolk, and particularly as dragonriders—we care for each other. We're all we've got."

She looked at Jepara and smiled. "Now that you're one of us, you're part of that, too," she said softly. Jepara looked up at her with a hint of wistfulness.

"And we take care of each other," Xhinna went on. "Which means we accept praise rather than crow over our success, we give aid when needed, we work to keep all our spirits up."

She paused to let her words sink in, before finishing: "One day, gold rider, you may be a Weyrwoman in your own right, and the whole Weyr will look to you."

"They look to *you* now," Jepara said. "We *all* look to you."

Xhinna nodded, unable to avoid that truth. "When Fiona comes back, she'll be the Weyrwoman, and I'll be happier."

There was a moment of awkward silence, and then Jepara spoke. "We'd better get back to R'ney." Her tone was much lighter than before. "He'll think we're slacking or something."

When they returned to camp, the wherries were hastily—and clumsily—butchered and fed to the twenty ravenous dragonets. In the end, the four wherries were just enough to fill them.

"We're going to need more food," Jepara declared as she tried to rub wherry ichor onto a nearby leaf.

"And something to clean with," Taria agreed. She beckoned for Xhinna to come close to her and whispered, "We need help."

"We'll have to make do with what we have," Xhinna said.

"Until when?"

"At least until we can stockpile enough provisions that Tazith can get a good night's rest," Xhinna said. Taria raised an eyebrow, but Xhinna merely shook her head, saying, "Later."

They spent the rest of the day taking stock and organizing their

"Sky Weyr." Xhinna still hated the name, preferring to call it a camp and having a greater deal of sympathy for Fiona's repugnance at naming the old camp "Eastern Weyr." They managed to find enough fruit to satisfy the twins so they would settle down for an afternoon nap, while Jepara took charge of a scouting party to search the surrounding forest.

In three days, Xhinna, R'ney, Jepara, C'nian, and Hannah had developed themselves into an expert hunting group, bringing home up to six wherries each outing. Taria, not comfortable straying far from Coranth, had volunteered to stay at the camp and watch the twins, but she'd still managed to locate several stands of nutfruit trees, as well as several with the sorts of edible leaves that they'd enjoyed back in Eastern Weyr.

"Tonight, I think," Xhinna said to Taria as the sun set and they started their climb up into the canopy from the fireplace over which they'd roasted their evening meal. F'denol took watch on the lowest branch. After their first cookfire, they'd heard Mrreows and other marauders in the night, and Xhinna wanted to be certain that they weren't surprised by some tree-climbing carnivore.

"Now?" Taria asked. Coranth was healing; they'd found the plants they needed to make a good salve and managed to boil some cloth to replace her blanket-bandages, but the green was still weeks away from complete recovery. If anything happened to Tazith, the camp would not long survive.

"We need help," Xhinna said.

Taria nodded reluctantly and moved closer to Xhinna, hugging her tightly. "You come back."

"I will."

"And not three Turns older," Taria growled as she released her.

"Mind the twins," Xhinna said.

"Always."

Tazith circled the camp once in the growing dark.

Do you know where to go? Xhinna asked, sending her dragon the final image.

Yes, Tazith replied and, with Xhinna's assent, took them *between.*

The cold nothingness that was *between* lasted longer than the usual mere three coughs. They broke out into daylight, circling the old Eastern Weyr. Tazith started a steep descent toward where they'd last seen K'dan and the others.

Xhinna let out a breath she hadn't realized she'd been holding when she saw K'dan and Bekka waving up at her.

"Hurry," she called, "we've got to get out of here!"

"Qinth is too hurt," Bekka said.

"Thread is coming," Xhinna told her. "We haven't time."

"What do you propose?" K'dan asked, looking at the netting rigged under the blue dragon.

"I'll take her first," Xhinna said. "With J'riz and Colfet. I've got the others set up already."

"Where?" Bekka asked.

"When?" K'dan guessed, nodding in satisfaction when he saw Xhinna's look. "Three Turns again?"

"Yes, we're all back in time on the Western Isle," Xhinna told him.

"Fiona said not to go there," K'dan reminded her.

"I think Fiona said it because we *did* go there," Xhinna said. K'dan frowned on that for a moment, then nodded. Xhinna continued, "We must move quickly."

"Where's Coranth?" Bekka asked.

"Injured," Xhinna told her. "She got clawed by a Mrreow when we took the last of the hatchlings." She shook her head sadly as she added, "You weren't here when I came back for you."

"Because you're taking us now," K'dan said with a tone of awe in his voice he normally used when referring to one of Fiona's schemes. Xhinna found that she couldn't speak, only nod.

"Well, let's get moving, then," Bekka said, unhooking the netting and moving it toward the stricken green.

"She's small enough that I think we can lift her," Xhinna told J'riz. "If we're careful, it won't hurt her too much."

Too much was the operative phrase; dragon and rider both moaned with the pain as the green was gently moved into the netting and then tied on to Tazith's harness.

"I should stay here," Colfet said when Xhinna motioned for him to climb up in front of her.

"No time," Xhinna said, shaking her head. "I need you to keep camp."

The old seaman gave her a surprised look and grimly climbed up on the blue. Xhinna mounted and helped J'riz up behind her. He was becoming a young man, but Xhinna still remembered him as the cute boy who'd been such a help and a handful; so she was both pleased and surprised when he slipped his arms around her waist and leaned against her back as Tazith leapt into the air.

Below them, Qinth gave one whimper and was silent.

How is she? Xhinna asked Tazith.

She is very brave, Tazith said with pride and affection for the green dragonet.

Let's go, Xhinna said, imagining their camp.

Their arrival was greeted with cheers and a swift unloading as R'ney and C'nian gently helped Colfet and J'riz unhook the injured hatchling and lower her to her carefully constructed weyr. Xhinna waited just long enough to make sure that everything was right before going back again through time to the Eastern Weyr.

"I can take two," Xhinna said as K'dan helped Bekka guide her Pinorth toward the harness.

"A gold and a bronze?" K'dan asked in surprise.

"That's about all we've got," Xhinna reminded him with a lop-sided grin, Qinth being the only dragonet that *wasn't* gold or bronze. "We've managed that before."

Shrugging, K'dan helped his Lurenth into the harness and then handed Bekka up before climbing up behind her.

"It's been several days since the twins last saw you," Xhinna told him as Tazith gained enough height to go *between*. "I hope you aren't planning on resting anytime soon."

"No, not at all," K'dan said. "Sleep is overrated, really."

THREE
▼▼▼▼▼▼▼▼▼▼▼▼

A Leap to Screams

"It's only temporary," Xhinna said as she explained the camp layout to Colfet and K'dan the next morning. Bekka had turned a shade of green at their strange height and, too unnerved to speak to anyone, had gone quickly to sleep as soon as her queen was fed.

"I see," K'dan said drolly. "And after this?"

"We didn't have time to scout, with Coranth being injured," Xhinna said. "We needed a high place that was safe from the Mrreows and tunnel snakes."

"This certainly is that," K'dan agreed, still unable to keep the amusement out of his voice.

"Harper," Colfet growled at him, shaking his head warningly.

K'dan's grin slipped and he sobered. "You did fine, Xhinna." His grin came back again, though, as he added, "Even Fiona would have a hard time outdoing this!"

"There is that," Xhinna allowed, catching on to K'dan's teasing. "I suppose she'll be jealous."

"Only if she ever finds out," Bekka spoke up from her perch. "Of course," she added with more spirit, "*I'll* be certain to tell her."

"Any time after you check on Coranth and Qinth," Xhinna said. Bekka groaned but started—gingerly—to get up.

"Why did you have to pick a spot so high?"

"To avoid the Mrreows and the tunnel snakes," K'dan reminded her.

"I prefer a Weyr," Bekka said as she edged toward Coranth. Taria moved toward her with the grace of one used to negotiating the springy treetops, causing Bekka to halt in alarm. "Won't they break and drop us all to the ground?"

"Not broom trees," a voice called from the distance. It was J'riz. "They're stronger at the top than at the bottom. And they're like ironwood at the bottom."

Warily, Bekka allowed Taria to lead her to the injured green. Presented with a professional challenge, Bekka soon forgot all about the height. She even managed to walk herself over to J'riz and Qinth without the least whimper.

When she was finished with the injured weyrling, she made her way—slowly—to K'dan and Xhinna.

"We're going to need more supplies," she told them. "We need better bandages, and we should have numbweed to ease Coranth's pain."

"We'll have to search for numbweed," K'dan said.

"On foot," Xhinna added. Seeing his questioning glance, she explained, "Only Tazith can fly for the moment, so he's our only source of food for the hatchlings." She explained how they'd managed to catch wherries by the half-dozen.

"That'll do until we can arrange pens for herdbeasts," K'dan declared.

"No," Xhinna said, shaking her head. "If we pen the herdbeasts, we'll attract the Mrreows." K'dan started to protest, but she raised a hand. "We don't know if the Mrreows can climb."

"Oh." K'dan's brows furrowed in thought. "So we're stuck up here until Coranth can fly."

"At least," Xhinna agreed. "Or if we can find enough fruit or vegetables to tide us over—and build a supply of wherry meat that'll last long enough to let me scout."

"Doesn't Tazith need a rest?" Bekka asked, eyeing the blue with a frown. "His color isn't too good."

"He says he's all right," Xhinna lied. Bekka took one long look at her and snorted derisively. Xhinna blew out a sigh and admitted, "He's managing."

"We should find a way to give him a rest," Taria spoke up, joining the group. Xhinna nervously noticed several of the weyrlings looking in their direction.

"We could organize ground parties," Jepara said. "We could go in groups, looking for herdbeasts or wherries."

"And, queen rider, if anything were to happen to you . . . ?" Xhinna prompted.

"Then it'd be the same as in Threadfall," Jepara said. "We've got to take risks, Xhinna." She paused, meeting Xhinna's eyes. "You know that."

Taria closed the distance between them and stood on her toes to mutter into Xhinna's ear, "Delegate. You know you can."

Xhinna gave her a half-hearted glare, which Taria shrugged off with ease, returning the challenge with raised eyebrows.

"Let me go," Colfet spoke up. "I know something of nets and spears."

"Actually," Xhinna said in surprise, "why don't we go fishing?"

"Because we're on land, Xhinna," Bekka reminded her.

Xhinna mimicked two hands holding a pole and Colfet chortled.

"Fishing for herdbeasts or wherries?" the seaman asked.

"Wherries, probably," Jepara said, catching on. "They usually stick to clearings, but if we were to hang the proper lure, I'm sure we could catch several."

Jepara, Colfet, and K'dan took charge, setting up four parties of three riders each, leaving the rest to guard the camp. Xhinna was given strict orders by Bekka, Taria, K'dan, and—surprisingly—Jepara to rest herself and her blue.

K'dan sweetened the order by saddling her with two well-stuffed children and orders not to let them miss their nap. As it was impossible for Xhinna to keep sleepy children awake, she soon found herself resting her head against her blue with one sleeping twin on either side.

▼ ▼ ▼

Xhinna woke to the sound of excited voices and rose to see the twins beside her talking animatedly, eyes shining.

"No, it's too early!" Taria cried in the distance. Xhinna looked around in alarm. What was too early? A cry, half-rage, half-pain, came from Coranth, and Xhinna spun to see the green fling herself awkwardly into the air, bellowing a challenge to all around. Coranth was rising to mate.

"K'dan!" Xhinna called, beckoning to the harper to come get his children.

Tazith woke, hot and hungry. He was in the air after Coranth before Xhinna could say a word. *She hasn't had firestone,* a part of Xhinna thought quietly. The part that was with her blue relished that thought, seeking only to catch the green.

No, Xhinna thought, exerting her will on her dragon. *She must eat first.*

Herdbeasts here, Tazith called to Coranth, punctuating his thought with a bellow even as he veered toward the open plain.

"Xhinna!" Taria's voice was full of worry, fear, and excitement. Xhinna grabbed her tightly, whispering hoarsely, "Don't let her gorge."

"She's injured," Taria said.

"So we make this quick," Xhinna replied as she felt Tazith guide a buck toward Coranth. "Tazith will help."

"He's the only one," Taria said tremulously. Tazith was the only blue anywhere nearby, and the only male dragon old enough to be interested in a mating flight.

"He'll do," Xhinna promised even as a squawk told of Coranth's first kill. "Don't let her gorge."

Taria closed her eyes and leaned into her, her breath coming fast as she grappled with her lust-enraged green. Xhinna closed her eyes and felt—

Soaring, flying, tearing through space. Tazith watched as Coranth downed another herdbeast, giving an awkward cry as the beast's death-throes brushed her injured leg, but she was full of the heat, the passion, she wanted to tear, rend, chew and—

No, only the blood! Taria called to her. Coranth fought her, but her rider's will was adamantine, unbreakable. With a shriek of rage, Coranth plunged her fangs into the dying beast and sucked furiously on the blood that poured out. Tazith sent another buck her way and she dispatched it, too, sucking the hot, flowing blood greedily.

Then, with a taunting shout, she was airborne. The pain of her leg was nothing. She was a green, and below her was only a puny blue. Well, it was Tazith and he was strong and quick—Coranth dipped back down temptingly and swooped up again, but before she got far she felt something grab her—Tazith! How did he do that? And then—

There was no thought, only feeling. Bliss, joy, ecstasy.

They were falling like leaves through the sky. Idly, Tazith cupped air and Coranth imitated him.

"Now," Xhinna said hoarsely, "we bring them home."

Taria nodded mutely against her.

"We are *not* losing those eggs," Xhinna declared later when she and Taria and the rest of the camp had recovered from the euphoria of the mating flight. Taria gave her a grateful look and squeezed her fingers.

"There's no chance she can clutch here," K'dan said, glancing around at their airy heights.

"But the ground's too risky," Bekka said. "She can barely defend herself, let alone a nest." She'd tended to Coranth's injuries as soon as the green had landed. The strenuous flight had opened the wounds again, though it had caused no new damage.

"We could defend it for her," Xhinna said. "We could set a watch, keep guard."

"It would be easier with a green's clutch," K'dan agreed. "It'll be smaller. But then what?"

"And where?" Jepara asked. They had caught three small wherries with their new "fishing" technique—hardly enough to feed the twenty-three ravenous weyrlings and two exhausted full-grown dragons. Colfet had offered to organize a real fishing party, if Tazith could provide transport, but even that would not add significantly to their supplies.

"You brought us three Turns back. Why?" K'dan asked Xhinna.

She shrugged. "It seemed the right time to be," she said. "I suppose I was thinking . . ."

"What?"

"I was thinking that perhaps we could stay here until the weyrlings were mature," Xhinna said. She gave Taria a wry look, adding, "I never thought we'd have mating flights."

"Fiona said we weren't to feed the greens firestone," K'dan recalled, his face set in thought.

"And we didn't," Xhinna said. "We didn't even feed the blues, if you recall."

"Only the browns and bronzes," K'dan said with a nod. It had not made sense to train the blues in firestone without training the greens, or so Fiona had said. T'mar had agreed with her suggestion, knowing that the new hatchlings could learn the skill quickly enough back at the Weyrs.

"And Coranth just rose . . . ," K'dan continued.

"Do you think the greens that went back with Fiona might have risen, too?" Xhinna asked, her eyes wide.

"Or they're about to," he said.

"There were thirty-six greens in the last clutch," Taria remarked.

"And if they clutched like the others, then there'd be sixteen eggs, more or less, in each clutch," Xhinna said.

"And then we'd have five hundred and seventy-six fighting dragons," Bekka breathed in awe.

"Five hundred and seventy-six dragonets," K'dan reminded her.

"Give them enough time and they'd be fighting dragons," Bekka countered, drawing herself up to her full height. K'dan gave her a second glance: Bekka had always been mature for her age, but now that she'd reached her physical maturity, it was hard for him to remember how old she truly was because she hadn't grown a millimeter taller. He nodded in acknowledgment.

Turning to Xhinna, he said, "So your plan is to bring them here?"

"Um, it wasn't exactly a plan," Xhinna said. "And how could we get the greens and the blues to come back from the Weyrs?"

"What about the Mrreows and the tunnel snakes?" Bekka pointed out. "Unless your plan handles *them,* all we'll have is more empty eggs."

The thought of another field of destroyed eggs caused them all to recoil.

"Well, we'll have to make a test with Coranth's clutch anyway," Xhinna said with an apologetic nod toward Taria, who said nothing, but her fingers fluttered against Xhinna's.

"And we've got about three months to figure out how," Bekka said.

Xhinna and Tazith returned exhausted from another expedition across the southern tip of Western.

Her days for the past month had consisted of ferrying hunting and fishing parties out to their sites, scouting the land, and bringing the parties and their catch back afterward. Sky Weyr was solely dependent upon her and her blue for transportation with injured Coranth the only other full-grown dragon. And, she admitted to herself, it wasn't enough. Day by day they were losing ground. There was no margin for error. A bad day's hunt meant that either riders or hatchlings went hungry—so the riders went hungry. Everyone in the camp was gaunt, save the twins, who were extravagantly fed and spoiled by all.

"No luck," Xhinna reported to Taria, who had become something of the camp's headwoman. Xhinna herself had become more Weyrleader than Weyrwoman. She consulted with K'dan and Colfet, but they deferred to her, partly, perhaps, because she had the only dragon able to fly, but also partly, she thought, because she had started with the job and they saw no reason—yet—for change.

If there was one good thing about their situation it was that Xhinna and Taria were together more than they had ever been before: They shared their private time with a passion that they'd never known previously, a sense that every moment was a gift to be cherished, every caress an act of love, and every soft word a caress. They had arguments, some vociferous, but that was nothing new—they were only arguments, nothing more. What was different was how much esteem they shared for each other as they exchanged the news of the day and realized how, quietly, each had done so much, so well.

"Maybe tomorrow," Taria said, pulling Xhinna over and stroking her short hair. Xhinna closed her eyes, luxuriating in the contact and the compassion.

"I love you," she said, opening her eyes to meet Taria's shiny dark brown ones. Taria smiled and leaned down to kiss her. It was a gentle touch, lips on lips, soft, a promise of more later, a motion with more meaning than intent.

Once again, Xhinna marveled at her luck. How could she have found someone so good as Taria? How could she ever have found the courage to open up when so many times before she'd been disdained, rejected? And then, to Impress Tazith, the most marvelous, amazing dragon ever to grace Pern's Weyrs! She was the first woman to ride a blue and that made her a target for those who would say she couldn't handle a man's job, even more so than Taria or the other girls who'd Impressed greens. She knew this and she would rise to the challenge. She would not fail. She *could not* fail. But why?

Xhinna snorted with amusement as she found the answer: Fiona.

"What?" Taria asked.

"Fiona," Xhinna muttered with a grin. She felt Taria tense under her, confused and worried. Xhinna reached up and ran her fingers through Taria's hair. "I was thinking that if it weren't for her, we wouldn't be here."

Taria relaxed. "I'm jealous of her."

"Why?"

"The way you talk about her," Taria said with some reluctance.

"Mmm?" Xhinna murmured, opening her eyes once more to look into Taria's face.

"It's . . . I don't know." Taria shook her head. "It's like you idolize her."

"I do," Xhinna agreed quietly, moving her hand down to stroke Taria's cheek. "I *love* you." She caught Taria's eyes. "See the difference?"

"But you can't be a queen rider like her," Taria protested.

"I'm not," Xhinna said.

"You act like one," Taria said. "Or a Weyrleader."

"I do what needs doing."

"Precisely," Taria replied. "That's what makes you a Weyrleader."

"Well, if so, you'll always be my Weyrwoman," Xhinna promised. Taria giggled, shaking her head, and then, shyly, pressed her cheek into Xhinna's hand.

"We need more food," Bekka said a sevenday later as she met with Xhinna, K'dan, and Colfet. Taria was keeping the twins occupied, but she sat nearby with one ear to the discussion. "We're wasting away."

Twice in the past sevenday, when fierce rains and thunderstorms had driven all prey to ground, the hunters and fishers had returned without enough to feed even half-rations to the humans. On the last occasion, the hatchlings had gone hungry.

"We may stunt the dragonets' growth," Bekka added, glancing longingly toward her Pinorth. "Only Qinth is thriving."

"That's because we're giving her the best of all the pickings," K'dan said.

"We need to move to someplace where we can gather a herd, plant crops, fish," Xhinna agreed, shaking her head dejectedly. "I haven't found that yet."

She had taken to bringing at least one other rider with her on her forays. Night after night they'd return with the blue's color nearly matching the dawn sky, he was so tired.

"If we go to ground, the Mrreows will get us," K'dan said. "If we stay here . . ."

"We could go back to the Weyrs," Colfet suggested.

"I don't think so," K'dan said, his lips pursed tightly.

Xhinna gave him a questioning look.

"I have to wonder why no one's come yet," he said.

"They would have to *time* it," Bekka said.

"Maybe they don't know where we are," K'dan suggested. "Or maybe they're afraid to *time* it after what happened to Fiona and the others."

"It doesn't matter. At this rate, we'll lose everything," Bekka said. She glanced at Xhinna. "What are you going to do?"

"What are *we* going to do," Xhinna corrected her. Bekka's eyes flashed angrily. Xhinna ignored her and glanced questioningly to Colfet and K'dan.

"We've got one flying dragon, two injured dragons, and twenty-two other hatchlings," K'dan said, ticking off the numbers on his fingers. His eyes suddenly lit as he said, "Who are now old enough to go *between*."

"Just," Xhinna agreed. "But they're not old enough to fly."

"Didn't the weyrlings from Fort go *between* with their riders?" Bekka asked, her eyes animated with excitement. "Could we do that?"

"Maybe," K'dan said. "But it's dangerous. And all those times they had Lorana or Fiona leading them." Bekka gave him an inquiring look and he explained. "Even T'mar had to admit that Lorana has an uncanny sense of time and place. Fiona seems to have inherited it."

"Inherited?" Bekka asked.

"Well, *inherited* isn't exactly the right word, but Fiona might have gotten the ability from Lorana," K'dan said. "They can talk to each other sometimes."

"Like dragons?" Bekka asked, eyes aglow as she reached out to her own queen. An instant later, her eyes narrowed and she studied K'dan. "Can you do it, too?"

"No; I've tried," he admitted.

"Well," Bekka said, "what are we going to do?"

"Dragons can do anything," Taria said.

"If they've the strength," Xhinna said. She shrugged as she added jokingly, "And the firestone." Her grin died on her lips as her words gave her an idea.

"What?" Taria prompted.

"Firestone," Xhinna said. "We can use firestone."

"How?" K'dan asked.

"We could set a fire, burn a section of the forest, clear a space where we could keep a herd."

"Wouldn't that make things easier for the Mrreows?" Bekka asked.

"Not if we chose a high place, a plateau somewhere," Xhinna

said. "I'd thought of it before, but clearing all the trees and under-growth . . . But with firestone we could do it in a day or less!"

"Xhinna," Taria began slowly, "do you remember that fire we saw the other night?"

"When it was raining?" Bekka asked, frowning. "I thought it was lightning."

"But we didn't hear any thunder," Xhinna allowed. "And if we set a fire during a downpour it wouldn't last long—"

"And the rain would sink the ash into the soil, preparing the ground for new growth," K'dan added, his eyebrows lifting in admiration.

"But we don't have any firestone," Bekka objected.

"Yet," Xhinna agreed with a smile.

They had to wait two more days before they had enough food to allow Tazith the time to go *between* back to Eastern Weyr and collect the firestone needed. She wasn't *timing it* because she was going to Eastern Weyr in the same time—three Turns in the past from that terrible day when the tunnel snakes had destroyed the clutches—and, because no one in the future had ever mentioned this trip, she knew that she would not and *must not* be discovered. She came in the dark of the night and only took four sacks, Tazith silencing the watch dragon with a quick thought. She ensured that the other sacks were disarranged so that the loss would not be apparent.

Afterward, Xhinna took her blue to the rocky promontory where they'd camped after the disastrous Hatching.

"You're supposed to think of your second stomach," Xhinna said. Tazith opened his jaws to let Xhinna toss a small stone into his mouth. The blue started chewing loudly, his molars crunching hard on the rock, splintering it.

Second stomach, Xhinna reminded him. She felt Tazith agree, his outer eyelids closing as he concentrated on his chewing. He swallowed. They waited. And waited.

"Do you need more?" Xhinna finally asked when nothing happened.

No, Tazith said, then urgently, *Stand back!*

Xhinna jumped aside as the blue opened his mouth and a short spurt of flame came out.

"You did it!" Xhinna cried, jumping up and down. "You did it, Tazith!"

More, Tazith said, opening his jaws. Now *I need more.*

Xhinna threw several more stones to him and he began chewing once more, thinking at the same time, *It feels different, this.*

That's because you've never flamed before, Xhinna thought back.

I like it, Tazith said. Xhinna could feel the sense of power coursing through him and she moved around to his side to pat him on the neck, but when she reached up toward his eye ridges, he flinched away. *I need to concentrate.*

Sorry.

Tazith concentrated. This time he made a respectable flame, which Xhinna admired from her position just behind his head.

Try burning that, she said, directing his attention to a stubborn bit of grass growing up through the stone. Tazith turned and opened his jaws to flame once more. The grass shriveled, turned black, then crumbled to ash. *Excellent!*

With this I can set a fire? Tazith wondered.

Well, with a lot more firestone, Xhinna allowed, looking critically at the three sacks she'd left tied on her riding harness. *Are you ready? Or do you want to try some more?*

Let's go there, then we can try, Tazith said. Xhinna nodded, seeing the sense in going to the plateau they intended to flame. She grabbed the sack of firestone she'd left on the ground and clambered up her dragon's side to her mount on his neck.

I want to see if I can get firestone to you from here, Xhinna said after she'd tied on the fourth sack. Tazith turned his head back toward her, and Xhinna threw a small piece to him. It arced by his mouth and fell to the ground. *Sorry.*

Try again, Tazith told her calmly, with no rancor. This time Xhinna got it right in his mouth, and Tazith chewed the stone happily. *Much better.*

Are you ready? Xhinna asked, bringing up the image of the rain-spattered ground and the dark clouds that had scudded over their camp five days earlier.

Ready.

In a moment they were airborne, then *between.* They arrived right over the tree-crowded plateau, and Tazith dived, flaming. Xhinna cried with pure joy as her blue's flames set the first tree alight. She guided him around to the center and they built an arc of flame. She fed him more firestone as he needed it, until the act became nearly instinctive. *This* was what she was meant to do, *this* was what she had been born for: to fly a blue, to flame, to sear!

She laughed with joy as the flames grew, even as the skies above opened with rain. Soon the entire plateau was alight, as tree after tree burst into flame and the fire spread—gradually the rain would soak the surrounding forest sufficiently to quench the firestorm, but by then, an area would have been cleared sufficient for their needs.

Come, Tazith, let's go home, Xhinna said as she surveyed their handi-work. *You've earned a rest.*

I'm not tired, Tazith assured her even as Xhinna felt the weariness of their efforts overtaking both of them.

Not much!

"**W**ell, it's not much of a herd," K'dan allowed as he helped release the last of the dozen herdbeasts they'd caught. The smell of burnt wood had been mostly washed away by the rains. Large patches of grass had been left untouched by the fires consuming the trees above, and in the areas that had been burned, new green shoots were already poking up out of the ground.

Tazith had labored mightily to move several fallen, blackened tree trunks to form a rude corral. K'dan and half the bronze riders had done their best to help, but it was quickly evident that one blue dragon could easily do the work of seven humans—and in half the time. Instead, the humans applied their tool-using skills to making the space secure enough to keep the beasts corralled for at least a day.

"Of course," K'dan remarked as he straightened from chinking smaller branches into a gap, "this is pretty far from our camp. It makes for a bit of a trek."

"It does," Xhinna agreed. "Which is why you should bring back as much meat as the camp will need for the evening."

"You're not thinking of going now?" K'dan asked, eyes narrowed as he took in Tazith, lying where he'd collapsed from his last load.

"I can't see things getting any better." With a sour expression on her face, she added, "And we can't guarantee that Tazith won't get injured the way Coranth was." She shook her head. "I'm afraid if we don't go now, we'll never be able to."

K'dan moved closer to pitch his voice only for her. "We don't know what happened to snare Fiona. What if *you* don't come back?"

"What if I *don't* go?" Xhinna asked.

K'dan met her eyes, shook his head, and spread his hands in surrender.

"I'll be back," Xhinna said.

"We'll be waiting," K'dan promised. He managed a small nod. "We'll start a fire here so you'll have warm food when you return."

We're going to get help, Xhinna said as the blue raised his head. Wearily, he rose to his feet and Xhinna climbed to her seat on his shoulders. *Are you ready?*

Yes, came the reply and, to match it, Tazith took a few lumbering steps and leapt into the sky. *Where are we going?*

Telgar, Xhinna said, calling the vision up in her mind even as she registered surprise that she hadn't called it home.

The blue rumbled beneath her, and then they were *between* in the place of no sight, no sound, no feeling.

She counted to herself: one, two, three, four . . . she knew it would be a longer jump than normal as she was moving forward through time as well as halfway around the planet.

Suddenly she tensed. Did she hear something?

Can't lose the babies! Can't lose the babies!

Fiona? Xhinna thought, hearing the woman's fear and panic, feeling it grip her just as she heard another voice, a man's:

The Weyrs! They must be warned!

But they were saved! They *were* warned, Xhinna thought desperately. This time made no sense, it was a pocket of fear and panic—

And it threatened to overwhelm her. Her fear for the weyrlings, for injured Qinth, her fear of losing Tazith, of losing—

Go back, a voice said, breaking through the others. *Go back, now!*

Fiona? Xhinna cried in fear and hope.

Go back! Beneath Fiona's voice, Xhinna felt an echo, another voice: Lorana's. *Go back! Free yourself!*

I can't! Xhinna wailed as the sounds of the panicked voices seemed to grow louder.

Can't lose the babies! Can't lose the babies!

The Weyrs! The Weyrs must be warned!

It is an echo, a glimmer of an instant, Fiona told her. *Push back. You must go back now, while Tazith still has the strength.*

But if Xhinna couldn't get through, she wondered, how would they know at Telgar where to find the weyrlings in the Western Isle?

Red Butte! Lorana's voice came to her. *Leave us a message at Red Butte and we'll find you!*

Tazith? Xhinna thought with a whimper. She could feel his strength fading, feel the fatigue biting into him, compounded by the cold of *between*, by the fear and panic of the voices around them.

I will not lose you, Xhinna thought to herself. *I will not lose you! I will not lose you!*

Her determination burned fierce, hot, like a bonfire. She remembered the joy of flaming the plateau, of all that they'd done and—

She broke through.

The cold and nothingness of *between* disappeared and Xhinna found herself high in the air. Tazith gave a strange rumble, and they began to plummet toward the ground.

Tazith! She felt no response from the blue. *Tazith!*

FOUR
▼▼▼▼▼▼▼▼▼▼▼

The Growl of
a Mother

Xhinna woke with a start.

"Careful!" a man's voice warned her.

"It's not every day dragon and rider fall from the sky," another man added with a chuckle. Xhinna's brows furrowed. She knew that voice.

"J'keran?"

"The same," the brown rider told her agreeably. "You were quite hard to catch, I'll have you know."

"It took a bronze and a brown both," the other man added.

Xhinna opened her eyes as she realized the identity of the other man: X'lerin, rider of bronze Kivith.

"Is this Telgar?"

"No," X'lerin replied, chuckling, "we're here in your aptly named Sky Weyr." He turned away from her and called out, "She's awake, she's all right."

"As if I didn't tell you that an hour ago!" Bekka's voice came back dripping with irritation.

A hand gripped hers and Xhinna turned to see Taria's tear-stained face.

"I was worried," the green rider told her.

"And well you should have been," J'keran rumbled. "It's not every day someone tries a fool stunt like that."

"The 'stunt' worked, didn't it? Seeing as we're here," X'lerin reminded him.

"Indeed, here," J'keran agreed, his voice sounding less than pleased.

"Fiona?" Xhinna asked.

J'keran barked a bitter laugh even as X'lerin shook his head. "She sent us."

"We volunteered," J'keran said, his voice a mixture of pride and bitterness.

"We're all T'mar could spare," X'lerin said by way of agreement.

"Two browns, five blues, four greens and, of course, X'lerin's bronze," J'keran enumerated. "With your blue and your friend's green, that gives us just fourteen, barely half a proper wing."

"Well, there'll be no Thread to fight," X'lerin said jauntily.

"Tell us the rest, then," K'dan spoke up from beyond Xhinna's sight.

J'keran started to answer, but stopped at a glare from the younger X'lerin. Instead, with ill grace, he gestured for the bronze rider to explain.

"I've notes from Fiona, Lorana, T'mar, and Shaneese," X'lerin said, gesturing toward his dragon in the distance. "T'mar told me that we would have to stay here until the danger of jumping into the time knot—"

"Hmph!" J'keran snorted.

"—until the danger has passed." He glanced over at Xhinna. "So that means we're here for the next three Turns or so."

Xhinna looked stricken.

"It was the right choice," K'dan told her. "Under the circumstances, it was the only choice."

"We saw Thread," Xhinna said.

"So we understand," X'lerin said. "Did you remember what Fiona said to you?"

"About Red Butte?" Xhinna asked.

"What about Red Butte?" K'dan echoed.

"Fiona said that we could leave a message at Red Butte and they'd get it," Xhinna told him. She frowned at X'lerin. "You got a note?"

"I can't say," X'lerin replied, his eyes twinkling. "Lorana was rather firm on the notion of not 'breaking time.'"

"Xhinna, you're not dead so your stomach's going to start grumbling any moment now," Bekka put in. "Mine already has, so why don't we show our new riders some Sky hospitality and feed them?"

Xhinna sat up, was pleased to discover that she felt fine if, as Bekka had guessed, a little hungry, and, with one swift movement, rose to her feet. She felt Tazith's presence and sent him a quick mental caress.

"It's really springy up here, isn't it?" X'lerin commented.

"It takes a bit of getting used to," K'dan agreed, "but it's not bad. Not bad at all."

"I hope you brought supplies," Xhinna said as she led the way through a tight gap in the upper branches of the broom trees and down toward their dining area. "We've enough herdbeasts and about the same sorts of fruits, but we've no grain or other such —"

"Fiona made sure we carried as much as was possible," X'lerin assured her. "But that won't be enough for three Turns."

"Does it really have to be that long?" Taria asked, trailing along at the rear of the group.

"T'mar said that K'dan would probably know best," X'lerin said, pausing in his efforts to follow the path Xhinna blazed through the branches as they descended. He glanced around. "I don't think I've ever been up this high in a broom tree before."

"It *is* unusual, isn't it?" K'dan responded. "Apparently Xhinna's Tazith first tried it."

"Is Kivith too heavy?" Xhinna wondered suddenly. "We hadn't really planned on making it permanent, just until we could find a better location. The hatchlings—including K'dan's Lurenth—all seem to enjoy the height."

"Kivith assures me that he is quite pleased at the moment," X'lerin said.

"Something to do with a whole flight of queens and he the only mature bronze," J'keran quipped.

"I think it's too early to consider such things, J'keran," K'dan told him evenly.

"Better too early than too late," J'keran replied, not at all repentant. He leered at X'lerin as he added, "I'm sure there'll be a proper bronze to attend to the matter."

"J'keran," X'lerin said, "perhaps you'd best get back to the rest of the wing and help with the off-loading of supplies."

"Check with Javissa—she'll find someplace to put them," K'dan added frostily. "I do hope that Fiona thought to send coverings—something we could use to cover the supplies and for tents in the rain."

"Javissa's here?" Xhinna asked in surprise.

"She insisted," J'keran said with a note of respect in his voice. "She didn't want J'riz to—"

"J'riz's Qinth is recovering," K'dan said. The brown and bronze riders looked amazed.

"Bekka doesn't like losing a patient," Xhinna said dryly.

"She is *some* healer," X'lerin said. Shaking his head, he added, "I wouldn't have given the little green more than a day."

"How did you know about it?" K'dan asked, eyes narrowing suspiciously.

X'lerin gave him a wry grin. "Ah . . . I believe Fiona mentioned something about a note left at Red Butte?"

"So we know something that has to go into this note we've yet to write," K'dan commented sardonically.

X'lerin looked alarmed. "Fiona said we weren't supposed to tell you anything!" He sighed, then in an effort to change the topic, asked, "And how is this Qinth?"

"Qinth proves that dragons are even tougher than we thought," K'dan said. "Did you bring anyone else with you?"

"Javissa's daughter, Jirana," X'lerin said. "She insisted that she'd be needed as much as her mother."

Xhinna noted that J'keran was still with them. "Tell Javissa that I'm glad she's here and ask her to coordinate with Taria about storing the goods."

"I don't think I can find my way back," J'keran said wryly.

"I'll show you," Taria offered.

"Lead on, green rider!" J'keran said with a mock bow.

"Did you bring any *klah* bark?" K'dan asked. "I'm pretty certain we're almost out."

"Not enough for three Turns," X'lerin told him ruefully.

"*Klah* and rolls for four, please!" Xhinna yelled down to the group at the fire near the base of the tree.

"On the way," C'nian called back.

"Sit," Xhinna said, gesturing to the makeshift seats marked by nothing more than pads strategically placed on horizontal branches.

"We'll have to eat in shifts," X'lerin remarked as he found a spot.

"We can seat six in a pinch," Bekka said stiffly.

"I don't think he meant to be rude," Xhinna said to her, referring to J'keran.

"No, he probably did," X'lerin said, shaking his head.

"He was always a bit of a hothead," K'dan agreed. "I remember Fiona regaling me with his antics as a weyrling."

"And the knot *between* really shook him," X'lerin added.

"Not only him," K'dan declared, giving the younger man a probing look.

"No, not only him," X'lerin agreed.

"Tell us."

X'lerin sighed. "As I said, I've got notes from Fiona, Lorana, Shaneese, and T'mar."

"We can *read* them later," K'dan said.

X'lerin gave K'dan a pained look. But before he could start his account, C'nian's voice called up from below.

"Ready!"

"Thanks!" Xhinna called back. They had rigged a platform and rope that served to carry items up and down between ground and treetop camp. Now she pulled on the rope to bring up the food prepared below. A tray set on the branches between the padded seats served as a table.

"I'll serve," K'dan told her agreeably. "Just sit."

There was a pitcher of *klah*, mugs for all, and a basket of warm rolls.

"There's no butter, nor sweetening," Xhinna said. "If you want cold meat—"

"This is fine," X'lerin assured her. They sat in companionable silence for several moments as they ate and sipped their *klah*.

Finally, X'lerin nodded to K'dan. "As I said, being stuck *between* shook many people—"

"Fiona in particular," K'dan guessed.

"Fiona in particular," X'lerin said, nodding. "She was lost all alone in *between* and abandoned until Lorana came back for her. And when she did, Fiona wasn't breathing."

"But she recovered?" K'dan asked.

"She did," X'lerin assured him. "We were only back a few days before she woke up in the middle of the night, convinced that she'd heard Xhinna."

"Well, I'm glad T'mar was wise enough to listen to her," K'dan said, thinking back to a time when he had doubted Fiona's intuition.

"Her, Lorana, and Talenth," X'lerin said. "Even so, D'gan was totally—"

"D'gan?" K'dan broke in. "He's alive?"

"Yes," X'lerin said. "I'm sorry, I should have explained better." He took a breath. "No one at Telgar understands it completely, but when we tried to jump forward in time to Telgar, we crossed with the riders who'd tried to jump to fight Thread—the lost riders of Telgar Weyr."

"Yes, I thought as much," K'dan said.

"And we got caught, part of us locked in Fiona's cry and part locked in D'gan's cry—"

"'Can't lose the babies,'" Bekka repeated. She turned to K'dan. "She was talking about her babies."

"'The Weyrs must be warned' was D'gan's cry," K'dan remembered. He shuddered. "I remember when I first heard that cry." The others looked at him. "Lorana said it, echoing him."

"And now she's brought him—and all those lost riders—back to Telgar."

"Oh," Xhinna said with sudden understanding.

"That must be . . . awkward," K'dan said.

"We'd only just started to see some of that . . . awkwardness when Fiona heard Xhinna's cry," X'lerin said.

"D'gan was opposed to your going," K'dan guessed.

"D'gan doesn't know you went," Xhinna said.

X'lerin raised his mug to her with a smile. "Precisely."

"You'd hardly be noticed in the throng of all those old Telgar riders," K'dan said. He tipped his mug and took a hefty gulp of *klah*. "I can't imagine him yielding his leadership to T'mar with any grace."

"And the problem won't necessarily be solved by the time we return," Bekka noted. When the others looked at her, she explained, "It might be three Turns for us, but it may be less than a day for them."

"Indeed," K'dan said.

There was a tone of worry in his voice that made the others glance away from him until Xhinna reached across the table to put a hand on his arm. "She'll be fine, K'dan." The harper looked over to her. "They'll all be fine."

"What matters for us, now, is what we're going to do," Bekka declared.

Xhinna dropped her arm and turned to X'lerin. "So, Weyrleader, what should we do?"

"Me?" X'lerin gasped, sitting bolt upright. He threw a hand beseechingly toward K'dan. "You're oldest. By the First Egg, you were *my* Weyrlingmaster—*you* should be Weyrleader!"

"I'm already Werylingmaster, father, and harper," K'dan said, shaking off the offer. "And my dragon's just out of the shell." He jerked his head toward the bronze rider with a smile. "No, X'lerin, I'd say your position is clear."

"Um," X'lerin said, glancing around the table. "Ah . . . who managed everything before?"

Bekka cocked her head toward Xhinna. "*She* was in charge."

"I ride a blue," Xhinna protested. "I was just doing what was needed."

"Fine," X'lerin said firmly. "What's needed now is for you to brief me." His lips quirked upward. "After that, we'll see."

The first priority was stowing the goods the others had brought. After that, Xhinna found herself introducing the rest of the group to the bronze rider and, strangely, in charge of the evening hunt—at least coordinating it, as X'lerin insisted that her Tazith had strained himself too much to do more work that day.

Even so, Xhinna managed to get aloft on Tazith because she had to show the new riders some of the tricks they'd learned in driving game to hunters, and also because she was the only one who knew how to find the various spots that R'ney, Jepara, and the other hunters preferred for their traps.

"What do you know of J'keran?" R'ney asked softly as he rode behind Xhinna on their way back to camp with two large wherries— his catch—slung beneath Tazith's belly.

"He was one of the ones who went back in time with Fiona to Igen Weyr," Xhinna replied noncommittally, her senses alerted by the lack of tone in the other's voice.

"Hmm," R'ney said. "He seems rather . . . abrasive."

"He's been through a lot, and the loss of F'jian affected him more than some," Xhinna said. She shrugged. "To be honest, I didn't pay much attention to the riders at Eastern because I spent so much time with Fiona and the babies."

"He seemed to be making an effort to be sociable with Taria," R'ney said. "There was a green rider, V'lex, who looked upset."

"Well, things will sort themselves out soon enough," Xhinna said, trying to keep any sense of misgiving from her voice.

"I'm sure they will," R'ney agreed.

Tazith descended to the clearing nearest the cooking area, and then, getting busy unloading the wherry carcasses, they had no opportunity to continue the conversation.

Among other things that X'lerin's wing brought with them was a decent supply of herbs and—

"Seeds!" Bekka cried in triumph when she first saw them. She rapidly pawed through the small packets and quickly stuffed a few into her pockets, saying to a perplexed Javissa, "These'll grow here. We can start a garden."

"Jirana can help," Javissa said. "But for now, I need to find some of the peppers and a few other herbs to spice the meat tonight."

"Did anyone think to get redfruit?"

"And bitter bulbs," Javissa assured her with a smile. "We'll have spiced wherry tonight."

"That and the bread—"

"I'm sorry, the bread won't be ready until the morning," Javissa said. "We haven't started the dough yet."

That evening a great feast was prepared on a roaring fire in the clearing nearest the treetop Weyr. There was *klah,* fruit juice, fresh hardnut, a smattering of greens, and plenty of roast wherry for all.

"If I'd known what the cooking was going to be like, I would have volunteered quicker," V'lex exclaimed as he came back for another helping.

"Well, you should've known, dimglow, as you had much the same in Eastern," J'keran snarled, pulling him out of the line. "And if you think you're going to gorge yourself to sleep—"

"J'keran," X'lerin cut in smoothly, "I think tonight is a night when we can all eat our fill."

"A jump *between* times is tiring and uses a lot of energy," K'dan added.

"Well, at least wait until the others have all had theirs, then," J'keran grumpily told the green rider.

V'lex flushed, but turned away and moved to the back of the line.

"You should let the weyrfolk here eat first," J'keran continued, raising his voice to make it carry. He glanced toward Taria and winked. "After all, they've been on short rations for too long."

Seeing Xhinna tense, K'dan said quickly, "Xhinna did her best."

"I'm sure," J'keran said in a tone that belied his words. "It's hard enough for a blue, but given his rider . . ." He let his words trail off. He cut a quick glance in Xhinna's direction, smirking when he caught the expression on her face. He turned to Taria, placing his back to the others. "Did you want some more?"

Taria shook her head and moved away quietly to sit beside Xhinna. R'ney joined them after filling his plate for a second time. He glanced in J'keran's direction, but said nothing.

"He's not usually like this."

Xhinna looked up and saw V'lex standing before them. He gestured at the log on which she was seated. "May I join you?"

"Certainly," she said, shuffling over to make room.

V'lex sat down, nodded to Taria and R'ney, and then said quietly to Xhinna, "He's baiting you, you know."

"He's a brown rider, he has Turns more experience than I do—he outranks me in all things," Xhinna said tonelessly.

"He could never have done what you did," R'ney declared stoutly. "Single-handedly you saved us all." He nodded toward the young queen riders who were grouped around X'lerin and K'dan, chatting and giggling. "They know it." He jerked his head toward the silent group of bronze weyrlings and added, "So do they."

"Well, things will be different now," Xhinna said.

"Different isn't always better," R'ney said.

Xhinna nodded, buoyed by his confidence in her, but saddened that those words hadn't come from Taria.

The new arrivals soon adapted to the routine of life in the broom trees. X'lerin's bronze even located the perfect spot for their "weyr"— right at the very edge of Sky Weyr's forest. Every morning when they rose, X'lerin slipped onto Kivith's back and the bronze simply fell out of their high loft to glide easily down toward the main camp, where he'd deposit his rider before continuing on to the burnt plateau for a meal if he felt hungry, or to the sea beyond for a dip, usually waking Colfet, who had set himself up in a small cot by the shore. Often the old seaman would return to camp on the bronze's back with fresh catch for breakfast or for an afternoon stew.

That Kivith's path took him over the whole camp, as well as the burnt plateau, allowing X'lerin to scout the whole area each morning, was not lost on Xhinna.

"It just seemed the thing to do," X'lerin had said with a modest shrug when Xhinna complimented him on his and Kivith's planning.

He was nearly half a Turn her elder, but still half a head shorter and not likely to get any taller; he'd once told her that he came from a long line of short people. He seemed comfortable with his lack of height; he was well-muscled and wiry, with hazel eyes and a sharp-hewn face that smiled often.

This morning, however, more than a month after the newcomers had settled into their own weyrs, Kivith let out a challenging bellow as he reached the end of the camp, startling everyone awake.

Mrreows, Tazith said, relaying the bronze's warning to Xhinna as she raced from her bed toward his weyr.

Tell them not to kill them, she told him. *Have the net crew go after them. Let's see if we can catch one.*

A cage had been built the sevenday before, with R'ney and J'riz leading the effort. Xhinna was pleased to see that the brown rider had taken the young green rider as one of his own; they worked well to-gether, J'riz following R'ney's designs with silent grace, almost seem-ing an extension of the ex-smither's will. R'ney seemed a natural father: He enjoyed the presence of the lad, and didn't mind when his sister and their mother, Javissa, occasionally accompanied them on their various construction projects.

For her part, Javissa, who had taken over from Taria the role of headwoman of Sky Weyr, was spending more and more time with the old seaman, Colfet. Sometimes X'lerin had his bronze carry Javissa down to Colfet's hut before breakfast. The two would return not only with fresh fish, but also with the contented expressions of two who had shared the silence of the dawn and the meditative pleasure of sit-ting together with their poles and waiting for fish to be lured onto their hooks.

Taria had put her finger on the value of the seaman when she'd said, "He's got the calm of the sea."

It had been Javissa and Colfet who had come up with the idea of capturing a Mrreow so they could study it. Taria had blanched at the notion, still remembering the pain her Coranth had felt when the Mrreow had scored her leg with its claws. Xhinna was tempted to side with her, but the tantalizing possibility of being able to control the tawny-furred beasts was too important: If they could prevent the Mrreows from attacking, then no other dragon would be mauled like Coranth.

Now Tazith relayed Xhinna's order as she climbed onto his neck. Out of the corner of her eye she caught a flash of green rising into the sky.

Tell Coranth to stay back, she said. The green was heavy with egg and Xhinna didn't want anything to happen to her.

She'll stick with us, Tazith replied. Xhinna grinned at Taria's tactic: with Taria on her tail, she'd not let herself get too close to the Mrreeows, either.

Taria's caution probably saved them both a mauling as the Mrreeows fought ferociously to free themselves from the nets, one tearing a strip out of a brown who'd come too close.

Kill it! Xhinna ordered, waving at the group of blues she'd assigned to just this duty. One of them swooped low enough to let the rider fire an arrow deep into the Mrreow's head, killing it instantly. The brown—J'keran's Perinth—dropped the net with the dead Mrreow in it, wheeling away back toward the Weyr.

Tell Bekka, Xhinna said to Tazith.

She knows, the blue replied a moment later. *She's ready.* The blue had a fierce tone in his thoughts. Xhinna could feel a matching rage for revenge rising within her, but she fought it back down, sending him a calming thought.

We should kill them all, Tazith thought, rumbling low in his chest. Around him, the other dragons rumbled their agreement.

But not that one, Xhinna thought, referring to the one that lay wriggling in the net below brown Jorth. *Have W'vin bring it to the cage. And have X'lerin get the cover.*

The cover was constructed just like the walls of the cage: tree-trunks spaced closely together. It was large and heavy enough that it took all of Kivith's strength to lift it. As Xhinna watched, W'vin released the catch on the net just above the cage and the Mrreow slipped out of it onto the ground below. Xhinna was amazed at the big creature's speed and agility; it had scarcely landed before it was back on its feet and leaping toward the top of the cage. X'lerin and Kivith were quick with the cover and had it down before the Mrreow could escape, but the creature had come much closer to freedom than Xhinna had expected.

Take us in, Xhinna said to Tazith. They landed close by the cage and the Mrreow leapt toward them, growling angrily in its raspy voice. Tazith bellowed to quiet it, but instead, the Mrreow batted a claw through the gap in the cage and roared back.

"Careful!" Taria cried, yanking Xhinna back. Xhinna had been so engrossed in watching the Mrreow that she hadn't even noticed Coranth land.

The Mrreow gave another low growl and turned away from them, pacing around the perimeter of the cage, looking for a way out.

"She seems smart," Taria noted, easing up on Xhinna's arm and taking a step closer to the cage. She stepped back immediately as the Mrreow turned her tawny eyes in their direction.

"Very smart," Xhinna agreed. She turned as she felt the wind from dragon wings landing behind them. It was X'lerin's Kivith, and behind him was W'vin on Jorth.

"Keep back," Xhinna warned them, as the Mrreow turned toward the new arrivals and leapt, growling.

"What's wrong with her belly?" W'vin asked, pointing.

"She's pregnant!" Taria exclaimed. To Xhinna she muttered, "Boys!"

"She doesn't look well," X'lerin said thoughtfully as he studied her.

Xhinna squinted for a better look. Yes, the Mrreow didn't look well at all. There was blood dripping from her mouth.

"The fall hurt her," Taria said. She sounded sad. "Do you think she'll die before she delivers?"

"The other one was a male," X'lerin said, gesturing behind them toward a tawny carcass that lay tangled in a net, an arrow protruding from its skull. "Perhaps they were a pair."

"Looking for a safe place for their den," Taria said with a sympathetic catch in her voice. Xhinna understood: Coranth was due to clutch any day now, and they were no closer to finding a safe place for the eggs.

"We should kill it," X'lerin said, glancing toward the Mrreow as it made a pained sound—a high-pitched whine. "Shall I have P'nallo land?" he asked, referring to their best bowman.

"Look, she's birthing!" Taria said urgently, pointing. The Mrreow had flopped over onto the ground, sides heaving even as more blood spilled from her snout. "We can't kill her."

"And what will we do with her get?" Xhinna asked. "They won't survive without her."

Taria grimaced, torn between her wish to let them be born and the prospect of their early death. "We could feed them scraps," she said.

"They drink milk," Xhinna said, pointing to one of the teats poking out of the Mrreow's flank. "They won't be able to eat."

"Well, we've got milchbeasts in our herd, maybe they'd drink that," W'vin suggested. "Babies do, and like it."

He ignored Xhinna's look of surprise. "If we raised them, maybe we could tame them. If we could train them, maybe we could use them to keep other Mrreows from attacking us."

"These are nothing like dogs," Xhinna said distractedly. Already, the first baby Mrreow was emerging from its mother. Xhinna stood, transfixed, as the dying Mrreow, with a faint growl of pain, turned to lick the sack from the baby, cleaning it. The baby made a soft sound, nuzzled toward its mother's belly, found a teat, and started suckling. A moment later, X'lerin asked, "What's that noise?"

The baby Mrreow was making a buzzing, rumbling sort of noise, but it didn't sound like distress.

"It's happy," Taria said, smiling. "It's with its mother and it's drinking."

"Just like the herdbeasts—they don't make that sound but you can see how happy their calves are when nursing on their mothers," W'vin agreed. He moved a step closer toward the cage. The Mrreow raised her head and gave a low growl. Then her flank rippled and she gave a piteous cry as her muscles pushed out another baby. Blood flowed freely from her nose and she laid her head back on the ground, making a smaller noise, like a dog's whimper.

Taria started forward, pulling her dirk.

"What are you doing?" Xhinna asked, grabbing her free arm and tugging her back.

"She can't lick the sack—the baby will suffocate," Taria declared. "I've got to help."

"She'll *kill* you!" Xhinna cried.

Taria turned back to her, her eyes spangled with tears. "We can't just let it die like that!"

The Mrreow gave another whimper of pain as her flanks heaved again and she pushed out a third baby.

Tazith, Xhinna called, picturing what she wanted even as she told the others, "Get back!"

She pushed Taria behind her and pulled her own knife even as Tazith leapt into the air and spun quickly, slamming his tail smack into the middle of one of the trunks that formed the cage. Then she forced her way through the gap and crouched, knife poised in front of her.

The Mrreow lifted its head and growled low, but it couldn't move to defend itself as yet another contraction started the delivery of a fourth baby. The contractions pushed the baby Mrreow halfway out before the mother gave one last moan, her eyes closed.

"I think she's dead," W'vin said, coming through the gap just behind Xhinna. "Look, she's not breathing."

"Cut the babies out of their sacks," Taria pleaded. W'vin glanced at Xhinna. With a sigh, she moved forward and knelt by the nearest Mrreow, knife still at the ready. She cut its sack and then turned to the next even as the first started a gentle mewing sound.

"I'll get the last," W'vin said, kneeling and gently pulling the last baby from its mother. Deftly, he split the sack and freed the baby within. It, too, made a small whimpering mew and began thrusting its head fitfully against the brown rider's hands, as though searching for a teat.

"We've put a double door on the cage, kept the lid off, and someone's with them most every day," Xhinna told K'dan and X'lerin at the end of a sevenday. She frowned as she added, "Taria's named hers Razz."

"And what do you think?"

Xhinna shrugged, looking off into the distance to gather her thoughts. "I think that it's too early to tell," she admitted. Her voice hardened as she added, "Part of me just wants to kill them now or, maybe, let them go back into the wild but—if they attack the hatchlings!"

"The hatchlings are safe up here, aren't they?"

"They are," Xhinna agreed reluctantly. "And Taria is convinced that the scent of our Mrreows might keep other Mrreows away from us."

"I suppose that's possible," X'lerin said. K'dan nodded in agreement.

"Looking after them is going to take away from other work," Xhinna said.

"As long as no one shirks their duties, I won't complain," X'lerin said.

"J'keran hates them," Xhinna said.

"That's almost reason enough alone to keep them," K'dan said sardonically. X'lerin gave the harper a surprised look and K'dan added, "Your brown rider has been making noises about how poorly the weyrlings are being trained."

"I assume you put him in his place," X'lerin replied crisply.

"Actually, I couldn't think of a single word to say."

"A speechless harper!"

K'dan leaned closer to the bronze rider. "I'm starting to get worried about how the younger riders are reacting to him."

"And you?" X'lerin said, glancing at Xhinna.

"I'm just a blue rider," Xhinna protested.

"Oh, stop that!" K'dan snapped at her. "There's no rider on Pern who is 'just' anything, least of all you."

Xhinna's eyes widened.

"Do you think Fiona chooses her friends lightly?" K'dan continued. "Or that she'd leave her children—our children—with just *any-one*?"

"No," Xhinna said in a small voice.

"K'dan, please don't break her," X'lerin spoke up.

K'dan's fierce expression crumpled and he reached a hand toward the blue rider. "Sorry," he said. "It's just that I will not have you tearing yourself down."

"He's right," X'lerin said, looking at her. "There will be plenty who look at your Impression as a mistake and will question your right to ride a blue. So it's up to you, blue rider, to show them how wrong they are. This"—he spread his hands out to encompass all the Weyr—"is a great start."

"But if I hadn't come here—"

"If you hadn't come *here*, back in time, where would you have gone?" X'lerin interjected. "You knew you couldn't jump back to Telgar or our time, and you saw Thread falling. Where would you go?"

Xhinna shrugged, but said nothing.

"Xhinna, you will be wrong many times in your life," K'dan told her patiently. "But when you make a decision, stick to it. So far all your decisions have been good ones."

"And understand this, Xhinna," X'lerin added, "it's a foolish wingleader who doesn't listen to all his—" He winked at her. "—or *her* riders."

"A blue could never lead a wing!" Xhinna exclaimed.

"Why?" K'dan glanced at X'lerin. "Just because it's never been done, blue rider, doesn't mean that it *can't* be done." He shook his head ruefully. "After all our Turns with Fiona, we should *both* know that by now!"

Despite all their efforts, one of the Meeyus—as Jirana had insisted upon calling the baby Mrreows—sickened over the next sevenday. It died in the young girl's arms and she was beside herself with grief. She had become something of a prime advocate for the baby Mrreows and somehow had homed in on Xhinna's antipathy; the blue rider often found herself at loggerheads with the younger girl, who had only ten Turns but seemed to treat Xhinna more like an uppity older sister than the person in charge of their safety.

And then there was Taria. Not only did she seem more intent on the Meeyus and their survival than on finding a suitable place for Coranth's imminent clutch, but it also seemed that watching the baby Mrreows as they grew and made their—admittedly, cute—baby noises was arousing a desire for something else in the green rider. Something that Xhinna could never give her: children.

That Taria was passionate for and delighted by children was something that Xhinna had known and acknowledged since they'd first met. Indeed, Xhinna shared that love—she enjoyed snuggling with the small twins, cheering on the efforts of toddlers, the looks of awe she'd get from the older children. She wanted a child of her own someday—maybe more than one—and when the time was right, she'd have one.

But the time wasn't right. No more than the time was right for Taria.

And yet—

Xhinna frowned as she recalled the number of times she'd heard Taria's delightful laugh punctuating the speech of some deep-voiced male. Sometimes it was R'ney, other times W'vin, and even J'keran.

Well, she thought, mentally rubbing her hands to shake off her line of thinking, this isn't getting anything done.

Tazith veered eastward, leaving the burnt plateau and the Meeyus' cage behind as they continued their search for a safe Hatching Ground for Coranth. They reached the coastline and she waved as she passed over Colfet's ship. It was nothing more than a wide dugout with a small sail, but the seaman had a crew in training and was working with a small group to build another hull. They'd gotten much better at fishing and had been returning decent catches of brightfish and the prized redfish.

Xhinna considered for a moment whether it would make sense to establish trade once more with the Northern Continent, but shelved the idea for later as she had Tazith turn due south to follow the shoreline.

Here and there were sandy patches, but none that looked large enough to accommodate Coranth and an entire clutch of eggs—or defensible.

Perhaps a small island? Something not too far away but nice and sandy, lying in the warm sun? She decided to try that later, if nothing turned up in her current search.

They flew on for several hours, until Tazith grew tired and Xhinna's eyes were dry and irritated from squinting too long. With a headache pounding behind her eyes, she had Tazith take them back to the Weyr.

"What have you got for a headache?" she asked Bekka, whom she'd found, as usual, with J'riz and Qinth.

"Him," Bekka said, nodding toward J'riz.

"What?"

"Kneel down," Bekka ordered her. Then she said to J'riz, "Can you reach?"

"I can reach," the boy said, moving up behind Xhinna. As the blue rider started to turn her head to see what he was up to, Bekka snapped, "Stay still!" Adding, "Unless you want to keep that headache."

Xhinna felt J'riz's fingers on her head, moving gently, probing, moving and then—"Aaah!"

"Don't stop," Bekka urged J'riz, saying the words that Xhinna couldn't because suddenly she was sighing in relief from the easing of the pain behind her eyes.

J'riz's small hands, with their thin fingers, found knots in her neck and eased them, found tension behind her ears and eased that, rubbed her temples gloriously, and Xhinna found herself sighing once more, eyes closed in bliss.

"She's really tight," J'riz said to Bekka. To Xhinna he added, "You're like one giant knot."

"Sorry," Xhinna apologized.

Bekka snorted. "Lie down," she ordered. "J'riz, do that thing with your feet."

"She's pretty big," J'riz said consideringly. He moved around in front of Xhinna. "If you'd lie over there," he said, pointing, "I think it'll work." A moment later he added, "Otherwise, we'll have to go to solid ground before it'd be safe to walk on her back."

"Walk on my back?" Xhinna asked Bekka.

"Just be quiet and do what I say for once," Bekka told her with the same tone of exasperation that Xhinna herself often used when her orders were questioned by the younger riders.

"Okay," she said, throwing her hands up in surrender and moving to the indicated location. She lay down, aware of but barely feeling the broom tree leaves underneath the thick canvas they'd spread over them.

A moment later, she felt J'riz sit on her butt. The boy was light. He started running his hands down her back, on either side of her spine, and then under the shoulder blades, finding knots and easing them, soothing bunched muscles. A while later, she felt him rise and suppressed a sigh of disappointment.

"Don't move," Bekka growled. This time her tone held a clear reminder that this girl was not just a healer but a queen rider—and Xhinna obeyed.

Lying as still as she could, she felt J'riz stand carefully on her back, one foot on either side of the base of her spine. Gently he walked up, careful to keep his feet close to her spine. She heard a *crack!* and then felt an odd sensation, as though someone had suddenly stopped making an irritating noise or the world was suddenly clearer, cleaner—less painful.

"Oh," Xhinna breathed in contentment.

"Shh," Bekka said. "Breathe normally."

As J'riz continued his work, Xhinna found it easier to relax, slipping almost into sleep. Bekka spoke.

"I've been looking for someone like him for ages now," she said. "He's small enough that he can massage babies without us having to worry, but compact enough that he can move *your* spine when needs be."

"Move my spine?"

"A body gets out of kilter, some muscles work harder than others, and soon enough, your spine's out of whack," Bekka said. "I didn't know all about this until I was at the Healer Hall." She paused. "But my mother knew enough about massage to help the babies get to sleep—you know they're all out of sorts when they're born, squished as they are—so the massage helps them relax enough to get their spines, and their skulls, back in alignment."

"Skulls?"

"Only in babies," Bekka said. Xhinna could hear her shrug echoed in the tone of her voice.

J'riz got another crack out of her and then Xhinna realized what Bekka had been saying. "You're training him to be a healer?"

"Can never have too many," Bekka said, agreeing. "And a journeyman's allowed an apprentice."

"A helper," J'riz corrected, stepping off Xhinna's back. "A master's allowed an apprentice."

"Means nothing to a midwife," Bekka said dismissively. To Xhinna she said, "You can get up now."

"That was wonderful, green rider," Xhinna said, glancing down at the boy's brilliant green eyes. He truly was beautiful, and he was growing quickly into an incredibly handsome young man.

In many respects, he reminded her of Fiona: They both thrived on attention. That was probably just as well, Xhinna thought, for a boy—nearly man—as pretty as he was would garner *lots* of attention whether he wanted it or not.

And, Xhinna realized, with Bekka to watch out for him, he'd be safe. She realized that he needed to be safe, that he needed someone who was like Bekka: not just big sister, but something more.

"Thank *you*," J'riz said, unaware of her thinking. His voice cracked between the first word and the second and Xhinna laughed, chucking a hand at his ribs, as she said, "Now I know why Bekka does the talking for you!"

"She's not that different," J'riz said, again losing control of his voice, this time on the third word. "Her voice changed, too."

"Of course," Xhinna agreed.

"But she's not that bad," J'riz said, glancing up at her, his green eyes flashing as he gave Bekka a sideways look, "for a girl!"

"You're still ticklish, green rider," Bekka said, raising her hands menacingly.

"But I'm faster than you!" J'riz laughed and darted away.

"I'll leave you to it," Xhinna said, smiling at Bekka. Then she looked at J'riz, who continued to keep just out of Bekka's reach, and said with a nod, "Thank you, green rider."

"No prob-*lem*!" J'riz squeaked as Bekka caught him with a tickling hand on the far end of her lunge. "Bekka, you'll wake Qinth and then we'll be oiling again."

Xhinna left them even as she heard Bekka's Pinorth rouse from her nap and send a demanding plea toward the two riders.

"Oh, no, see what you did!" Bekka cried. "You woke the bigger dragon, you fool!"

That evening Xhinna was surprised when she didn't see Taria at the cooking fires for dinner.

"She's eating by the Meeyus," an exhausted-looking Jirana said. She yawned widely. "I was watching them all day, and Taria and J'keran volunteered to relieve me."

"Actually, only Taria volunteered," X'lerin put in as he moved over to seat himself by Xhinna. "J'keran has extra duties."

"Extra duties?" K'dan asked, joining them. "Does this have anything to do with our missing supplies?"

"Missing supplies?" Javissa turned her sharp eyes to the group and moved briskly toward them. She gave her daughter a sharp look. "Go to bed."

"I'm not tired!" Jirana protested, her exclamation belied by the huge yawn that followed.

"Now!" Javissa said, waving toward the rope ladder that led to the tops of the broom trees. "And mind you go carefully!"

"Taria says that she's been excellent with the Meeyus," X'lerin said approvingly as Jirana headed up the rope ladder.

"If she'd slack up on her chores, then I could fault her for it," Javissa said. She turned to cast a fond look in the direction of her youngest. "She's been doing them perfectly. But . . ."

"The Meeyus are giving her a chance to be grown up," K'dan said.

"She's so *eager*," Javissa said wistfully. "It's not enough that she'll have the Sight—she wants it immediately."

"Can you blame her?" K'dan asked. "She's living in the shadow of not only her father but also her brother."

"And she probably just wishes she could get on with her life," Xhinna added.

"There's more than that," Javissa said, glancing from Xhinna to

X'lerin to K'dan. Her lips thinned as she came to some decision. "She wants the Sight to see if there will be a future for Pern."

"Oh!" The word burst from Xhinna's lips.

"I'm sorry—," K'dan began, but stopped as Javissa raised a hand.

"It's on all our minds, Harper," Javissa said. "It can't be kept from the children, particularly her."

K'dan frowned even as he nodded. "Tiona and Kimar talk about it."

"Well, I believe that Tenniz didn't send us here for no reason," X'lerin said.

"Ah, but he didn't send us here," Javissa said apologetically. "He sent Lorana to the Dawn Sisters and *she* found the Eastern Isle."

"Fiona sent us a note," Xhinna reminded her. When Javissa looked confused, Xhinna added, "Remember? The note we got back in Eastern Weyr? Or rather, she will—Turns from now."

"But we're not sure why," K'dan said.

"I have to trust that it's to save Pern," X'lerin said.

"I hope so," Javissa agreed fervently. She jerked her thumb back toward the broom trees. "And my little one so desperately wants to be a part of it."

"In the meantime, Xhinna, any luck in finding a suitable clutching spot?" X'lerin asked.

Xhinna shook her head. "Tazith and I spent the day looking west, but it's all the same—flat, with broom trees and grasses."

"No place safe from tunnel snakes, then," X'lerin declared.

"Or Mrreows," K'dan added.

"Well, we'll keep looking tomorrow," X'lerin said. "Something will turn up."

"I hope so," Xhinna said. "But we're running out of time. Taria's Coranth could clutch any day now."

"And, even if we find a suitable spot, we'll only solve half our problem," K'dan said.

The others looked at him and he explained, "Where are we going to find Candidates?"

FIVE

▼▼▼▼▼▼▼▼▼▼▼▼

By Hearts Sundered

In the end, Coranth decided for herself. She chose the nearest sandy beach within flying distance of their Weyr, a spot north of Colfet's cove.

Xhinna was furious with Taria for not getting instructions from her, furious with Coranth for her choice, and hurt that neither thought to tell her or Tazith so that they could return rather than continue their long scouting.

Instead, the first Xhinna learned of it was when she arrived back at the Weyr and was congratulated by a smiling X'lerin.

"Where's Taria?" Xhinna asked, looking around. "Where's Bekka?"

"At the Hatching sands," X'lerin said, sounding confused. "You didn't know?"

Xhinna shook her head.

"I'll have Kivith give Tazith the image," X'lerin said immediately. "I was just arranging a guard," he explained. "We'll be there directly. J'keran's there now with Perinth."

"Good," Xhinna said.

"This is going to stretch us out, isn't it?" X'lerin said, frowning.

Xhinna nodded. "We've got the Weyr, the Meeyus and the herd, Colfet's cove, and now these sands."

"We haven't seen any Mrreows since . . ."

"But we don't know about the tunnel snakes," Xhinna said, itching to get airborne and glancing anxiously toward Tazith.

"Go!" X'lerin said. "We'll be along shortly."

Xhinna gave him a grateful nod and took off.

Are you ready? she asked Tazith, realizing how tired and sore she was and guessing how tired her steady blue must be—although he would never admit it to her. She radiated love to him: He was amazing, he was tireless, he was the best blue on all Pern.

I am, Tazith agreed, neither modest nor boasting, merely accepting her word at full value. *Shall we go?*

Xhinna clenched her jaw as she circled down over the sandy beach and picked out Taria among the others. The green rider looked up at her and then quickly to her side where R'ney stood. He offered her his hand and she took it before looking back up toward Xhinna and waving. Why did Taria feel she needed R'ney's support? Xhinna wondered.

By the time Xhinna landed, she'd worked herself up into a near fury, ready to lash out at Taria, at Coranth, at R'ney.

Shh, there is nothing wrong, Tazith told her. His tone was as matter-of-fact as his earlier acceptance of her praise.

Unless I make it wrong, Xhinna thought to herself, taking a deep breath and letting it out slowly. She ran toward Taria, grabbed her and scooped her up, spinning with her in her arms as she planted a great kiss on her partner's lips.

"How many did she have?" she asked excitedly, waving an acknowledgment toward R'ney as she let Taria back down to the ground.

"Eighteen!" Taria said proudly, glancing toward her proud but exhausted green.

"Talenth only had three more when she first clutched!" Xhinna told her.

Taria's face fell. "Talenth is a queen—you can't expect that from a green."

"I don't," Xhinna said, suddenly feeling defensive. "I meant it as a compliment."

"Oh." Taria sounded like she didn't give that much credence.

Xhinna moved toward the nearest egg and touched it lightly. It was warm. "It's soft."

"It'll harden," Taria declared, glancing toward her green. "She chose this place all by herself."

Xhinna glanced around critically. "Is it far enough from the sea?"

"It's high tide now," Taria said, pursing her lips tightly. She gestured at the gap between the edge of the sea foam and the nearest egg. "And there's a whole dragonlength's distance."

"What if we get rough weather?" Xhinna muttered. "How will we protect the eggs then?"

Taria flushed angrily. "This is the best she could do," she shouted, and Coranth raised her head, eyes whirling toward red as she reflected Taria's anger. "Who are you to judge, you didn't find anything better!"

"I'm not judging," Xhinna said, confused at how the conversation was spinning out of control. "I'm merely thinking, planning."

"You shouldn't have let Tazith chew firestone," Taria said.

Xhinna did a double take at this abrupt change of topic.

"This'll be the last time they clutch," Taria said, shifting her body in R'ney's direction. "So you'd better hope they all hatch."

"X'lerin's on his way with guards," Xhinna assured her. "We'll keep a watch day and night."

"Good."

She's acting like she just had a mating flight, Xhinna thought in surprise. Her eyes narrowed as she saw the way R'ney moved, half toward Taria, half away from Xhinna.

Could they . . .

Yes, Tazith told her calmly. Xhinna's face blanched as she looked from R'ney to Taria and back.

"X'lerin's coming," she said abruptly, turning back to her blue. She jumped up onto him and urged him skyward.

Airborne, with her back to everyone and everything, Xhinna let her tears flow.

"Xhinna?" Bekka asked cautiously when she saw the rider dismount onto the broom trees of Sky Weyr. "Why aren't you at the beach?"

"Headache," Xhinna said, glancing hopefully toward J'riz. The boy was fast asleep, lying next to where Bekka sat, propped up on one arm.

Bekka glanced toward J'riz, a smile playing on her lips, then back to Xhinna. Her face darkened.

"Oh, dear," she said. She turned toward her queen. "Tell you what, help me oil Pinorth and I'll see what I can do to massage you myself if J'riz isn't awake when we're done."

"Thanks," Xhinna said. Bekka motioned toward her queen and Xhinna led the way.

At barely three months old, Pinorth was still a good bit smaller than Tazith. Oiling her was an easy task, mind-numbing, thoughtless work that allowed Xhinna to distract herself completely with the familiar motions and quiet joy of a job well done.

"When she rises . . ." Xhinna began, looking at the well-formed queen and seeing her full grown, rampant, a force in the sky.

"That's Turns to come," Bekka said, shaking her head with a fond look at her queen. Absently she patted Pinorth's neck, then reached over to scratch at her nearest eye ridge. She met Xhinna's eyes frankly. "Is this your first big fight?"

"Maybe our last," Xhinna said, working to keep the fear out of her voice and not at all surprised that Bekka could imagine the cause of her headache.

"Only if you're an idiot," Bekka said. "And I never saw that in you."

"She and R'ney—"

"And what do you expect?" Bekka cut in. "You practically threw them at each other! All it lacked was you publicly blessing the union."

Xhinna took a step back, stricken. Had she? Had she done this to Taria and not realized it?

"She wants children," Bekka said, changing tack. "*You* want children." She gave Xhinna a shake. "Didn't you learn anything from Fiona?"

"I—"

"To be honest," Bekka cut in, "I think you should be grateful it was R'ney and not J'keran."

"Xhinna!" K'dan called from one tree over, moving swiftly toward them. When he was close enough he said, "X'lerin's Kivith told my Lurenth and . . . well, I thought that if you wanted to talk . . ."

"Bring him to the beach, talk on the way," Bekka told Xhinna. She glared at the bronze rider. "And, if you don't mind, K'dan, you might consider sleeping people—" she nodded toward J'riz "—as well as sleeping dragons."

A smile played across K'dan's lips and he gave her a half-bow. "My apologies, gold rider, I shall bear that in mind."

"Especially as now, no doubt, you'll be asking me to watch your brood while you're gone."

"Would you?" K'dan said, his smile growing bigger.

"**S**he's a good person," Xhinna said as Tazith bore her and the harper skyward.

"Bekka?" K'dan asked.

"Yes."

"She bears a lot on her shoulders."

"Oh, we all do!"

"Yes, indeed," K'dan agreed. His tone grew more thoughtful. "You more than others."

"Certainly not more than X'lerin."

"X'lerin only has to learn how to be a Weyrleader," K'dan said, "which is something he's had more than three Turns to consider."

"And I?"

"You have to learn how to be the first woman blue rider since the Ancients came to Pern," K'dan told her.

"I've got Fiona and Lorana and, I hope, you to guide me," Xhinna said.

"They would be happy to do so were they here," K'dan agreed. "As for myself, I can only guess the way."

"What should I do?" Xhinna asked in a burst of despair.

"Ah," K'dan said, "I was hoping to ask *you* that!"

"What?" She'd been talking about Taria and R'ney but K'dan seemed to have changed the subject.

"Do you think that you're the only one here who doesn't know what to do, blue rider?" K'dan said. "Do you think that X'lerin knows more? You should know better, because you and he trained together."

"But—" Xhinna cut herself short. Did no one know what to do? Everything was different here. The rules of the Weyr weren't quite what was needed—they need something similar but not quite. Xhinna gave K'dan a startled look.

"Ah, you've figured it out!" K'dan said with a chuckle. "We're on uncharted waters, as our friend Colfet has said. We don't know our way forward." He sighed. "It was easier when we were at the Weyr, when all we had to do was fight Thread."

"And we can't even do that—we don't have enough dragons," Xhinna said with a sigh.

"Yes, we have to solve *that* problem, too," K'dan agreed. "But for now, Xhinna, the question is—what are you going to say to them?" He jerked his finger to the riders on the beach below.

"I don't know."

"Well, we can't stay up here all day," K'dan told her. He leaned forward so that his lips were closer to her ears. "If I were Fiona, I'd probably say go with what your heart tells you."

"I don't know what my heart is telling me!"

"At which point, she'd probably say: 'Good.'"

Despite herself, Xhinna laughed.

"Best get it done soonest," K'dan said as he helped her climb down off Tazith's neck. He turned her toward the oncoming throng. "If you want my advice, I'd say: Start with the one most hurt."

Xhinna took a deep, steadying breath and nodded jerkily. She waved K'dan ahead, veering toward R'ney. The brown rider viewed her approach apprehensively, saying as soon as she was in earshot, "Xhinna, I'm sorry. The excitement of the clutching, and Taria—well, there are no excuses."

"Only apologies," Xhinna said. The brown rider lowered his head in shame. Xhinna moved forward and touched his shoulder lightly. "Mine should be the first."

R'ney gave her a startled look.

"You're a good man, hardworking, conscientious," she told him. "I've always known that Taria wanted children and that someone would have to help in that." She shrugged. "I was surprised and hurt that Coranth clutched without me, that Taria didn't tell me, and then to find out that you two had . . . made your decision without my knowing . . . well, it was too much for me all at once."

"It wasn't so much a decision, as a heated moment," R'ney said. "And if it hadn't been, perhaps we would have kept our senses enough to tell you."

Xhinna shook her head. "Well, I'm glad you didn't." R'ney gave her a look of surprise. "It had to happen sometime, and this really couldn't be a better time."

"Really?"

"Yes," Xhinna said. "Consider that in ten months' time, all the dragonets, including yours, will be ready to start their first flights."

R'ney nodded cautiously, trying to follow her logic.

"After that, things will get hectic, particularly as somewhere around that time we can expect our mature dragons to rise again, so now is the best time to start a new life in our Weyr.

"But let's keep that to ourselves, okay?" she asked, giving him a wink.

"Certainly," R'ney replied, surprised at her recovery. "And I can assure you that it won't . . . I won't . . . we won't—"

"Have another moment of passion?" Xhinna filled in, easing him out of his embarassment. Guiltily, R'ney nodded. "I certainly hope you don't mean that! Taria wants more than *one* child, you know. And you've got a duty to Pern."

"I wasn't thinking of duty," R'ney admitted miserably.

"R'ney, I can't think of anyone I'd like more to see as father to Taria's children," Xhinna told him emphatically. She turned, looking around. "Now, I've got to talk with her, too."

"Can I come?"

"Brown rider, you made yourself part of my family when you fought to save the hatchlings," Xhinna told him. "Of course you may come."

Taria was too shocked by the approach of both R'ney and Xhinna, moving together companionably, to think of running away.

"I'm sorry," Xhinna said, her words crossing Taria's. The green rider did a double take and Xhinna moved shyly toward her and then suddenly they were together, arms wrapped around each other, hugging tightly, crying and babbling at the same time, neither able to hear the other.

"I wanted you here," Taria said, waving toward R'ney. "And then . . . the feelings from Coranth . . . the Meeyus . . . Razz . . . I wanted what they had."

"It's okay," Xhinna said, hugging her and stroking her hair. "It's okay. It's your right, it's your body, it's your choice."

"But I should have asked you," Taria said, pulling away far enough to look into Xhinna's eyes. "It wasn't right."

"It was passion, Taria," Xhinna said. "It's the passion that I love in you."

"I think I'm pregnant," Taria told her quietly, her eyes glancing beyond her to R'ney, then back. "Is that all right?"

"It's perfect."

"They'll only be blues and greens, most likely," X'lerin said when he, Xhinna, and Bekka met at the beach the next morning to examine the eggs, "because the sire was a blue."

"And if he'd been a bronze, would that make a difference?" Xhinna asked. K'dan marched over to join them; he'd come earlier to take his turn at guard.

"We don't know," X'lerin said with a shrug. "There was only Qinth from the green clutches, so we can't be certain."

"We're wondering if Tazith's chewing firestone would make him sterile, like the greens," Xhinna said, glancing toward Taria, who looked back in surprise at the question.

"I doubt it," X'lerin said. "The bronzes and browns chew firestone, and we've never had problems with them."

"I hadn't thought of that," Taria said in a low voice, chagrined.

She moved closer to Xhinna, absently leaning against her in a gesture of apology and solidarity.

"So do you think we should throw the mating flights open to all, when they start?" Bekka asked, clearly continuing a prior conversation with X'lerin. Xhinna and Taria leaned in closer to the conversation, Xhinna's arm going around Taria's waist as they moved forward. Taria reached with her near hand and clasped Xhinna's hand, pulling herself in tighter against the taller blue rider.

Xhinna reached out with her free hand for R'ney, who arched back, hands raised, ceding the tender moment to her alone.

"Perhaps a few, at least," X'lerin said cautiously. He shrugged, adding, "After all, we're going to be here for Turns."

"But only those from the current clutch and maybe the next clutches will be old enough to fight by the end of our three Turns back here in time," Bekka protested.

"True, but Weyrs will still need werylings," X'lerin said. He turned back to the clutch on the sands, his hand open. "And this is a good start."

"And if we can hatch this clutch, perhaps there'd be reason for the others to come back," K'dan added.

"You mean so they could mate and clutch more hatchlings?" Bekka asked, her brows furrowed in thought.

"Yes," K'dan replied, nodding firmly.

"You're thinking to repopulate Pern's Weyrs in three Turns?" X'lerin asked.

"With enough queens and greens, we could do it," K'dan declared.

Just as there was no way to hide the eggs on the sands, there was no way that the news of Taria and R'ney's new relationship could remain secret in Sky Weyr. Xhinna defused any tension by very obviously dragging R'ney over to sit with her and Taria. She noted with humor how T'rennor, rider of green Kisorth who had lost all her eggs in the Hatching sands at Eastern, smiled hopefully in R'ney's direction.

With less enjoyment, she saw the way V'lex eyed the brown rider reflectively, saw J'keran's angry glower, heard W'vin extend his congratulations to all.

"V'lex isn't my type," R'ney declared when Xhinna teased him about it later.

"And what is?"

"Well, like Taria," R'ney said, "or you, only different." He saw Xhinna's raised eyebrows. "He's too thick and slippery." He added hastily, "Oh, by all accounts he's a good rider, and he's flown in far too many Falls for his prowess or his courage to be questioned, but . . ."

"Tall and wiry works better for you," Xhinna concluded, letting him wriggle free of his red-faced silence. R'ney nodded. "I'll keep that in mind."

"I can make my own acquaintances," R'ney said with a touch of frost in his voice.

She smiled to let him know she was teasing him and R'ney ducked his head in acknowledgment.

"As I well know," Xhinna said, her lips curving up as she reached to punch him lightly on the shoulder. She glanced around at the gathering and said, "Well, as soon as your Rowerth can manage, we'll see if we can't get you to meet more riders elsewhere."

"That'll be a while," R'ney said with a sigh. They glanced up as F'denol and Jepara approached, hands linked.

"Congratulations," the bronze rider said to Xhinna and Taria, "you're the first to clutch here in the Western Isle."

"I think it's generous of you to be so free," Jepara said to Xhinna. Her tone didn't match her words.

"Taria is not mine," Xhinna told her firmly. "I don't own her."

Jepara's face hardened and Xhinna saw the way her hand clenched F'denol's.

"If I *did*," Xhinna continued, "then I'd be the sort to say that you should be seeking out the company of a High Reaches rider."

"But—" Jepara gasped then subsided as she absorbed Xhinna's words. Jepara was from High Reaches, it would be expected that she would return there—and that, according to Tradition, she would partner with a High Reaches bronze rider. "Oh."

F'denol reddened, looking embarrassed at the queen rider's discomfort. Xhinna gave him a grin to ease his worries, saying, "I'm not like that. Hearts do what they do, and we're best when we adjust." She made a shooing gesture toward them with both hands, adding suggestively, "Wasn't there someplace you wanted to be?"

F'denol needed no further urging, but Jepara moved more slowly, a certain reluctance in her stride.

"There's one who only wants to play," R'ney observed with an edge to his voice.

"And F'denol's not built to handle her," Xhinna agreed. The miners' daughter was a handful and getting more so every day. Bekka wanted nothing to do with her, nor did X'lerin, who, alone among the bronze riders, showed both sense and tact in dealing with her.

Jepara found her position as gold rider a role she relished: paramour of so many dragonriders, queen of all she surveyed.

"You're the one who can tame her," R'ney said. "You're immune to her charms and she's attracted to your power, especially as she can't understand its source."

"And how, brown rider, did you get to be so astute?" Xhinna asked archly.

"Five older sisters," R'ney said with a sigh. "You get to know what's happening pretty well."

Meeya, the sweet young rider of Calith, came forward to congratulate them, batting her eyes at R'ney in an obvious attempt for his attention. Xhinna led the conversation elsewhere and steered her in toward G'rial, the bronze rider from Fort. Xhinna thought he possessed the sort of quiet strength that the girl seemed desperate to have.

"Good choice," R'ney murmured when he had the chance. "He's smart enough to know when to say no, and that's rare."

"In a man?"

"In anyone," R'ney replied. He glanced after Jepara and then back toward Meeya. "You know," he said thoughtfully, "they both remind me of my sisters."

"Really?"

"Yes," R'ney said, grinning. "I remember when Sevra, the youngest and prettiest—and she knew it—decided she could get away with baiting Nerena, who was the shyest and meekest."

"And?" Xhinna asked. "What did your parents do?"

"Nothing," R'ney said with a smirk. "They knew Nerena pretty well. One day, when Sevra had been at her worst for over a sevenday, Nerena blew her top and cut off all Sevra's hair while she slept." R'ney shook his head. "She thought she had the *best* hair."

"And what did you parents do then?"

"They said, 'Sevra, maybe now you'll not taunt your sister so much,'" he replied, shaking his head and grinning at the memory. "You've never seen such outrage. Sevra learned two lessons from that."

"Two?"

"Maybe four, now that I think on it," R'ney said, lifting a hand and ticking off fingers as he said, "She learned that if you push someone too far, no matter who, they'll fight back. She learned that no one will support her when she's wrong, no matter how pretty and demanding she is. She learned what it was like to be the ugly duckling in our smithhall; it took months for her hair to get back to its old length. And," he finished, ticking off the fourth finger, "she learned that there's no point in demanding justice when you're being unjust yourself."

"A lot of lessons," Xhinna said, feeling a pang for sisters and brothers she never had.

"I learned a lesson, too," R'ney said.

Xhinna raised an eyebrow.

"Just because she's shy and modest, doesn't mean a person won't stand up for herself." He paused just a moment before adding, "Did you know that Jepara has taken to calling Meeya 'Meeyu'?"

"Oh," Xhinna said, rolling the notion around in her mind as an evil grin spread across R'ney's face. Then she smiled, too. "You'd think she'd be smart enough to realize that those baby Meeyus will be Mrreows one day."

"You'd think," R'ney agreed. Xhinna raised a hand and laid it on his shoulder. "You know, brown rider," she said, "it's worth repeating. I really couldn't think of a better father for Taria's child—if that's to be."

R'ney turned red and placed his hand gently on top of hers. "I would like to take credit for having planned it in advance, but in all honesty I can't," he told her. "In other circumstances, the same thing might have happened with anyone nearby."

Xhinna shook her head at him. "Which of your sisters does Taria most remind you of?"

"Nerena," R'ney said without a moment's thought. He raised his hands and shook his head, saying, "But you can't think—"

"No," Xhinna told him soothingly. "But if someone like, say, Sevra were there, or someone even like V'lex . . ."

"It would have been much easier to control my emotions—theirs being such less pleasant personalities," R'ney admitted. He cocked his head at her, looking down into her deep blue eyes. "And how do you know this?"

"I've been dealing with children for Turns now," Xhinna said, smiling up at him. "Adults are only grown-up children, after all."

"And we all mature at different rates," R'ney said thoughtfully, glancing again in the direction of Jepara. "Is that why you tolerate her?"

"That and to honor a dead man who taught those I respect," Xhinna said, her eyes going distant.

"Mikal of the Harper Hall?" R'ney guessed. Xhinna shook her head. "Weyrleader M'tal of Benden?" Again, Xhinna shook her head. R'ney spread his hands in surrender.

"No one important," Xhinna said, thinking back to her conversation with Fiona. "Just a man who made a mistake and was never allowed to recover from it."

"D'gan of Telgar?" R'ney asked, then shook his head. "But they say he's still alive, so he's got a chance."

"Not him, either," Xhinna told him. She could see he was perplexed, so she continued, "I was thinking of Vaxoram. He was the bully Kindan—K'dan—bested back at Harper Hall just before the Plague."

" 'Step by step,' " R'ney quoted, showing that he was familiar with the tale.

"Exactly," Xhinna said. A breeze wafted by and she smelled the scent of food being prepared nearby; her stomach reminded her that she should eat soon, her conscience reminded her that she needed to be certain that Taria had eaten, too. "I'm hoping we'll give her the chance Vaxoram never had."

"And how are you planning on doing that?" R'ney asked skeptically.

Xhinna pulled him close and whispered into his ear. When she was finished, he straightened, his eyes twinkling. "Oh, you'll teach her a lesson Nerena would have loved!"

"Would have?" Xhinna caught the bittersweet tone in his voice.

R'ney dismissed his pain with a shrug. "She died in the Plague, keeping the rest of us alive."

"Nerena is a pretty name," Xhinna said into the silence that followed. R'ney cocked his head at her. "I think that Tarena wouldn't be bad, don't you?"

"You mean—for—" He cut a hand toward the Hatching sands and Taria. "—if it's a girl?"

"I've a thing for girls," Xhinna admitted with a small smile. "They're more biddable, to my way of thinking."

"Biddable!" R'ney snorted, shaking his head. "Blue rider, you need to acquire a mirror for when you next say that."

"Okay," Xhinna said, patting him on the shoulder. "Perhaps not more biddable, but it would be a good name for a girl."

"Girls, as you may have noticed, are dangerous," R'ney said. Xhinna looked at him, brow raised. "At least for me," he allowed. "They find it incredibly easy to wrap me around their thumb."

"So, a girl it is, then," Xhinna declared.

The brown rider nodded in satisfaction, savoring the name: "Tarena."

"And, perhaps, Tareny if it's a boy?" Xhinna suggested, enjoying the brilliant expression that spread across the brown rider's face.

▼ ▼ ▼

"**N**o, I've no objection," X'lerin said when Xhinna found the time to approach him several days later with her request. "R'ney's a good man and this will help him." He smiled. "Besides, it will heal any ruffled emotions about the hatching sands."

"True," Xhinna agreed, deciding not to be ruffled with the bronze rider for broaching the subject; as she'd said to R'ney, there were secrets that were kept in the Weyr or Hold, and there were those that were openly acknowledged. This was one of the latter.

"What do you think of W'vin?" X'lerin asked.

"He's a steady, good man," Xhinna said.

"And J'keran?"

Xhinna paused a long time before answering. "He does his work, he's a good trainer, he's—"

"Tired, bitter, scared, worn out," X'lerin broke in, saying the words she was trying to avoid.

Xhinna took a breath to protest on the brown rider's behalf but let it out again, nodding her head once in curt agreement.

"You wouldn't believe how often I've found him drunk," the young bronze rider said mournfully.

"But after all he's done—all they've done—isn't it our job to give him and all those with him new hope, new encouragement, and the rest they so desperately need?" Xhinna asked. She continued, "I've seen him fighting, I've seen him come back Fall after Fall when his friends and fellow riders haven't, I've seen the light go out of his eyes, the fear come into them."

"Are we all going to be like that?" X'lerin asked, allowing just the slightest of his dread to leak into his voice.

"No," Xhinna declared passionately. "That's what we're here for, we're here to see to it that we live, that Pern lives, or that if we have to die, it's for only the best reasons."

"Sky rider," X'lerin said. He said it not for the title but to honor *her*—Xhinna. It was the title that many of the riders, particularly those whom Xhinna had brought back in time herself, had started calling themselves.

Xhinna grinned at him, acknowledging the compliment.

"So we'll have to show them reasons to love life again, just as we learn the difficult lessons that they've learned in staying alive through all these Falls," she said. "When we come back, we'll come back with enough dragons to save Pern, enough weyrlings to replace them, and enough experience to handle the worst Falls ever."

"And how will we do that?" X'lerin asked. "Get that experience, I mean."

Xhinna smiled at him and tapped her forehead. "That, you'll learn when the right time comes." She paused, her smile fading. "For now, what do you suggest we do with J'keran and the others?"

"Keep them busy, but not too much," X'lerin said after a moment's thought. "Put them on duties that mix them with more of us 'youngsters,' let them work with the weyrlings, get to know the new queen riders and bronze riders."

"And figure out a way to brew something with kick—more than what J'keran's made so far," Xhinna said. X'lerin gave her a surprised look. "They're going to need to get very, very, very drunk a number of times in the next three Turns. They'll need a chance to drink some of their nightmares into oblivion." She frowned sadly, knowing it wasn't the best solution, but she'd seen it work often enough that she wasn't willing to give up on it just because it would mean having to clean up after drunken men, having to sort out blows, having to assert authority over them.

"But if they get drunk, what if they don't listen to us?" X'lerin asked.

"There are six queen weyrlings here," Xhinna reminded him. "How badly do you think they're really going to behave?"

"Point."

"And you, Weyrleader, will have all this time to impress those queen riders with your skills."

"And which of all these young queen riders did you pick out for me?" X'lerin asked.

"It's not my job to suggest that you use your eyes, man," Xhinna told him brusquely. X'lerin braced at her tone. She relented, adding, "But to my tastes, I find Meeya's shyness a bit too much; Jepara needs a strong hand and a man smart enough to see past where she is now to where she will be when she's older."

"She'll be Weyrwoman," X'lerin said without any doubt.

"Not with that attitude of hers," Xhinna said. "The bronzes have as much choice as the queens in who rules the Weyr. If she doesn't mend her ways, she'll be queen-second for all her days."

"She's strong-willed."

"She's spoiled and she toys with people," Xhinna said. "She hasn't yet begun to see them as real, as subject to pain, as worthy of love."

"But she's Halla and Pellar's daughter!"

"And that's the mistake everyone makes with her," Xhinna said. "They think of her famous parents and they don't see the child." She recounted R'ney's tale of his two sisters.

"Oh, so she needs someone to cut her hair!" X'lerin said when she'd finished.

"No, she needs someone to paddle her bottom until she can't sit," Xhinna said. "But for a reason so good that she can't argue the punishment."

"I wouldn't care to—" X'lerin began, shaking his head.

"And *that* is why she's so spoiled," Xhinna cut him off. "Because no one cares to."

"In all honesty," X'lerin told her in a quiet, sincere voice, "I'd really prefer if you rode a queen."

"Why, thank you!" Xhinna said, truly flattered. She changed her tone and smiled devilishly as she said, "And if I did, I'm sure that my queen would be happy to outfly you."

"Probably," X'lerin agreed. "There certainly is one thing you've taught me already."

"One thing?"

"Don't judge a rider by his—or her—dragon's color."

"Even gold," Xhinna agreed.

SIX
▼▼▼▼▼▼▼▼▼▼▼▼

A Knot on
the Shoulder

"No good deed goes unpunished" was an old saying—an Ancient-Timer saying according to some—and Xhinna realized, ruefully, that it was still valid when X'lerin gave her his latest surprise two days later.

"Wingleader?" Xhinna echoed, eyes wide. "You want *me* to be a wingleader?"

"And that's an order," X'lerin said to Xhinna, with a smug look. K'dan stood nearby, a huge grin spreading across his face as he, clearly forewarned, took delight in Xhinna's amazement.

"We're only just making it official," the harper told her. "After all, it's either that or Weyrleader—"

"But I ride a blue!"

"And we've already told you that it's not the dragon, it's the rider," K'dan reminded her.

"So I'm to be wingleader and my wing is . . . ," Xhinna asked, hopeful that she'd found the glaring flaw in their—for K'dan was clearly as responsible for *this* as X'lerin—distracting plan.

"Well, mostly you, Taria, and the queen weyrlings," X'lerin said diffidently. "I'll assign some others from time to time."

"And my duties?"

"Not different from what you've already been doing," X'lerin said. He eyed her shoulder. "But I want your rank knot on by night-fall." In a smaller voice, he added, "And we want you to *lead* the queens."

"You're serious?" Xhinna said. "You want me to lead the queens?"

"Deadly," X'lerin told her.

"What about K'dan? He's the Weyrlingmaster!"

"I'll have my hands full with the others," K'dan said. "Not that I won't be drilling the queens when the time comes, but we felt—"

"We felt that they needed someone like you," X'lerin interjected.

"What?" Xhinna asked, brows high. "A girl?"

"No, a leader," X'lerin retorted. "I've got my hands full with my wing and the queens are too much on their own for any bronze rider." He cut his eyes slyly toward K'dan as he added, "Even a harper."

"We're merely recognizing your authority in a way that can't be argued," K'dan added. Xhinna turned to look at him—so they expected her to be challenged. Her thoughts turned immediately to Jepara. Apparently X'lerin had come up with a solution to her intransigence that kept him away from it. It was, she realized, not such a bad solution, especially given that X'lerin's dragon was the only mature bronze in the small Weyr, which sometimes required him, as the authority of last resort, to delegate difficult tasks and distance himself from painful decisions.

"Wingleader?" Xhinna repeated. "So I'll be leading the queens and—what?"

"You're going to be scouting a lot and you'll need help. This will make it easier all around."

"Some won't like it," Xhinna pointed out.

"Do you mean J'keran?" X'lerin asked, raising an eyebrow. "I'll manage him."

Actually, she'd been thinking of Jepara and the other young queen riders, but Xhinna could think of nothing else to say, glancing from young bronze rider to older harper until K'dan burst out in laughter.

"You should see your face!"

Xhinna glared at him.

"Check with Javissa, I'm sure she can find you something from our stores to make a suitable rank knot," X'lerin told her, his eyes twinkling with delight.

She started to move off but stopped and turned back. "If I'm to be a wingleader, shouldn't I have a wingsecond?"

"Of course," K'dan said at once.

"Who do you have in mind?" X'lerin asked. "I'm afraid that I'll need all the older dragons—"

"And Coranth is guarding her eggs," K'dan noted.

"I was thinking of someone else," Xhinna said. "Someone with his own authority."

"Oh!" X'lerin said, suddenly enlightened. "Excellent, a marvelous choice." He nodded firmly. "Go for it."

Xhinna was already annoyed when she caught up to R'ney a sevenday later. She'd spent most of the past week dealing with various moans, groans, and whines from the young queen riders—not to mention no small amount of time dealing with the obstreperous Jepara. But when his brown weyrling threw clumps of dirt all over her clean clothes, her anger overheated.

"Stop, stop!" she yelled. "By the First Egg, R'ney, what do you think you're doing?"

"Xhinna!" R'ney cried, rushing around Rowerth's hind legs and briskly brushing the damp soil off of her. In his haste, he only succeeded in grinding more in. "I didn't hear you come—I'm sorry."

Xhinna let out a deep sigh, telling herself that, as K'dan had recently reminded her, the first duty of a leader is to control herself, particularly her temper. Xhinna's protest that she wasn't a leader, merely a blue rider, had been met by contemptuous snorts from both X'lerin and K'dan.

"It isn't the color of the dragon but the force of your personality," K'dan had told her. X'lerin had nodded in firm agreement. They'd gone on to talk about what it meant to be a leader and how some, regardless of their dragons, were better suited than others—J'keran was the counterexample.

Now Xhinna forced herself to ask more reasonably, "What are you doing?"

"Digging."

"Digging—why?" Xhinna asked, tamping down more firmly on her temper.

"To see how deep we need to go," he replied, in a tone that implied that his answer should have been obvious.

"How deep?" Xhinna repeated, wondering if the smither was entertaining some wild notion of making tunnels. If so, she'd remind him right quick about the tunnel snakes.

"To the rock, of course," R'ney replied. His enthusiasm faded enough for him to gauge the level of her confusion and he flushed. "I'm sorry, I was thinking that perhaps we could level the dirt off the top of the plateau and make our Weyr here."

"Take *all* the dirt off the plateau?" Xhinna asked in surprise. She thought for a moment. "How long would that take?"

"That's what I'm trying to find out," R'ney told her. "I have to know how far down we need to go and how quickly a dragon can dig before I can do the calculations." He smiled as if expecting praise for his resolution of two problems in the same operation.

"And where are you supposed to be right now?" Xhinna asked.

R'ney's face fell. "Taria's with Razz and Jirana."

"You left a pregnant mother and a child together with a Mrreow?" Xhinna roared, unable to contain herself. Bekka had only needed one quick inspection of Taria before pronouncing her officially pregnant.

R'ney wilted for a moment, then said mulishly, "The Meeyu is sleeping and they're on the outside of the cage."

"Oh," Xhinna said in an apologetic tone, "sorry." In an attempt at further apology, she waved her hand at the hole that had provided the dirt still festooning her best riding gear and asked, "So what did you find?"

"I'd only just started, blue rider," R'ney replied. He was too gentle—mostly—to roar back at her. The few times he had, though, she'd thoroughly deserved it and had, as soon as she'd cooled down, been grateful for his criticism.

"One of the duties of a second," R'ney had said as he dismissed her apology back then, "is to have the courage to tell his leader when she's wrong."

"Keep doing that, please," Xhinna had told him.

"Is this another of those times when I'm wrong and need to apologize?" she asked now, feeling humbled.

R'ney thought about it for a moment and then shook his head. "No," he said, "this is one of the times when you should bite my head off and feed it to the Mrreows for endangering our young."

"Okay," Xhinna said. "By my count, then, we're about even."

"I don't keep count," R'ney told her. "But if I did, I'd say that I was in your debt from the first."

"Well, then, I'd say that *now* we're even because I was keeping count," Xhinna told him drolly.

The brown rider gave her a steady look, then snorted and shrugged, shaking his head.

"But, digging out all the dirt, is that really possible?" she asked.

"It's certainly possible. It's only a question of digging."

"But how much and for how long?"

"I was trying to find out," R'ney reminded her. Xhinna shrugged an apology and gestured for them to move to the front of the small brown dragon.

"How'd you get Rowerth here, anyway?" Xhinna asked. "Coranth?"

"Taria offered to ferry him in exchange for my supervision of her and Jirana when they were with the Meeyus," R'ney said. "Rowerth wanted some exercise, and K'dan had mentioned that the dragons use their back legs to launch themselves, so I thought digging . . ."

"It might be a good idea for the hatchlings to get out more," Xhinna said. "And we've enough dragons now that we could bring them to the shore. They like prancing in the water."

"I hadn't thought of that," R'ney confessed. "I planned to ask Taria to have Coranth bring Rowerth to bathe when we were done. I figured we'd get dirty." He glanced down at his own tunic and flicked a clod of dirt off it.

"Could Tazith help dig? He'd be faster," Xhinna asked.

R'ney shook his head. "Not that I don't appreciate the offer, but—". He paused as Rowerth began furiously scooping out more dirt with his hind legs. The little brown—not quite so little anymore—was clearly thrilled with the play he'd been asked to do.

"I'd already calculated the baseline for Rowerth, and I'd have to recalibrate for Tazith," R'ney said. Xhinna raised one eyebrow at him and shook her head slowly in the way she'd come to realize made the smith remember that she hadn't his smithcraft training. R'ney sighed.

"It's easier this way," he said simply. She shrugged and stood back, watching until she got bored.

"I'll check on the others," she told him, heading off to the Mrreow cage. Tazith begged to stay behind, entranced by the little brown's play.

"Talk nicely with R'ney and he might let you join in later," Xhinna called with a wave toward her blue. Tazith rumbled wistfully and craned his neck down by the brown rider, faceted eyes whirling a light green as he hoped to charm the smither.

"Not yet, Tazith," R'ney said, reaching up idly to scratch the blue's eye ridges. "Let's let Rowerth see what he can do first."

Jirana was awake when Xhinna got to the cage. She was just outside the bars, leaning in with one arm to pet the nearest Meeyu. Xhinna broke into a run when she saw her and tackled the child, scooping her up and rolling her out of the way.

"Never do that!" Xhinna cried as Jirana burst into frightened tears. "You can't trust the Mrreows!"

"I was only petting it," Jirana cried. Taria woke up at the commotion and looked over in alarm.

"I must have dozed off," she said in apology. Her eyes narrowed as she took in the tableau. "What are you doing with Jirana?"

Xhinna explained quickly and Taria shook her head. "They wouldn't hurt her."

"Not like Coranth," Xhinna retorted hotly. "They'd maul her first, probably hamstring her, and then—" She broke off, seeing the growing terror in Jirana's eyes. She took a deep breath and brought her worries under control. "Sweetie," she told the young girl, "you can't just think that every soft furry thing is going to be good all the time."

"She's right," Taria said, giving Xhinna a pointed look. "Sometimes you can't be too careful."

"No," Xhinna corrected, "you can *never* be too careful." Taria had grown moodier and more worried as her pregnancy really took hold and the Hatching neared.

"Shouldn't you be off finding Candidates?" Taria asked. The eggs were due to hatch in another three weeks at most, as the old Teaching Ballads warned:

> *Count three months and more,*
> *And five heated weeks,*
> *A day of glory, and*
> *In a month, who seeks?*

The three months were the time from mating to clutching, the "five heated weeks" the time on the usually warm Hatching Grounds at the great Weyrs. The "day of glory" was the Hatching and Impression itself, and then, as they'd recently discovered, "in a month, who seeks" meant that the month-old dragonets could actually go *between* from one place to another, even though they usually took between two and three Turns to reach their full growth.

"Are you two fighting again?" Jirana asked, having recovered from her fright. She looked at Xhinna and then Taria. "I thought you loved each other."

"We do," Xhinna told her. "But we can love each other and still disagree."

Taria snorted. "And people, even dragonriders, can be wrong," she said. "The smart ones are those who admit it."

"I was coming to tell you that I've arranged to go Search," Xhinna said as she released Jirana. She was surprised when the girl grabbed her hands and began to rub them.

"I like your hands," Jirana told her softly. "I feel safe in them."

Taria glanced sharply at the little girl, then up into Xhinna's eyes. Her lips quivered for a moment, and then she confessed, "I do, too."

The tension seemed to drain out of the air as Xhinna met her eyes.

"I get scared sometimes," Xhinna said softly. She felt Jirana pause in her rubbing, then resume it again as though she were performing some sort of healing massage, like her brother J'riz.

"I'm terrified all the time," Taria replied. She glanced down at her belly, still flat, at the Meeyus in their cage and then, fleetingly, toward the sandy beach where Coranth's eggs lay.

"V'lex and Sarinth are with the eggs," Xhinna reassured her.

"I should bring Coranth back to her eggs," Taria said, rising. She motioned for Jirana, but the girl ignored her, sitting firmly in Xhinna's lap, rubbing her fingers in patterns around the backs of Xhinna's hands.

Tazith? Could you come here please? Xhinna called.

Tazith flew in a moment later, landing nearby.

"We're ready now," Jirana said, getting up from Xhinna's lap and extending a hand to help her to her feet. Xhinna grinned at the little girl's offer, but accepted it solemnly and used a bit of Jirana's weight to help her to her feet. "Do you feel better now?"

"Yes," Xhinna told her, "I do."

"My mother gets mad when I fight," Jirana said.

"I get mad when I fight," Xhinna admitted. "Sometimes it's hard not to, though, isn't it?"

"You mean it doesn't get easier when you get older?" Jirana asked in surprise.

"It gets easier to stop being mad," Xhinna told her. "And it gets easier to decide *not* to be mad. But sometimes you still get mad."

"Oh." Jirana raised her hands for Xhinna to pick her up. Even at ten, the child was small enough that she was nothing to carry, and Xhinna slung her on one hip with the practice of a child-minder and walked toward Tazith. Jirana leaned in suddenly and kissed Xhinna's cheek. "I love you."

"I love you, too," Xhinna said, returning the kiss with a big, loud smack. Jirana giggled, then gestured for her to raise her up to Tazith. Xhinna complied and climbed up behind her, rigging the riding straps for the two of them before urging Tazith into the sky.

Once they were airborne, Jirana leaned back and tilted her head so that her words could carry to Xhinna's ears. "Can I come with you?"

"I'm bringing you back to your mother," Xhinna said, "isn't that enough?"

"I want to come with you," Jirana said.

"I don't think your mother would like that," Xhinna said. "It might be dangerous."

"Not with you," Jirana replied confidently. "If my mother says it's all right, will you let me?"

Xhinna smiled. "We'll see."

"It seems they can swim just fine," K'dan said as he watched Lurenth prance in the waves. It had been an unanswered question as to whether the weyrlings could swim until K'dan had asked his bronze to try the water. Watching Lurenth cautiously approach and then just as anxiously retreat from the waves that lapped the shore had brought a smile to everyone's lips. Lurenth had turned back to *whuff* at his rider before sternly braving his way into the waves and then out beyond them.

I'm floating! Lurenth had declared, gamely turning onto his back and stretching his wings, sculling his way forward with his hind legs.

"Yes, you are!" K'dan had called back, laughing at his dragon's joy. "Don't go too far, or Tazith will have to bring you back."

I won't, the little bronze affirmed.

"Well, that's excellent," Xhinna said, sending a thought to Tazith instructing the blue to keep a close eye just the same. "We can get them all down and exercising."

"That'll help with their muscles and growth," K'dan said. "But it'll make them hungrier."

"I think better hungrier than flabby," X'lerin said as he moved down the sands to approach them. "I'll have W'vin arrange for the rest to be brought down in rotation."

K'dan nodded. "Until we're sure they're safe, it's best not to have too many in the water at once."

X'lerin frowned. "I've never heard of anything like a sea tunnel snake."

"No," K'dan agreed. "And I checked with Colfet. He says that he's never heard of anything in the sea that would attack a dragonet."

X'lerin nodded, turning around to glance at the distant eggs that lay on the sands.

"It's nothing like the Weyrs," K'dan said as he followed the other bronze rider's gaze.

"We're going to need Candidates soon," Xhinna said.

K'dan turned back to face her. "What do you propose?"

Xhinna shrugged, turning a questioning look to X'lerin, who gestured for her to continue. She told K'dan, "I can't see any choice but—"

"Hold on," K'dan said, raising a hand. "I was thinking about this . . ." He jerked his head for them to follow him. X'lerin raised his eyebrows toward Xhinna, who shook her head to show that she knew no more than he.

"It's over here," K'dan said, leading the way. "I made sure to draw it above the high tide line."

"Draw what?" X'lerin asked.

"This," K'dan said, pointing to a series of lines and squiggles on the sand before them. He bent down and picked up the stick that clearly had been his writing instrument.

"And what is this, harper?" X'lerin wondered.

"Well . . . ," K'dan began slowly, "I can't claim to know more than anyone else on this, but I've been thinking about what happened to Fiona and the others—"

"That's why you've been asking me!" X'lerin exclaimed.

K'dan nodded. He glanced over to Xhinna. "And Xhinna tried to go forward to Telgar—"

"And nearly died for her pains!" X'lerin put in.

"But none of the Records ever mention something like this," K'dan said, "at least as far as I recall."

X'lerin nodded. "In *that*, you are our master."

K'dan's lips twitched even as he shook his head in disagreement.

"Anyway," he said, gesturing to the drawing on the sand, "I was thinking that perhaps *between* has a shape to it."

"A shape?"

"Well, perhaps not a 'shape' so much as something that defines it," K'dan said. "That *between* is a way through both space and time, so I thought that time and space have a meaning in *between*."

"I don't understand," X'lerin said. Beside him, Xhinna nodded vigorously in agreement.

"I don't know if it can be put into words," K'dan said, pointing again to the drawing, "which is why I tried to draw it."

"And this drawing shows?"

K'dan pointed with the stick to the part of the drawing farthest from them. "Let's say that that line represents where Fiona and everyone else went. Our 'present' if you will."

"About three Turns from now," X'lerin said by way of agreement.

"A bit more, I think," K'dan said. "I've checked with Colfet. He's been looking at the stars and he thinks we're back in the summer three Turns before the Third Pass."

He pointed to a spot on the drawing. "That dotted line represents the time when D'gan and the old Telgars jumped *between*."

"And that other line?" X'lerin said, pointing to the line that ran from some point in the future to the top line of the drawing, the "present" line.

"That's the line representing Fiona's jump *between* times," K'dan said. He pointed at the big hole where the two lines met. "And that hole is the knot that formed when they crossed paths."

"And?" X'lerin prompted.

"We know from Xhinna that the knot was still there when she tried to jump," K'dan said. "And we know from your arrival that the knot doesn't prevent people from jumping *back* in time, only from jumping forward."

"Or we were just lucky," X'lerin said.

"Did you feel like you were stuck, unable to move?" Xhinna asked him, a shiver going down her spine as the memory of that horrible moment flowed once again in her mind.

"No," X'lerin said. "As I told you, it was like a normal jump *between* times."

"Nothing like when you were caught going forward with Fiona," K'dan observed.

"No, not at all," X'lerin said. "You know how relieved we were." He pursed his lips tightly and turned to Xhinna. "We were all afraid."

"Shh!" K'dan snapped. X'lerin gave him a surprised look. "You're referring to the message Xhinna sent but hasn't written yet."

"Yes," X'lerin admitted, his shoulders slumping.

"I can leave that message when I go in Search," Xhinna said.

K'dan raised his stick and drew a new line close to them. "I think you'd be safest if you went *back* in time from here and then came forward once more." He drew connecting lines from the "now" position to some place back in time and then back again.

"Yes," Xhinna said, frowning at the drawing. "That could work."

"It would be safest if you didn't change times at all," X'lerin protested.

"Safest, but we're going to have to time it at some point," K'dan said. X'lerin raised an eyebrow. "Weyrleader, in the next three Turns, we're going to need firestone and the only place we can get that is back in time."

"At the Igen mine?" Xhinna asked.

"Yes," K'dan agreed. "It's the only place that's large enough where our presence might be kept a secret."

"And we need to keep it a secret because no one back in time knew about us," X'lerin guessed.

"Perhaps because we *didn't* go back in time?" Xhinna suggested.

"If we didn't go back in time, then we don't get firestone," X'lerin reminded her. "And we'll need it if we have to stay here until we're beyond the time of the knot *between*."

"And if you go back in time, maybe some of those who were missing after the Plague could be saved," K'dan added.

"But, K'dan, aren't they already dead?"

"Not if you rescued them!"

▼ ▼ ▼

"**I** should come with you. You're weyrbred—you won't know what to say," Jepara said when Xhinna explained her plans to her gold riders. Xhinna couldn't hide her surprise at the other's offer. Jepara pressed on, "As a Lord Holder's daughter, it's my right."

"We don't know if this will work," Xhinna told her, shaking her head. "If we fail—" Her words trailed off as she heard Taria gasp. She nodded toward her, then continued, "If we fail, we don't need to lose two dragons—yours would not survive your loss."

"Two?" Jepara repeated in confusion. And then she caught Xhinna's meaning and her eyes turned involuntarily toward where her Sarurth lay sleeping. "Well, then who's going to take over if you don't come back?"

Taria hissed, too angry to form words.

"Just as long as it's not you," Meeya chimed in.

"No one's asking you, *Meeyu*," Jepara snarled back. "Shouldn't you be milking milchbeasts for your kin?"

Meeya glared at her, but before she could respond, Xhinna intervened, "That's enough!" She cut her glare between Jepara, Taria, and Meeya.

"Bekka will take over—"

"Me?" Bekka cried in protest.

"—until I get back," Xhinna continued, ignoring the interjection. "It won't be long—this whole conversation has probably dragged on longer than the trip will take."

"You need to take *me*."

Everyone turned toward the sound of the small voice. It was Jirana. Seeing her, Jepara snorted derisively.

"I have to go, to show you the way, to help with Laspanth."

"Laspanth?" Xhinna asked.

"My queen," Jirana replied, sounding sleepy. "The green queen."

"Sweetie, you should get to bed," Xhinna told her in a kindly voice. "You sound all worn out."

"She sounds addled," Jepara said. She turned back to Xhinna. "But she's right in a way. There are eighteen eggs on the beach. How are you going to carry enough Candidates on one tiny blue?"

Xhinna ignored the jab implied in "tiny" and started to answer when Jirana responded dreamily: "Only five are needed. Five will hatch: three greens and two blues."

Xhinna shook her head, stood up from where she sat, and moved toward Jirana. "Come on, little one, I'm taking you to your mother."

When Xhinna picked her up, the little girl shook and her eyes opened wide. "Xhinna?" She seemed surprised. "Did I really say all that? About a queen and five hatchlings?"

"What, don't you remember?" Jepara called.

"It was like a dream," Jirana said, "I thought maybe I was just sleeping."

"Let's get you to your mother," Xhinna repeated, not surprised to find that Taria had joined her.

Taria leaned closer to Xhinna and said for her ears alone, "Was that the Sight?"

"Yes," Jirana replied, having better ears than Taria had imagined. The little girl yawned and leaned against Xhinna's chest. "That was the Sight."

"It's early," Javissa said when Xhinna recounted the events to her later. She glanced down at Jirana, who was deep in sleep; she'd nodded off during the short walk from the meeting and couldn't be stirred, even when Javissa bundled her up in a blanket. "The first Sight usually comes with adolescence."

"So do you believe it?"

"I don't know." Javissa shook her head. "It's possible, but it's also possible that she's imagining it."

"I need to go soon," Xhinna said.

"There's danger?"

"Yes," Xhinna said, recalling her conversation with K'dan and X'lerin. "We can't be sure if timing it won't get us trapped."

"She said she'd get a queen?"

"And that only five Candidates were needed for Coranth's clutch," Xhinna said.

"And what of the others?"

"She didn't say," Xhinna told her.

Javissa looked up to the stars that were just peeping through the night sky. When she lowered her gaze, her eyes met Xhinna's. "I never expected this."

"You say she's too young?"

"I do," Javissa agreed, her lips pinching together in a quick frown. "But the way you described her, she behaved just like her father when he saw the future."

"Could she be pretending?"

"No, she never saw her father when he had a Sight," Javissa replied. A smile touched her lips briefly. "And she's an honest child, mostly. I don't think she'd scheme up something like this."

"So what do we do?"

"If you can wait until morning, when she's awake," Javissa said, "I'll ask her if she still wants to go."

"It doesn't matter so much when I go as *when* I go to."

"Well, then," Javissa said, turning to glance down tenderly at her only daughter, "let's see what the dawn brings."

"I can't believe you're going to listen to a little girl," Taria chided her the next morning when they met on the beach. "There are eighteen eggs on the sands, not five."

"I know," Xhinna agreed. "But we've got to start somewhere and Tazith can only carry so many—"

"He could carry one more if *she* didn't go," Taria sniffed. She shivered as a cold breeze blew in from offshore where clouds were gathering and threatening a misty, perhaps even damp, morning.

She is very light, Tazith said to Xhinna.

"What?" Taria demanded, catching the distracted look in Xhinna's eyes.

"Tazith says she's very light," Xhinna reported.

"Huh, he would!"

"Look, Taria, K'dan agrees that it makes sense to scout out for Candidates back in time," Xhinna said. She made a face. "To be honest, if I could, I'd prefer to leave Jirana behind—"

"What?" Taria exclaimed. "Why?"

"Because K'dan could be wrong," Xhinna told her. "It could be that no one can go *between* times."

"X'lerin and the others—"

"I should have said, can go forward *between* times," Xhinna corrected herself with a wave of her hand.

"But you're not," Taria said, "you're going back—" She broke off.

"And then I've got to come back," Xhinna said, nodding to affirm Taria's unspoken conclusion. "*That's* where the problems will come, if any."

"Why can't X'lerin go?" Taria asked. "He's the Weyrleader."

"It makes more sense for me to go," Xhinna said. She said nothing, waiting for Taria to think of the reasons herself.

"You're expendable," Taria said at last.

"It's my fault we're in this mess—it was my decision to come here," Xhinna said, not quite disagreeing.

"That's unfair!" Taria said. She half-turned to glance at the distant broom trees that housed Sky Weyr. "Did X'lerin say that to you?"

"No," Xhinna replied, "I said it to myself."

"You take too much on," Taria said.

"Someone's got to find the Candidates. Who better than Tazith?"

Taria's lips tightened; she couldn't argue with that—it was well-known that blues were good at searching out Candidates and it was obvious that Sky Weyr couldn't afford to risk X'lerin and Kivith, the only mature bronze.

"But why take *her*?" Taria asked, pointing to the distance. Xhinna turned and saw Jirana rushing across the sands toward them, Javissa and X'lerin following farther behind.

"Tazith says she gives good coordinates," Xhinna said.

"What do *you* say?"

"If she really *does* See, then I have to take her with me."

"Xhinna, Xhinna!" Jirana called, nearly doubled over and out of breath as she reached them. "I'm ready!"

"You should catch your breath first," Taria told her absently.

Jirana smiled up at her, her dark eyes flashing. "I can do that when we're in the air."

"Only five?" Taria said to the girl.

"That's all I saw," Jirana told her.

"Could you be wrong?"

"Oh, yes!" Jirana said. She saw Taria's look and added, "That was my first time, so I can't say that I've got everything right. And—" She shrugged her shoulders. "—I don't quite remember all of it."

Taria cut her eyes to Xhinna imploringly.

"So are you sure you need to come, little one?" Xhinna asked. She waved a hand toward Javissa. "I'm sure your mother would appreciate it if you stayed here."

"I have to go—it's my duty," Jirana said, shifting her gaze between Xhinna and her mother.

Javissa pulled the little girl into her arms and hugged her tight. "If you're certain, go."

Jirana pushed back far enough to peer up into her mother's eyes. "I'm certain, Momma."

Javissa's lips curled up and she bent down, kissing the top of her daughter's head. Gently, she turned her around and pushed her toward Xhinna.

"Weyrleader," Xhinna said, nodding toward X'lerin, giving him final say in the manner.

"Good flying," X'lerin said.

"Come on," Xhinna said to Jirana, motioning her toward Tazith who, in deference to the child's scant height, lowered his forelegs and shoulders to the ground.

"Thanks, Tazith!" Jirana said as she scampered up onto the blue's neck.

That was very kind, Xhinna added as she climbed up behind the little girl. She rigged the riding straps and gave Tazith a silent command.

Hold on, Tazith cautioned as he righted himself. A moment later he took two steps forward, leapt with his back legs, and was airborne, clawing upward into the sky.

In front of Xhinna, Jirana let out a cry of pure joy.

I have the image, Tazith said, relaying it to Xhinna. She caught a flag at half-mast, realized it was the Crom Hold flag.

Let's go, she said, even as she tried to puzzle out one niggling color in the image.

They were *between* when she realized what it was. Beneath the Crom Hold flag she'd seen another, smaller flag. Yellow. The Plague flag.

SEVEN

▼▼▼▼▼▼▼▼▼▼▼

A Deed Redone

"We need to go back," Xhinna said as soon as they burst into the sky above Crom Hold. Dawn was just breaking: The sun had just crested the horizon, casting the inner walls of the Hold in sharp relief. "We've gone back too far—"

"No, we haven't," Jirana said. "We're right where we need to be." She pointed down, behind them. "Tazith, turn around and go behind that hill. Land there."

"No!" Xhinna said. "Jirana, that yellow flag is the Plague flag. We've gone back to the time of the Plague, we've gone back too far."

We've gone back only seven Turns, Tazith assured her.

"Then why is the Plague flag still flying?"

"Why don't you ask them?" Jirana said, pointing to a small group of tents in the distance.

At Xhinna's urging, Tazith turned and winged his way toward the tents. Xhinna could tell that even from the high towers of Crom, the tents would be obscured by the knoll in front of them.

Drop down, Xhinna told Tazith and soon the blue was behind the knoll, equally obscured from Crom.

"They're flying the same flag," Jirana said, pointing toward one of the nearest tents. "But not the yellow pennant."

"Maybe they don't have one to spare," Xhinna said. "Jirana, we can't risk the Plague—"

"They look like they're starving," Jirana said, referring to the small knot of people stretched out not far from the flagged tent. She turned and pointed east. "There, isn't that the Red Star?"

Xhinna turned her head to follow the girl's finger and picked up the dim light of a red orb nearly obscured by the brilliance of the morning light. Yes, it was the Red Star.

"How many Turns is it from our Pass?" Jirana asked, glancing back over her shoulder at Xhinna.

"Tazith says we've gone back seven Turns," said Xhinna, who was beginning to catch on to the younger girl's reasoning. Jirana nodded and smiled.

"Then we're ten Turns before the start of the Pass, and the Plague ended two Turns before this."

"So why is the fever pennant flying at the Hold?"

"Xhinna, this is where we *need* to be," Jirana said. "You're going to have to trust me on this."

Xhinna pursed her lips tightly, sending a different image to Tazith even as she said, "Little one, I can't."

A moment later, dragon and riders were gone from the morning sky.

"**X**hinna!" Jirana cried as soon as they burst back from *between*. "What did you do?"

"I have to leave a message," Xhinna said as Tazith, at her request, started a lazy downward spiral.

Jirana spotted what was below them. "That's the Red Butte, isn't it?"

Xhinna nodded.

"You brought us forward in time," Jirana said in surprise. She gestured down to the plateau. "My father is buried there. You brought us here to the time after he died."

"I know," Xhinna said. "I had to find out," she added, more to herself than to the child in front of her. "I had to know that we could make the jump forward again."

"And you didn't tell me."

"Little one, what good would it have done to tell you?"

"At least I'd have known."

"I thought that if you knew, your fear might help trap us," Xhinna told her.

"But there was no trap, was there?" Jirana said. "At least, I didn't *feel* anything."

"No, it was like a regular jump *between* times," Xhinna agreed.

"So you know that K'dan's right—that the knot is only at that one time, when D'gan's Weyr jumped to fight Thread and Fiona's Weyr jumped forward."

"Yes," Xhinna said, not hiding the relief in her voice. "And I can leave a message for Fiona in the future."

Deftly, Tazith landed on the wide plateau and Xhinna jumped down. Immediately, she reached up for Jirana, who objected, "I can get down by myself."

"You'll take my help or you'll stay up there," Xhinna said. "I won't bring you back to your mother with a broken leg." As Jirana relented and threw her legs over the blue's side, Xhinna added, "Beside, the ground is harder than you'd think."

On the ground, Jirana took quick note of their surroundings. "It's hot up here. And dry."

Xhinna nodded. "We won't stay long."

"Over there," Jirana said, pointing east.

The plateau was large and riddled with crevices. Xhinna looked at her doubtfully. "How can you know?"

"I was here, in my dreams," Jirana said. She gave Xhinna a sad look. "I left an offering for my father." Without another word, the youngster strode off, her face set in determination.

Xhinna followed after, raising a hand to her brow to better shield her eyes from the sun.

"It's there!" Jirana shouted, breaking into a run just as Xhinna spotted a whiter patch among the rocks. Xhinna picked up her pace, not quite running—having a care for her footing and the heat—and soon saw the white rocks that Lorana had used to cover Tenniz's shallow grave.

"I'm here, Father," Jirana said, standing by the cairn. "I've Seen and I know what it's like." She made a small, sad noise. "I'm sorry I couldn't have told you." Oblivious to the sound of Xhinna approaching behind her, she continued, "Did it make you sad, too, knowing all those things?"

"Jirana?" Xhinna said, kneeling beside the young girl. "What is it that you Saw?"

"The first thing a person Sees is their death," Jirana said.

"Oh."

Jirana reached behind her and caught Xhinna's hand in hers. "It's not as bad as you think," she said. "I was old—older than you."

"What else?"

"I can't say," Jirana said stoutly. "I can't break time any more than Fiona can."

Xhinna wrapped her free arm around the child's chest and hugged her tightly.

"Tell me what you can," she suggested.

"I did," Jirana said, turning suddenly in her arms and staring Xhinna in the face, her face grim, "and you didn't believe me."

"We have to be careful," Xhinna said, a little defensively.

"You don't trust people," Jirana said. "You try to do it all yourself." She shook her head and then turned back to her father, saying, "Maybe *you* can do it, but *we* can't."

"Are you talking to me or your father?" Xhinna asked in a soft, encouraging voice.

"Both of you," Jirana said. "He's dead, so he can't hear me; you're afraid, so you *won't* hear me."

She dropped Xhinna's hand and moved out of reach, turning to say, "What message are you going to leave?"

"Once I leave the message, we can go back to Crom," Xhinna said, trying to find a way to placate this suddenly too-strange child.

"Not to the same time," Jirana said. "They'll have seen Tazith and they'll be scared."

"Scared?"

"They'll think he was scouting."

"For whom?"

"For whoever is hiding in the Hold."

"Dragons are beholden to the Weyrs, Jirana," Xhinna said, trying to gently remind the child of the facts. "A dragon wouldn't scout for a Hold."

"Unless the Weyr ordered it."

"But Crom's beholden to Telgar and—" Xhinna broke off as Jirana nodded. Telgar, ten Turns in their past, was still led by D'gan.

"Nerra rules Crom," Xhinna said.

"Now she does," Jirana agreed, "in *our* time, Turns in the future."

Xhinna pursed her lips tightly.

"Did you ever find out *how* she came to rule Crom?" Jirana asked.

"She took the Hold back from her brother, who had blockaded himself inside while the holders starved," Xhinna recalled. And then her eyes went wide. "Oh!"

Stoutly Jirana declared, "I *told* you we were in the right time."

Tazith vetoed Xhinna's first image, telling her it was too close to when they'd left, so she imagined them once again over the knoll but ten minutes later than when they'd left. She paused for a long time before giving Tazith the order to jump back in time.

"They could still be dying here," Xhinna said. "We could be wrong—"

"Then we'll die," Jirana said. "It's possible."

"I thought you—"

"Xhinna, the Sight doesn't show what *will* happen, only what *might* happen," Jirana said. "My mother told me that, and she was told by my father."

"But the hatchlings, this queen of yours—"

"There are *might be*'s, not certainties," Jirana told her. She shook her head as they slowly glided toward the ground, adding, "I could be wrong. I'm new at all this."

" 'Every day is new,' " Xhinna said, recalling an old song she'd once heard at Fort Weyr, Turns earlier.

" 'And so are we,' " Jirana finished, turning back to give Xhinna a big smile. "Are you going to trust me?"

"Let's see what happens first," Xhinna temporized. She glanced about the camp. "Why are they all just standing there?"

"I think they're too sick to move," Jirana said.

"With the Plague?" Xhinna cried, thinking to tell Tazith to claw his way back up.

"No, hunger," Jirana said, shaking her head. Tazith touched the ground. "Let me go to them," the little girl said, gesturing for Xhinna to help her down.

"What?"

"If I'm wrong, I'll wave you off," Jirana said. "That way Tazith won't lose you."

"No," Xhinna said firmly, sliding her right leg over Tazith's neck and sliding down. On the ground she reached up for Jirana. "We'll do this together."

Jirana smiled in thanks, threw her legs over, and let Xhinna catch her as she slid down.

Once they were both standing on their own feet, Xhinna ordered Tazith back into the air. When the blue rumbled in protest, she patted his foreleg and said, "Jirana says we'll be safe, so up you get!"

Call if you need me, Tazith said.

Stay behind the knoll, Xhinna reminded him as he rose higher into the sky.

If I stay here too long, I'll have to land, the blue responded.

Fly in circles for a bit, Xhinna said. *I'm sure we'll know one way or the other before you get exhausted.*

"We need to go *there*," Jirana said, pointing toward the tent with the Crom flag.

They had only a couple hundred meters to go, but to Xhinna it seemed much farther. She could see people rise and then fall back down onto the dusty ground as she passed; she could see others not even moving. If this wasn't the Plague, it was, as Jirana had said, starvation, Xhinna thought. All around her the people were gaunt, tired, their eyes dim, hollow.

They were stopped at the entrance to the tent by a tall, strong man who stood in their path.

"State your business."

"We ride in Search," Xhinna said, straightening her spine in a vain attempt to match the other's height.

"Search? A girl?" the man asked. He glanced to the air. "Where are the bronzes?"

"Why come *here*?" another called from the crowd that was slowly gathering.

"Did you bring any food?" a woman added.

"No," Xhinna said. "I'm sorry, we didn't know."

"What, does Fenril tell you that everyone is well-fed now?"

"I haven't spoken with Fenril."

"You are from Telgar, are you not?" the guard demanded, glancing down at the short dirk hanging from her belt. "That's the Telgar mark on your dirk."

"I—" Xhinna paused, trying to figure the best way to proceed.

"What, are you a renegade?" a voice from the crowd called out.

"D'gan would never let a girl near a dragon, unless it was a queen," the guard said, his eyes probing Xhinna's.

"The dragon chooses the rider," Xhinna said.

"A blue rider—we would have heard of this," someone else called from the crowd.

"What's your name?"

"Xhinna."

"That's not a Telgar name."

"It's not a dragonrider name, even," another added.

"Xhinna . . . ," Jirana said, her voice tinged with fear.

"We ride in Search," Xhinna repeated to the guard. "Will you let us pass?"

"What of your friend?" the guard asked, glancing down at Jirana, who looked away.

"She's trader born," Xhinna said, hoping that would ease their way.

"Trader!" a voice from the crowd called. "Have you come to trade, little one?"

"Please," Xhinna said to the guard, "let us pass." Above them, Tazith bellowed, sensing her disquiet. "Tazith, shh!" she said aloud, even as she relayed the thought to the blue.

The guard's eyes flickered from Xhinna, to the blue in the sky, and then back. "That's really your dragon," he said in surprise.

"Of course he is!" Jirana exclaimed.

"No girl rides a blue," the guard declared. But he was already stepping aside and pulling the tent flap open.

"Except Xhinna—she's the first," Jirana said as she reached for Xhinna's hand and half-tugged her into the tent.

Inside, they stopped dead. All eyes were on them, and it was obvious that their conversation with the guard had been heard by everyone.

Xhinna gazed around the room, looking for a familiar face. At the far end, one chair stood apart from all the others, but no one sat on it. The chair was roughly made—bits of wood and cloth lashed together—but the cloth was of good fabric, as though the builder had tried to make up for the poor quality of the wood.

Finally she recognized the woman she'd been hoping to find. "My Lady Nerra?"

The others in the room mumbled, and two large men moved in front of the young woman protectively. The woman raised her arms and pushed her way between the men.

"Who are you? How do you know my name when I swear we've never met before?"

"That's Lady Nerra?" Jirana said in a stage whisper. She nudged Xhinna. "Bow, you must bow!"

Xhinna turned to see the little trader bowing low before Nerra and then, apparently deciding that it wasn't good enough, going down to one knee, all the while tugging at Xhinna.

Xhinna stood her ground, saying to Jirana, "If you know Lady Nerra, then you know she sets no great store in ceremony."

"I don't?" Nerra said, arching one brow haughtily.

"Not—" Xhinna caught herself before she could say "in my time" and finished lamely, "so I've heard."

"Then you've heard wrong," the entrance guard said, his voice booming as he made his way to stand between Xhinna and Nerra.

"Stand aside, please, Jefric, and let me speak with your lady,"

Xhinna said, putting an arm on the man's side with gentle pressure. To her surprise, he moved.

"How did you know my name?" he demanded, his hand going to the hilt of his sword. "Did Fenril send you?"

Xhinna's eyes narrowed. "Fenril's still in the Hold?"

"Where else would he be?" Nerra asked, stepping forward, her gaze focused on Xhinna. "What do you know?"

Xhinna glanced down at Jirana, reached to touch her on the shoulder, and beckoned for her to rise. Jirana made a face, but obeyed.

"My lady, I know too much," Xhinna said. "I must be careful what I say, so that I don't do any harm."

Jirana nudged her. Xhinna made a restraining motion with her hand.

"We can't *tell* her," Jirana said in a poorly managed whisper.

"Tell her what?" Jefric asked. He looked down at Jirana and then knelt before her. "Tell her what, little one?"

Jirana squirmed under his gaze, but said nothing.

"My lady, we must ask—is there still Plague?" Xhinna asked, driven by some nagging memory.

"It's been nearly two Turns since any succumbed," Jefric growled. "And still the gates of Crom are closed against us."

"Fenril's drunk most of the cellar and spends every night whimpering in fear," Xhinna said.

Nerra's head whipped up. "Who told you that?"

Jirana gasped and pulled on Xhinna's hands, dragging the taller girl down so she could whisper in her ear. "Two Turns!"

"Yes," Xhinna said, smiling at Jirana, "I had the same thought." She stood and, with her hand, pulled Jirana once more to her side. "My Lady Nerra, would you like to be restored to your Hold?"

"Hah!" Jefric barked a laugh. "And how do you propose to do that? Are you going to scale the heights or—"

"Jefric," Nerra said in a calm, commanding voice. The guard stopped and looked at her. When she had his attention, she said, "She rides a blue."

"Come nightfall," Xhinna said, "Tazith could carry four at a time."

She glanced toward Jefric. "If the gates were open, could your men take the Hold?"

Jefric's face slowly cracked into a grin. "Of course, my lady."

"Wingleader," Nerra said, pointing to Xhinna's shoulder knots.

Xhinna blushed. "How many would you need to open the gates?" she asked, already knowing the answer.

"Four, Xhinna," Jirana piped up in exasperation, "don't you—"

"Jirana! Time!" Xhinna reminded her tersely. The little girl closed her mouth with a snap and then, with exaggerated motions, pantomimed that she was sewing it shut. Xhinna turned her attention back to Nerra. "If we could wait until darkness . . ."

"That would give us time to prepare," Nerra agreed. She cocked her head at Xhinna. "And what would you want in return?"

"I ride in Search," Xhinna reminded her.

Nerra started to shake her head. "Most of my people are sick, and the men will be needed in the fields—"

"We're not looking for men," Jirana piped up.

"My friend speaks the truth," Xhinna said.

"There's a queen on the sands?" Nerra asked, surprised.

"Not yet," Jirana chirped. "But—"

"Jirana!" Xhinna told her quellingly. Jirana's shoulders slumped and she looked chagrined. Xhinna turned back to Nerra. "If things go as we hope, we might be able to take more later."

"I see," Nerra said, her brows creasing. She moved toward the fabric-covered chair that had stood empty all this time, gestured for Xhinna and Jirana to take seats nearby, and then sat. She turned toward Jefric, saying, "Do you know what to do?"

"With the gates open, we'll have no problems," Jefric affirmed.

"You won't—," Jirana began but bit her words off before Xhinna said anything.

Nerra glanced at Xhinna, then back to Jefric. "Why don't you get the others ready, then?"

Jefric hesitated until Nerra told him, "I'll be fine."

"Very well, my lady," Jefric said, giving her a full bow before smartly turning on his heel and moving toward the entrance. The others fell in behind him, and soon the tent was empty except for Nerra, Xhinna, and Jirana.

"So . . . we are alone," Nerra said in the silence.

"We still need to be careful what we say," Xhinna told her apologetically.

" 'You can't break time,' " Jirana quoted in agreement.

Nerra's eyes widened. "You're from the future?"

"The less you know, my lady, the better it is for everyone," Xhinna said.

"I'm not so sure," Nerra said after a moment. She caught Xhinna's look and added, "Oh, I agree with you in general, but, for example, you mentioned that you might be back again. Riding on Search?"

"Perhaps."

"So it would help if I could have an idea as to when you'd come and how many Candidates you might need," Nerra said. She saw that her comment had struck home and added, "And it would help if I could know how many to expect back."

"I see," Xhinna said, her lips pursed thoughtfully. A moment later she answered, "We don't really know at the moment."

"Thousands, if we're lucky," Jirana piped up.

"Thousands?" Nerra repeated, eyes going wide.

"Jirana!"

This time the little girl was unrepentant. "She has to know. If this is going to work, they're going to have to come from somewhere."

"Some*when*," Nerra said, a smile playing across her lips as she saw the surprise in Xhinna's eyes. Her smile faded and she asked, "Is it very bad, where you come from?"

"It will get better when we get those thousands," Xhinna said.

Nerra nodded absently; her gaze had settled on Jirana and she was searching the girl's features questioningly. "You look familiar."

"We haven't met," Jirana said.

"You're trader stock, you said as much," Nerra said almost to herself. Her eyes lost focus as she delved into her memory, and then they widened as she looked again at the girl sitting before her. "Are you related to Tenniz?"

"You can't say *anything*, my lady!" Jirana said pleadingly. "He doesn't know, please don't tell him!" She paused a moment, then said in a lower voice, "Your word as Lady Holder."

"But I'm not a Lady Holder."

"Yet," Xhinna said.

Nerra turned to her, mouth agape, and sat back in her chair. "The Conclave would never—"

Xhinna said nothing, nor did Jirana. The look on their faces alone was enough.

"But D'gan—" Nerra started again, and then closed her mouth once more as new thoughts stifled her. She was silent for a long while. Finally, she turned to Xhinna and asked in a whisper, "Thousands?"

Xhinna nodded. She told Tazith, *You should land and get some rest. We'll be flying again at nightfall.* Aloud, she said, "I've told Tazith to get some rest."

Nerra nodded, still distracted by her wild thoughts. A moment later, with a decisive sweep of her hand, as if pushing her thoughts aside, she sat up and said, "What's it like, riding a dragon?"

"You'll find out tonight, my lady," Xhinna replied.

"Until then, perhaps you'd like to rest," Nerra said, rising from her chair and beckoning them toward the exit.

"That's a good idea," Jirana agreed with a wide yawn. "We've been timing it."

"Jirana!"

Xhinna woke and it was a moment before she recalled that she was in the tent that Nerra had assigned them. In the cot beside her, Jirana snored softly.

Tazith? Xhinna asked, stretching her senses toward him.

Night has fallen, the blue dragon replied easily.

We'll be going soon, Xhinna assured him.

Voices outside the tent caught her ear.

"They could be spies," a man said in protest.

"If they are spies, then the dragon would have given us away already," a woman—Nerra—said in reply.

"Four won't be near enough if there's treachery," Jefric—Xhinna now placed his voice—said.

"I'll have my crossbow," Nerra said. "If there's treachery, she'll die."

Xhinna made a loud noise, leapt from the cot, and stormed out to face them.

"There won't be any treachery," she declared, glancing angrily at the lady holder. "You won't need a crossbow."

"The towers are full of guards—she shouldn't even go," Jefric said hotly.

The tent flap twitched and Jirana stepped out. She gave Jefric a dirty look, then said to Nerra, "Leave your weapons behind, my lady."

"What?" Jefric said, aghast.

"The power of your words alone will win your victory."

Nerra frowned, then turned to Jefric. "She's right," she said firmly. "If I'm to rule, then I need to rule with my voice."

"Your voice won't open the gates, my lady," Jefric protested.

"I wouldn't be so sure," Xhinna said, reaching a hand down to ruffle Jirana's hair.

When they were airborne, Jirana staying reluctantly behind, Jefric leaned forward from behind Xhinna and growled into her ear, "If anything happens to my lady, I'll kill you."

"If anything happens to her, it won't matter what you do to me," Xhinna replied.

Jefric was silent for a moment as he thought about what she'd said, then grunted reluctantly.

"The high tower, over there," he said, pointing.

"No, the courtyard below," Nerra called from her position in front of Xhinna. "If your little friend is right, that's where I'll get my support."

Xhinna nodded and instructed Tazith to land.

"One thing, my lady," she said as they closed with the ground.

"What?"

"It would be best if it did not become general knowledge that a woman rides a blue," Xhinna said.

"Very well," Nerra said after a moment. "Your voice is low enough that most will consider you a young man. Keep your helmet and jacket on, and none will see except what they expect to see."

"That will work?"

Nerra laughed. "If it doesn't, it'll be the least of our worries!"

Quite on his own, as soon as they touched the ground in the courtyard, the blue let out a huge bellow, startling and alerting everyone in the courtyard.

"Now you've done it!" Jefric swore, sliding off the blue and drawing his sword in one fluid moment.

Nerra dropped to the ground in front of him and turned, raising her hand. "Sheathe your sword."

The other two guards took up positions on either side of her, glancing warily as the courtyard came to life.

Tazith bellowed again, his voice echoing around the courtyard and into the Hold beyond.

Xhinna vaulted from his neck and moved toward the others in time to see Nerra straighten her shoulders and say something to herself. Xhinna thought she was quoting Jirana: *"Your words alone."*

Catching sight of Xhinna, Nerra said, "Your blue is welcome to perch on the tower."

Xhinna nodded and relayed the order to Tazith, who bellowed once more, added a warbling chirp of pleasure, then leapt into the night sky, beating his way easily up to the nearest of the courtyard gate towers.

With a nod, Nerra turned away from the Hold and toward the gates. She walked easily, ignoring the clatter of guards assembling behind her.

A guard moved from the gates toward her.

"Tormic!" Nerra called cheerfully. "I know the hour is late, but please open the gates."

"Nerra?" the man said in surprise. He glanced around her, saw

Jefric and the other two, then looked up to see Tazith peering down from the tower.

"Yes," she said. "I would like the gates opened, if you please."

Tormic's eyes widened and he seemed to be struggling to find an answer.

"If you'd like, I'm sure Jefric and Nerritor would help," Nerra said, motioning to the men behind her.

"But—but—"

"Tormic, our people need us—they need our aid," Nerra said, looking the man straight in the eyes. "It is time for Crom to Hold once more."

Tormic braced at her words and bowed once, deeply, before turning around and bellowing, "Open the gates!"

Nerra made a restraining gesture with her fingers to Jefric and the other guards, ordering them to maintain their positions as she moved forward with Tormic.

"Good evening, Javennor, I see you've drawn the short straw again," she said to the nearest guard. When he returned her gaze with astonishment, she asked, "What happened, did you bet on the wrong horse?"

Tormic stifled a laugh even as Javennor's eyes grew wider.

"We need the gates open, if you please," Nerra said. "Or would you rather the dragon help?"

Javennor's wide eyes strayed to Tazith above him and, jerking his head in a quick negative, he turned with Tormic toward the gates.

As simply as that, the gates swung open, revealing the resolute-looking group of Nerra's men waiting beyond. Nerra called out to them, "Crom Hold, form ranks!"

In an aside to Tormic and the other gate guards, she added, "That means you, too."

The gate guards hesitantly joined the armed band moving in from outside. Nerra stood in front of them for a long moment until she was satisfied that the ranks were properly dressed, then said to Jefric, "I shall meet my brother now."

As the group marched by Xhinna, Nerra beckoned to her with an arm. "I'd like you to witness this, dragonrider."

Xhinna dipped her head. "Of course, my lady," she said, trying to deepen her voice to sound like that of a young man.

Together they marched to the Hold entrance. Jefric nodded to Tormic and the two stood at either side, pushing the double doors open.

Nerra walked straight to the end of the great hall and sat on the chair in the center of the raised dais there. She turned to Jefric. "Please invite Fenril to join us."

It took a while to find Fenril and, based on the sounds coming from outside the hall, a certain amount of force, as well. At last he entered in stained nightclothes, one arm pinned behind his back by Jefric.

"I found him in the drudges' quarters, my lady," Jefric said, his voice filled with deadly rage. His mouth worked for a moment as he fought for words. "He was, ah, entertaining."

"Brother?" Nerra said, glancing at the man standing before her. "Would you care to explain?"

Fenril whimpered, but said nothing.

Nerra flicked her gaze away from him, eyes blazing. It was a long moment before she could bring herself to look once more at him and say, "Brother, why is it that the people of our Hold have been denied the food they harvested, the food saved for such a terrible Plague as the one that passed through us nearly two Turns back?"

"Still," Fenril mumbled.

"Pardon?"

"Still Plague," Fenril said defiantly.

Nerra turned to Tormic. "Is this true?"

Tormic reddened as he stammered, "M-my Lady, Lord Fenril said that the Plague was outside the Hold, that we were in danger—"

"Not so," Nerra said, cutting him short. "No Plague, except for that of empty bellies, starving people. And that ends now."

"Our stores are running low," Tormic said.

"We'll share what we have," Nerra said. "There are farms desperate for seed—seed that should have come from the Hold." She turned back to Fenril. "Father, with his dying words, set upon me the charge of this Hold. You have denied it for these past two Turns and our people have starved from your neglect. What say you?"

"I—I—," Fenril stammered, shaking his head. "Not right. D'gan would never support—"

"It is up to the Conclave of Lord Holders to confirm a Lord Holder, not a Weyrleader," Nerra told him sternly. She waved to one of her guards, who moved to place a restraining arm on Fenril's shoulder. "Until that time, brother, you will be kept under guard—"

"On what charge?"

"Treason," Nerra told him calmly. "To the holders in your charge, to your father, and to me." She nodded at the guard. Paying no attention to Fenril's gabbled protests as he was led away, she turned to Tormic. "I need to see the Storemaster soonest."

"Food," Jefric prompted in a quiet voice.

Nerra's eyebrow rose as she added, "And I'm informed that we could do with something to eat." She gave Tormic an apologetic shrug. "I'm afraid it's going to be a long night."

"That's all right, my lady," Tormic replied. "The lads and I were getting rather bored."

"Well, we wouldn't want that!" Nerra laughed. "As soon as I hear from the Storemaster, I'll need you to lead a wagon with supplies down to the camp."

"Blue rider," Nerra said as she pored over the Hold Records arrayed on the Great Hall's large table some three hours later, "if I could impose on you again, there are some in my camp who need nourishment and can't walk on their own."

"Tazith can carry only a small number," Xhinna said, still careful to keep her voice low.

"I know," Nerra said with a weary sigh. "Just do the best you can." She nodded toward Jefric. "I'll need you to go with the blue rider, to organize things."

"My place is at your side, my lady!" he protested.

"I'm sure that Tormic here will fill your position for the moment," Nerra said, glancing significantly at her guardsman. "And you're the only one who can manage the camp."

Jefric lowered his head in reluctant agreement. He raised a hand toward Xhinna. "Blue rider?"

They made their way out of the Great Hall to find Tazith already in the courtyard, eager to be stretching his wings once more.

"She'll be all right," Xhinna assured the worried guard as they rose into the air.

"And you would know because you're from the future?" Jefric guessed.

"*That* should not become known to many," Xhinna replied. "My little friend will tell you that it's dangerous to know too much of the future."

"And why is that?"

"Because one can make grave errors," Xhinna said.

"Like leaving my lady behind on her own?"

"In this case, I really do think she is safe," Xhinna said. Her lips curved upward. "And I notice that you did not protest too much."

Jefric grunted. "'Tis true. I've known Tormic for most of his life. He's an honest lad."

Xhinna was about to respond when Tazith abruptly descended, landing them gently, if quickly, on the ground beside the camp's main tent.

"Why didn't you bring me?" Jirana's voice broke the silence of the night, and they saw her small shape dart forward from one of the tents. "I was *so* worried!"

"You were tired and Tazith could only carry so many," Xhinna said, grabbing Jirana and hauling her into her arms for a comforting hug. Jirana made a face, pushing back and making it clear that she wanted to be let down.

Back on her feet once more, the young trader girl said, "Well, it's okay. I spent the time well." She glanced up at Jefric. "Did everything work out?"

"Exactly as you predicted, little one," Jefric said with a respectful nod.

"I didn't predict, I—" Jirana slapped a hand over her mouth and glared furiously at the old guard.

"'Timing it,'" Jefric said, leaning down so that his words only carried among the three of them. "It did not take us long to understand what that meant."

"The future isn't certain," Jirana said quickly. "You must never rely on it—"

"Even if you come from it?" Jefric asked her with a smile. He shook his head. "Regardless, everything went as you predicted. Crom Hold has its rightful ruler once more."

"Good, because there are many who are starving here," Jirana said. Jefric nodded; this was no news to him. "I talked with some of them already." She glanced up toward Xhinna. "How many can Tazith carry? There are some here who are so starved they can't walk."

"That's what we came back for," Xhinna told her.

"Good," Jirana said. She grabbed Xhinna's hand and pulled her along. "I've had the first group collected at our sleeping tent." She looked up at Jefric. "Can you get some of the fitter folk to help us carry them?"

"Immediately," Jefric said, giving the young girl a look of respect.

"And when you come back, we'll need glows," Jirana said. "Also, if you could bring back warm soup, not too thick—"

"Is that wise?"

"The headwoman here says so," Jirana said.

"You've met the headwoman?" Jefric asked in surprise.

"I have," Jirana allowed. "But we were busy with those worst off; we didn't get much chance to talk—"

"Oh, there you are!" an older woman's voice called out from the darkness. "It's about time!"

"There was the Hold to recover," Jefric said defensively.

"And how long did that take?" the woman demanded. "I can hardly think that Lady Nerra spent the last several hours partying." The woman who left the shadows was much the same age as Jefric; shorter, but not by much. She turned toward Xhinna. "And you, blue rider, what's your excuse?"

Before Xhinna could draw breath to reply, Jefric waved a hand toward the woman, saying, "May I introduce you to my wife, Elsith?"

"Elsith?" Jirana repeated in surprise. "It sounds like a dragon's name."

"It's a perfectly respectable name," Elsith retorted. "And I've yet to hear of a dragon who's taken it." With a snort, she added, "Though I don't doubt I'd let her, if it came to that. Names can be shared, more's the honor."

"Delighted to meet you, Elsith," Xhinna said, extending a hand.

Elsith's brows narrowed as she took Xhinna's hand. "It's coarse enough, but it's not a man's hand." She moved forward and peered up at Xhinna. "And you're riding a blue?"

"We'd prefer to keep that among ourselves," Jefric warned.

"Crom knows how to keep quiet," Elsith said firmly. "And if we don't move these people soon, more of them will be silenced forever."

Jefric quickly organized a group of men to move the most sick to Tazith who, with Xhinna riding and eyeing her charges carefully, flew back to the courtyard.

Javennor and a group of guards were there to take charge as soon as the laden dragon arrived. No sooner had Xhinna lowered the last sick person to the ground than she and Tazith were airborne once more, heading back for another load.

When she returned after the fifth trip, Jefric called to her, "That's the worst of them. You can rest."

"I'd better get back to Nerra," Xhinna said. "Did you want to come?"

"And me!" Jirana piped up from the distance, trudging toward them with more determination than stamina.

"I should stay here," Jefric said, glancing back to the large tent, as he boosted Jirana up to Tazith's neck.

Xhinna was too tired to do more than nod. With a weary thought, she urged Tazith skyward once more. Gamely, the blue rose and beat his way back to the Hold's courtyard.

Javennor rushed forward when the blue landed, only to stop in surprise when he saw that the only riders were Xhinna and Jirana.

"Jefric says that's the worst of them," Xhinna told him as she slid down and held up her hands for Jirana.

"And who's this little one?"

"She's with me," Xhinna told him. "She's been helping Elsith at the camp."

"How bad is it, at the camp?" Javennor asked even as Tazith reared into the night sky and flew to his perch on the courtyard tower.

"The ones that were brought were the worst," Xhinna said. "But there are many back there not that much better."

Javennor pursed his lips and nodded. "Well," he said, "things will get better with herself back in charge."

Xhinna nodded, then waved and, with a hand on Jirana's back, guided the youngster into the Great Hall.

Inside they found Nerra surrounded by several others. She looked up as they entered and furrowed her brows.

"Jefric decided to stay at the camp," Xhinna explained. "He said that they'll need more wagons with supplies in the morning."

"I'd already thought of that," Nerra said with a nod. She turned back to the clay tablets in front of her and rubbed a hand across her weary eyes.

Xhinna moved behind her, laid a hand on her shoulder, and leaned close to say, "After a Fall, the riders sleep for hours." Nerra looked at her blankly, and Xhinna explained, "After this night, you've got to be as tired as if you've ridden a Fall."

"There's too much—"

"There's nothing to be done now that can't wait until morning," Xhinna said. "You're exhausted, you need your rest."

Behind her, as if in emphasis, Jirana yawned loudly.

"Very well, blue rider," Nerra said. She glanced around the table and addressed those gathered there. "I've been reminded that even dragons need sleep."

The others chuckled, some wearily, some in relief.

"We'll begin again at first light," Nerra told them. "Until then, let the normal guard be kept and a light kitchen for those in need."

"**X**hinna, Xhinna!"

Xhinna woke to the sound of Jirana's voice and the little girl shaking her. She pulled away from the noise and the shaking. "What?"

"We've got to help them, Xhinna!" Jirana said, reaching out to shake her again. "We can't just leave."

"I know," Xhinna said, focusing bleary eyes on the intent trader girl. "I hadn't planned on leaving yet."

"But—"

"Little one, you forget that Tazith can take us back *when* we want," Xhinna said, pushing herself upright. "We've all the time we need here."

"Oh," Jirana said, placated. She added, "The necessary is through that door and there's *hot* water."

Xhinna moved to gather up her clothes, only to find that they weren't where she'd left them.

"Here's a robe," Jirana said, tossing it to Xhinna. "They're washing our things and will have them back shortly." She waved at a pile of clothes stacked on a chair. "Someone left those for us."

Xhinna grunted, pulled on the robe, and made her way to the necessary. She luxuriated in the hot water while Jirana prattled on in the other room, but dried herself hurriedly when someone—blessed person!—brought in a tray with *klah* and fresh-baked breadrolls.

After she'd dressed and eaten, she found Nerra once again bent over the table in the Great Hall.

Nerra waved as they approached. "Good morning! Did you sleep well?"

"Yes, and you?"

Nerra smiled. "For over two Turns I've dreamed of my bed." Her smile widened as she confessed, "It was better than I'd imagined."

Then her smile faded as she looked at the tablets spread out on the table in front of her. "Other things are not so good."

"What can we do to help?"

"I—I didn't think to ask—"

"You tithe to Telgar—it's the least we can do," Xhinna replied with a shrug.

"But your mission—"

"It will keep," Xhinna replied. "We ride in Search, but the time is not immediate."

Nerra nodded in understanding.

"How best can we help you?"

"What we need most is to contact the outlying holds minor and cotholds, to learn their needs," Nerra told her. She nodded toward a small man standing beside her. "Pinnor here is our Storemaster; he's known to them."

"Well, Pinnor, when can you ride?" Xhinna asked.

"As soon as my lady wishes," Pinnor said, his eyes on Nerra.

"I'm afraid I'm not familiar with most of the landmarks of Crom—" Xhinna began.

"But aren't you a Telgar rider?" Pinnor asked.

"It's a long story," Xhinna said.

"One that the blue rider will not bore us with now," Nerra added in a tone that brooked no argument.

"I'm sure if you can describe where you want to go, we'll find it," Xhinna told the Storemaster.

"Very well," Pinnor said with a barely hidden sniff. "If you'll give me a moment to get my things, I'll be ready."

Xhinna nodded and Pinnor left. Nerra leaned over to her and said, "He's a bit of an old stick, but he's good at his job." She frowned. "I don't think he quite believes how bad things are in the outlying holds."

Xhinna nodded. She wasn't sure how bad things were out there, either.

"If your blue can handle another, I'm at your service," Tormic spoke up from the other side of Nerra. When Nerra looked at him in surprise, he explained, "Jefric should be here by mid-afternoon and it might be that a man-at-arms will be needed."

"I'm afraid you might be right," Nerra said. "Explain to those in need that we'll get to them as quickly as we can."

"They'll be glad to see the news come a-dragonback," Tormic said with a grateful look toward Xhinna.

"Ah," Nerra said, her lips twisting into a frown, "you might explain to them that we've limited resources in that regard."

"I will," Tormic agreed sourly. He glanced to Xhinna and added, "No offense to you, blue rider."

EIGHT

▼▼▼▼▼▼▼▼▼▼▼▼

A Journey Through
Twilight

It was, in the end, worse than either Xhinna or Pinnor had feared. The first four holds they reached were lifeless, barren.

"These were good holds, good lands," Pinnor said sadly as they surveyed the last of the four.

"It was the Plague," Xhinna said. "Too many people were ill at the same time."

Pinnor jerked his head in savage agreement. "We lost many in the Hold itself."

"I've no doubt," Xhinna said. "Where to next?"

"Next?" Pinnor repeated, still eyeing the waste below them. He heaved a sigh, then said, "I suppose we should see about Keogh."

Keogh was thriving, but the holders there greeted the blue dragon warily.

"We've nothing more you can take from us," someone called when Tazith landed. "Go away!"

"I come from Crom Hold," Pinnor called. "I've been sent by Lady Nerra."

"Lady Nerra is dead," a man said, stepping to the front of the crowd.

"Not so," Tormic called. "She is in Crom Hold." He peered closely at the man. "Is that you, Javver?"

"Javver was my father; I'm Jarren," the man declared. "Who are you?"

"Tormic of the guard."

"Crom guard?"

"The same," Tormic replied. He waved a hand toward Pinnor. "And this is Pinnor, Storemaster."

"Storemaster?" Jarren repeated, his expression darkening.

"Lady Nerra sent me to find out what supplies are needed," Pinnor said.

"Needed?" someone in the crowd muttered. "Land's what we need most!"

"Land? What about seed to plant it?" another objected.

"The last four holds we've seen are all barren, lifeless," Tormic said. "I'm sure the Lady Nerra would have no qualm if you were to take hold."

"First, we need to see what stores are on hand—," Pinnor began.

"Ho! So you would take our food!" someone in the crowd cried out.

"Quiet!" Jarren shouted. "If he's here from our rightful Holder, it's our duty."

"There are many starving throughout Crom," Xhinna called from atop Tazith. "They need help."

"I'll not see another man starve when we've enough," Jarren growled, turning back to the others behind him.

"We've some seed at the Hold," Pinnor said. "We'd be happy to share."

"We needed seed two Turns back," Jarren said. He waved to the distant plains. "There are fields out there lying fallow for want of seed."

"We can provide it. Just let me know what you need, and we'll see what we can do," Pinnor said, reaching up to Xhinna who handed him down his pack full of slates and writing tools. He glanced around. "It's hot out and I really need a place to lay out my work . . ."

"Come with me, Storemaster," Jarren said. He looked pointedly at the crowd. "The rest of you—back to work. There're fields to plow, crops to plant."

After Keogh, they went to Campbell's Field and found it just as inhabited and bountiful. When Pinnor had finished there, it was getting dark.

"We should return," he told Xhinna. "Lady Nerra will want to know what we've discovered."

"And we can use some rest," Tormic added. Beneath them, Tazith rumbled in agreement.

"I've found them," Jirana announced when Xhinna returned from the last of the holds a sevenday later. "We can go now."

Xhinna was especially tired, as the day before she and Jirana had finally ventured forward in time to plant a large chiseled marker near Tenniz's cairn. It had been the Storemaster's suggestion to shape a stone into a wide prism with their message for the future inscribed on all sides. The message was simple: "Back three turns in Western. Send help."

"Found whom?" Xhinna asked, rubbing a sore knot on her neck as she peered down at the young girl.

"The Candidates," Jirana said as though it were obvious.

"Oh, you did, did you?" Xhinna said. "All on your own, without the help of either me or my blue?"

"Well, you were busy," Jirana said with a shrug.

"To hear Nerra tell it, you were quite busy yourself," Xhinna said. "Or was it some other trader girl who spent all her time nursing the sickest back to health?"

"It wasn't just me," Jirana said. "Elsith was there, too." She made a face. "They don't have a healer—their healers all died in the Plague."

"The Plague was hard," Xhinna said.

"That's when you lost your parents, wasn't it?"

Xhinna nodded.

"I'm sorry," Jirana said. She moved to wrap her arms around Xhinna's waist.

Xhinna gave her a half-smile and a quick hug. "And I suppose Lady Nerra will just let us take these Candidates away?"

"Weelll . . . maybe we should ask her," Jirana allowed, then added in a rush, "But I'm sure she'll say yes."

"Is this the Sight?"

Jirana groaned. "No, it's just—well, you'll see."

"And where will I see?" Xhinna asked teasingly.

Jirana flushed and bristled. "The Great Hall," she said. "We'll meet them in the Great Hall."

She grabbed Xhinna's hand and dragged on it.

"And what of Nerra?"

"She's in the Great Hall, too," Jirana said, tugging harder and suddenly falling forward as Xhinna stopped resisting her.

"Well, why didn't you say so?"

"Arnnff!"

The Great Hall was much cleaner and more cheerful than when Xhinna had first entered it. Bright new tapestries had replaced the old, dingy, fire-smoked ones; the floor was well swept and the glows were fresh and plentiful. The atmosphere in the room was cheerful and relaxed.

Nerra sat at the end of the Hall on the raised dais in the central chair. She was listening intently to two holders who were entreating her on some matter when Xhinna and Jirana entered from the back. Catching sight of them, Nerra straightened and made a graceful gesture to the two holders. "Will you excuse me for a moment?"

The holders followed her look and nodded in assent, stepping to the side as Nerra jumped out of her chair and rushed over to Xhinna. As she approached, she asked Jirana, "Are you certain?"

Jirana nodded and Nerra gave her a wry look. To Xhinna she said, "You'll be leaving us?"

"We need to complete our Search and return," Xhinna told her.

Nerra nodded, then caught Jefric's eyes and motioned him over. The large man, newly appointed captain of the Hold guard, moved swiftly and quietly, giving Xhinna a polite nod and tousling Jirana's hair. The youngster made a face and batted his hand away.

"You know," he said to Xhinna with a measuring glance at Jirana, "if you wish, we could keep her here."

"I think her mother would object," Xhinna told him easily, playing along.

Jirana made a growling noise in her throat, and Jefric smiled and tousled the girl's hair again.

"Jefric, would you bring Jirana's guests here?" Nerra asked. Jefric nodded brusquely and strode off. Nerra turned to Xhinna. "If you'll wait here, I'll conclude this other business."

Xhinna waved a hand in agreement and, placing a hand on Jirana's shoulder, drew back to the tapestries lining the side of the hall.

Nerra's business with the two holders took only a few moments more. Bowing, they left, seeming happy with Nerra's pronouncement. Once they were gone, Nerra jumped down from her chair and came over to Xhinna.

"I'm glad that's over!" she said. "I've managed to sort those two out to their satisfaction, which is more than they'd hoped." When neither Xhinna or Jirana spoke, she explained, "Those two are—were—in contention over who should take over one of the abandoned cotholds."

"Is there much fighting like that?" Xhinna asked.

Nerra shook her head. "Sadly, no." She saw Xhinna's look of confusion and explained, "I'd rather have more who were eager to restart a hold than those who are too listless to—" She broke off at the sound of approaching footsteps.

Jefric led a group of four into the room. They stopped at Jefric's order, and he came to join Nerra, glancing down toward Jirana as he asked, "Are these the ones?"

"Yes," Jirana said.

Xhinna eyed the small party and tried to hide her dismay. They were quiet, grouped in a small knot except for one girl with dirty-blond hair who stood apart from the others. They seemed to be in their teens, one just barely.

The girl who stood apart looked at Xhinna idly, nearly with contempt, but then did a double take when she saw Xhinna's rank knot. She seemed to recognize it, and her gaze went to the doors at the end of the Hall as though seeing through and beyond them to Tazith.

That one for certain, Xhinna thought, seeing the longing in the girl's hazel eyes. The girl was still gawky with adolescence, likely to have fourteen Turns, maybe somewhat more. Xhinna guessed she was an orphan of the Plague. The girl met her gaze and lifted her chin with feigned pride; Xhinna had made that same pose herself too many times not to recognize it for what it was.

"Alimma," Jirana said, moving forward, "this is Xhinna. She rides in Search."

"Search?" Alimma repeated, her eyes shining briefly with hope, then dimming. "Did you want me to find you some likely boys?"

She is one, Tazith said with a certainty that surprised his rider. *Two are meek—they'll ride greens but fight well; the other is strong but hurt.*

"No, thank you," Xhinna replied, tousling Jirana's head as she added, "The looking's already been done."

Alimma's eyes lit.

"Which one of you knows how to handle fractious children?" Xhinna asked, eyeing them carefully.

"I do," the thinnest of them replied. She had a haunted, fragile look about her. She looked starved, gaunt. Xhinna thought that she could put on at least a stone or two in weight if given the chance.

"Danirry lost her family in the Plague when she had fifteen Turns," Nerra explained, her eyes going dark with a rage that Xhinna could almost feel radiating from her. "She was shunted from aunt to uncle, and never fed."

"You've seventeen Turns?" Xhinna asked.

"Only queens take girls," Danirry said.

"Or greens or blues," Xhinna said. She could not help taking on a tender expression as she added, "Like my Tazith."

"You're a wingleader?" Alimma asked, pointing to her rank knot.

Xhinna nodded. She was surprised at how the notion no longer seemed strange to her.

"Are you?" Danirry asked. Xhinna could see a faint glimmer of hope spark in the girl.

Xhinna nodded again. "We ride in Search, and our need is immediate."

"Cliova, Mirressa," Nerra said nodding to the two quiet girls standing somewhat behind Alimma, "what say you?"

Cliova gave Alimma a questioning look and the other nodded once in a small, quick jerk, her eyes still on Xhinna. Seeming to sense Cliova's anxiety, Alimma reached a hand back for Cliova to grasp.

"I'll go, if you want me," Mirressa said, giving Xhinna a coy look. She had a high, childlike voice. Xhinna guessed that she had perhaps thirteen Turns, maybe less.

I can see why some bronze riders hate this, Xhinna thought. Mirressa was cute in a childish way but no more; to have one so young make eyes at her left Xhinna feeling uneasy, like she needed to wash her hands. Then she realized that Mirressa was scared and trying to appear older than she was.

She has strength, Tazith told her. *Mother strength.*

Yes, now Xhinna could see it. She could imagine this girl grown into motherhood, fiercely fighting for her children, taking on all opponents—and winning.

"We've a chance that there will be greens in the Hatching," Xhinna said to her. "Would you be willing to ride a green dragon?"

"And fight Thread?" Mirressa asked, suddenly coming alive, her voice no longer simply bubbly but determined.

"Yes."

Mirressa stepped forward. "I'll do it."

"Are we going now?" Jirana asked suddenly. "We've got another stop and I need to use the necessary first."

"I'll take you," Mirressa said, stepping forward and extending her hand. Jirana took it unhesitatingly and followed Mirressa from the Great Hall.

"We'll get our things," Alimma said, turning to leave and pulling Cliova with her. Danirry said nothing, glancing silently at Nerra and then back to Xhinna, giving the blue rider a scrutinizing look.

Xhinna walked over to her and reached out a hand. Danirry stared at it for a moment, then raised her hand to take Xhinna's in return. Xhinna lifted the hand to study it and frowned.

"I bite them when they get ugly," Danirry said, glancing at her fingernails, which were bitten to the quick.

"Then you should never bite them," Xhinna said, smiling at the surprised look on the girl. "You've got pretty hands, and they'll look prettier with nice nails."

Danirry jerked her hand from Xhinna's as though stung. Xhinna turned to Nerra, who gestured, urging patience.

"Don't you need to get your things?" Xhinna asked.

"No, nothing's mine—I should leave it for the next girl," Danirry said.

Xhinna bit her tongue on a sharp retort. This girl was clearly convinced she was worthless. She wondered why both Jirana and Tazith thought she would Impress. Xhinna's nose twitched, and she realized that Danirry had not cleaned her clothes in a while either.

"Danirry, why don't you go check on Mirressa and Jirana," Nerra said, gesturing toward the exit. The girl nodded once and scuttled away, her shoulders slouched, her bare feet dragging on the floor.

"A dragon won't put up with that," Xhinna said as soon as the girl was out of earshot.

"She gives the others her food; gives them the new clothes," Nerra said, shaking her head with a sad smile. "She's lost half a stone's weight since she came here."

"What happened?"

"The Plague, the famine that followed, aunts and uncles who had too little of their own, who fed her last, worked her hardest," Nerra said. She frowned, eyes narrowed. "She came here from somewhere nearby, but won't say where. She arrived in my camp two days before you, half-dead with hunger." She paused. "She bartered down to the very last thing she could offer for food, until that final time." Nerra sighed. "She's not the first and won't be the last, I'm afraid. But after that, she lost interest in eating."

"We'll take care of her," Xhinna said. She could guess how Danirry could become the fighter Tazith and Jirana had seen in her. The thought of what the girl had gone through filled her with rage. "Did you find the one who made that last 'barter'?" she asked, her voice low with anger.

"She was old enough—though far too thin for anyone to think she was of age," Nerra said.

▼ ▼ ▼

When the others came back, each with a small carisak, Xhinna asked, "Are you ready?"

Danirry was, surprisingly, the first to nod. Alimma was not far behind her. Cliova seemed to take Alimma's nod as indication of her own agreement, and Mirressa could do no more than bob her head nervously.

"When will we see you again?" Nerra asked, moving to hug each of her charges.

"I think you'll see us—all—soon," Xhinna told her. "But we'll have nearly three Turns more ourselves."

"And I'll have a queen," Jirana declared brightly. "The best queen in all Pern." There was some hidden sadness behind her cheer, something Xhinna couldn't quite pin down. The girl must have felt her unease for she turned to Xhinna and raised her arms, demanding to be picked up. Xhinna's eyes narrowed in suspicion even as she complied, and the little girl whispered in her ear, "Nothing lasts forever."

Xhinna shivered. What must it be like, she thought, to know what will come and be unable to change it? She hugged Jirana tightly. "Whatever it is, little one, I'll be there for you."

"I know," Jirana said in a ragged voice.

"There are only four here; I thought you said five," Xhinna said, changing the subject.

"One more," Jirana agreed, "but not from here."

Xhinna narrowed her eyes. "Please?" the little dark-haired girl pleaded. "It'll be all right, I know it."

Nerra escorted them to the courtyard and stood, with Jefric at her back, waving as Tazith lifted into the sky with his increased burden.

"Igen next," Jirana said. Xhinna glanced at her in a mix of surprise and concern. "I've got the image, can Tazith get it from me?"

Tuzith?

She gives a good reference, the blue responded, relaying the image to Xhinna who closed her eyes for a moment to "see" it better.

In the image, the sun was low in the evening sky and black dots were visible in the Weyr Bowl. Xhinna recognized one of the larger ones as a trader dray.

Without further urging, Tazith went *between.*

The dots below them enlarged into shadows and men as Tazith made a gentle landing in the center of Igen's Weyr Bowl. The men had stopped, and Xhinna could tell that they were perplexed by her arrival.

"Greetings, dragonrider," a man said as he stepped forward from the shadows.

"Grandfather!" Jirana claimed, jumping down from Tazith and flinging herself into his arms. "It's me, Jirana!"

"Jirana?" Azeez scooped her up with a deep laugh and hugged her tightly. "You've gotten bigger and heavier." He paused to examine her more closely. "Wiser, too."

"I've got the Sight, Grandfather," Jirana said in a voice mixed with pride and terror. "I got it early because the need was great."

"You did, did you?" Azeez asked. "And what did you see, little one?"

"I saw you here," she said in a slightly defensive tone. Her voice dropped as she added, "And I saw other things that I can't talk about yet."

"That's hard, little one," Azeez said, scooping her head with his big hand and pulling it against his shoulder comfortingly. "That's hard."

Jirana pushed back against his hand so she could look up into his eyes. "Not all of it. I'm going to get a queen and her name will be Laspanth and she'll be the best queen on all Pern."

"Well, that *does* sound nice," Azeez admitted. "Your father always said that there was good with the bad."

"And I don't die until I'm really, really old," Jirana said. In a smaller voice, she added, "It's not so bad, don't worry."

"How many Turns have you now?" Azeez asked, slipping her away from him to examine her face carefully. "You should only have seven, but you look—"

"I have ten!" Jirana exclaimed. "I'm just small for my age." She smiled at him. "I'm going to be the youngest ever to Impress a queen."

"Why are you here, little one?" Azeez asked. He glanced beyond her to Xhinna, still perched on Tazith with the four girls from Crom.

"To Search," Jirana told him, sounding surprised that he hadn't guessed. "We're here for—"

"Me!" a boy's voice cried. A boy slightly taller than Jirana raced into view. "Me, pick me, have the dragon pick me, Jirana!" He paused as he caught sight of her. "What happened to you? You're so big!"

"I've ten Turns now," Jirana told him proudly. "So I'm older than you." She shook her head as she continued, "And it's not you, anyway, it's—"

"Me!" the boy cried again. "I know it is."

"Jasser—" Azeez began.

"It's *me*," Jasser insisted. "I know it." He looked up accusingly at Jirana. "You came back for me, you know it."

"Jasser!" a girl's voice cried. "Mother says if you're not back this instant—"

"Aliyal, it's Jirana! She's come back and she's older—she's come back because she loves me!"

"I do not!" Jirana said, squirming out of her grandfather's arms and turning to stand in front of the boy. "You've got red hair and no trader's got that."

"Jirana!" Azeez growled.

"I wouldn't say anything bad about red hair," Xhinna called warningly.

"Aliyal, we came for *you*! We ride in Search," Jirana said, dodging around Jasser and racing to leap into the arms of a young willowy teen whose red hair shone even in the gloom.

She is the one, Tazith confirmed.

"Green Coranth has clutched and we need Candidates," Jirana told the teen, gesturing to the women on Tazith's neck. "There'll be blues and greens, mostly."

"Search?" Aliyal repeated in surprise. "But—the greens?"

"Or blues," Xhinna said from her perch on Tazith.

Aliyal's face broke into a huge, hopeful smile as she turned to Azeez and said, "Oh, could I?"

I can carry eight—they're small, Tazith told Xhinna.

Only seven, Xhinna told him, surprised that he'd got the number wrong; he was usually spot on with such things. Tazith flicked his wings from his sides and ruffled up a light dust from the ground below.

"Mother, can I go, too?" Jasser spoke up. "You know Aliyal will need me."

A woman came bustling out of the dray and stopped suddenly, taking in the tableau of dragon, riders, and Jirana. "Oh!"

"Aressil—" Azeez began consolingly.

"Is this what you want, child?" the dark-haired woman asked, glancing at her daughter with Jirana still in her arms. "You're of age—it's your decision."

"Don't go without me!" Jasser cried. "You need me to comb your hair."

"I can comb her hair," Jirana snipped.

Jasser stuck his tongue out at her. "You'll get it all tangled."

"Jasser, I need you here," Aressil said, moving toward the boy.

"I won't stay," Jasser declared, pulling away from his mother. "I'll run away and find her, you know I will."

"You're not coming," Jirana said. "I didn't see you."

"That's because you're blind!" Jasser shot back. "If you saw Aliyal, then you must know I'd be there. I can't leave her: She needs me."

Xhinna glanced at the mother and saw from Aressil's expression that, as she'd guessed, the reverse was probably true and it was Jasser who needed his sister more.

Aressil moved closer to Tazith, looking up at Xhinna and asking wistfully, "There isn't room for two more, is there?"

"Oh," Jirana said with sudden insight, glancing up at Aressil. "You don't want to lose them both."

From their perch on Tazith, the Crom girls heard the entire conversation.

"If we left our things, could Tazith carry them all?" Mirressa suddenly asked.

Yes, the blue told Xhinna. He must have answered Mirressa directly, for the girl quickly unfastened her carisak from its straps and threw it to the ground.

"My stuff isn't as important to me as her children must be to her," Mirressa said. Alimma sighed, and two other carisaks fell to the ground a moment later.

Tazith warbled in a tone that Xhinna recognized as amusement, even as it startled the others. *Their things are light; I can manage.*

"Aressil, you can come with us," Xhinna called. "We'll make room." To the girls she said, "Tazith says that he can manage the carisaks, too—they're light enough." To Azeez, she added, "Could you hand them back?"

And so it was arranged, the carisaks returned along with two hastily assembled light carisaks for Aressil and Aliyal, even as Jirana complained, "But that's not what I *saw!*"

"You don't see everything, you know," Jasser taunted from his place behind her. Xhinna had put the lightest in the front to ease the burden on Tazith's shoulder muscles. The straps were strained, and her position was awkward with her legs spread wide.

Tazith took a long run before pushing himself up into the air and, with only two beats of his wings, took them *between.*

NINE

▼▼▼▼▼▼▼▼▼▼▼▼

A Knife in
the Dark

"They've barely next to nothing," Taria complained the night that
Xhinna returned with her Candidates. "And that little one—she really
has seventeen Turns? She looks like she won't last a sevenday."

"She'll do fine, Tazith said so," Xhinna told her comfortingly,
working hard to maintain a calm and even tone. Taria had made her
annoyance with the new weyrfolk obvious in the disdainful look with
which she greeted them—her expression made it obvious that, as far
as she was concerned, they were all girls, there weren't enough of
them, and they seemed so woebegone—and things had gone downhill from there. "And we'll make up what they lack from our stores or
our own supplies. I'm pretty sure some of my older clothes will fit
them easily."

"You don't have any old clothes—you left them all at Eastern,"
Taria snapped.

"J'keran has volunteered—"

"J'keran?" Taria interrupted. "He isn't going to time it, is he?"

Xhinna was momentarily taken aback by Taria's sharp reaction.
Finally, she said, "I think he's already gone, along with W'vin and
V'lex."

"What if he—they get caught in that knot?"

"K'dan was careful to give them a good image," Xhinna said.
"Tazith and I both checked it."

"But—" Taria snapped her mouth shut and stormed off, leaving Xhinna hurt and confused.

"There's more left, but not much," W'vin told X'lerin and K'dan when the three dragons returned later that afternoon. They stood in the clearing not far from the broom trees that constituted their aerial home. "We've got all the clothes, more canvas, more rope, and anything edible that was left."

"It was a heavy load," J'keran said, "but not too much for our browns." He smirked at V'lex as he added, "I think even V'lex's Sarinth worked off some fat this trip."

X'lerin caught V'lex's hurt look and said, "Well, I appreciate it, all of you." He gestured to the full cargo nets that lay on the ground below. "I'll have some of the bronze weyrlings help you with the stowing."

J'keran's eyes narrowed. "Where's the rest of our wing?"

"Hunting," X'lerin replied easily. "Xhinna found a nest of wherries and they've all gone after them."

"Ah, Wingleader Xhinna," J'keran muttered softly. "I'm sure that's the *best* use of her abilities."

"It doesn't matter, J'keran," X'lerin replied, "as I am the one who set the work."

"And she did so well in finding five Candidates," J'keran said. "I can see why you'd want her hunting wherries."

"We've time enough to get more," X'lerin told him coldly. He nodded to W'vin and V'lex, saying, "Once you get the goods stored, you can join the hunt or rest as your dragons need."

"Weyrleader," W'vin said with a firm nod to X'lerin and a beckoning look toward V'lex and J'keran. They each gave X'lerin quick nods, though J'keran's was sketchy, barely perceptible—just short of insult.

A noise overhead heralded the return of the hunting party. X'lerin glanced up as the others were departing and declared loudly enough for his voice to carry, "Ah, good! They've each got a wherry! We'll be able to celebrate our bounty tonight."

In a quiet voice that carried only to X'lerin's ears, K'dan said, "He's pushing you, you know."

"I know," X'lerin replied with a sigh, running a hand through his hair. "I know."

"I think he's angry that they didn't get lost."

"Caught *between*?"

K'dan nodded. "We need to keep an eye on him."

"I've heard that he's got a new brew going," X'lerin said. "He'll be trying the first batch tonight."

K'dan's brow creased. "How can it be any better than the others?"

"Rumor," X'lerin laid stress on the word, "has it that he's found a secret ingredient and does a double brew."

"Wonderful," K'dan said in a tone that belied the word.

"**W**e've only got a little time," Xhinna said as she reached up to help the girls down onto the sands. "They'll be serving dinner soon—roast wherry."

Alimma was the first down, followed by Mirressa and Aliyal. The other two followed more slowly, insisting that they could climb down from Tazith's neck by themselves. Alimma looked around wide-eyed at the eggs clustered on the sands, dim in the evening's fading light. Xhinna could see her counting and waited until she said, "Eighteen?"

"Yes," Xhinna said. "The first clutch of a green on Western Isle."

"Is that where we are?" Mirressa asked, turning around to look back inland to the stand of broom trees from whence they'd come.

"Why can't we live down here?" Cliova asked hopefully. She'd found the height of the broom trees frightening and at first had closed her eyes and refused to move. Fortunately, Timar and Kiona had chosen that moment to race by, shouting and chattering, causing Cliova to open her eyes and follow their antics with amazement. After that, she was willing to try a few steps, but not on her own—she insisted upon holding Alimma's hand until the other threw it off in annoyance.

"Tunnel snakes and Mrreows," Xhinna replied. "The tunnel snakes are like the ones at home, only bigger."

"Mrreows?" Alimma asked.

"They are four-footed, large, and furred, but not like dogs," Xhinna explained. "We named them for the sound they make when they're angry. If you ever hear that sound, you should get to safety."

"And where's that?"

"Up in the broom trees," she told them, gesturing to the trees in the distance. "They can't climb that high." A moment later, to ease their fear, she added, "They're afraid of fire and the dragons."

"So we're safe?"

Xhinna shrugged. "We can't be sure; they attacked during the Hatching and—"

"Will they attack again?" Mirressa asked.

"We hope that with all the dragons watching, we'll be safe," Xhinna replied.

Mirressa shivered. Cliova looked back to the distant broom trees with longing. "Shouldn't we get back now?"

"Of course," Xhinna said. "You can get back on Tazith while I check with the guards."

"Guards?"

"We keep a dragon and rider or weyrling and rider to guard the eggs," Xhinna explained.

"Will they hatch soon?"

"Do you remember your Teaching Ballads?" Xhinna asked as she headed toward the bronze rider standing guard.

Mirressa's very sweet voice sang out:

> "Count three months and more,
> And five heated weeks,
> A day of glory, and
> In a month, who seeks?"

She looked at Xhinna, adding, "Is that what you mean?"

Xhinna chuckled. "You should sing for K'dan," she called back to Mirressa. "He'll have you as his apprentice."

"A harper?" Mirressa asked dubiously.

"Indeed!" Xhinna said as she joined J'sarte, who stood beside his bronze Nineth. To him she said, "Anything to add?"

J'sarte chuckled. "Just don't tell Bekka if you've any knowledge of healing."

"My mother was a midwife," Cliova called from her perch on Tazith's neck.

"Oh, you're doomed," J'sarte said, laughing harder. "Bekka's mother was a midwife."

"And she rides a queen," Mirressa said in awe.

Xhinna told J'sarte, "I'll send someone down to relieve you."

"Thanks," J'sarte said. "I'd hate to miss out on the feast." To the girls on the dragon's back, he called, "Ladies, good evening!"

"Good evening!" Alimma called back loudly.

"It seems you picked well," J'sarte told Xhinna in a voice pitched for her ears alone.

"We'll see," she said, patting him on the shoulder. She turned and, with a departing wave, made her way back to Tazith.

"Who was that?" Alimma asked as Xhinna set Tazith to climbing in the darkening sky.

"J'sarte, rider of bronze Nineth," Xhinna told her easily, glad of the question—it was first sign of interest Xhinna had seen in Alimma— and gladder that the holder girl was in front of her and couldn't see her gleeful expression. "Remind me to send him relief."

"Okay," Alimma said firmly.

"'**F**ive heated weeks' is the time from clutching to hatching," K'dan told Cliova when she approached him that evening in the clearing below the broom trees. Xhinna and the others joined them around one of the three large fires that had been built on what they had started to call the Meeyu Plateau, as the cage was not far away. "Coranth clutched four weeks back, so the Hatching should come any time in the next sevenday."

"Any time?" Cliova gasped. "Even at night?"

"It's doubtful," K'dan assured her. "The Records put Hatchings during the day, but I suppose a night Hatching is not impossible."

"Sometimes dawn, sometimes after noon," J'keran added from the next fire over. He had an arm around Taria, who looked quite comfortable. Xhinna noted that, from time to time, he would look around surreptitiously before bringing a flask to his lips. Once she saw him offer it to Taria, who giggled happily.

Xhinna rose, thinking to go over to them, but was stopped by a hand tugging on hers. She looked down to see Jirana. Noting the child's pinched expression, she knelt and asked, "What is it?"

"I'm worried," Jirana said. "The eggs—they aren't safe."

"Hannah's watching them with Vanirth," Xhinna assured her.

"No, they're not safe," Jirana repeated pleadingly. She looked away from Xhinna and muttered to herself, "Maybe it's too late."

"Too late for what?"

"To save them," Jirana said.

Tazith, Xhinna called, *see how Vanirth and Hannah are doing.*

The little queen is dozing, Tazith replied. *She was annoyed that I woke her. She says she bored and sleepy.*

And Hannah?

The same.

Xhinna's eyes narrowed and she rose. *Let's go there,* she told her blue, moving toward his distant bulk.

"I'm coming," Jirana said, trudging along after her.

"It's probably nothing," Xhinna reassured her. "It's late and you should get to sleep."

"I'm coming with you," Jirana repeated adamantly. Xhinna stopped, spotted Jirana's mother in the distance next to Aressil, and waved, pointing down to Jirana and then over to Tazith. Javissa caught her motion and nodded, waving back in approval.

"Don't fall off," Xhinna told the girl tersely as she picked up her pace.

Jirana snorted. "That's not how I'll—"

Xhinna stopped, turning abruptly back to the girl. "Not how what?"

"Nothing," Jirana said a little too quickly. Xhinna frowned at her, but decided not to press the issue at the moment, returning to her march toward Tazith.

In a few quick wingbeats they were airborne. Tazith swooped down again briefly to snatch a few timbers from the woodpile, and when they arrived at the beach, he dropped the logs on the ground at the far side of the warming fire. Hannah and her queen both roused at the noise and looked up suddenly.

Tazith landed nearby, and Hannah strode over to greet them.

"Is everything all right?"

"You're not my relief?" Hannah asked with disappointment. Xhinna leapt down and shook her head. "I'll bring D'valor down when we get back."

"Oh, good, because I'm half asleep," the young woman confessed. She gestured toward the sea. "That steady sound, it just lulls my eyes closed."

"We should have more guards," Jirana said. Privately, Xhinna agreed, but it was always a trade-off between guards and hunters.

"What about the Candidates?" Hannah suggested. "They could get to know the eggs."

"They wouldn't know if the tunnel snakes or Mrreows came by," Xhinna said.

"So? Pair them with one of us oldsters," Hannah said. Xhinna raised her eyebrows in acknowledgment and then, with a wave to Hannah, took a quick stroll around the eggs. Jirana accompanied her.

"See?" Xhinna said to her when they'd returned to the fire. "Nothing to worry about."

Jirana shook her head. "Maybe not tonight."

Xhinna sighed and tousled the girl's head. "Come on, you! I'll get you back to your mother and bring D'valor down here before Hannah freezes."

"Oh, please!" Hannah called feelingly from the fireside.

Jirana's words were not forgotten by Xhinna. With X'lerin's approval, she doubled the guards on the Hatching sands. As the days crawled toward the end of the sevenday when the eggs should hatch, she grew less worried about Mrreows or tunnel snakes and more concerned about the low number of Candidates.

"Why don't you go back and get more?" Taria asked, looking at

Xhinna with annoyance when the blue rider mentioned it again. They were sitting on the beach, watching the weyrlings, her Tazith and a detachment of other mature dragons frolicking in the sea. How they managed the colder water was beyond her; it took no more than an instant in it to turn Xhinna nearly as blue as her dragon, teeth chattering uncontrollably. Taria claimed she liked it, but Xhinna hadn't seen her in the water more than twice in the past sevenday and never for very long.

"K'dan and X'lerin are worried about us taking more risks timing it." Xhinna hesitated before adding, "Especially because of what Jirana said."

"So they believe a little girl instead of their own eyes?" Taria snapped, gesturing at the eighteen eggs that lay spread around them. Xhinna sighed. She knew that Taria liked Jirana well enough and trusted the girl, but Taria was feeling the same strain that had tugged on Xhinna: If the trader girl were right, then more than twelve of these eggs wouldn't hatch. And if that were so, if only one in every three eggs survived, what would it mean for Pern?

"Well, we've got Jirana, Aressil, and Jasser if it comes to that," Xhinna said, temporizing. "And there's Colfet, too."

"You can't be serious!"

"I'll bring it up with X'lerin," Xhinna said, relenting. "If he approves it, I'll go."

"And bring back another five?" Taria asked scornfully. "What do the Records say—five Candidates for each egg?"

"I don't know where we can find ninety Candidates on short notice," Xhinna said.

"It shouldn't *be* short notice—you should have got more!"

"And feed them with what?" Xhinna asked, throwing an arm in the direction of the burnt plateau. "Clothe them with what?" She shook her head. "And we've no place to put them."

"Well, why didn't you do something about it? You're the great wingleader!"

"R'ney thinks—"

"R'ney, R'ney, R'ney!" Taria interrupted with another scathing tirade. "It's R'ney do this, R'ney do that—it's no wonder I don't see him anymore, you're besotted with the man!"

"He does good work," Xhinna said. "He doesn't like to stop until he's got the job done right."

"Well, maybe you should assign *me* as one of his jobs. He hasn't bothered to be around much lately!"

No, Xhinna realized, he hadn't. It had been J'keran who'd spent the most time with Taria. It had been J'keran who had figured out what could be brewed for alcohol, and it had been J'keran who had been keeping Taria up all hours—the green rider had staggered back to her bed in the middle of the night nearly every night since Xhinna had returned with the Candidates.

"He needs to relax," Taria had said when Xhinna brought it up. "You said so."

"But the baby—"

"I don't drink that much," Taria had said. "Don't you think I would be careful with R'ney's child?"

Xhinna had turned away at the question, the first of many digs and reminders that the child was Taria's and R'ney's, not hers.

Day by day she felt herself becoming more distant from Taria, as though each day the eggs lay on the Hatching sands, something died in her friend, as though each day Taria grew more pregnant, she lost some spark of life, some sense of control or hope.

"She's moody," Bekka had said when Xhinna first mentioned it. Later, when Xhinna mentioned it again, Bekka said, "You should talk to her."

But now, talking to Taria, she found herself fighting with the person she loved more than any other.

"I don't think you care about the baby, I don't think you care about Coranth's eggs," Taria said, flinging the words at Xhinna. "You certainly don't care for Razz, it's a wonder any of the Mrreows are still alive."

Ah! Xhinna thought, back to the Mrreows. She had rejected Taria's suggestion from the first and wouldn't budge on it—she could not imagine for a moment that having a Mrreow, however tame, around the dragon's eggs would be anything other than a threat to dragon and human alike. X'lerin and K'dan agreed with her, although she wondered: If *she* thought otherwise, would they be persuaded by her arguments?

"But if we teach them to live with the dragons and respect the humans, they could *guard* the eggs from the tunnel snakes!" Taria had protested.

"And eat the hatchlings and maul the humans," Xhinna had replied, shaking her head vehemently. "It's just too dangerous, Taria, we can't risk it." She had paused for a moment before adding, "You know more than most—think of what one did to Coranth!"

"Weyrlings will claw and bite when they're newborn. The Mrrc ows just need to be trained," Taria had said. She'd pursed her lips and glowered at Xhinna. "You just don't like them."

"We can't risk it," Xhinna had repeated with finality. That had been a mistake. Taria's eyes had widened in hurt, and she had turned away from Xhinna, refusing to talk further.

And now she looked ready to do it again. Moody! Like a baby! Xhinna fumed, not knowing how to handle this woman who was so different from the calm, poised person she'd met at Telgar.

Taria must have felt the strain, too, for she lifted her eyes to Xhinna and began reasonably, "Look, if you say we're going to lose a dozen hatchlings, why not risk having Razz's help?"

"And what about the others?" Xhinna asked. "You can't say that Razz can do it all on her own. She's got to eat, she's got to rest." She paused. "You didn't name the others nice names—they're Bite, Claw, and Scratch, remember?"

"We didn't spend as much time with them," Taria complained. "If we'd had one person with each of them, all the time taking care of them—"

"But we didn't, and we don't know if they'd be different," Xhinna said. She offered some praise. "Maybe it's just your way with Razz that makes her easier to deal with."

"Maybe it's *your* way of running things that makes the others nasty," Taria snapped back.

"I've got to bring the weyrlings back," Xhinna said, rising. Brushing off some sand, she started toward Tazith.

"That's your best excuse? The weyrlings can't wait?" Taria asked, gesturing to them as they cavorted in the sea, playing amongst the waves. "Why don't we work this out? Don't you want eighteen eggs in this clutch?" She paused and threw in another dig. "After all, it's the only one you'll have."

Xhinna frowned, shaking her head. "Tazith can mate again; there'll be more clutches."

"Not with my Coranth," Taria declared, her eyes flashing. "Not if you won't take the least precaution to save her eggs."

"We've got a guard," Xhinna reminded her. "I doubled it."

"Ever watch the queens when they come here?" Taria asked, glancing toward the gold forms in the sea beyond them. "Ever notice how they behave?"

"They're just giving Coranth space," Xhinna said, using her old answer to this old argument one more time.

"Maybe," Taria said. "Or maybe they don't like the ground here. Maybe they know something we don't."

"Bekka's Pinorth would have told us," Xhinna said. She didn't tell Taria that she'd had Bekka ask Pinorth to make a careful tour of the grounds and that the little queen had found nothing amiss. She made a placating gesture toward Taria. "Look, this is new for us, for all of us. I'm worried, you're worried, we're all worried."

"Then why don't you *do* something?" Taria demanded. Xhinna started to respond, decided it was futile, and closed her mouth, shaking her head sadly.

"I'm doing the best I can, Taria," she said after a moment, when she had managed to find her voice once more. "We all are."

"But what if it's not good enough?" Taria asked her with feeling. "What then? How does Pern survive if you're wrong?"

"There'll be other Hatchings," Xhinna said. "We can try something new—"

"But the weyrlings will be *dead*, Xhinna!" Taria wailed, waving her arms in the air. "They'll be *dead*. We can't get them back; we can't make new ones."

Xhinna took a deep breath, startled by Taria's renewed outburst, and tried again, slowly. "K'dan said—"

"Shards to K'dan!" Taria shouted. "Shards to X'lerin and all the others—they aren't here! They put you in charge and you're *killing* our hatchlings!" Tears streamed down her face. "You're killing them, and you'll do nothing to stop it." Her lower lip trembled as she added, "I don't think you want them. Maybe you don't want to remember it, Xhinna, but you're a woman. Not a wingleader, not a blue rider, a woman! And *we're* supposed to protect the young."

Xhinna's eyes boggled at Taria's words and so many things bubbled through her mind that she couldn't say any of them.

"Go on, Xhinna," Taria said, waving her away. "Go bring the queens back to the Weyr. Pretend you're a wingleader with them—maybe they'll believe you."

Xhinna started to say something, to rage at her, but she didn't have the energy. She'd done so much for this Weyr, worked so hard. She had no energy left for this lunatic bickering. With a sigh, she turned toward the beach and Tazith.

That evening, Xhinna resolved to go find more Candidates on her own. If Jirana was right, and the eggs didn't all hatch, it would do no harm; and if she was wrong, then there should be enough humans for all the hatchlings—even if she had to make two trips.

She decided that if she went only with Tazith and the lightest of straps, she could easily bring back eight more in the first trip, and she might manage another eight in the second, providing Candidates to spare.

She was climbing onto Tazith when she heard someone approach. It was Jirana.

"Where are you going?" the girl asked.

"I'm going to get more Candidates," Xhinna said.

"But it's too late, the eggs are rocking already."

"Eggs don't hatch at night," Xhinna said.

"But they're rocking right now," Jirana insisted.

"Come on, I'll show you," Xhinna said, lowering a hand to the girl, who clambered up. The child was wrong, just guessing, Xhinna told herself as they rose and glided toward the hatching sands. Taria was there, and so was J'keran, on guard—

Xhinna's blood pounded when she heard the sounds coming up from the sands below. She heard Taria and J'keran plainly enough and let out an angry sigh. What they were doing clearly wasn't guarding.

"We should go back," Xhinna said, "it's past your bedtime."

"I've heard those noises before," Jirana said matter-of-factly. "I've heard them with Taria and J'keran before."

That was something Xhinna didn't want to hear, and her blood boiled as she thought of all the taunts her friend had thrown at her, when for nights she and the brown rider had been partying when they were supposed to be guarding—

"Hear that?" Jirana said, cupping hands to her ears and turning her head for the best sound. "The eggs are rocking."

Unable to hear anything over the pounding of the surf, Xhinna urged Tazith lower. She kept her head turned away from the place where she'd heard J'keran and Taria—the green rider was her own woman and could make her own choices.

Then she heard the noise, like shells cracking. In an instant she was on the ground, running from egg to egg and kicking them, shouting with all her might. "Get away! Get away! Get away from them!"

Tazith! Get help, rouse the Weyr! The eggs, the tunnel snakes are attacking them!

"What are you doing?" Taria cried, rushing up half-clothed and throwing herself at Xhinna. Xhinna dodged her and continued kicking and rocking the eggs. Three just rolled over and over and away, toward the sea.

"What, are you killing them?" Taria cried, throwing herself back on Xhinna. "I'm sorry, I'm sorry, but don't kill the eggs!"

"They're already dead," Xhinna cried, trying to point to the small holes in their base as they rolled down into the sea. "Don't you see?"

"Don't kill them, don't kill them," Taria wailed, her efforts getting feebler and feebler. J'keran rushed up and shoved Xhinna out of the way.

"Xhinna!" he cried, his hand going to his belt knife. Xhinna, suddenly enlightened, pulled her own knife, preparing to hack open another suspiciously light shell, to show them the destruction inside—

She grunted as J'keran threw his full weight on her, shoving her to the ground.

"I won't let you!" he growled. Xhinna rolled just in time, although J'keran's knife tore the sleeve of her tunic. "She's with me, that's all there is to it. You know the rules!"

In the background, Xhinna vaguely heard Jirana wailing next to the remains of one of the ruined eggs. Xhinna rolled onto her feet only to dodge the brown rider as he tried to slam her once again onto the ground.

"J'keran, hold!" Xhinna cried. "The eggs are dead, J'keran!"

"Only if you kill them!" J'keran cried, overwhelmed by rage and righteousness. "You'd kill all Pern in your jealousy."

"No," Xhinna said. She heard the cracking again and dodged away from him, turning toward the sound. If she could just get J'keran to—

She missed his motion and his knife came slicing down her back, as a thin line of pain and then a hot, searing agony. Behind her, Tazith roared in challenge and leapt into the air, ready to tackle the brown rider, prepared to challenge his dragon.

And then, suddenly, before Xhinna could slip aside, regain her composure, *try* to reason with the drink-addled man, she slipped on a rock, knocked her head against the ruined egg, crashed it open, and—vaguely she heard a series of bellows above her as her sight dimmed and her breath fled her lungs.

"Now that's one thing I never thought of," a soft voice said as Xhinna stirred to wakefulness. "Fighting with another rider."

"I doan recommen' it," Xhinna said with a thick tongue. The other person was Bekka—she knew just from the healer's scent, that mix of lemon and something astringent. "How long . . ."

"Shh," Bekka said, putting fingers on Xhinna's lips. "You've done your talking for the day." She paused until she was certain the blue rider would obey, then lifted her fingers and brushed Xhinna's cheek tenderly. "You can ask your questions through Tazith."

"He'll tell me," a small voice spoke up. Jirana sounded tired, tremulous, relieved, and still very, very scared.

Whatever it is that frightens you, it's coming closer, Xhinna thought, forming the words with Jirana in mind. She heard the girl gasp and realized that Tazith had relayed her words exactly. *I'm sorry.* Xhinna apologized. *You should tell someone. You aren't supposed to* know *so early.*

"I can't," Jirana said out loud. "You cannot break time."

"Oh," Bekka said even as Xhinna thought the same. "We know that," she added softly, "but don't forget that sometimes you can cheat it."

Not this time, Tazith relayed from the young girl to Xhinna.

Little one, Xhinna thought, sending the dark-haired trader girl a soothing feeling, a caress of thought, a sister's encouragement, a mother's love.

"You'd better ask your questions—I'm going to need a nap soon," Jirana said aloud. Xhinna knew from the *touch* of her—the nuanced tone that Tazith used when relaying Jirana's words and emotions— that Jirana had slept by her side, had not left her for more than the necessary.

"Nine days," Bekka said, wringing out a rag over a basin and placing the damp cloth on Xhinna's head. "I thought we were going to lose you."

I'm tough.

I wouldn't let you go, Tazith said in a voice that seemed to hold an echo of Jirana—a voice that was still a child's, with a tone that was only a woman's. *You have to stay.*

The hatchlings?

Only five, Jirana thought to her with a sadness that matched Xhinna's own emotions. "Two blues, three greens."

"Riders just as we thought: Alimma and Danirry the blues, the rest the greens," Bekka added.

Taria!

Jirana said nothing, but Xhinna felt her turn to Bekka.

"Taria and J'keran fled," Bekka said. "I wanted to find them, but K'dan stopped me."

Why?

"She asks why," Jirana supplied.

"Because of that vile drink J'keran had been brewing," Bekka said. "K'dan said something about bad brew that I don't understand— sensible people drink wine—and told me that until the effects wore off, the two of them were a danger to one and all." She sniffed. "The stuff was bad in small doses, dangerous in large ones, and lethal if they'd drunk another bottle."

Taria! Xhinna cried, full of fear for her pregnant friend.

She heard the sound of brisk footsteps approaching. Two sets, one smaller than the other.

"Okay, you get out of here and find your mother," Bekka said peremptorily to Jirana. "She's awake. We kept our promise, and now you've got to sleep. You're skin and bones."

"Okay," Jirana said glumly. Xhinna felt Jirana's hand press lightly on her eyelids, warning her not to open them, and then she felt small lips kiss her cheek. "I'll come back as soon as they let me."

Probably sooner, Xhinna sent sardonically through Tazith. *You get your sleep, little one.*

"We'll take care of her," Bekka said, giving Jirana a soft, affectionate whack on the butt to keep her moving. The heavier footsteps retreated with Jirana; Xhinna guessed that it was J'riz who remained.

Bekka started moving Xhinna delicately but purposefully, making comments softly to J'riz. The blue rider thought for a moment to protest such an invasion of her privacy, but she decided against it— she wasn't supposed to talk. Besides, she couldn't fault Bekka's logic in training him, even if she did have to suppress a smirk when she thought how it kept him near the healer.

Another moment of inspection and then, painfully, Xhinna was rolled onto her stomach and her robe lifted so that Bekka could inspect the wound that, judging from her comment and the touch of her fingers, ran all the way from the bottom of her shoulder blade to the base of her hip.

"Your hip and the fall saved you," Bekka said. "If his knife had gone deeper, it would have not only ruined your kidney but ruptured your intestines, and then the only thing I could do would be to give you lots of fellis mixed with that idiot drink of J'keran's."

"Rotgut, K'dan called it," J'riz said softly.

J'keran was out of his head, Xhinna reminded herself as they rolled her back over—painfully—to a more comfortable position. He thought I was jealous, in a rage, as addled as he was. It's a wonder I'm alive.

"Gonna bea' ihm to pu'p," Xhinna spluttered through lips too dry to speak, a throat suddenly raging with thirst and roasting with fever.

"If that's what you think best, blue rider," Bekka responded. But her tone begged Xhinna to reconsider.

Xhinna tried to nod and shrug at the same time, but sudden pain lanced through her side and she lay back, gasping slowly, desperately, for enough air.

"I'll stay with her," J'riz offered. Distantly, Xhinna heard Bekka and the young green rider exchange words, perhaps arguing. "If I don't, she'll only come back the moment you leave," the boy said. She being Jirana, Xhinna realized.

A warmth spread through her and she let herself relax. So *that's* what it felt to be loved by a child. As her thoughts faded away, she suddenly understood Taria's fear and her desire. Yes, a child would be good. Probably impossible but—good. Someone like Jirana or Fiona. Maybe Bekka. Or a boy like pretty J'riz. She felt his hands stroking up her arms, two fingers wide, then down, as though she were a strange drawing he was trying to read in the dark.

Dark. Sleep started to close in on her and she heard someone breathing softly beside her. Rocks cracking, shells burrowed, dragonets dying, creeling like J'riz's Qinth with the pain, crying like Coranth from claws that gouged deep. Kill them all, save the babies.

Shh, a voice said inside her. *Rest*.

"**W**ingleader," X'lerin said when Xhinna first wobbled out on her own two feet a fortnight later. Well, not quite on her own two feet:

Bekka was there supporting her, and Jirana clung to her hand, ready to steady her if anything went wrong.

A burst of applause and cheering startled her more than the bright sun in her eyes.

"I present your newest riders," X'lerin said, gesturing to the five women. They stood in a cluster surrounded by dragons, the hatchlings nearest, blues and greens on firm broom trees, grown browns and bronzes circling overhead in slow, graceful turns.

"Danirry, rider of blue Kiarith, step forward," Xhinna said, her voice carrying clearly over the morning's breeze.

Danirry gave her one nervous look and Xhinna smiled at her, beckoning with one hand, which she'd freed with some effort from Jirana's grasp.

The rank knots had been hard to make. With cloth so scarce, Xhinna had chosen to sacrifice the remains of her tunic, which had been blood-ruined on the back and in tatters from the knife cut and subsequent tearing to give her first aid. She had insisted on having a hand in making each one, but in the end she'd had to relinquish the bulk of the work to others. It was a Weyr tradition that the wingleader made the rank knots and the Weyrleader bestowed them. Xhinna had been moved to tears when X'lerin, K'dan, and W'vin had insisted that *this* time, *they* would make the knots instead.

"Kneel," Xhinna said to the girl standing in front of her. Danirry was still gaunt, though she had begun to fill out, and now her eyes glowed with love for her blue dragon. With Jirana's help, Xhinna slipped the rank knot over Danirry's wrist and slid it up to her shoulder, pinning it there.

"Rise, rider," X'lerin said, "and join the ranks of Sky Weyr."

It still felt funny to Xhinna to say "Sky Weyr," but X'lerin had embraced the name with a fervor that had surprised her.

"I am Danirry," the girl said as she rose, her voice carrying clearly around the cluster, "rider of blue Kiarith, rider in Xhinna's wing, rider of Sky Weyr!" She raised her right hand into the sky and clenched it tightly into a fist, jerking it back down in the ancient gesture calling riders to fly.

She stepped back, but not to the other girls; instead, she stepped toward X'lerin and gave him a slight bow.

"Danirry of Sky Weyr, I greet you," X'lerin said, nodding back. She moved to W'vin next, then J'per, and so on until she had exchanged greetings with all the Weyr, including, to Xhinna's surprise, Jirana, Aressil, Javissa, Jasser, and Colfet.

Her greetings done, Danirry was supposed to join the end of the ranks of the weyrlings, but apparently, she—and Alimma, judging by the nod of encouragement the other woman gave her—had other ideas.

Danirry moved toward the weyrlings, then circled back to stand behind Xhinna.

"Wingleader, I, Danirry, Kiarith's rider, stand behind you."

Before Xhinna could respond, Alimma stepped forward and knelt.

Xhinna accepted the change in ritual with a droll look at the young woman in front of her, motioning to Jirana, who helped her once more with the shoulder knot before stepping back quietly.

"Rise Alimma, rider of blue Amanth," Xhinna said, deciding to play along with their unannounced revision.

And again the words were exchanged, the greetings made, and Alimma, rather than joining the ranks of the weyrlings, came to stand behind Xhinna, next to Danirry, proclaiming loudly, "Wingleader, I, Alimma, Amanth's rider, stand behind you."

And it did not end with the five new riders. Just after the last—Mirressa—finished her declaration, Bekka came forward to kneel before Xhinna. They had not done this ritual with the queens or bronzes, as they were due to fly with other Weyrs when they were old enough.

"I am Bekka, rider of gold Pinorth, rider of Sky Weyr!" Behind her, little Pinorth bugled in firm agreement.

Xhinna could not speak, she was so moved by Bekka's declaration.

"You're supposed to say—," Jirana prodded gently.

Xhinna's eyes went pleadingly to X'lerin and K'dan, but the two bronze riders merely smiled and nodded encouragingly. When she still hesitated, X'lerin said, "Go on, Wingleader."

"Rise, rider, and"—Xhinna fought for breath amid her sobs—"join this Weyr."

Bekka rose and turned to face the circle as she shouted, "I am Bekka, rider of gold Pinorth, rider of Sky Weyr!"

Jepara was next, then Hannah, Latara, Meeya, and then the bronze weyrlings, C'nian, G'rial, and all the others.

Xhinna felt herself trembling with emotion, bursting with pride, and she thought furiously, searching for the right words to say to thank them all.

She gestured to Bekka and Jirana to help her. Slowly she moved to stand in front of X'lerin.

"Weyrleader, I present the riders of my wing," she said, gesturing proudly to those standing behind her. "We await your orders."

TEN
▼▼▼▼▼▼▼▼▼▼▼▼

An Easy Problem

Xhinna was exhausted and still trembling when she went to sleep that night; Bekka chided her for doing too much her first day back on her feet.

"What happened to Wingleader?" Xhinna asked her.

"Wingleaders can make asses of themselves, like anyone else," the healer told her, shaking her head. "I told you to rest after the ceremony. You didn't have to insist on helping the weyrlings with their oiling."

"It was only the girls," Xhinna said, adding hastily, "and J'riz."

"Hmmph!" Bekka snorted. "*I* could have helped him."

"Well, I'll sleep late tomorrow," Xhinna promised.

"Yes, you will," Bekka said, raising a cup of fruit juice to Xhinna's lips. "Drink this."

The juice had a slight bitter aftertaste: fellis juice.

"Yes, it's fellis juice," Bekka said when Xhinna made a face at her. "And we're running low on that—we used most of it on you."

"I'll try not to get knifed by crazed brown riders in future," Xhinna said.

"See that you don't," Bekka returned without a hint of sympathy. "You've done enough damage to yourself to last a lifetime—you don't want to add more." She paused for a moment. "And how many times did you use the lower branches today?"

One of the problems with Sky Weyr's broom trees was that they lacked a place for the necessary. "The lower branches," generally referring to one spot in particular, had become a euphemism for the same.

"Twice, as if you weren't there both times," Xhinna said. Bekka made a face and Xhinna arched a brow in response.

"You need to drink more," Bekka said. "You're not peeing for two, like—" She cut herself off quickly.

"Taria," Xhinna finished for her. Bekka looked away quickly. "She's out there, somewhere."

"Or somewhen," Bekka said. "Have you decided—?"

"What to do about her and J'keran, if and when they come back?" Xhinna guessed. She shook her head. "No."

"Well, you can't do anything for a while still; you've no strength," Bekka reminded her. She took a deep breath and added in a rush, "And if you think you can slip out by yourself, I should tell you that I've had Pinorth order Tazith not to fly you anywhere until I say it's okay."

Xhinna turned to her in surprise, then pointed a finger at her own chest, and said defiantly, "Wingleader."

Bekka shook her head, pointing a finger at herself. "Healer. It's my job to see to it that you are alive to do yours."

Xhinna shrugged, and her shrug turned into a yawn. She was so weak; she could feel herself starting to tremble.

"Besides, if you tried, your body would fail you," Bekka said with concern. "You need another month or more before you're fully back together and . . ."

"Say it," Xhinna ordered. She could sense the young healer's reluctance.

"You might never get your full strength back," Bekka said. "You might not even be able to fly a Fall."

"Why not?"

"I did the best I could," Bekka told her, shaking her head, "but your muscles were badly torn. If you're not careful, they'll never be right and you'll always be in pain."

"I can handle pain," Xhinna swore.

"*You* can, but your back may decide *it* can't," Bekka said. "And if it goes into spasm when you're flying, like when you're trying to catch a sack of firestone . . ."

"I'll get better," Xhinna declared.

"Yes," Bekka agreed. "But there are other things you can do, other things than flying a Fall."

"Like what?"

"Like your other duties to Pern," Bekka said. "To provide heirs worthy of you, to care for them and be there for their triumphs."

"I can do that and still ride Falls," Xhinna said.

"You could have before," Bekka told her, shaking her head sadly. "But whether you still can ride Falls, we won't know for a while."

"And if I take it easy, will that help?"

"All I can say is if you *don't* take it easy, you certainly won't be able to fly a Fall," Bekka said, chewing her lower lip anxiously.

"I am *going* to fly Falls," Xhinna declared. "Tazith is going to flame Thread from the skies, and he'll be the best blue on Pern."

"Well then, blue rider, if that's what you're *going* to do, the first thing you need to do is get some rest."

"Okay," Xhinna said, lying back down again. "And then?"

"Then, we'll see," Bekka said. "If you want to get back into full form, we're going to have to take it easy at first, and then we'll have to get your muscles back into shape." She shook her head. "I don't envy you."

"Why, will it be hard?"

"It'll hurt worse than anything, even having a baby," Bekka warned her.

"Fiona says that having a baby doesn't hurt," Xhinna replied.

"Fiona doesn't remember how she shouted when she gave birth," Bekka corrected her. "She begged me to remind her, but I must have forgotten." She smiled wryly, then shook her head as she added, "Or maybe not. She's asked me for the best exercises to ease birthing."

"That's wise," Xhinna said, yawning again and closing her eyes. "Fiona's wise."

"Go to sleep."

Xhinna tried, but found it hard to relax. It was only when she felt the warm form of Jirana curl up in front of her that she heaved a deep sigh and slid into slumber.

She woke cold and shivering. A moment later she heard indistinct voices and felt someone slide up behind her. It was a woman. Taria?

No, this woman felt different. Xhinna tensed until she felt the woman's hands on her shoulders, heard her voice murmuring soothing sounds. Javissa.

Jirana must have enrolled her. Xhinna remained tense, uneasy with this other presence, but Javissa murmured to her, soft words that made more sound than sense. She was here to help, she was a warm body to keep her warm, help her recover, get better. She was here because Jirana asked; she was here as her daughter's mother. Javissa stroked her hair softly, whispering the words mothers always used to console their daughters, soft murmurings that soothed. Xhinna trembled, her muscles rebelling, but she made them relax. Javissa was warm, she was soft, she was like Jirana, only bigger. She cared. She loved her daughter, so she loved her daughter's friends.

Xhinna's mind picked at that for a moment before she allowed herself to relax fully. If Jirana was someone she loved like a sister, could she not accept Javissa's extension of this sister-love? What, Xhinna wondered, would it be like to have a mother love her?

An image of Fiona swam into her mind. Fiona, who had taken her in when she'd been virtually shunned; Fiona, who had stood for her, who had loved her like a sister but treated her, at least sometimes, like a daughter. Fiona, who wasn't quite a mother, nor quite a sister.

Warm, Xhinna drifted deeper as an image of Taria came to her mind, holding her, loving her.

She awoke hot, tingling in all her senses. She knew this feeling. She leaned forward and planted a delicate kiss on Jirana's hair before rising from between daughter and mother. She was pleased to see Javissa reach forward and drag Jirana into her arms. The two might sleep through or wake drowsily from what was to follow, but they'd experienced it before and wouldn't be frightened.

Hot, tense, she moved out from safety and into the air whipping around under the temptations of the morning sun. The sky was red, the sun just creeping over the horizon.

She heard Tazith's heated plea and let him fly free, soaring, twirling, arcing toward the burnt plateau and the pen full of herdbeasts, hot and ready to feed.

She heard the rest of the camp stir, heard the excitement in their voices.

Even before Tazith blooded his first kill, Xhinna felt the exultation that was the union of two dragons, a hot, demanding throb that beat in her flesh, pounded on her heart, caused her breath to come quickly.

Coranth. Even as she knew it, she felt the green fade from her thoughts. Behind her, she heard a dragon roar and take flight. Kisorth, T'rennor's green.

Kisorth! T'rennor! Xhinna thought. T'rennor: no!

For all that she wanted Tazith to triumph, to have the joy of mating, she loathed the thought of being with the green rider. It was not that he was a man—it was that he was the wrong man: too meek, too easily led, too willing to be the butt of jokes for the fleeting attention it provided. V'lex had immediately taken him under his wing—as V'lex and J'keran had spent much time together, none of which improved T'rennor's self-esteem. In fact, the opposite was occurring: T'rennor seemed daily to become more pitiful. Xhinna knew that X'lerin was aware of it, too, but neither he nor Xhinna had yet found a way to help the younger man and, it was true, for all their flaws on the ground, J'keran and V'lex were superb riders who were happy to teach T'rennor all that they knew, provided he did not outfly them.

T'rennor's Kisorth blooded two kills and then was in the sky. Tazith took off after her and had the lead, but brown Jorth burst into the sky, gaining and overtaking Tazith with his stronger wings. J'per's Ginoth appeared and also gave chase. Sarinth clawed her way high into the sky, bellowing taunts at the two browns and the blue below her. She dived on them, and the browns lumbered aside, but Tazith lurched in and caught her—and then another dragon wrapped paws around him, pulled him free, and threw him away.

Tazith cried more in frustration than in pain—the claws had been sheathed. He struggled to regain his position even as Sarinth cried a taunt at him, and the browns resumed the chase. Tazith bellowed in anger.

Why had J'keran's Perinth interfered? It was not his flight, he should not—and then Ginoth caught the green Kisorth and Xhinna's thoughts left her as the emotions of the mating swept over her and all the weyrfolk.

Come on back, Tazith, Xhinna thought to her blue. *You were great!*

Tazith, disgruntled, wearily began his flight back to the Weyr.

"Someone has been raiding our stores," Javissa said later when she came to report on the stocks to Xhinna.

"Taria's pregnant," Xhinna said. "They probably came to feed their dragons and took what else they needed."

"So?"

"We'll let it pass," Xhinna said. "This means at least that they're alive and surviving." She had a haunting image of a gaunt, pale Taria dressed in rags, her belly distended with child and hunger. "I'd prefer they take what they need from us, rather than starve."

"But without their hunting, we've as many mouths to feed but two fewer to provide," Javissa said.

"We'll make do," Xhinna told her peremptorily. "Anyway, you forget Alimma and the others."

"You're right, we've twelve new mouths to feed—five hatchlings and seven humans, when you include Aressil and Jasser."

"Seven new workers, then," Xhinna said.

"You leave Danirry here with me," Javissa said with sudden ferocity. "She's too thin to work hard and needs to eat more."

Xhinna grinned at the change in the woman's demeanor. "I can't keep her here by herself," she said, "or she'll feel singled out and the others will think she's privileged."

"Well . . . then give me Mirressa, too," Javissa said. "She's got more meat on her, but she also needs a mother's touch."

"I'll let you have them for a sevenday, then we'll rotate," Xhinna offered. "I'll take Aressil."

"And do what with her?"

"I thought that she might help R'ney with his wild schemes."

"She'd be good at that," Javissa agreed. "And we've got to find a place for those eggs—a good one—before Sarinth lays them."

"Yes," Xhinna said with a tone of forbearance. She smiled at Javissa. "Anything else, Mother?"

"You're to stay here in the Weyr," Javissa said. "And keep Jirana by you at all times, or Bekka will confine you back to quarters."

Xhinna fumed at that restriction; she'd planned to go to the old sands and then to the burnt plateau to talk with R'ney.

"Don't go fractious on me, child," Javissa said, "I've had it all with J'riz and now Jirana." She shook her head. "Don't think, wing-leader and all, that you can get anything by me, or that I won't tan your bottom if you do."

"Tazith might have something to say about that," Xhinna replied softly, taking Javissa's threat with a grain of salt.

"He's a smart dragon," Javissa said thoughtfully. "He'd probably catch you and hold you down until I was done."

You should listen to her, Tazith said.

"Well," Xhinna said, knowing when to make the best of a situation, "if I'm here, then maybe Danirry and Mirressa won't feel singled out."

"Then it's settled."

"But certain headwomen should think twice before taking on airs," Xhinna warned.

A smile grew on Javissa's face and her eyes twinkled devilishly. "And what makes you think I didn't?"

The downside of the arrangement turned out to be proximity to Danirry. The blue rider followed Xhinna around like a lovesick child. Mirressa was only slightly less difficult. She was so biddable that Xhinna could not imagine her ever saying "no" to anyone. Friendliness and loyalty were one thing, downright subservience was entirely another, and Xhinna started planning on how to help Mirressa into a more healthy relationship with the others around her—before someone like J'keran plied her with drink and addled her wits.

The worst of it with Danirry was that Xhinna couldn't quite settle her own feelings about the new rider. Her sense told her that at some point, Danirry would feel compelled to become her lover, that she might grow out of it in the future—the other woman was still too traumatized to consider relationships anything but fleeting. Xhinna suspected that part of Danirry's recovery involved her first being attracted by Xhinna and her position of power, and then pulling away as she became her own person and owner of her heart, body, and spirit.

Thin and small as Danirry was from malnourishment, Xhinna thought she looked like a younger version of herself—or Taria. Hence the attraction and also the fear.

Xhinna had known when she'd first accepted this group of women that she was treading a difficult path. Being known as the first weyrlings of a green's clutch and the first fighting riders to train under a female wingleader, they would be judged, their every failure seen as a sign that even if women might ride dragons, they could not *lead* dragons against Thread. And the judgments upon them would fall tenfold upon Xhinna.

"Good enough with those others have trained," she could imagine the older riders saying of her, "but not really up for it where it counts." They'd nod knowingly and one would say, "Aye, a gold or even a green is a woman's mount. A blue's unnatural."

These women, under her leadership, would prove them wrong—and it was up to *her* to make it so, whatever the price.

So, what was the right price to pay for Danirry's self-esteem?

And how much of this is about her and how much about me? Xhinna asked herself harshly. She began to see how easy it would be to abuse her power, to convince herself that she was only acting in the interests of the Weyr.

These were the sorts of questions she usually brought to Taria. Together they would talk them over for hours until by some strange fusion of words and gestures, they would arrive at an unspoken conclusion.

So what would Taria say? Xhinna wondered as she asked Rowerth to have R'ney come meet her. The answer came to her instantly: She would say I love you; you will do what's right.

That was her old Taria. What would the new one say?

When R'ney arrived, Danirry had attached herself to Xhinna as her official supporter and stabilizer. Bekka, the mischievious fool, had actually had the gall to *tell* Danirry to make sure Xhinna was all right, a charge the young woman took on with near ecstatic dedication. She'd even helped Xhinna to the necessary, a ploy that the wingleader had adopted both out of need and hope that perhaps Danirry's poorly hidden ardor would abate when she realized that her wingleader was human—and female—after all.

R'ney—drat the man!—took in her discomfort with one raised eyebrow and a hastily erased smirk. But, she suddenly realized, he might have a solution. Surely he had been in similar straits; he could at least tell her how *he'd* coped.

For that matter K'dan and Fiona probably had dealt with such affections hundreds of times and—

Oh! Xhinna thought, suddenly enlightened. Fiona *had* dealt with such affection before. Xhinna herself had been the source of it. "How are you, Wingleader?" R'ney asked, bringing her from her hidden set of problems to her more immediate set.

"Tetchy, tired, wobbly, and irritated," Xhinna said.

"Don't forget alive," R'ney reminded her.

Xhinna glowered at him, and then firmly turned her attention to the Weyr's problems. "We've got twelve weeks—three months before Sarinth will clutch," she reminded him. "Where will we put them? How will they hatch?"

"And how will we keep them safe?" R'ney added.

"That, too," she agreed with a twist of her lips.

"I've a long-term plan, which might do in another Turn or two," R'ney began, stroking his chin and pulling his hand away to glance at it irritably. Apparently the brown rider was not satisfied with his razor; he had the barest trace of stubble but it annoyed him all the same.

"We've got twelve weeks," Xhinna reminded him. "A Turn might help but not for the next two hatchings—"

"Two?" Danirry asked, her eyebrows going up.

"Queens—and greens, probably—rise twice a Turn in a Pass," Xhinna said.

"But we're not in the Pass now, are we?" Danirry asked, glancing anxiously up at the skies above and using her fear as an excuse to grasp Xhinna's arm.

Xhinna moved forward, pulling away and turning to face the other blue rider. "No, we're three Turns back," she said. "We won't see Thread for Turns yet."

"You did that?" Danirry asked in surprise. "You brought us back in time?"

Xhinna nodded. "We needed to get away from a Threadfall; it seemed the wise thing to do."

"Back in time . . ." Danirry murmured thoughtfully.

Xhinna turned back to R'ney. "Okay, you're so excited: Tell me about this long-term plan of yours," she said with a sigh.

"Rain," R'ney said, grinning broadly.

"Rain?"

"Yes, we use the rain," the brown rider told her, giving her an expectant look.

Xhinna frowned. "To catch more water?" she guessed. No, judging by his expression. "To fill a lake?"

"No, to get to the stone," R'ney said. "It's simplicity itself. We burn, dig, and break—and the rains do the rest."

"I'm not a smither," Xhinna reminded him, letting some impatience creep into her voice. Danirry laid a hand on Xhinna's shoulder in an offer of support.

Tazith, ask Kiarith if he doesn't feel itchy, Xhinna said to her blue in desperation.

"Oh, Kiarith is awake and he's itchy!" Danirry said suddenly. Xhinna turned to her, trying to look surprised, only to find her breath suddenly taken away.

There, standing in front of her, was a completely different person. The gaunt ghost Danirry was not there; the fawning, love-struck

Danirry was also absent. Instead, there stood a vision of beauty, a young woman growing into adulthood, a look of joy and belonging etched deep in her eyes, a smile on her lips, a passion for life radiating from her.

"See to him," Xhinna said, finding the strength to wave a hand in dismissal. "R'ney can look out for me."

"I'll come right back!" Danirry promised.

To her surprise and annoyance, Xhinna found herself saying, "Hurry."

R'ney waited in tense silence until Danirry was out of earshot and then asked, drolly, "Wasn't that supposed to be: Take your time, we don't need you?"

Xhinna turned back to him: his eyes were dancing with merriment. "Oh, hush!"

A moment later, R'ney asked her in all seriousness, "Do you know what you're doing, Wingleader?"

"Actually, I was hoping to ask you," she admitted. "I thought perhaps you've been—"

"No," R'ney said. "Once the other way around."

"And?" Xhinna prompted, willing to take any advice she could find.

"We had a grand time together," R'ney said, shaking his head sadly. "And he died."

"Oh," Xhinna said. "I'm sorry."

"Don't be; we weren't," the brown rider told her. He raised his eyebrows in the direction the other blue rider had gone. "If all things are equal, I'd say grab for it with all you've got."

"All things are probably not equal," Xhinna said sadly. She quickly gave R'ney a rundown of what she'd learned from Nerra and her own subsequent observations. "If I choose wrong—"

"She'll survive," R'ney said firmly. "You can't fix all the people on Pern, you know."

"No, but she's *mine*, so I'll do my best for her," Xhinna said.

"Naturally," R'ney agreed. "And what is that?"

Xhinna shook her head and blew out a sigh. "I don't know."

"Well, not that I think you need to divert your attention or anything, but just in case, perhaps we can get back to our plans," he suggested.

"Go on," Xhinna said warily, waving for him to proceed.

"As I said, we'll let the rains do the hard work," he told her. "We burn off our target area, dig out ruts all along its length, and, as I said, let the rains do the rest."

"What?" Xhinna asked. "How?"

"Have you ever watched rain falling on newly turned earth?"

Xhinna thought for a moment, her eyes narrowed. Then she shook her head.

"Ever been to a Gather?"

She nodded, even more confused.

"And seen how the horses dig up the ground?"

She nodded again.

"And what happens when it rains?"

"You get mud," Xhinna said, wondering what by the First Egg the brown rider was going on about and if he would ever get to the point.

"And if it's a hill or a place where there's lower ground, what happens to the mud in the water?"

"It sinks into the ground, doesn't it?"

"Some," R'ney agreed. "But when there's too much mud and there are deeper places for the muddy water to go—say, downhill—where does the water carry all that mud?"

"Downhill," Xhinna said, annoyed at such an obvious question.

"And when enough rain falls and takes away all the mud, what's left?"

"Nothing?"

R'ney shook his head, his eyes twinkling. "Bare rock."

"Wait, instead of *us* digging up all the earth, we dig up some channels and let the rains clear the rest of the dirt?"

R'ney nodded, looking relieved. "I was afraid I was going to have to draw a diagram."

"You should have—your explanation took far too long," Xhinna told him. Then she felt a hand touch her waist and she turned around.

"Did I miss much?" Danirry asked, peering up at the wingleader with a smile.

"No," Xhinna said, just as R'ney said, "Yes."

The girl looked from wingleader to wingsecond and back, confused. Xhinna laughed and laid her hand over Danirry's in reassurance.

Somehow, Xhinna promised herself, she would do the right thing by Danirry. It was just another one of the duties of a leader she'd never before considered.

Danirry took the touch for an invitation and, wrapping her arms around Xhinna's waist, moved in close, resting her head on Xhinna's shoulder.

"You can lean on me," she told Xhinna, "I'll hold you."

R'ney raised an eyebrow and gave Xhinna a warning look but, unfortunately, the blue rider's head and chest were almost *exactly* what Xhinna needed for her sore shoulder and she found herself leaning back ever so slightly.

"So, first you get your half wing of dragons to flame all the new growth back to char, then they dig grooves along the plateau, and then what?"

"We just wait," R'ney said with a shrug. He lowered his brow once more and jerked his head at the girl behind her, but Xhinna ignored him.

"And while we're waiting, brown rider, what do we eat?" Xhinna asked.

For a moment he looked thunderstruck, and Xhinna couldn't help feeling delighted. But he recovered quickly, saying, "I thought I'd leave that to you and the Weyrleader." He paused just long enough for her to see it coming, then added, "But I can see you've got enough on your shoulders, so I'll have think on it myself."

His stress on the word *think* wasn't lost on her, and she stuck her tongue out at him in as dignified a wingleader manner as she could manage. R'ney paused for one moment, brought himself up to his full height, and stuck his tongue out in return.

"May all your problems be as easy as mine," she told him with a glare.

"Honestly, Wingleader, I wouldn't trade my problems for yours for all the gold on Pern," R'ney said. His words seemed to startle him, and suddenly he looked as if he wanted to hug her.

"What?" Xhinna asked, wondering just how things could get worse.

"Gold!" he exclaimed, turning toward the burnt plateau and pointing.

"You found gold?" Xhinna asked. Danirry was wobbling a bit, so she straightened up. The girl might have her blue's determination, but she still had none of his stamina. Xhinna hoped that would change.

"No," R'ney said, shaking his head. "But we could!"

"How?"

"All that water," he told her. She shook her head at him, confused. "We'll be taking an entire plateau's worth of soil! There's got to be enough gold dust in there for—" He shook his head. "—I don't know how many grams, maybe whole kilos."

"Gold?" Xhinna repeated. "How do you know there's gold there?"

"It's the same type of soil where we found gold back home," R'ney told her with a pitying look.

"But it takes time and effort to get gold," Xhinna protested, recalling scatterings of conversations with Fiona.

R'ney raised his hands and shook them in disagreement. "No, no, no! You see, all we have to do is build the sluices right and we'll get the gold coming straight out."

"Especially if we did it in several places," Danirry added. With Xhinna's weight removed from her, she'd sidled around to stand on the wingleader's left. "It would be easy then."

"You've miner training?" R'ney asked, suddenly interested in her.

"No," Danirry said, "but our old harper insisted we learn all about mining, as well as the Ballads and reading and writing."

"Wise of him," R'ney said, his expression dismissing her once more.

"You'd be better with a cyclone chute—it'll fling the gold out," she added. R'ney's eyes boggled. "And if you build it right, the gold'll fall down into a catchment and the dirt will continue on over it."

"You, young rider, have just become my assistant!" R'ney declared. He glanced at Xhinna pleadingly. "I can have her, can't I?"

"I was told to stay with the wingleader!" Danirry objected, moving back behind Xhinna as if for protection. "She needs someone to watch over her."

"I do," Xhinna agreed calmly, savoring the way R'ney's eyebrows went up in disbelief and the set of his jaw as he prepared to argue with her. "But Mirressa's also got that duty." Behind her Danirry made a small noise of discontent, not quite a whimper. "What I really need are good eyes and ears that can go where I can't and report back."

She reached around and tugged Danirry in front of her. "Tell me, blue rider, would you like to ride Tazith?"

Danirry's face lit with wonder and excitement. And again, for a moment, Xhinna could see the beautiful person behind the frightened eyes.

The match proved perfect, and under R'ney's concerned guidance, Danirry began to blossom. They were both ecstatic at being allowed to fly Tazith and, between frequent races to oil their weyrlings, fought like children over who was rider and who passenger. That R'ney was neither threat nor competition was especially easy on the blue rider, and Xhinna was amazed to see near-daily transformations in the way Danirry acted and behaved.

Mirressa was a much easier person to handle, so, remembering R'ney's sisters, Xhinna assigned Jepara to her.

"She's a sop!" Jepara complained the next day. "She'll do anything—anything—I tell her to."

"And why does this bother you?" Xhinna asked.

"Because—because—oohhh!" Jepara threw her hands up in disgust, unable to find words to describe her feeling.

"So fix it," Xhinna said quietly. Jepara stopped mid-tirade and turned to her with eyes wide in astonishment.

"You can't be serious?" Jepara said. "The girl's got no spine! You might as well put a puddle on her green's back, instead of a rider."

"The green chose her," Xhinna said. Jepara started to say something, probably to castigate Mirressa's green, but Xhinna forestalled her with a raised hand. "And *I* chose you."

The queen rider stopped moving and stood, fuming, her eyes locked with Xhinna's in a contest of wills.

"I think that behind all that puddle, there's a real person who's been hiding all this time, waiting for someone like her Valcanth to find her, to see her true worth."

"Greens aren't very smart," Jepara snapped. She colored slightly as she remembered that Taria rode a green, but pressed on unrepentant. "They don't always make the best choices."

"Which is why they have riders," Xhinna told her calmly. "And why their riders have Weyrwomen to guide them."

"Well . . . how will I know when I've succeeded?" Jepara demanded. "How will I be able to tell when that puddle of mud grows a spine?"

"When that puddle of mud cuts off all your hair or turns your bottom red," Xhinna told her, fighting back a grin.

Jepara's jaw dropped and she raised a finger at the wingleader. "You—how did you—he told you! It was *your* idea!" One of her hands snaked around to her behind and she gave the Weyrleader a long, simmering look. "I couldn't sit for a sevenday," she said, growling.

Xhinna didn't try to pretend ignorance and merely stood her ground.

"You—oh!" Jepara said, twirling around angrily, waving her hands in the air. She settled herself, then said in a controlled, icy voice, "Very well, Wingleader, it shall be as you order."

Xhinna decided that silence was the best option and nodded at the queen rider, who walked off, chin in the air, toward where Mirressa was helping Javissa with chores.

Perhaps, Xhinna thought, things were looking up. All she had to do was find Taria and kill J'keran and all would be right with Sky Weyr. Well, maybe not kill, she corrected herself; even if the brown rider's transgression warranted it, there had to be a better way. The man had been addled out of his wits, after all.

ELEVEN
▼▼▼▼▼▼▼▼▼▼▼▼

A Cry in
the Silence

Xhinna could tell immediately that something was wrong when she woke in the middle of the night. She'd been certain that she'd jinxed herself with the thought that things were going all right and now, she was certain, they were due to go wrong—seriously.

The first thing she noticed was that Jirana was not keeping her front warm. The second thing she noticed was that somebody—but not Javissa—was lying against her back.

Whoever it was was shivering and crying. And cold, very cold.

Hadn't the girl given up on her and grown some sense? Xhinna thought to herself with an inward groan. Danirry had spent enough time with R'ney and the other new riders—surely she'd worked through her infatuation.

"Danirry . . ." Xhinna began quietly, trying to figure out how to get the blue rider back to her own bed without making matters worse.

Instead, the body behind her stiffened and, with an indrawn hiss, rose swiftly, running away.

"Danirry, no!" Xhinna cried, wincing as she propped herself up and slowly—achingly—stood up.

And then, just before she heard dragon wings rustling, a number of things clicked into her mind. The body had been different from Danirry's: round in the middle.

"Taria, no! I can explain!" Xhina cried as the green dragon leapt into the air, beat its wings down once and was gone—*between*.

"Xhinna?" Danirry's voice called from a different direction.

Xhinna had no chance to respond before Danirry was at her side, a questioning, concerned look on her face.

"Just a bad dream," Xhinna said.

TWELVE
▼▼▼▼▼▼▼▼▼▼▼▼▼

Stretching Bonds

"That's three in three nights," X'lerin said. He was reporting on their herdbeast losses. They were gathered on the rough platform that R'ney had laid down near Bekka's infirmary, on branches just beneath the top of the broom trees. The light of mid-afternoon came through in splotches, tinged green by its journey through the leaves above, and did not do enough to warm the air.

"We can only be certain that two were killed by Mrreows," R'ney said, glancing meaningfully at Xhinna.

"What about putting a cover on the cage?" she asked from where she sat, glad to be allowed to sit up for short periods. Her scar twinged, but she ignored it. The cage for the herdbeasts that had been built nearest their cooking fire was sturdy enough and big enough for several beasts at once; covering it would be a difficult and time-consuming task.

"It would stop the Mrreows," X'lerin agreed, leaving the other predator unnamed.

"But we'd have to lift the cover to add more stock," R'ney said. He mimicked grabbing and tugging with his hands, his expression doubtful.

"We can't afford to lose so many," X'lerin said.

"And extra guards won't help," Xhinna added.

"Particularly with the other losses," X'lerin said.

"It's hard to say no to someone who's begging," Xhinna agreed with a neutral expression.

"What worries me is the sorts of conversations they may be having," R'ney said, frowning.

Xhinna sighed. That Taria had chosen to leave the Weyr spoke volumes about Xhinna's leadership; she was constantly aware of that. That some might be sympathetic to Taria and J'keran was also a given. What worried Xhinna more was that some would consider it acceptable to permit theft of their own hard-won food. That might mean more than sympathy—it might mean active aid and rebellion.

Xhinna's enforced rest had eroded her authority among those who had to see her *doing* to believe she was leading. She'd heard snippets of conversations among the older riders when she'd been feigning sleep: "She's not a proper wingleader; when she rides at all, it's just a blue!"

When she'd mentioned it to R'ney, the brown rider had grown very silent. His silence told her that he'd heard the same and worse. Under her questioning he admitted as much. Xhinna felt that the resentment stemmed from worries about the clutches to come and whether the eggs would hatch.

"All Pern riding on her!" one of the older green riders had snorted derisively when he thought she was asleep. She recognized the voice: It was V'lex. Apparently she had failed to keep her opinion of him from showing, and he was reciprocating in kind, with interest. T'rennor followed along meekly, which was unnerving.

Many of the male blue riders resented her, more for her gender than her authority.

"You're a threat to them," R'ney had said, scowling. "Not only are you better than they are, but you're a girl, too." He shook his head. "They're afraid you'll take all the greens from them and they'll be shamed through all Pern."

"They can keep their smelly old boys and stinky greens," Xhinna said. She ducked her head in apology to the brown rider. "No offense."

"None taken," R'ney had said, smiling. "I'll be quite happy if you leave me those stinky men."

"Smelly boys," Xhinna corrected absently.

"Even better," R'ney had said, smiling.

"If we post only those we trust, they'll feel punished," Xhinna said. Fuming, she cried, "I've just got to get well!"

"I don't think that will be enough," X'lerin said with a frown. Xhinna saw R'ney shoot him a restraining look, but she would have none of it, saying to X'lerin, "Go on."

"Seeing you up and about will not convince those who have decided that you're not a proper rider," he said unhappily. "The only thing they'll judge you by is your success at the Hatching."

"But even T'mar couldn't guarantee that when we were back in Eastern," R'ney protested.

"And that's another thing," X'lerin began, reluctant to add more problems to the pot. But Xhinna gestured for him to go on and the bronze rider said, "There are many, particularly among the older riders, who think that you tricked T'mar and Fiona into bringing us all here."

"Tricked?" Xhinna asked, eyebrows raised. "T'mar and Fiona?"

"Hot heads and slippery tongues," X'lerin said. "But they think they should have stayed back at Telgar and left you to shift for yourself."

"I don't like where this is going," R'ney said.

"Without the older dragons, we can't survive," X'lerin told Xhinna frankly. "The ones born in Eastern are solidly with you, but the ones who came with J'keran . . ."

"And we've got to find Candidates, too," Xhinna said.

"We've got time," R'ney said, trying to buck up her spirits. "We've got two months, at least, before Sarinth lays her eggs."

"Sarinth," Xhinna repeated sourly. A sudden suspicion stirred her. "And what are the odds that V'lex has been talking with J'keran?"

"That," X'lerin said slowly, "is a very likely possibility."

"And a very scary idea," R'ney agreed.

Xhinna nodded. If V'lex convinced T'rennor to flee the Weyr before his green clutched, going to wherever Taria and J'keran were hiding out—a dark thought came to her.

"What if there was only one Mrreow attacking?" she asked the other two suddenly. "What if it was being trained?"

"Razz?" X'lerin asked, referring to Taria's favorite Mrreow.

"It's possible," R'ney said, nodding.

Xhinna pursed her lips into a frown. A second, even darker thought she kept to herself: What if the attacks by Razz had been a demonstration? And a display to convince others to rebel?

R'ney, X'lerin, and K'dan were glad when Xhinna finally took her first steps in a month up to the top of Sky Weyr. She chose her footing carefully among the strips of canvas that had been laid down as walkways, guided by Jirana. She was still shaky, which surprised and annoyed her—she hadn't felt so bad when she'd been slit by J'keran's knife.

She pushed the worry aside, releasing Jirana's hand and straightening to her full height. Oh, it felt good to stand again!

"I suppose it's too early to ride Tazith?" she asked wistfully. She had an entourage: Jirana, Mirressa, and Bekka had all insisted on being present as she showed off her recovery to the Weyrleader, Weyrlingmaster K'dan, and her own wingsecond, R'ney.

"Can you touch your toes?" Mirressa asked.

Xhinna shook her head.

"Well, then, I expect you know the answer."

Xhinna frowned. She steadied herself and slowly leaned over, her hands palm out toward the ground. She got no farther than mid-thigh before the pain stopped her.

She straightened once more, fighting to keep the pain from showing on her face. It didn't matter. Jirana moved behind her and, pulling her tunic from her trousers, inspected Xhinna's scar.

"No bleeding," she reported, lowering Xhinna's tunic.

"Good," Mirressa said.

"Well, I'd be surprised if there were. We took the stitches out a fortnight back, she should be all healed," Bekka said. "But if she stretches too much, too fast, she *might* tear the scar."

"So we take it slowly," Jirana said in a voice that hid a warning.

"We take it slowly," Xhinna agreed. She looked around. The Weyr was empty: The weyrlings had been carried to the beach for drill and a swim; the older dragons were out hunting or searching for suitable Hatching Grounds.

Given V'lex's continued influence on T'rennor, Xhinna decided that she could use Kisorth's imminent clutching as a reason to talk with the older green rider both about the depredations on their stock and her concenrn about finding a safe location for Kisorth to clutch. V'lex, when Xhinna inquired, seemed not the least concerned. The interview had been awkward and his attitude had been just short of insulting. Still, she was convinced that the green rider was in contact with J'keran.

Since they had last talked about the issue, the depredations had slackened to one herdbeast every two days and then, after a fortnight, they'd suddenly stopped altogether with one final, grisly assault on a herdbeast, its clawed remains scattered throughout the holding pen, rendering it unusable. R'ney had found a new location and, with Colfet and—surprisingly—Jepara, who had proved as fair a hand with an axe as with a bow, had put a new pen together in a day.

An itch twitched along Xhinna's scar, recalling her from her reverie, reminding her not to overexert herself. She smiled at Mirressa. The green rider had matured so much since Impressing her Valcanth. She was still too eager to please, too meek for Xhinna's tastes, but she was starting to develop an inner conviction, a strength that would grow all the stronger as her green grew to maturity. She might still say "yes" far more often than was good for her, but she'd at least started to say "no."

Xhinna grimaced, then asked Mirressa, "How many?"

"How many times do you have to touch ground?" Mirressa asked, confused. "Just once."

"It's hardly ground," Xhinna said, indicating the canvas-covered tops of the broom trees they stood on. "But I meant, how many times should I try this now?"

"Oh, you mean to stretch?" Xhinna nodded and Mirressa pursed her lips in a way that made the young green rider look cute enough to kiss. "Try three more times, and then you should give it a rest."

"Three more times," Xhinna repeated with a gleam in her eye. She bent down and found it no easier, but the stretching, while painful, felt good, right. Jirana wanted to check her scar once more, but Xhinna shooed her away testily. "Wait until I'm done!"

Twice more she bent over, slowly, straining the scar, feeling it give, and bending lower before the pain and the stretching forced her to stop.

"Okay, now I'm looking," Jirana declared, sliding Xhinna's tunic back up and, with a hiss, gesturing for Mirressa to look. Bekka took a quick glance, then gave Mirressa a challenging look, requiring opinion.

"No," the green rider said, "that's all right. It should be a little red." The green rider's fingers traced the scar lightly, pressing here and there in what was just barely more than a tickle. Xhinna, who was used to such inspections, managed not to twitch in reaction.

"And now, Wingleader, that you've completed your calisthenics and been vetted," R'ney said drolly, "perhaps you'd care to engage in the management of your wing?"

Xhinna managed not to glower at him, conveying instead an authoritative nod in his direction.

"Very well," R'ney continued, drawing a breath to begin. "Bekka reports"—he nodded in the direction of the healer—"that our stocks of bandages have been depleted." He gave her a telling glance. "I have no idea why they've been used so profligately . . ."

Xhinna ignored the taunt and let his words roll over her, even as she smelled the fresh blossoms of the broom trees and the other scents of spring. There would be more showers soon, and then, as R'ney had excitedly declared, the mud would flow. The barren hill that lay beneath the burnt plateau was rainfall by rainfall creeping more into view and the appearance of bare rock could so excite only a smither— or those worried for the future of Pern.

The new pen was working well and there'd been no more Mrreow incursions, further convincing Xhinna that the prior assaults had been planned. She fumed at that, but revenge would have to wait.

"Are you listening?" R'ney asked softly. Xhinna shot him a glare and nodded. "Just checking," he said, continuing. "Meeya has reported some luck in turning wherry feathers into pillows, but Colfet reports that we're running low on canvas."

"Any luck with the gold?" Xhinna asked.

R'ney and X'lerin exchanged looks. Ah! Xhinna thought, so that's why they're looking so complacent.

"Shouldn't we get Javissa here with Aressil to talk about our trade options?" Xhinna asked, cocking her head at them inquiringly.

"Wouldn't that be counting your eggs before they clutched?" R'ney asked.

"Not if I'm any judge of character," Xhinna said, grinning as bronze and brown rider exchanged exasperated looks. "So, R'ney, how much did you find? And am I to gather that because Aressil isn't here, she's busy chortling over your new hoard?"

"She is, in fact, down at the flume now with Danirry, cataloging our findings," R'ney admitted.

"How many grams?" Xhinna prompted, wanting to cut to the heart of the matter without any of the word dancing that the brown rider loved—and with which, apparently, he had also infected X'lerin.

"About two thousand," R'ney said, smirking at Xhinna's reaction.

"We thought you'd be pleased," X'lerin said. Xhinna cut a look over to K'dan, but the harper shrugged and said, "I've been working with the weyrlings—this is as much news to me as it is to you."

Xhinna was not entirely surprised at this admission, but it was a shock to realize that for all K'dan's age and wisdom, it would not have occurred to him to keep a closer eye on R'ney and X'lerin in this matter, particularly when they started acting so smug. She would have. But then, she was naturally inquisitive and . . . she'd had months of practice. Before that, she'd had even more time with children, and as she was coming to realize more and more, children were great teachers of human nature.

"We're going to need to worry about Candidates soon enough," she said, musing aloud. "We could probably bring the gold with us for trade."

"Gold for people?" R'ney asked dubiously.

"No, gold for trade," Xhinna said. "Gold could help make life here easier, more enticing." R'ney looked relieved.

"True," K'dan said, glancing down at the thick leaves and branches supporting him. "Life here does seem a bit insubstantial."

"Airy," R'ney agreed.

"It would be nice to have a proper Weyr," X'lerin said.

"So what would we buy with our gold?" Xhinna asked, bringing the conversation back to solid ground.

"Bandages and medical supplies," K'dan said immediately. "Bekka's made a list."

"Clothing," R'ney said. "Fabric and needles." Aressil had proved to be a dab hand with tanning, and she and R'ney had quickly turned Cliova, Aliyal, Hannah, and J'sarte into competent tanners—although the older weyrlings preferred their healer lessons to the smelly, hot work of tanning leather.

"We'd do better hunting if we could get proper bows and arrows," X'lerin added. "P'nallo's done very well with what we have, but he swears that steel-tipped barbs would give us twice as many kills."

"We're having to fly farther and farther to find game," R'ney added.

"We can talk about that later," Xhinna said. "When will we get our first grams of gold?"

"I have a kilo of dust bagged and ready," R'ney told her, smiling happily at her surprise.

X'lerin chuckled loudly, pointing at Xhinna's face. "And you *wonder* why I made you a wingleader!"

"What?" Xhinna said.

"A kilo!" X'lerin repeated, shaking his head at R'ney and chuckling again at Xhinna's look. "Who else would have a wingsecond like that?"

"Blue rider," V'lex said, nodding respectfully as he sat down opposite Xhinna. When X'lerin had told her that he was sending the green rider to talk with her, she'd been surprised and just a bit skeptical.

But now J'keran's favorite was in front of her, a respectful, apologetic look on his face.

"I know who's been taking our stuff," he said in a rush.

"I do, too," Xhinna replied.

"And?"

"I don't like thieves," she said. Seeing him about to protest, she raised a hand as she added, "But I won't let dragonriders—or their dragons—starve." She paused, watching his reaction, then asked, "Have you seen them recently?"

V'lex shook his head. "J'keran's changed, Wingleader. He's a different man."

"Sober?"

"He's given up the rotgut," V'lex temporized. He paused for a moment, looking this way and that, not meeting her eyes before he said, "T'rennor's Kisorth will clutch soon." He slid his eyes up to meet hers. "X'lerin says that he's put you in charge of the Hatching."

So, Xhinna thought in surprise, you've grown a spine while J'keran's been gone. The V'lex of old would never have dared criticize the brown rider. And his interest in Kisorth's clutch—Xhinna made a note to keep an eye on the two green riders; it seemed that V'lex had taken a stronger interest in T'rennor than she would have thought possible, which might have important consequences for the whole weyr.

Green and blue riders, she was discovering, were hard to keep in one category. With browns it was even more so. Only the bronzes and queens were steadfast in their preferences. The rider of a female green could be the dominant partner in a relationship, although that role was more prevalent among blue riders. And while the male riders of greens were more likely to prefer male partners, it wasn't always the case. Based on her experience of the past four Turns, the only thing that seemed certain to Xhinna was that when dragons rose to mate, passions flowed freely, with the controlling passion being that of the dragon's over the rider. At all other times, riders were free to follow their own hearts.

"We need every dragon on Pern," Xhinna said. "Bronze, brown, gold, but particularly green and blue."

"Green and blue?"

"Green rider, you and I both know which dragons make up the bulk of the Weyrs," Xhinna said. "Which ones fly the most Falls, take the most injuries, work the hardest without fail?"

"Blues and greens," V'lex replied, a light shining in his eyes. "The browns and bronzes do their bit, but they're always bigger, they find everything easier."

"Well," Xhinna said with a slight smile, "they'd rather have to, being so big and clumsy." She shook her head. "Don't get me wrong! We need the browns and the bronzes, we need their stamina, their strength, but—" She raised a hand and opened it, gesturing questioningly. "—how do you think they'd fare if they flew Thread alone?"

"Not well," V'lex admitted. "Why my Sarinth and I have been through more Falls than—" He broke off, reddening and shaking his head. "I'm sorry, Wingleader," he said. "It's not your fault that you were too young and your dragon too new to fight a Threadfall."

"But I will," Xhinna said. "And when I do—when we do, Tazith and I, we'll be counting on you older riders to guide us while we newer riders will be doing all we can to support you." She paused, then added, "Just as you've been doing with T'rennor."

V'lex nodded. He glanced up at her, really looked in her eyes, and she saw something new, something different in him. V'lex might never be the sort that Xhinna could like personally, but his half Turn of flying Thread had made him someone she would respect.

"J'keran said you were a coward in that fight," V'lex said, eyeing her carefully.

"I was," Xhinna said. "I was wearing only a tunic and I was trying to convince him that I wasn't his enemy. I didn't want to fight and, in the end, I didn't fight—I was trying to show him that the eggs were hollow, that the tunnel snakes had gotten to them."

"That's what I said," V'lex told her. She didn't think the green rider had told J'keran that from the start, though. She imagined that this admission was from a more recent conversation. "But, you know, he said that the eggs weren't hollow, that the one you tried to knife was full."

"If it was, it didn't hatch," Xhinna said. "Only five eggs were good."

"But he said that egg was full," V'lex repeated, shaking his head. "He told T'rennor that—" He broke off suddenly, realizing he'd said too much, and dropped his gaze to the ground.

"But T'rennor's not listening to him anymore, is he?" Xhinna asked softly. V'lex looked up at her and nodded. "He's listening to you." The green rider said nothing. "And so what matters is what you're going to tell him."

"It shouldn't be this hard," V'lex said grumpily. "A rider should rise and flame, throw firestone, burn Thread, and rest." He frowned again. "And greens aren't supposed to fall in love with other greens."

"Perhaps that was the tradition," Xhinna said, and he looked up at her questioningly. "Traditions are good when the times are the same." She made a gesture, throwing the question to him.

"But times aren't the same," he said, finding some new hope in that realization. "If they were, we wouldn't have the greens clutching." He licked his lips and continued hastily, "If my Sarinth were still young, hadn't chewed firestone, then she'd be clutching, too."

Xhinna nodded, not quite certain what point the green rider was trying to make, but supporting him in his effort.

"And my green would have hatchlings," V'lex said in a voice that stirred strong emotions in Xhinna's gut. Oh, yes, she knew this emotion, she understood this man suddenly with a feeling of great clarity. V'lex wanted children. More than that, he wanted children for his beloved green. And if she couldn't have them, then he wanted them for those who could, like Kisorth.

There were depths in this man, Xhinna realized, that Fiona, with her blunt enthusiasm, would never have seen, never even have known were there, desperate for nurture. In far too many troubling ways, this man was like Taria in male form: one of the natural parents and caregivers that nurture all those around them. She could see how V'lex, surrounded by desperate males, all lonely and far away from their home and even their own time, would have been willing, eager even, to provide all the comfort he could. It was part of his nature: He would give without question if it provided ease to others.

Fiona had once remarked that she couldn't understand why he was so popular. Xhinna could understand that now. The Weyrwoman operated by demanding and receiving adoration and admiration; she loved everyone and expected love in return, thrived on it. It just wasn't in her nature to yield to the demands of others—she simply wasn't made that way.

And because she wasn't made that way, and also, Xhinna admitted, because Fiona had been so young and uncertain in herself, she couldn't have seen where V'lex should have behaved differently. Fiona probably did not even realize what he had done to this day, merely assuming that the green rider was happy because he was in such high demand, just as she was happy in the same situation.

V'lex was also somewhat like Mirressa: a person who simply could not say "no" even if it was in her best interest. And so his time in Igen had cemented him in the role of the butt of jokes, the first to come running and the last to leave. When the old Igen riders had joined the Weyr, they had naturally attracted those most like them. It must have been a huge relief for V'lex to have someone else—T'rennor, for example—suffer as he had, glad of the attention, miserable with the shame.

If it hadn't been for J'keran's attentions to Taria, Xhinna would not have noticed, leaving the fighting dragons to X'lerin. X'lerin wouldn't have noticed because, untrained, he had to accept J'keran's authority within his wing. Without malice or anger, she wondered idly if V'lex might have indirectly launched the brown rider in Taria's direction. Not that it mattered—J'keran, so drained by the repeated Falls and the losses, would have gravitated toward Taria, someone much like V'lex in nature, someone who would satisfy his desire to mold and dominate. As much as J'keran and the others had created V'lex's behavior, the green rider's behavior had affirmed J'keran's; the two were like poles of a magnet, tilting the one always away from what attracted the other.

However, with J'keran gone, V'lex began to chart his own course, the course that led him closer and closer to T'rennor and the green that would clutch at the same time as Coranth. In some ways, the old friends—V'lex and J'keran—had become rivals.

V'lex was breaking with tradition.

"Have you started scouting for Hatching Grounds?" Xhinna asked, leaping to the next logical conclusion. V'lex straightened in surprise. "It's what I would have done," she told him calmly, glad to see that she'd guessed rightly that he was looking on the sly. "It's what I *did*—until Coranth took the option out of my hands."

"I haven't found any place better than Coranth's," V'lex admitted. He glanced into Xhinna's eyes and held her gaze. "It's not very good, is it?"

"And that's why you were wondering about that egg?" she guessed, referring to the egg that she and J'keran had battled over. The green rider nodded.

"If those eggs hatch," V'lex said, "T'rennor will have a different chance than I did." He paused for a moment, giving Xhinna an opening to question him, but she knew what he meant—that T'rennor would be able to be more than a mere green rider: He would have the chance to be parent to dragonets and weyrlings.

"T'rennor already has a different chance," Xhinna told him staunchly. V'lex looked startled. "He's got *you*, green rider. That gives him an example that I doubt you ever had."

V'lex considered her words and his stance altered, became more upright and decisive. Yes, a different man, Xhinna mused. I was wrong to judge him. "So, green rider," she asked, holding out her hand, "are you ready to break more traditions?"

A smile slowly spread across his face. He reached for her hand and then, with a graceful pull, brought her into a tight hug. Emotion warped his voice as he spoke firmly into her ear, "Yes, Wingleader, I am."

"Good, then here's what I want you to do," Xhinna said, hugging him tightly before pushing back so that she could meet his eyes.

"What, Wingleader?"

She told him. She was careful in her explanation and blunt in her language, causing him to blush at least twice.

"*Just* as hard?" V'lex asked when she'd finished.

"Harder," Xhinna said emphatically. "I want no one to think you were kindhearted."

"But—"

"You're going to ride Fall with them, so do what you must, green rider," Xhinna said firmly.

"J'keran—"

"Isn't here," Xhinna reminded him. "And he rides a brown. So he doesn't understand about blues and greens."

V'lex's eyes lit and he nodded emphatically. "No, Wingleader, he certainly doesn't!"

"I'll let X'lerin know."

"And the boy?" V'lex inquired. "J'riz?"

"Certainly the boy," Xhinna said. "He rides a green; he needs to know."

"So that's four greens and two blues?" V'lex asked, verifying the numbers.

"Danirry will have to catch up, she's off with R'ney on survey," Xhinna said. "But I expect you to schedule that with her, don't let her shirk."

"She's the scrawny one, isn't she?"

"She was starved and sold the last thing she had for food," Xhinna told him.

"Did they catch the man?" V'lex asked, his features suddenly hard, his hand going to his belt knife. Xhinna's respect for him rose another notch.

"No," she replied with the same set expression. V'lex noted it and for a moment they stood reevaluating each other, finding the defensive, guiding parent that was part of the core of each of them.

"You'd've taken care of him if they had," V'lex said, loosening his grip on his knife and smiling at Xhinna.

"Justice is now in letting her heal, letting her see that not all men take," Xhinna said.

"I'll bear that in mind."

"She's got a strong will and a good heart, green rider," Xhinna said.

"And she looks manly," V'lex said, as though it were a compliment. He nodded to himself. "She'll ride her blue well, she's got a good conformation."

"She's not a *dragon*, V'lex!" Xhinna said in exasperation. "It's 'physique' you mean."

"Physique, then," V'lex said. "I'm not all that good with words."

"Well," Xhinna said to ease any hurt feelings, "she might prefer conformation to physique."

"She might at that," V'lex agreed. He smiled at the wingleader, adding, "And, if you don't mind, I think I'll try to make her 'physique' more womanly—put enough weight on her bones that she won't be pulled off her dragon by the first sack of firestone tossed her way."

"Do that, please."

"So we're going to have V'lex and T'rennor instruct the blue and green weyrlings," Xhinna concluded the next day when she met with X'lerin.

"And with them involved with the blues and the greens, they're not likely to think of running off to J'keran," X'lerin said, nodding in approval.

"I don't think V'lex is likely to throw in with J'keran now," Xhinna said.

"Why don't we find them?" W'vin asked. "They can't be too far if they're stealing from us."

"They could be Turns away," Xhinna reminded them. "They could be Turns in the past, even in the future—"

"What about Thread?" X'lerin asked.

Xhinna shrugged. "In the past, then."

"But you don't think so," Jirana said, piping up from beside X'lerin's wingsecond. Xhinna glared at her, willing her to be silent, but the youngster continued, "You love her—why don't you find her?"

Xhinna sighed as she saw how W'vin and X'lerin reacted to the question. It was the too-reasonable question she'd hoped she wouldn't have to answer, the one that hurt the most, that caused her to cry silently when she was sure everyone was sleeping.

"I can hear you," Jirana said quietly, looking Xhinna in the eyes.

Xhinna gave the brown-eyed girl a sad smile and ran a hand through her short dark hair.

"We don't know—yet—how to protect the eggs from the Mrreows and the tunnel snakes." She paused. "Taria was certain that the Mrreows would kill the tunnel snakes, but I'm convinced that the Mrreows are as much a threat to the dragonets as the tunnel snakes."

"So you're gambling," X'lerin said, looking at her in surprise and sympathy. "You're gambling with the life of the one you love."

"And her child," Xhinna admitted with a catch in her voice. "But if she's right and I don't let her try, then what will I do to Pern?"

"You know," Jirana said as she came over and hugged Xhinna, "you might try talking to people more."

Xhinna glanced cautiously at X'lerin. He grimaced, saying, "I'd guessed."

"You did?" Xhinna asked in surprise.

The bronze rider nodded. "I guessed and I decided to do nothing because I think you're right," he told her. "Until we have a full clutch of dragonets hatch out, healthy and whole, we have to try whatever we can."

"And so we're going to try with two clutches," Xhinna said, looking at Jirana. "With Coranth's and with Kisorth's."

"That will double our chances of success," X'lerin agreed. "But when her clutch hatches, how will we know?"

"She's got to get Candidates," Xhinna said.

"So have we," X'lerin said, frowning. Suddenly, his expression changed. "Oh! *Oh!*"

"I think it's hard, but I don't think it's hard-hearted," R'ney told her a fortnight later. Xhinna had taken him to a far shore to discuss her decision privately.

"Bekka says the baby won't be in any more danger, now that they've stopped with that drink of theirs," Xhinna said.

"And you practically gave them the best of our supplies," R'ney said, twitching a grin when he caught her surprised reaction. He pointed to himself. "I have spies everywhere."

"Even with Taria?"

R'ney shook his head ruefully. "Sadly, no." He looked down at her. "And they'll clutch soon?"

"Two weeks, maybe three," Xhinna said.

"And after that, we'll have five weeks to get all the Candidates."

"True," Xhinna agreed. "I've some thoughts on that and now that I can fly again, I'll bring them up with X'lerin and K'dan."

"And Bekka, Jepara, Jirana, and your whole gaggle of girls, no doubt," R'ney said, grinning at her reaction. "And in the end they'll say, 'Whatever you think, Xhinna.' And you know why?"

"Because I'm a girl," Xhinna said. She smiled at his look of surprise. "Because I'm the first blue rider who's a woman, and they know that everyone will be looking to me to see whether a woman can do the job."

R'ney said bitterly, "Even if you manage to handle all that's in front of you, there are some who will still say that girls can't ride fighting dragons."

"Particularly blues," Xhinna said.

"Especially blues," R'ney agreed with a firm nod. "The naysayers would be completely addled and wherry-brained, of course, but that won't stop them a bit, or they'd have died out Turns before."

"So you're not angry?"

"I'm worried, scared, horrified, and . . . slightly terrified at your resolve," R'ney said. "But I suppose if Lorana can lose her child to save Pern, you would consider no less."

"It's not my child," Xhinna said. "It's yours and Taria's."

R'ney snorted. "And who has the name for the child? Who will spend at least half the time diapering the baby?"

"You will," Xhinna said with a grin. "I'm planning on sleeping elsewhere until it's toilet trained."

R'ney snorted again with even greater derision.

"Well, perhaps a third of the time," Xhinna allowed. "I wouldn't want to deprive you of your joy."

R'ney smiled and waved off her taunt, glancing around abstract-edly at the island around them. It wasn't very large, certainly not enough for a settlement, but it had tree cover and plenty of lush un-dergrowth. "Do you suppose we could put herdbeasts here?"

Xhinna started to laugh, but stopped when she examined the is-land. "Yes, I think we could."

"There doubtless would be tunnel snakes," R'ney said with a sour look. "This whole island mass seems rife with them. I can understand why our esteemed ancestors never considered this low-lying damp piece of misery for a home, but there are certainly no Mrreows or we would have heard them."

"The herdbeasts are smart enough to move when the tunnel snakes mass," Xhinna said. A stray thought niggled her. Something to do with tunnel snakes. Eggs couldn't move. *Oh!*

"R'ney," she began slowly, "V'lex said something odd about the eggs from Coranth's Hatching."

"V'lex has gotten some sense, I'll grant but—honestly, Xhinna, he's not much better than a child at most things."

"That's not fair," Xhinna said. "He's not the smartest, but his heart's in the right place."

"Well, he's certainly amenable," R'ney agreed with a carefully neutral look. Xhinna growled and shoved a fist into his arm, not hard, but enough to get his attention.

"He said that J'keran swore that the egg I hit was solid," Xhinna said. "But I thought you said you saw eggs rolling down to the sea."

R'ney stroked his chin absently, his eyes set on the horizon, unsee-ing. After a moment he glanced back to her. "Five hatched, six rolled down to the sea," he recalled. "The weyrlings disposed of the others."

"Do you—"

R'ney cut off her words with an upraised hand, stroking his chin once more with the other, as he continued, "Jepara said hers was heavy, so C'nian helped. Meeya couldn't budge hers until G'rial and D'valor came back from rolling theirs into the sea." He gave her a bleak look. "Yours was cold, but there *was* a formed hatchling in-side."

"Did I kill it?" Xhinna asked, horrified.

"No, Wingleader, it was already dead," R'ney told her. "We didn't see any marks, but perhaps a tunnel snake . . ."

"I see," Xhinna said. Something still bothered her, something he'd said, but she couldn't bring it to focus.

"So, if Taria's using Razz to drive away the tunnel snakes, what are we going to do for Kisorth's eggs?" R'ney asked.

"I don't know."

She hadn't meant to, but somehow Xhinna found herself sleeping alone. The winds that swept over the broom trees made it so she was always cold. Alimma and the other weyrling riders were all camping with V'lex and T'rennor, eyeing Kisorth's bulging belly in fascination, prepared to help the moment the green started clutching, even though no one had found a better location than the sands. Blue rider P'nallo had joined them and Xhinna guessed that it would be less than a fortnight before all the blue and green riders—except her—were camping in the same location. In that much, her plan of putting V'lex in charge of their training had worked magnificently.

Jirana was with her mother, who'd been staying with Colfet more and more.

All of which meant that Xhinna was left to huddle under her blankets cursing the brilliance of her plan that had everyone in the camp warm and snug *except* her.

She thought of creeping over to R'ney, but the brown rider was exhausted from another day of surveying with Danirry on Tazith, performing the searches that Xhinna was still too weak to do herself. Xhinna was glad to see Danirry coming out of her shell around R'ney; clearly she felt safe with him, and the effect was that she was slowly recovering from her trauma, learning that some men, at least, could be trusted not to take advantage of her. But all that came at a price for R'ney: The brown rider had little free time in which to engage in his own interests. As it was, he spent all his spare time with Rowerth, oiling and feeding the brown, leaving him to the care of the queen weyrlings only when he had to be away. Xhinna thought that, as with

Danirry, R'ney was putting his dragon's needs entirely before his own, and she worried that the strain was beginning to tell. All of which meant that she couldn't bother R'ney.

She shivered. She was just too fardling cold. She thought of crawling in with Jepara, apologizing but begging the very real need for warmth. No, she thought grumpily as she scrunched further down under her blankets, if the eggs could handle the cold sands on the beach, then she could—

"That's it!" Xhinna cried, throwing off her covers and pulling on her robe. "R'ney, that's it!"

Heedless of her earlier decision, she rushed over to where the brown rider slept. "R'ney, I've got it!"

R'ney, however, was not alone, and realizing that, Xhinna felt herself blush mightitly.

"What?" R'ney asked.

The body next to him quivered and a head popped out. Danirry. Her mouth made a big O of surprise when she caught sight of Xhinna, and she said, in a small voice, "I was cold."

Xhinna smiled and clambered in on the other side of R'ney, elbowing him over to get into the warmest spot.

"Shards, you're freezing!" he yelped when her foot connected with his.

"And so was that egg!" Xhinna said, grabbing for his pillow and laying her head on it, feeling warm and suddenly very satisfied.

"What egg?"

"The one of Coranth's, the one that was dead," Xhinna said, closing her eyes and letting the delicious warmth creep all over her. She could have kissed R'ney when he wrapped an arm around her and drew her closer. "The sands aren't hot," she explained as she snuggled happily against R'ney's flat chest.

"And the eggs froze," he said with awe and sorrow in his voice.

" 's right," Xhinna said. "We'll plan in the morning."

And in moments, to R'ney's amusement, the young wingleader was gently snoring.

▼ ▼ ▼

"So what's the plan?" R'ney asked as he nudged Xhinna awake at first light. "What do we need to build?"

Beyond him, Danirry murmured in her sleep, objecting to the distraction.

"Plan?" Xhinna asked sleepily, wondering if perhaps Danirry didn't have the right of things and that they should wait to rise until the sun warmed them—and then she sat bolt upright. "The eggs—we need to keep them warm."

"Oh," R'ney said.

"The fire-lizard eggs had to be kept near a hearth, didn't they?" Danirry asked, propping her head up on one arm.

"And the Hatching Grounds are always warm—hot even," Xhinna said, remembering how she'd crept onto the sands so long ago in the vain hope of Impressing the queen egg that had held Fiona's Talenth.

"But how did the eggs freeze?" Danirry asked. "The sands were so hot during the day."

"During the day," R'ney said. "But at night . . ." Without warning, he threw the blankets off all of them.

Xhinna screamed as loudly as Danirry at the sudden cold and slapped at R'ney, who gave her an unrepentant look. Danirry clawed for her blankets and pulled them over her, uncovering Xhinna's feet.

"And it rained several times, too," R'ney said.

"Don't even *think* of getting water just to show us," Xhinna growled.

"Of course not," R'ney said as he rose from the bed, carefully tucking Danirry back in and kissing her cheek in apology. Sardonically, he told Xhinna, "I might freeze my wingleader, but I've grown out of wetting my own bed."

Xhinna rose and found her slippers as R'ney wrapped her robe around her shoulders. Thrusting her arms gratefully into the sleeves, she smiled and then nodded toward the eating area.

"Why don't you see if there's warm *klah* and, if not, rouse the guards," she said.

"I will if it's really going to take you that long to get dressed," R'ney said.

"It will." Xhinna planned to wrap a large blanket around herself and change within its warmth. She missed the warmth of the Weyr, the comforts of a well-established kitchen, of walls to keep out the wind. Living in the trees had gotten beyond charming and had moved into seedy.

"When are you going to build us proper Weyrs?" she grumbled to R'ney. A large part of his surveying was dedicated to that problem.

"I've got your Skies—"

"My Skies?"

"The blues and the greens," R'ney said. "They've taken to calling themselves 'Skies.'"

Xhinna shook the word off, motioning for him to continue, determined to talk with Alimma or V'lex when she could. "So the 'Skies' . . . ?"

"The Skies are scouting for quarry sites as well as proper Hatching Grounds," R'ney told her. "And W'vin and some of the others will ferry the first dozen herdbeasts to that island we found once they've caught them."

"It's a fair ways to go for food," Xhinna complained, even as a rope twitched beside them and she began to pull it up. At the end was a large bucket holding a pitcher of warm *klah*, courtesy of the fire guards. She could smell the scent of baking rolls rising from the ovens. Xhinna leaned over and shouted into the darkness below, "When your relief arrives, come on up and join us!"

"Will do," Bekka called back cheerfully. With Mirressa training with the blues, Xhinna had decided to turn vice into virtue and set Bekka and J'riz together on the dawn watch. After one or two groggy days, they learned to go to sleep earlier, finding bedding places on the branches not too far from the tops of the broom trees and waking in time for the last of the night and the first rays of morning. Bekka had even figured how they could see the Dawn Sisters, her personal talisman and guiding light. "They're a lot like me," Bekka had said when Xhinna had teased her about it. "They're up with the sun, bright and shiny. Besides, they led Lorana here."

Xhinna turned back to R'ney. "So, when you find the right sort of rock, what then?"

"Then we'll start the foundation for our hold."

"Not Weyr?"

"I suspect many of the dragons will sleep elsewhere," R'ney said. "So I think it should be a hold."

"And how big?"

"Well, we'll need rooms for Bekka's classes, storerooms, workrooms, a laundry room, a washroom with baths and the necessary, a kitchen, and a dormitory," R'ney said. He shook his head. "We can't afford to make individual quarters."

"It seems extravagant, given that we'll be leaving all this," Xhinna said.

"Which is why we're avoiding any unnecessary building, as much as we can," R'ney said. "As we don't have to worry about Thread, we're planning on building awnings around the main structure. As we expand, we'll put our quarters outside, do most of our cooking outside, and do our hardest work under canvas."

He proceeded to launch into a detailed description of the buildings, the awnings, and the planned expansions. Xhinna was impressed. "You've thought of everything."

"Not just me," he said, "Danirry's been an immense help, and it was Colfet who suggested the mass production." He poured a mug of *klah*, passed it to her, and filled one for himself. "So, what about this new problem you've found?"

"An old problem," Xhinna said, "and one that we hadn't properly considered."

"How warm do the eggs need to be kept?" R'ney guessed. He pursed his lips. "We could build bonfires, but the effort would be immense."

"Can we afford to be wrong?"

"Either way?" R'ney asked. "Too hot and we'll surely cook the eggs, not hatch them."

"We've got to keep them warm, probably as warm as a dragon," Xhinna said.

"So have a dragon sleep on the eggs," he said.

Xhinna shook her head. "The eggs are too fragile."

"Sleep beside them, then."

"That'd warm only one side," she said, frowning. She thought for a moment. "Maybe if we put the rider on the other side and had them switch regularly?"

"If Kisorth lays as many as Coranth, we'd need eighteen dragons and riders," R'ney said. "We've got a dozen."

"Have the weyrlings sleep with them, as well—that would give us three dozen."

"But the grown dragons would have to fly the weyrlings there and back each day," R'ney protested. "That's a lot of additional work."

A rustling of branches announced the arrival of Bekka and J'riz, each bearing a basket of steaming warm rolls.

With a grin, Bekka said, "Stop talking, eat!" She tossed a roll to Xhinna, who caught it and then flipped it from hand to hand until it was cool enough to grab and butter.

"If this works," R'ney added darkly.

"It's got to," Xhinna said, glancing meaningfully at him, willing him not to mention Taria's experiment. The brown rider nodded.

"We could set up some tents," J'riz suggested. "We could move our healer classes under them on the sands until Kisorth clutches."

"That's a good idea," Xhinna agreed. The tents were nothing more than sewn sails thrown over a smattering of rough-hewn wood. Colfet had shown them how to make quick wooden pins; with a wooden hammer, some rope, and pegs, they could erect fair-sized coverings in thirty minutes.

"We'll do that first thing," Bekka said. "That'll give us some shade."

"We don't have enough to cover a whole Hatching Ground from the rain," R'ney said to Xhinna.

"Well, that'll be your problem," Xhinna told him. "You and Danirry figure something out."

"Danirry will be with the Skies today," R'ney reminded her.

"Fine, get them to set up the tents," Bekka said.

"I'll talk with X'lerin," Xhinna said. The others glanced at her. "I think it's time Jirana and I went back to Crom."

"For Candidates?" Bekka asked, surprised. When Xhinna nodded, she said, "But we don't know how many we'll need!"

"We can get more when Kisorth clutches," Xhinna said, "but we can start with eighteen now."

"That's a lot of extra mouths to feed," Bekka said.

"But a lot of extra hands for work," R'ney countered.

"And we're going to be needing the hands—and the warm bodies, soon enough," Xhinna said. "I'd rather get them in small batches and let them get used to our ways than have to bring in a whole wing's worth in one go."

"And when will you be doing this?" R'ney asked.

"It's probably better to bring them back by light," Xhinna said, pursing her lips in thought. "I'd like to leave after breakfast, I think."

"If you're getting eighteen, you'll be making a lot of trips. Tazith can only handle eight at best," Bekka objected.

"I'll see if X'lerin will let me bring V'lex, as well," Xhinna said and was amused to see the startled reactions of the others. "And perhaps J'per."

"I won't be able to do this when I've Impressed Laspanth," Jirana said as she clambered up Tazith's foreleg early the next day.

"What?"

"Well, she'll need me full time and I won't be able to do this mind stuff," Jirana said. "That's only because of Laspanth, you see."

"No," Xhinna said as she clambered up after the dark-haired girl. "Not at all."

"That's all right," Jirana said, patting Xhinna's knee before reaching for her riding straps and tying on. Xhinna had rigged her harness to secure Jirana and six others.

Sarinth says they're ready, Tazith told her as she looked up at the blue and green hovering in the air above.

"Ready?" Xhinna asked the girl in front of her. Jirana nodded.

Let's go, Xhinna thought to Tazith. He leapt into the air, took two beats, sent the word to the two other dragons, and the three of them jumped *between*.

When they returned, three hours later by Sky Weyr time and six hours later by their own time, Xhinna was exhausted and could barely manage to keep the gabbling girls surrounding her from falling off before they landed on the soft-packed sand of the beach.

Jirana leapt off easily and raced to help Bekka and J'riz arrange a group of weyrling riders to handle the excited, frightened, shocked girls down from both their first ride on a dragon and their first time *between*.

Fortunately, the girls had not had to navigate the painful echo of the time-trapped D'gan and Fiona—that seemed to be heard only going forward through time, not coming back.

The first six were quickly joined by another nine girls, as well as three scrawny boys. Tazith had selected them, with some help from Jirana, who had seemed more eager to sleep than to talk.

"It's because I'm in this time too much," the girl had explained when Xhinna had tried to rouse her. "It's like Fiona and T'mar—too many of them in the same time. It's hard."

"But they only noticed it after they Impressed."

"They're not me," Jirana had said stubbornly.

Now, back once more in her "proper time," as she called it, Jirana perked up and was bouncing up and down on the sand as she described her exploits to her older brother. J'riz, to her surprise and annoyance, merely ruffled her hair and congratulated her—gone were the days when she could drive him into flights of jealousy. Xhinna noted the exchange with a smile, thinking that the little trader girl had far too much attention showered on her, and that a little brotherly indifference would help to settle her head back on her shoulders. Jirana craned her neck back over her shoulder and stuck her tongue out at Xhinna; how the child had guessed Xhinna's thoughts she couldn't say, although she wouldn't have been surprised if Tazith had something to do with it—the blue seemed to be besotted with the child.

As if in confirmation, Tazith rumbled in agreement, adding, *Of course*. Xhinna craned her head up to catch the blue dragon looking down at her, his eyes whirling a soft green in the mid-afternoon light. She beckoned, and he lowered his head for her to scratch his eye ridges.

The nervous girls and boys stayed huddled together. Xhinna

started to move toward them, but stopped when Bekka charged ahead of her and into the group of newcomers like a dragon through a flock of wherries.

"Line up," the young blond healer called. "Line up now so that we can meet you."

Xhinna looked around and saw V'lex and T'rennor standing to one side, arms folded. V'lex smiled and waved. When she reached them, T'rennor looked at her and said, "Nothing like training others to learn yourself."

"Not enough boys to Search?" V'lex commented, watching the new group being guided into three rows of six each by J'riz, Jirana, Alimma, and two of the green riders.

"Most of the lads old enough are working the fields," Xhinna said. "Those three were the only male Candidates we could find in a hundred."

"Three in a hundred?" V'lex asked, aghast.

"Too many died in the Plague and the rebellion, Nerra told me. More daughters lived," Xhinna replied. "With so few men to take their holdings, and too many mouths to feed, many sent their daughters where they could."

"There were women in the fields, too," T'rennor said. "With the men dead, they had no choice."

"So we fly with women," V'lex said, nodding toward Xhinna. "If they're all like you, we'll have no problem."

"It's the browns and the bronzes that worry me," Xhinna said. "I don't think any of the boys here would be taken by one of them."

"Well, that's a problem for another day, isn't it?" T'rennor said easily.

"It is," Xhinna agreed.

"They all look so sad," T'rennor said. "They'll need feeding and care." He frowned. "It's a pity we couldn't have saved the others. So many died just after the Plague."

When T'rennor's Kisorth clutched five days later, the Weyr was ready. As soon as the eggs were hard enough, Xhinna assigned a weyrling and rider to each of the sixteen eggs on the sands. Jirana walked directly over to one small, brownish one and touched the shell gently. "Hello, Laspanth, it's me."

"Jirana, I don't think that's a queen," Xhinna said. "And besides, don't you want to wait until you're older?"

"Nope, it's her," Jirana said with childlike certainly. "And I'm the right age now." She squatted comfortably in front of the egg and peered intently at the shell. Then she looked up at Xhinna and whispered, "She's sleeping, she needs her rest."

The words were clearly a dismissal. Shaking her head, Xhinna continued on her rounds, checking on the other eggs, the weyrlings, and the Candidates, whom she insisted should help out. Bekka wandered among them, saying encouraging words to each and every one until she got to Xhinna, where she let her guard down. "What if it rains?"

"We'll put the canvas up," Xhinna assured her. "And we'll do it at night, too: It'll help trap some of the heat from the sand."

Bekka glanced around nervously once more and then, noticing a young rider looking their way, put on a brave smile again and patted Xhinna on the back.

It didn't help Xhinna to know that the young queen rider and healer was as worried as she. She didn't sleep that night, waking fitfully to make rounds through the mass of eggs, weyrlings, and riders. She wasn't the only one, but while others dropped off one by one through the night as exhaustion took them, she kept on roaming until the Dawn Sisters appeared in the sky.

Jirana, rolled into a blanket and curled around the egg she'd claimed, opened her eyes and gave Xhinna an angry look when she passed by.

"You're disturbing their sleep," the little girl said, meaning the eggs. "I'll tell you if they need help."

"It's my job," Xhinna told her sternly.

"Just trust me," Jirana said. Coming from a small, dark-eyed, half-sleeping child, these were words that Xhinna found hard to credit. Jirana sighed and reached out to grab Xhinna's hand. "Trust me," she repeated.

Xhinna smiled at her, patted the hand, and gently pushed it back into Jirana's pile of blankets.

"We need these eggs to hatch," she said. "We can't fail."

Jirana bit her lip and looked away from Xhinna, muttering, "You've just got to trust me." Then she closed her eyes and rolled back toward her egg.

Xhinna stared at her. The child was a mystery: She had led them right so many times and yet—it was still hard to believe her claims. No one had ever heard of a queen egg coming from a green, not even among the fire-lizards. And here was this girl claiming not only that her egg was a queen, but also that she was in communication with the queen and already knew her name.

It was against all tradition, Xhinna thought wearily as she made her way back to Tazith.

I trust the little one, the blue offered as he drifted back to sleep, curling comfortably around his rider.

I worry about her, Xhinna said. *She bears a lot on her shoulders. Maybe too much.*

As she drifted off, she thought she felt a tendril of love coming from the direction of Jirana and her egg.

"**W**ell, sixteen is a good start," X'lerin said a sevenday later as he examined the guarded beach. He turned to Xhinna and examined her face. "You, however, have bags under your eyes. You need to get more rest."

Xhinna shook her head, stifling a yawn. "I can't," she said. "No more than you; R'ney's working overtime, and the whole Weyr is camped out here on the sands."

A frown crossed the bronze rider's face and he leaned closer so that his words would carry to her alone. "What about Coranth?"

"I know she clutched, but we can't figure out where," she said with a frown. "She'll need Candidates, though."

"And where will she get them?"

"If she's got eggs Hatching, I'll send her all the Candidates she needs," Xhinna swore. "I don't care how we do it—we need more dragons."

"True," X'lerin agreed. "But if she's right about the Mrreows . . ."

"We'll deal with that if it's so," Xhinna said. She doubted that Taria was right. She knew the green rider, knew that she was holding on now out of pure stubbornness. Xhinna wasn't sure what Taria would do if it turned out she was wrong; she hoped she'd return and accept the consequences.

X'lerin paused as he spied Jirana, happily lying with her back against her egg. He turned to Xhinna with an eyebrow raised questioningly.

"She swears it's a queen, her Laspanth," Xhinna said, shaking her head.

"She's been right about so many things; it's a pity she's wrong about what she wants the most."

"So it can't be a queen?"

The young Weyrleader shrugged. "K'dan says there have been some stories about the fire-lizards, but they were more likely the tales of confused holders."

"The fire-lizards came from somewhere," Xhinna said. "I wonder why we've got both green and gold females if only one of them has eggs that hatch."

"Green fire-lizard eggs hatch if they're watched and kept warm enough," X'lerin said. "Or that's what K'dan tells me." He sighed. "He said that Verilan had an idea once that perhaps the blues and greens were first, and the golds, browns, and bronzes came after."

"I could see how that might be," Xhinna agreed. "The blues and the greens are smaller, more able to survive on less than the larger creatures."

"I hadn't thought of that," X'lerin said. "If you're right, then perhaps a green hatched the first gold."

"From a blue mate," Xhinna added. Her expression changed as she added, "All this clutching is giving people ideas."

X'lerin raised an eyebrow, so she explained: "Many of our woman riders here are either pregnant or trying."

"That won't be a problem, will it?" X'lerin asked, frowning.

"I don't know," Xhinna replied. "We've got more than two Turns before we go back to fight Thread, and they've got at least a Turn before their dragons are ready to fly, so this is the best time for them to start a family."

"So you're encouraging them," X'lerin guessed.

"Not that so much as just letting the facts speak for themselves," Xhinna said. "And it's helping the older riders, too."

"How so?"

"They've got an investment in the future," Xhinna said. "Not only do they see these riders as their future wingmen, but they also see their children as a part of them, part of the wings, part of the Weyrs when we come back."

"It gives them something to live for," X'lerin said.

"Exactly," Xhinna agreed. With a twinkle in her eye, she added, "And something to do in the meantime."

"So am I to hope that you're taking your own advice?"

"I will, when the time is right," Xhinna said.

"Didn't you just tell me that that time is now?"

"I've my duties," Xhinna replied, turning away from him.

"It's a duty of a wingleader to see to the future," X'lerin told her softly. "I know that not all blue or green riders can find it in themselves to be parents."

"I'll be a parent," Xhinna said.

"There's Taria's child," X'lerin agreed soothingly.

"No, I'll be a parent myself," Xhinna told him. She smiled at his look and added, "I've got a proper father in mind for my child—he just doesn't know it yet."

"And so you're waiting for the right time?" he guessed. "A mating flight, perhaps?"

"Perhaps," Xhinna agreed lightly. "Now if we're done here, I'd best do the rounds."

"I'll come with you," X'lerin offered.

Xhinna raised a hand, turning around to tell him, "If you don't mind, Weyrleader, I'd *much* prefer it if you and your riders would get us dinner."

X'lerin chuckled and held up his hands in surrender, then started toward his Kivith. As he climbed onto the bronze's back, he called down, "You should get some rest, Wingleader."

"I will when you do, Weyrleader!" she called back in the same teasing tone.

X'lerin shook his head, did a graceful bow in his seat, and urged the bronze dragon skyward in pursuit of the evening's meal.

In the end, it was Alimma who got Xhinna to rest. They had made it through another night and Xhinna was drinking *klah* to keep awake, mumbling to X'lerin about the day's patrols, when the blue rider came to her.

"Excuse me, X'lerin, I need to talk to the wingleader," Alimma said, grabbing the cloth of Xhinna's tunic and tugging her away.

"Let go!" Xhinna said, batting at Alimma's hand.

"No," the blue rider said. "You need rest."

"What are you saying?" Xhinna asked. "I've got work to do, we've got to—"

"Xhinna," Alimma said sharply, "everyone's looking to you—you know that." Xhinna nodded, opening her mouth for a fresh protest, but the other blue rider held up a hand, saying, "Hear me out, please."

Xhinna fumed, then nodded. She'd hear the girl out and then she'd give her a piece of her mind.

"Everyone's looking to you," Alimma said again. "And you know that many are looking for you to fail."

"That's why I—"

Alimma cut her off with her hand again. "That's why you've got to rest," she said. "You're unraveling, and it's affecting the rest of us." She gestured around her and Xhinna noticed that the other four blue and green riders of Coranth's first clutch were there, too. "It's affecting everyone in the Weyr. Jepara's worried, Bekka's been crying, Jirana only talks to her egg."

"I know, I know, I—"

"Shh!" Alimma said, raising a finger to her lips. "You rest; we'll take it from here."

"But X'lerin—"

"He knows what we're doing—that's why he let me take you away from him so easily," Alimma said. "R'ney's got the first room finished at the stone hall and it's quiet there. We've set a bed up for you." Xhinna tried to protest again, but Alimma spoke over her. "I promise we'll have someone with you who will wake you the instant there's a problem we can't handle."

"But it's light out!" Xhinna exclaimed, gesturing to the rising sun.

"It's daytime, and you haven't slept more than a wink in the past seven," Alimma said. "Bekka's waiting for you; she's got a drink to help you sleep."

"Fellis juice," Xhinna said, making a face. "I hate it—"

"Please," Danirry said, stepping forward from the others and touching Xhinna on the shoulder softly. "You promised to take care of us, so let us take care of you this once."

Xhinna nodded, still reluctant. At the new Stone Hold, R'ney greeted her, and Bekka smiled when she saw her, insisting on tucking her into bed personally.

"Drink up," the blond healer said, handing her a glass. "Let me know how it tastes when you wake."

It tasted good, much to Xhinna's surprise. And the bed was warm: There'd been a warming stone in it moments before she arrived, she was certain. The blankets warmed her further, and there was a long, soft pillow running along the wall like another person keeping her company. She dropped her head and an arm onto it, and quickly drifted off to sleep.

THIRTEEN
▼▼▼▼▼▼▼▼▼▼▼▼

Attack from Beneath

"They're back," someone said in the darkness. It was a male voice: R'ney.

Xhinna stirred and turned over, reluctantly releasing the long body pillow that had comforted her for—how long had she slept?

"You've been asleep for a day and a half," R'ney told her.

She smelled fresh *klah* and warm rolls; those scents and the sound of liquid spilling into a mug inspired her to propel herself from lying on her side to sitting upright. R'ney chuckled as he extended the mug into her outstretched hands.

"By the shell of Tazith, R'ney, you are a true friend." Xhinna sighed as she sipped the marvelous warm liquid down.

R'ney's chuckle became a laugh and he turned a glow; when she blinked in the sudden light, he said apologetically, "You need to see to butter a roll."

The brown rider—or someone—had brought a chair and small table into the otherwise barren large room. He had placed the tray on the table and now, at Xhinna's sinuous one-handed invitation, took a seat opposite her. He raised a hand the moment she opened her mouth. "Eat first, talk later!"

As she started to wolf down her roll, R'ney frowned and, putting on a fierce expression, added, "Slowly!"

Xhinna slowed and chewed her roll with exaggerated diligence.

"Better," R'ney allowed. "While you start your next roll, I'll tell you the news."

Xhinna dutifully reached for and buttered another roll. Really, if it weren't for the worry in his voice, she would have gladly just sat and gobbled down the whole basket. But she knew R'ney wouldn't be here if it wasn't urgent.

"We had another attack of Mrreows—a pair, and we've heard more in the woods," he said. "The worst of it is that the pair actually came down to the sands before we drove them off. They were quick and they went straight for the sands, scattering Candidates and weyrlings in front of them until—"

Xhinna swallowed hastily. "Was anyone hurt?"

"No, thank goodness," R'ney said.

"How'd you stop them?"

"I yelled and waved my hands," R'ney admitted. He lowered his eyes. "In another instant I would have been mauled, but Pinorth landed in front of me and grabbed the nearest Mrreow—throwing it high, into the sea." He paused at the memory. "Snapped his neck, too, from the sound of it."

"So we double our guard and make sure everyone has a knife," Xhinna said, marshalling her thoughts.

"Spears would be better," R'ney said. "And more bowmen, too."

"We can spend some time training the Candidates," Xhinna said. She cocked her head at him. "All this, you or X'lerin could handle on your own. Why did you rush here to wake me?"

"Because little Jirana swears that there's a litter of Meeyus nearby and she's convinced Jepara to rescue them."

Xhinna pushed her sheets aside, jumped up, and slipped out of her nightgown as she looked around for her clothes.

"Pass me my things," she told the brown rider.

At the beach they found Jepara and Jirana in the center of a knot of riders. X'lerin was in front and gave Xhinna a look of relief as she approached.

"Jirana says that there's a litter of Meeyus," Jepara said to Xhinna. "I want to rescue them before they die."

"Jepara," Xhinna began, wishing she'd had more *klah* to clear her head, "these Mrreows are not like fire-lizards; they're more like the hunting birds of the falconers. They're vicious and wild—that's their nature."

"We need them, Xhinna," Jirana said. She glanced toward X'lerin and the look she gave the Weyrleader was odd: half-pleading, half-fearful. It seemed almost as though Jirana winced in pain as she spoke the words. "We can train them."

"We tried that, Jirana, remember?"

"We need to try again," the trader girl said. She turned to X'lerin. "They're babies, they're hungry, they need our help."

"We don't have the food or the people," Xhinna reminded her.

"Please, sister," Jirana pleaded, "trust me in this, will you?"

"You ask an awful lot."

Jirana grasped Xhinna's arm and pulled herself up on her tiptoes, her brown eyes meeting Xhinna's earnestly. "We must do this."

"Why?"

"I can't say," the girl told her.

Maybe Taria was right, Xhinna thought. And if she was, then they would need all the Mrreows they could find.

"We could build a pen," Jirana said. "Right here on the beach, where I can watch them."

"You?" Xhinna asked. "All by yourself?"

"I'll get others to help," Jirana said, biting her lip as she tried to build a roster of aides. "Leera, for certain, and . . ."

"If we're going to do this, we'll have one person for each Meeyu," Xhinna said, shaking her head and glancing to X'lerin to see that he understood. "The extra Meeyus . . . we can set them back in the wild."

"They'll die!" Jirana wailed. "And we need them—you can't do that!"

"Well . . . perhaps we can get some of the Candidates to help," Xhinna said. A flickering thought passed through her mind as she recalled the small balls of fur and the cute sound they made when they were contented. She nodded decisively. "I'll take one myself and—"

"Me, too," Jepara said. Jirana started to jump for joy, but the gold rider told her warningly, "If I'm not satisfied that they're safe, I'll put them all down myself."

"But they're not safe," Jirana said seriously. "They're death to tunnel snakes."

"They'll attack dragons," Xhinna said with a warning glare.

"I think they get confused, or they don't know better," Jirana said. "If I could get Laspanth or—" She craned her neck up and around to Jepara. "—your Sarurth to talk to them, maybe they'd understand."

"First," Xhinna said, "we have to find them."

"Oh," Jirana said, brightening. "I know where six of them are." Her expression fell as she added, "We killed their parents."

Xhinna turned to X'lerin. "Perhaps P'nallo and . . ."

"Me," R'ney said. "I can ride with you and Jirana."

"I'll need someone to rig a cage," Xhinna told him.

"Danirry," R'ney said firmly. "She can get the Skies to help, if you wish."

X'lerin spoke up. "Actually, Wingleader, I'd prefer to send P'nallo and a few others to scout for the other Mrreows. We can arrange a different party to go after these Meeyus."

Xhinna nodded in agreement.

"We need to hurry," Jirana said. "And we need to get my mother to tell the herders to get us fresh milk."

Xhinna hustled the child toward Tazith even as the trader girl prattled off orders. As Tazith bore the three of them skyward, Xhinna had a horrible thought: What would Jirana be like as a weyrwoman?

Further increasing Jirana's reputation, the Meeyus were exactly where she said, exactly as old as she said, and exactly the same numbers she'd said. Xhinna found herself torn once more between belief in all the girl's predictions and incredulity that one so young, even Tenniz's daughter, could know the things she claimed to know.

There were six Meeyus, and they appeared to be about two months old. The largest male stood fiercely in front of the others, his growl not as deep as a grown male's, but persuasive nonetheless.

"It's okay," Jirana said, moving fearlessly toward him, her hand out. She had a bit of fresh meat, hastily acquired from the campsite, in her hand. "It's okay, we're here to help."

She dropped the meat and the Meeyu sniffed at it, then licked it and chewed on it, but could not quite get it down.

"They're still babies—they need milk," Jirana said. She smiled as she glanced back at the bold one, saying, "But they'll do." She reached forward again, with the tips of her fingers near the Meeyu's nose. The Meeyu backed up, fearful, then moved forward, sniffing her fingers and then licking them. In a few moments, he was curled in Jirana's lap, making that buzzing noise that was so enchanting to one and all.

"You can get the others now," Jirana said, looking up quickly from the placid Meeyu. "We should get them and go—they'll be hungry."

Xhinna and R'ney got the others. One was sleeping and Xhinna passed it gently back to Jirana, who received it into her lap without comment, bringing up her free hand to stroke the first Meeyu back to sleep.

One of the littlest skittered away from Xhinna as she reached for it and she found herself lunging, with one Meeyu firmly lodged between her side and the crook of her arm. The skittish Meeyu batted at her; biting back a cry as the small, sharp claws raked her wrist, Xhinna reached around them and grabbed the Meeyu by the scruff of its neck. Instantly its temperament changed and it gave Xhinna a look that seemed to say, "What did I do wrong?" It curled its paws up and hung limply.

"Their mothers carry them that way," Jirana said. Xhinna turned to see the girl grab her two by the scruffs and stand carefully. "See?"

Xhinna chose to fly back rather than take the Meeyus *between* and risk disturbing them. Her choice worked out well: It gave Danirry more time to construct the cage, and gave Xhinna time to reexamine the area as they flew.

She'd spent several weeks trying unsuccessfully to locate Taria's lair, deciding in the end that the green rider either had chosen someplace completely out of sight or had, indeed, jumped *between* times.

Javissa was ready with fresh milk when they arrived, and all the Candidates crowded around until the headwoman quietly set them back to work, saying, "You'll frighten them. You can see them later, when they're settled."

"I was thinking we could tie canvas on top, when we need to," Danirry said as she showed her effort to R'ney.

"Good idea," he said, examining the stakes that had been set in the ground. "I see that you didn't waste our best wood."

"Hardly," she replied. "Most of this is what we couldn't use on the flumes." She waved a hand at it. "Rough wood, rough work, but it's sturdy."

"How far down did you go?"

"I had the dragons bounce on them," Danirry said. "They're a good meter, meter and a half in the ground."

R'ney seized one of the stakes and pulled; it bowed but didn't move. "Good," he said, glancing over at her. "Good work, Danirry."

The blue rider beamed at the compliment.

"There needs to be a door," Jirana complained, coming up to the pair of builders. "How are we going to get in?"

"We can build that later," R'ney said.

"We need it now," Jirana protested. "Otherwise I'm going to have to climb up every time I want to visit Meesha."

"Meesha?" R'ney asked.

"Meesha," Jirana said lifting her arm with the male Meeyu nestled in it. "They need names, or how will they know who we're calling?"

"I don't do that with herdbeasts," R'ney said.

"I only call them dinner," Jepara added with a grin that broadened further at the bronze rider's agreeing snort.

"But we do it with fire-lizards," Jirana said. "And the way we treat them is the way they'll act."

"She's right," Xhinna said, stroking the Meeyu she'd kept, the one who'd scratched her. The other, more docile Meeyu she'd yielded to

Jepara, who was now holding it in her lap, surrounded by interested Candidates. "I'm calling this one Scruff."

"Scruff?" Jirana repeated, her brows raised. "That's—"

"Her name," Xhinna finished. "You name your Mrreow what you want, I'll name mine what I want."

"Yours?" Jirana said. "You're keeping her?"

"Yes," Xhinna said as Scruff burrowed her head against her side, like a child looking to suck. Idly she scratched the soft tawny fur, and the Meeyu started making that pleasant buzzing sound.

Jepara's was named Tawny. At Xhinna's silent urging, V'lex and T'rennor appeared and each, dubiously, took one. V'lex named his Mee, and T'rennor, not to be outdone, went with Yu. Xhinna tolerantly said nothing, reminding herself sardonically that the two, after all, were green riders.

Red-haired Aliyal arrived silently to take the last Meeyu, which she named Amber, for his eyes. Of all the new weyrling riders, Aliyal was the quietest. She was not shy, Xhinna knew, nor did she shirk work, but the green rider seldom spoke except among the other traders. Even so, she had somehow formed a close bond with Alimma, who treated her better than she treated Cliova.

Mirressa offered to help Jepara with her Meeyu and the queen rider graciously accepted, so that the bulk of the Skies were intimately involved with the Meeyus.

Xhinna hadn't quite planned it this way, but she certainly didn't discourage it. She was confident that, if she needed, these riders beyond all others would do what she ordered. And much as she loved and respected little Jirana, she was willing, if it became necessary, to kill all the Meeyus with her bare hands to protect the eggs and weyrlings of her Weyr. Little Scruff whimpered against her and Xhinna softened. "Have we got someone bringing milk?"

It seemed that everyone in the extended camp had to touch, pet, fondle, or hold one of the Meeyus in the next several days.

To keep the litter from getting too frightened, Xhinna decided that only those who had done more than their share on any particular day would be allowed to handle a Meeyu. The competition worked and industry picked up immensely.

The effort lasted for three days until Xhinna, sensing that she was straining the Weyr too much, decided to end it, allowing each individual Meeyu handler to set his or her own schedule.

Xhinna took to leaving her Scruff with Jepara or Alimma when she needed to be elsewhere, although she was determined to bring the Mrreow with her on Tazith when it got older, if it proved trustworthy. The blue dragon regarded the small Meeyu with a mixture of curiosity and boredom, verging on antipathy.

Jirana had managed to badger J'riz into making her a shoulder halter for her Meeyu; she attached a lead rope to it and walked her Meesha everywhere as if it were a Hold canine. The Meeyu was not quite as obedient as that, but seemed content enough to stay more or less at the trader girl's side. Pretty soon all the Meeyus had halters and leads, Xhinna's Scruff included.

Jepara shook Xhinna awake in the middle of the night. "Something's bothering Sarurth."

The difficult queen rider had chosen to sleep with Xhinna, ostensibly for warmth and proximity to Scruff, but really, Xhinna had quickly realized, for advice on relationships. Apparently X'lerin was being aloof to her, spending more time in the company of the other weyrwomen, and Jepara was near frantic with worry.

Their conversation had turned intimate and Xhinna was not surprised to learn that Jepara had not realized that one love was much like the other, no matter who gave it or to whom it was given. When they finally decided to sleep—after the topic had been talked over far longer than Xhinna cared—Jepara had rolled over with her back to Xhinna in a clear statement. Xhinna had smiled to herself, and was not at all surprised when, sometime later, Jepara heaved a huge sigh, rolled back over, and draped an arm lightly around her. Cold nights made for the strangest of bedfellows, Xhinna thought as she rested her head on the pillow nestled up against the egg she was warming. She considered rudely forcing Jepara to move around to the far side of the egg, but Tazith was already there and little Scruff would complain at being wakened, having just found the perfect spot at the back of Xhinna's knees.

Now, Xhinna could feel the little Meeyu tense against her and she reached to Tazith. The blue was awake.

Xhinna felt for the Meeyu's lead, found it, and gripped it firmly in one hand as she used the other to probe through her clothes. When she found the hilt of her knife, she rose, saying over her shoulder to Jepara, "Stay here."

The night was cold and the wind blew through her gown, causing her to shiver, but Xhinna continued onward with some sense of dread.

She saw a figure moving toward her. It was Aliyal with her Meeyu.

"Something spooked you, too?" Xhinna asked when she recognized the red-haired green rider.

"Amber woke me," Aliyal said.

Suddenly Amber veered left, flinging sand; at the same moment, Scruff leapt in the same direction. Wordlessly, the two women let the Meeyus have their lead, Xhinna edging forward, knife in front of her.

They heard the sound of a weyrling moving anxiously and Xhinna started running toward the sound even as Scruff strained at her lead. The Meeyu stopped in front of an egg and turned back to Xhinna anxiously, making her pleading *meeyew* noise.

Xhinna moved forward, gesturing with her hand for Aliyal to stay back, and cautiously touched the egg in front of her. One of the bronze dragonets came around the far side at that moment, sniffing at Scruff and blowing at Xhinna.

Something is wrong, the bronze—Feyanth—told her. *G'rial went for help.*

Xhinna paused, listening, her knife moving back toward the egg. There was a faint, scratching sound—coming from inside the egg!

Xhinna slammed into the egg hard, rocking it. Loud growling came from both Meeyus, and Scruff lunged under the egg, grabbing and pulling at something with his teeth. A tunnel snake.

"Take my knife, kill it!" Xhinna yelled, raising her knife hand up behind her as she strained to keep the egg leaned over, away from the Meeyu and the tunnel snake.

As soon as Aliyal took the blade, Xhinna put all her weight into keeping the egg tilted while the green rider grunted, swinging wildly. At last there was a sick, fleshy *thunk*. Scruff gave a satisfied sound and pulled back, and Tawny leapt forward, buzzing happily to join her littermate in gnawing on the warm morsel.

The egg is dead, Tazith reported sadly. Xhinna could see the sand under the egg growing darker as the egg's vitals leaked out.

"Eat it up, gnaw it, tear it all you want, you two," Xhinna encouraged the two Meeyus. "You deserve it."

With a tear in her eye, she stepped back, letting the dead egg rock upright once more. She felt a hand on her shoulder and turned as Aliyal handed her the still ichor-slimed knife.

"Well done," Xhinna said, taking the knife and sliding it into the sand to clean the worst of the mess off.

"I would have preferred to kill it before it got the egg," Aliyal said with a hard edge to her voice. She met Xhinna's eyes squarely. "I'd kill them all, by myself, if I could catch them."

Xhinna nodded; the green rider had reflected her sentiments exactly.

"I'm sorry, T'rennor," Xhinna said as Kisorth's rider watched the crew haul away the wrecked egg.

"You did your best," T'rennor said. Beside him, hand on his shoulder, V'lex frowned.

"It wasn't good enough," Xhinna said, glancing directly at the older rider. V'lex looked up, flinched, and then dropped his eyes. Xhinna turned away, toward X'lerin, who stood close by, watching the egg as the work party moved it to the shore and slid it gently past the surf, into the sea.

"Weyrleader," Xhinna said around the heavy lump in her throat. X'lerin lifted his eyes to her and shook his head slightly. "I may not be able to keep my vow—"

"No," X'lerin said with a fierce undertone in his voice, raising a hand to forestall her words, "don't say it."

"But—"

"You gave your word, I expect you to keep it," he said sternly. Around them, heads turned to watch the interplay. "We know now that the tunnel snakes can attack through the sand, and we know our Meeyus can find them, so your job has gotten that much easier." He gave Xhinna a slight wink, barely visible, as he said, "Now do it."

X'lerin wasn't blaming her, Xhinna thought with a wave of relief. The Weyrleader trusted her still.

"Very well," she said. "If you'll join us at the hold, I'm calling a meeting to discuss our options."

"Strategies," he corrected absently, tearing his eyes away from the sea, where they had wandered once more, and focusing back on Xhinna. "I believe that's the word you were looking for."

"Precisely," she said with a curt nod. She marched briskly to Tazith, nodded thanks to Jepara, who was watching Scruff this morning, and ordered the blue skyward.

Ahead in time, from whence they'd escaped, without these new eggs fully hatched, Impressed, and matured, Pern had no hope, only the last remnants of those fighting against steadily increasing losses until the last dragon on Pern died, overwhelmed by masses of unopposed Thread.

If she could not find a way, Pern would die.

Tazith started his spiral down to the half-finished stone hall. X'lerin's bronze was already there.

Xhinna sprang down quickly and trotted into the room where she'd slept. As she did she heard voices becoming clearer ahead: R'ney, Danirry, X'lerin.

"We can't put the eggs in the broom trees. How would they stay warm?" X'lerin was saying.

"And when they hatched?" Danirry said.

"Stupid idea," R'ney said, his voice weary. "Sorry I said it."

"Don't be," Xhinna said as she stepped into the room. She smiled. "It was an honest thought, keep going."

"We could bring them here," R'ney said.

"Wouldn't we need sand?" Danirry asked.

"I don't know," R'ney said. "If the sands are for warmth, then anything that keeps them warm will help."

"But we know the sand insulates from losing heat to the ground," Danirry told him.

"And the sand lets the tunnel snakes through," X'lerin countered in R'ney's defense.

"Could we carry all the eggs from the sands here?" Xhinna asked, glancing at X'lerin. She raised an eyebrow toward R'ney and Danirry. "If we used slings, couldn't we bring the sand they're sitting on?"

"Perhaps," X'lerin said. "But we've fourteen fit dragons and fifteen healthy eggs."

"And we figure with the sand we'd need, we'd need four dragons for each load," R'ney said.

"That much," Xhinna said with a grimace. She shrugged. "Well, it was an idea."

"It won't help anyway," R'ney said, shaking his head. "We've got another month or two—at least—before the rock here is clear enough to lay out an area large enough for all the eggs."

Xhinna frowned. "Just the area outside now would be enough."

"For Kisorth's eggs," R'ney corrected her. "But—for all the eggs we'll need?" He shook his head. "Whatever answer we find has to work for all of them."

Xhinna slumped her shoulders and nodded wearily.

"It's a pity that the eggs can't talk, like the dragons," Danirry said wistfully. "Then we could ask them if the tunnel snakes were near."

Xhinna rose and headed outside, toward Tazith. "Well, keep working on it. I'm going to check on the camp."

Through the rest of the day, whenever asked by a rider or weyrfolk, Xhinna would give the cheerful answer that they were working on a solution and she was certain they'd find one soon. And each time, as she saw the relief and trust light up their eyes, she felt worse. She had no answers—but she couldn't tell them that.

Bekka found her wandering the beach and stopped her long enough for J'riz to massage the tense muscles of her shoulders and neck. It was a momentary comfort, for when he was done, she felt the weight of all the Weyrs of Pern fall on her back once more.

It was almost dusk when Jirana accosted Xhinna and casually grabbed her hand, swinging their arms together. Xhinna, too tense to think clearly, instantly felt alarmed.

"What's wrong?" she asked, stopping to look at the girl.

"Nothing," Jirana said. Xhinna give her a harder look, grabbed Jirana's other hand, and boosted the child up on her hip so that she could look directly into the worried brown eyes.

"What's wrong, little one?" Xhinna asked softly.

Jirana wouldn't meet her eyes as she said again, "Nothing."

Xhinna felt a tremor: Jirana was shivering. "Are you cold?"

"No," Jirana said curtly, suddenly straining against her. "I'm fine, let me down."

"Why don't I sleep near you tonight?" Xhinna suggested.

"No," Jirana said, and darted away into the gloom.

FOURTEEN
▼▼▼▼▼▼▼▼▼▼▼▼

A Body Torn

Once more Xhinna woke with a feeling of dread. The thick morning fog had rolled back in from the sea, shrouding the sands in a blanket of muffling white. She felt for Tazith and found him awake, standing on all fours, nervously scanning around him.

She had chosen to sleep by an egg at the outskirts of the group, far enough from Jirana that the trader girl couldn't get angry, but close to hand. Two Candidates shared Xhinna's egg, sleeping soundly in their thick pile of blankets. Because she was often interrupted in the night or got up to patrol on her own, Xhinna had elected to be on the outside and they, young holders that they were, glad to be rescued from certain death by starvation, did not argue with her—a trait she had come to appreciate. And they adored Scruff who, despite all Xhinna's efforts to keep an emotional distance, had become such a sweet ball of fluff that she slept with them, tethered by a collar attached to a long rope.

Xhinna was just beginning to think that it was unnecessary, that the Meeyu had come to accept her as her mother. She wasn't quite sure whether she should take that as a compliment or an insult, but she'd given up worrying about it, glad that this Meeyu, at least, had proved more biddable than Razz's dead siblings.

Follow. The "voice" was muffled, faint, no more than the barest of whispers in her mind.

She turned her head, sensing: The faint sounds of a dragon rising came to her, muffled in the fog, from a direction she couldn't trace.

Flying in fog was dangerous—all the riders knew that. Xhinna had trained with K'dan and T'mar back on Eastern and they'd been demanding taskmasters—fog was no mystery to her: She treated it with the respect and wariness it demanded.

She heard a noise to her right and moved toward it. A figure emerged from the fog. Javissa.

"Have you seen Jirana?" the trader woman asked. "I thought I found her egg, but she wasn't there."

A deep sense of unease gripped Xhinna and she grabbed Javissa's arm. "Come with me."

As they ran toward Tazith, Xhinna saw two more figures appear: Bekka and J'riz.

"Come with us," she ordered, not stopping for questions. As soon as they reached Tazith, Xhinna hustled them up onto him. She was glad to see that both Bekka and J'riz had their small medicine pouches with them: The healer had insisted that all her apprentices carry them at all times. "You never know when you'll need them," Bekka had told Xhinna when asked.

"Someone's got Jirana," Xhinna said as she climbed up after them.

"How are you going to find them in this soup?" Bekka asked.

Jirana? Xhinna thought, passing her query through Tazith. Faintly she caught an echo, no more than a whisper and an image: darkness, fog, a large black spot. It was not enough to go *between;* the image needed to be clearer. *Can you see stars?*

Xhinna sat tensely, waiting for a response. She felt Bekka's hand grip hers, knew that Bekka had gripped Javissa's and J'riz's hands, tying the four of them together, felt a slight rush of power from them and then—there! An image of stars came to her, just above the fog and the dark spot.

Let's go, Tazith.

The blue was airborne in one leap, *between* in the next instant.

▼ ▼ ▼

The stars guided them. They came out over another bank of fog, broken in places. Seeing a darker spot, a break in the shoreline, Xhinna guided Tazith to land near it.

As she jumped down, she heard voices talking loudly, quickly stilled by one barked command from a male voice. She had expected J'keran and Taria, but what if there were others?

"You stay here," Xhinna said.

"I'm coming with you," Javissa said. "That's my daughter."

"And my sister," J'riz added, moving up beside his mother, his belt knife drawn.

"And my—" Bekka cut herself off. "My weyrmate, if nothing else."

J'riz touched her shoulder comfortingly and she grabbed his hand.

"We might need a healer," Xhinna allowed. "Let me go first. J'riz, you follow. And keep that knife out."

"Do you expect trouble?" Bekka asked. As if in answer, a Mrreow growled low in the distance, a hunting sound. A higher-pitched growl came from in front of them, followed by a girl's squeal, suddenly cut off.

Xhinna moved, darting from shadow to shadow, silent in her soft shoes. Bekka's heavier boots could be heard, but both Javissa and J'riz moved inaudibly. Bekka stopped moving, apparently aware of the noise she was making. Xhinna could hear a grunt from Bekka's direction and decided that the healer was removing her boots.

The darkness in front of them grew larger and larger until it revealed itself in the mist—a huge cave, carved out of the face of the shoreline Turns back by the river that flowed idly from it.

No wonder no one had found it, Xhinna thought as she scrabbled from rock to rock across the river to the wider expanse on the far side.

A Mrreow's roar broke the silence of the night, punctuated by a child's scream.

Xhinna shouted and broke into a run, knife ready.

"No!" a voice cried—Taria. "Razz, no!"

Xhinna heard more noises then, echoing throughout the cave: girls and boys crying out and rushing around.

"Come back, the dragons need you!" J'keran cried in frustration.

Another Mrreow roared, from near where the girl had screamed.

"Come back, they're attacking!" J'keran yelled again. "If you split up, they'll hunt you down."

Tazith, get help, Xhinna told her blue as she raced toward the location of the last roar and the child's shriek.

Dim glows provided just enough light for her to dodge the eggs as she came upon them. A hiss came from her side, and farther away she heard more shrieks and a muffled cry—it sounded like Taria.

"Tunnel snakes!" J'keran cried. "Come back, we have to fight them!"

That sounded so much like the old J'keran: stupid but brave.

"Jirana!" J'riz yelled.

Shards! Xhinna thought. She'd wanted to keep their presence a secret.

"Jirana, it's me, Xhinna!" Xhinna called, even as she dodged blindly to change her location. She paused, panting as quietly as she could, straining to hear. There! To the right, was that a whimper? "I'm coming!"

She took off again. There was a noise behind her. Some trick of light showed a flash of sickly blue, and Xhinna sliced the tunnel snake as it jumped from an outcrop above. She lopped off its head and continued to run toward Jirana even as she realized that the tunnel snake had been the largest she'd ever seen, fully half the size of one of the weyrlings.

"Jirana?" Xhinna called again. She heard footsteps, many sets— and then Bekka called out, "I've got her!" More quietly: "There, Jirana, it's all right. I've got you, you'll be all right."

But Xhinna had known the healer for Turns now, and she recognized that tone of voice.

With berserk rage, Xhinna went charging toward Bekka, slicing tunnel snakes or anything that looked like them and looking for the large amber eyes of the attacking Mrreow.

A roar alerted her and she spun, falling backward as she thrust her knife forward. A huge male Mrreow flew over her, snagged her knife, yanking it from her hands even as its roar turned to a bellow of pain.

She scrambled to retrieve her knife and turned to face the Mrreow if it returned. Panting hard, she tried to hear anything beyond the sound of her breath.

There was motion above again and she pivoted, slashing the air, splitting the tunnel snake in half before spinning around again at the first touch of a large paw.

The Mrreow had flung itself in the air with a menacing growl, and as Xhinna turned, thrusting out her knife to protect herself, she felt a second tunnel snake's claws rip into her scalp just before the Mrreow's paw connected with it and flung it far.

But it was too late for the Mrreow. Xhinna's knife and her intincts moved faster than her brain, and in the startled moment she had to recognize that the Mrreow had attacked the tunnel snake and *not* her, its momentum and hers drove the sharp dirk hard into its chest.

"No!" Xhinna cried, too late. She and the Mrreow continued in motion, and as they fell, Xhinna's weight drove the point of the dirk home. "No, no, no!"

The Mrreow hit the ground, Xhinna on top of it, her dirk beneath her. And then she spotted its collar. It was Razz.

"Bekka!" Xhinna cried. "Oh, no, no, no!" The tawny beast had been trying to *save* her, attacking the tunnel snake she hadn't seen. "Bekka!"

Blood gushed around the hilt of her dirk, flooding over her, pumping out with the force that only an artery produced.

"*Bekka!*" Xhinna shouted. She put her hand around the blade, trying to staunch the flow of blood, but it did no good. With a grunt, she pulled her dirk out with her hand still wedged around it, the blade nicking her flesh as it came free. Heedlessly, she threw the knife to one side, moving her bleeding hand to cover the deep wound that pounded out more and more blood. "Bekka!"

The blond healer appeared in the corner of her vision, just beyond the Mrreow's head. She took one look at Xhinna, at the blood—and Xhinna knew, even before Bekka shook her head.

"No!" Xhinna cried, pushing her hand harder against the wound. The bleeding was slowing, couldn't Bekka see that? It was all right, it was—she looked up at Bekka once more, then caught the Mrreow's eyes as they dimmed, their life ebbing.

And in that instant, Xhinna felt a feeble warmth from Razz's lungs, as though the dying beast were breathing her life to her, giving her a gift, trying to lick her one more time with her rasping tongue.

"Xhinna," a voice spoke beside her, faint beneath her own unceasing cries. "Xhinna, she's dead."

"No!" Xhinna cried. "No, she can't be!" Her tears were flowing freely, her sight was blurry, and she pulled roughly away from the hand that reached for her arm. "No, she was trying to save me," she cried. "It was a mistake, I couldn't stop and—and—*Bekka! Do something!*"

"She's dead, Xhinna," Bekka told her, swimming into view. The blond woman was crying, too, crying for her friend, crying for the Mrreow that had saved her. The Mrreow that Xhinna had—

"*No!*" Xhinna shouted, refusing the truth. She felt another hand come around her waist from the far side and heard R'ney's voice near her ear.

"Come away, Xhinna, come away now," the brown rider begged her. Xhinna squirmed, her elbow digging into his chest, and he fell back with a grunt that made Xhinna feel even more guilty, but—

"NO, you have to help her!" Xhinna cried, heedless of the blood streaming from her own head wound. "She's got to live! It was a mistake, I didn't mean it! She's got to live."

"She's gone, Xhinna," a soft voice beside her said. Taria.

"I didn't mean it," Xhinna said, turning a pleading look at the green rider. "I couldn't stop." She shook her head, tears flying. "I couldn't stop."

"I know," Taria said soothingly. "I saw. You didn't see, you just reacted."

"We've got to help her," Xhinna said, turning from Taria back to Bekka and then to R'ney, who stood nursing the side he had fallen on. "We've got to save her."

"We can't, Xhinna," Bekka said, stepping closer. She held a hand over the tawny beast's eyes and slowly lowered the lids. "She's gone, there's nothing we can do for her."

"Give me a bandage," Xhinna ordered the healer.

Bekka's eyes widened. "There's no point, Xhinna."

"Get—me—a—bandage!" Xhinna roared. In the distance, dragons bellowed in support. She felt a moment's awe at that: She hadn't known they would do that for her.

Tremulously, Bekka pulled a bandage from her carisak and passed it to Xhinna.

"And another," Xhinna said, as she bunched the first one and stuffed it quickly under her hand into the wound gaping below.

"It won't help—her heart's been torn," Bekka said as she passed another bandage over.

"I need something bigger—it's got to go around her," Xhinna said, ignoring the healer's words. She heard a dirk being drawn and a sharp tearing sound beside her. She turned and saw Taria ripping her shirt to shreds. "Cut mine, too."

Taria obeyed, passing Xhinna the bits she'd quickly knotted together from the wreck of her shirt. Xhinna held still for Taria to cut her shirt away; quickly she knotted the new strips to the end of the other shirt.

"I'll help," R'ney said, moving into her field of view and holding out his hand for the end Xhinna was trying to wrap around the large beast.

Bekka took the strip from him and continued it around the beast's back, cinching it up in line with the wound, then passed it to Taria, who passed the last bit back to Xhinna. They repeated the process with the strips of Xhinna's shirt so that the wrappings went around the dead Mrreow's chest twice.

After that, Xhinna stood up. "I'm sorry," she said, looking at the still form in front of her. "I didn't know." She glanced at Taria and her tears came again. "I was wrong—I should have listened to you."

Behind her, Tazith started scooping out the soft sand, digging a deep hole.

"We'll put her there," Xhinna offered, glancing at the green rider. "If you don't mind."

"No," Taria said softly, "that's perfect."

Xhinna nodded, then turned to Bekka. "Jirana?"

"She's resting," Bekka said. "She's got a nasty cut that will need stitches, but she'll be fine."

"Stay with her," Xhinna ordered. She sent out a call for X'lerin and the rest of the fighting wing, asking them to send half their strength here and set the rest on perimeter patrol. She moved around to stand behind the Mrreow's head. She reached down, laced her fingers together under it, and began to lift with her knees.

R'ney moved to the Mrreow's tail, but he couldn't reach around. Taria joined him on the far side. They couldn't budge it. A rush of noise flowed around them and suddenly there were more riders, each finding a place around the Mrreow's sides and lifting: X'lerin, W'vin, J'keran, Colfet, K'dan—what was he doing here?

"I killed her when she was trying to save me," Xhinna said from her position at the Mrreow's tawny head. "I want to bury her here by the sands she fought to protect."

The others nodded and heaved the body off the ground. They moved slowly, in silence, and gently placed the Mrreow in the hollow Tazith had dug.

"I'm sorry," Xhinna said, half to the dead Mrreow, half to Taria. "I should have listened."

She reached down and took a handful of sand and sprinkled it over the body. R'ney joined her from the other side, then Taria, X'lerin, W'vin, J'keran, Colfet, and K'dan.

They stepped away as Tazith gently pushed the rest of the sand over the dead creature.

When the hollow was full, Taria stepped up to her and said, "What are your orders, Wingleader?"

"Xhinna!" It was Bekka hurrying over to them. She was alone.

"Where's Jirana?" Xhinna asked.

"You'd better come," Bekka said, her eyes suddenly shiny with tears.

"What?" Xhinna demanded.

"She said for me to tell you she was okay," Bekka said, her face crumpling. She gestured hurriedly. "You'd better come."

Xhinna reached out and grabbed Taria, tugging her behind her. As they moved, she noticed that Taria's belly was huge, that otherwise the green rider was gaunt, hollow-eyed with terror and exhaustion.

"You look awful," Xhinna said over her shoulder as they moved.

"*You're* all green with tunnel snake," Taria said. She sniffed and made a retching sound. "And the smell!"

Jirana was lying on the ground, her eyes closed. Javissa and J'riz were beside her, the green rider's eyes flowing with tears while his mother just stroked her daughter's hair quietly.

"The Mrreow sliced her open," Bekka said as Xhinna knelt beside the girl, reaching forward with one hand to stroke Jirana's upright palm.

The girl opened her eyes and tilted her head toward her. "Laspanth?"

"She's fine," Xhinna lied, gently stroking Jirana's hand. "You'll be fine."

"It hurts," Jirana moaned. "I knew it would hurt—that's why I couldn't tell you."

"But—"

"Ask the queens," Jirana said, closing her eyes with a grimace. Xhinna leaned forward, impelled by some inexplicable feeling to catch the words Jirana only breathed: "Trust."

"She's young," Xhinna said, looking to Javissa and then Bekka. "She's strong."

Bekka shook her head. "Xhinna, she's not this strong," the healer told her quietly. "If she moves when I try to stitch her up, I'll tear her guts open."

"Fellis," Xhinna said, aware that others were gathering near.

"Not good enough for this," Bekka said. "And she's in such bad shape, I'm afraid that she might slip too deeply into sleep."

"We can't just give up," Xhinna said. She looked at Javissa, but the trader would not meet her gaze, still stroking her daughter's hair. "I'm not giving up," Xhinna declared. She looked at Bekka. "We are *not* giving up."

"No," Bekka agreed. "Of course not."

"R'ney," Xhinna called over her shoulder, "take charge here, clean this up, bring the eggs to our sands."

She bent down and gently put her hand under Jirana's head.

"We can't move her," Bekka said.

"We have to," Xhinna replied, sliding a hand under the girl's back and gently lifting her up. Jirana gave a whimper and Xhinna carefully adjusted her position so that the child was cradled in her arms.

"Guide me," Xhinna said to J'riz. The green rider nodded and slowly led her out of the cave. He climbed up Tazith and helped her raise the stricken girl. Bekka clambered up behind her.

"We're going to the sands," Xhinna told her even as she urged Tazith to climb—gently—into the sky.

"You've got your kit?" she asked Bekka.

"Yes."

"And you've got the needles and sutures?"

"Yes, Xhinna," Bekka replied testily. "But this is hard work and it's still dark."

Tazith, Xhinna said, picturing an image in her mind, and then they were *between.* She felt Bekka's astonishment and worry. The cold of *between* could do horrible things to an open wound. They came out above the beach, where Pinorth bugled in surprise. The sun was high above, and the sands were warm with the noon heat.

"Enough light now?" Xhinna called as Tazith began a gentle spiral to a soft landing on the sands.

"If the cold of *between* didn't kill her," Bekka said, jumping down and reaching up to receive the stricken girl.

Xhinna and J'riz did all they could to get her down gently, without stretching open the three long gashes in her abdomen. Weyrfolk rushed to help, including V'lex and X'lerin, who grabbed her, carefully keeping her level, and gently lowered her to a canvas spread over the ground, arrayed with tools.

Taria approached them with a much-relieved Javissa, saying, "Tazith told me what you did, so we came here early and got everything ready."

Bekka glanced at the supplies all neatly laid out and said to Xhinna, "It might work."

As they laid her on the ground Jirana stirred and murmured something. Xhinna leaned in close but only caught the tail end: ". . . anth."

Xhinna glanced up. They were in the center of the sands, far from the egg the trader girl had claimed as her queen.

"She's okay," Xhinna said, but the girl whimpered, her face puckering in pain.

"If she moves like that, Xhinna, I don't think anyone could close the wounds," Bekka said, looking up from where she knelt beside the girl.

"Don't do anything yet," Xhinna said. Bekka raised her eyebrows in surprise, but Xhinna shook her head, raising a hand as she raced to Jirana's egg.

Trust me, the girl had said. *Ask the queens.*

Tazith, send the queen dragonets here, hurry!

They come, the blue replied even as Xhinna felt him leap skyward and arc lazily overhead. *Can you help the little one?*

Xhinna had no reply.

"Xhinna, what is it?" Jepara asked as she approached with her Sarurth.

"Jirana's dying," Xhinna told her, and at the words, her eyes welled with tears. "We've got to help her."

"How?" Meeya asked as she and Calith came nearby.

"Bekka," Xhinna said, clutching the gold rider, "you can talk to the dragons, can't you?"

Bekka nodded, her forehead creased in puzzlement. Xhinna grabbed the healer's hand and placed it on the egg.

Trust me, the little girl had said.

"Everyone, gather around, hands on the egg," Xhinna said. "Jepara, talk to her."

"Talk to her?" Jepara repeated in surprise, and then, enlightened, she placed her other hand on the shell and closed her eyes.

"We need to ask Laspanth to help Jirana," Xhinna said, closing her eyes and placing her hands on the egg, the smallest finger of her right hand brushing the smallest finger of Meeya's left. Another finger brushed her left hand: Jepara.

Laspanth, Xhinna thought. *Help Jirana. Take her pain, give it to us, keep her still so that she can get better.*

Beside her, Xhinna heard Jepara gasp in surprise.

"Now!" Xhinna shouted, relaying the same thought to Tazith. She brought her full focus on the moment, on the egg, on the queens, on the small girl who had asked her to trust her and—

It was as though she'd never truly seen before, as if she'd never truly breathed before, felt before. The world of her senses was totally new to her, beyond description, and then—

Pain! She gasped, she went rigid, she didn't twitch or move a muscle, she just felt pain—roaring, furious pain—and with it, terror: She was dying. She rode down the terror, calmed it, soothed it, held the pain, examined it, compared it to other pains, the pain of her shoulder, the pain of childbirth to come, of Threadscore, of—

"Xhinna!" a voice cried. "Xhinna, it's done."

Xhinna opened her eyes and was surprised to find herself on the warm sandy ground where she'd collapsed next to the egg.

"Laspanth?" Xhinna whispered as she recognized that the voice belonged to Jepara.

"She's fine," Jepara said. "Bekka is done with Jirana. We should go see her."

Some twitch, some feeling just at the edge of her mind, tugged at Xhinna and she shook her head. "Bring the egg—Tazith, carry it."

"I've done the best I could," Bekka told Xhinna wearily. She nodded toward Jirana's cloth-covered stomach. "She didn't move a muscle, didn't make a sound."

Xhinna felt a painful twinge in her own belly and, wincing, lifted her tunic to stare down at herself.

"Xhinna, what's wrong with your stomach?" Bekka asked, peering at the reddened skin.

Xhinna didn't answer her, turning instead to the dark-haired queen rider beside her. "Jepara, how's your stomach?"

Wordlessly, the queen rider lifted her tunic to reveal three parallel red welts, matching Xhinna's.

"We took the pain, didn't we?" Jepara asked then, smiling at Xhinna. "It had to go somewhere."

"What about the others?" Xhinna glanced over her shoulder at the figure that trailed them silently. "Taria, lift your tunic."

Surprised, the green rider lifted her tunic above her distended belly. There were three welts across it.

Xhinna looked at her and remembered a hand going to her shoulder even as the dark-eyed woman said, "I had to help."

Xhinna lowered her tunic, moved over to Taria, and bent down to gently kiss each of the three welts. She turned her head and pressed her ear to Taria's belly and listened for a moment, her eyes widening in surprise as she made out the sounds of the life moving within. Then she rose, gently pulling Taria's tunic back over her belly, her hands going to the green rider's as she stood.

"I should have come for you earlier."

"I thought we could manage on our own," Taria said. "I knew what you were doing."

"You did?"

"Not at first," Taria admitted. "At first I was too confused, too dazed by J'keran's attention and that awful drink —"

"We've got better," Xhinna offered shyly.

"Not until the baby comes," Bekka growled tersely from beside the sleeping Jirana.

"I'm sorry about Razz," Xhinna told her friend.

"I know," Taria said. "I'm sorry we didn't find an answer."

Bekka shushed them as she noticed Jirana stirring. Xhinna turned to the girl, saw the pain on her face, and knelt down at her side, opposite Bekka.

"Jirana, it's all right, you were right," Xhinna said. "I spoke with Laspanth; I trust you."

Ask the queens, Xhinna heard clearly.

"Ask the queens what, sweetie?" Xhinna asked, tenderly stroking the girl's dark hair.

For help, Jirana said.

"We did that," Xhinna assured her. "We did that and they helped you. You need to rest now, get better. You want to be healthy when Laspanth hatches, don't you?"

The girl sighed and Xhinna felt her slipping into a deeper sleep.

"I'll stay here," Bekka said, gesturing to Jirana. "You go away— you're disturbing her."

Xhinna nodded and, with one last brush of Jirana's soft hair, rose. She was surprised when she felt a hand slip into hers: Taria.

FIFTEEN

▼▼▼▼▼▼▼▼▼▼▼▼

A Greeting Foretold

In the end, beyond talking quietly and hugging, Taria was too ex-hausted for more than sleep. Xhinna fed her carefully, a light broth, and kissed her on the forehead as she lay beside her, as though Taria had never left.

J'keran was an issue that would wait for another day.

Ask the queens. She shook her head in wonder at Jirana's words. The little girl was almost too trusting. Her gift made it hard for her to distinguish between what was real and what was wanted.

She wandered over to the egg that held Laspanth. She no longer doubted Jirana about that: She'd felt the strangeness of the dragonet inside, felt the quiet strength that was such a mirror of Jirana's own strength. A queen from a green—how could that be?

K'dan and X'lerin must have been right. In the evolution of fire-lizards, the queens, bronzes, and browns must have come after the blues and greens. The queens were smarter than all the others, the leaders of their clutch. But what about that first queen? She couldn't protect herself in the shell, how had she survived? How had she made her green mother dame and blue sire know about the tunnel snakes?

With a sudden insight, Xhinna moved to Laspanth's egg, placed her hands on it, closed her eyes, and opened her mind.

Laspanth, where are the tunnel snakes? she thought, hard, at the form inside the egg.

Nothing. And then— She heard it first, a rustling, rock-moving noise, slithering, sliding. And then suddenly it was as if the ground beneath her were lit with glows, showing map lines where tunnel snakes burrowed, digging and rising toward their helpless prey . . .

"Xhinna? What is it?" Bekka cried.

Xhinna realized that she had been screaming. "Rouse the Weyr!" she called, crying to Tazith, sending bursts of thought to the queen weyrlings, to Pinorth, to X'lerin.

"Xhinna, are you okay?" Bekka called anxiously, rushing to her side.

"Grab my hand!" Xhinna said, clasping Bekka's wrist tightly and pulling her hand to Laspanth's egg. "Reach out, feel, close your eyes, and see!"

Bekka gasped as she felt and heard the first whisperings of Laspanth's thoughts.

Beyond her, dragons bellowed in anger and excitement. Xhinna felt Tazith, pictured a large site underground, heard the blue digging furiously and then roaring with glee as he surprised a group of tunnel snakes and tore them to pieces with his jaws.

All around her, the dragons roared, the riders cried, and the night air was rent with the sounds of dying tunnel snakes.

A noise alerted Xhinna and she spun as she saw Jepara approach with Scruff on her lead, chewing on something greenish and spitting out bones, buzzing with pride in her achievements.

"She got six!" Jepara cried happily. "And Sarurth got three." She grabbed Xhinna and hugged her, as Scruff ran in circles, wrapping her lead around the pair of them. "And Sarurth can hear the tunnel snakes, she can spot them. She says that Laspanth showed her how."

Xhinna saw Taria approaching, eyes wide in surprise. Xhinna bent down and picked up the Mrreow. "This is Scruff—she killed six tunnel snakes."

"She's pretty," Taria said, letting the grime-stained Meeyu sniff her.

"I should have listened to you," Xhinna apologized once more.

"And I should have come back. The Mrreows aren't enough."

"They are now," Xhinna said. "The dragons find them, the Mrreows dig them out and kill them."

"Indeed, they are!" an ichor-covered Jepara agreed fervently.

Certain that all the eggs were once again safe, Xhinna went back to check on Jirana.

"It's a wonder she's still asleep," Bekka snorted in disgust.

"She's not," Xhinna said as she peered down at Jirana, watching her chest rise and fall. "But she's too tired to talk, too excited to cry, and too sore to do either." She stroked the child's hair once more, smiling down at her. "Behave, little one, or I'll talk to your queen."

A small smile played across Jirana's lips, and then she let out a deep, slow sigh and slipped into sleep.

Xhinna assigned J'keran to guard Jirana, saying, "If she dies, you die."

The brown rider had been abject in his apology, but it hadn't spared him her wrath. True to her word, she'd beaten him to a pulp, limiting her revenge to a swift kick where it hurt the most, followed by a double-fisted blow to his chin as he collapsed.

He had awakened, groaning, to find a knife pointed at his neck.

"Say it," Xhinna growled, standing above him. "You know the words."

J'keran swallowed, feeling the tip of the knife prick his skin. "Wingleader, I have struck another in anger; my life is forfeit."

"Louder, so the others can hear," Xhinna said, flicking her knife to the left and right before resting it, once again, under the point of his chin. J'keran's eyes followed her blade, saw those standing around him in a tight knot. He recognized X'lerin, K'dan, W'vin, bronze rider J'sarte, T'rennor and—V'lex.

"Weyrleader, my life is forfeit. I struck another in anger," J'keran said more loudly, his eyes darting toward X'lerin, his heart sinking as he acknowledged his shame. The person above him was no longer a mere girl, a mere blue rider, an upstart. He'd been wrong not to accept what he'd seen, arrogant to think that he might know better.

He had clenched his jaw tight as he felt the knife bite into his skin. He would not cry out; he would at least die with honor.

The blade stopped. "Your life is forfeit," Xhinna said, standing back, sheathing her knife, and gesturing for him to rise. "You live for the Weyr now."

J'keran rose slowly and knelt before her, head bowed, ignoring the drop of blood that spilled to the ground.

"Wingleader, my life is yours," he said.

"Heard and witnessed!" the crowd called. Behind him, he heard dragons roar, heard his beautiful, precious Perinth among them. He would live. He could fly again, fight Thread as he was meant to do.

He glanced up at Xhinna and was surprised when she winked at him, reached down and slipped her forearm behind his, and heaved him to his feet.

"Live long, brown rider," she told him quietly. As he looked into her deep blue eyes, he saw that she truly meant it.

"Thank you."

"One more thing," she said, raising a hand warningly. "You belong to the Weyr, and so for it I say: You may not drink again unless the Weyrleader gives leave."

"As you say," J'keran had said, bowing his head once more.

And now, he followed Jepara's orders without a word, collecting the best scraps from the newly-butchered herdbeast, placing them in a clean light bowl, finding a wooden hammer, and placing all the items near to Jirana's hand.

Then, at Jepara's gesture, he sat and waited as the sun slowly rose in the sky.

He said nothing when Xhinna woke and rose, throwing on her tunic and rushing off to gather the Candidates. She was back moments later at a surprise summons from Bekka, who glided from the sky to land behind the strange brownish-green egg. Sarurth walked sedately to the other side, forming a triangle of queens, with Jirana's bed and the egg in the center—they were thrumming in anticipation of the hatching.

The thrumming grew louder and Xhinna looked down at Jirana. "Ready?"

"Yes," the girl said, reaching up her arms as Xhinna leaned down and lifted her to a sitting position.

The thrumming grew louder and the egg cracked.

"Come on, girl, you can do it!" Jirana called encouragingly. She looked around and was surprised to find the wooden hammer placed into her hand. She beat—feebly—on the shell. Cracks grew, and the queen dragons thrummed loudly in greeting.

The shell cracked wide open, shards flying, as a small gold head thrust through.

"Hi!" Jirana called, dropping the hammer. "I'm happy to see you, Laspanth!"

And I, you, the newest queen on Pern replied. A moment later, wistfully eyeing the nearby scraps of food, she asked, *Is that something to eat?*

J'keran raised the dish up to Jirana, who happily fed a great gob of warm, fresh meat to her queen.

Xhinna, smiling so wide her face hurt, supported Jirana until the little queen was completely out of her shell and her hunger sated, at which point the trader girl asked to be put down so that she could have her queen lie with her.

As Xhinna settled the girl back on the sand, Jirana looked up at her, smiling. "See? You did it, Xhinna! You saved the eggs! You saved Pern!"

"No," Xhinna said, smiling back at her as she reached out to pull Taria to her side, "you did it, little one."

Jirana shook her head and, freeing one hand from Laspanth, pointed to Taria and Xhinna.

"We *all* did it."

‣ BOOK TWO ◂

The Sky Dragons

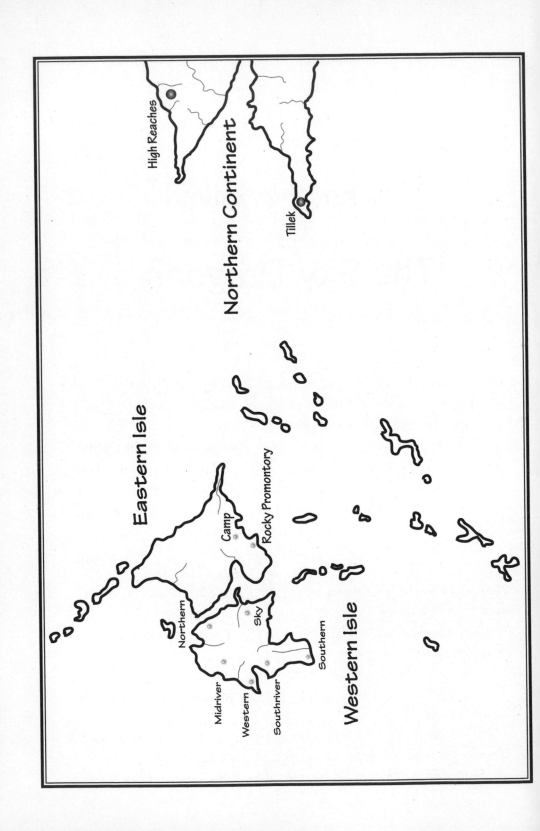

SIXTEEN

▼▼▼▼▼▼▼▼▼▼▼

The Battle of Friends

"Shards, Fiona, it may only be soft wood, but I'm still sore there, you know!" Xhinna cried, rubbing her chest where the Weyrwoman had scored—once again—on the front of her padded leather armor. "I've got a baby to nurse," she added in a lower tone, "and he's not going to like it if I'm wincing because of you."

"You can always yield," Fiona said, eyes dancing as she circled the point of her practice blade in the vicinity of Xhinna's chest. "And you've scored as much on me—*also* nursing!—as I have on you."

In the near distance, sheltered under the shade of a large canvas awning, Mirressa shook her head at the two women.

"See, your mommies are arguing again," she said in a singsong voice to the two babies sleeping on either side of her. Her voice carried as she intended and she waved mildly to Xhinna and the Weyrwoman, not at all apologetic.

"On your guard, Weyrwoman!" Xhinna called, raising her blade once more.

Instead, Fiona lowered her blade and raised her free hand in pax, turning away from Xhinna to glance down the long stretch of beach beyond them.

"I still can't believe it," Fiona said as Xhinna moved up beside her. Xhinna followed her gaze and nodded in mute agreement.

From where they stood, staring down the length of the coast, there was nothing for two kilometers but dragons, riders . . . and dragon eggs.

The midday heat baked the sand and blurred the farthest images, but Xhinna knew that there were more than ninety eggs ready to hatch in the next sevenday or less.

Around and over them a full Flight of dragons frolicked—three wings of thirty dragons each. And that was only the Rest Day Flight. Two other Flights were engaged in various activities: hunting, working, providing for the whole of Sky Weyr.

That industry in nearly the same numbers was repeated no less than five more times across the width and breadth of the Western Isle.

"Two thousand fighting dragons," Fiona said to herself, reaching to grab Xhinna's hand. "And no one in our time knows about it."

"Well . . ."

"None that are saying," Fiona agreed with a light chuckle. Nerra, Lady Holder of Crom, had been instrumental in helping them provide the Candidates for so many of the new dragons, aided in no small part by Javissa, Aressil, and a whole group of very tight-lipped traders.

Pulled from the wreck of the Plague, twenty-three hundred people had been brought here, to the Western Isle, to rebuild the dragon strength of Pern.

Fiona shook her head in wonderment. "I keep thinking . . ."

"What?"

Fiona turned to look up at the blue rider. "I just keep thinking that it's too good to last."

Xhinna nodded silently. She'd had the same feeling.

Footsteps crunched in the sand, causing them to turn. A small form approached. Jirana. Rider of the first of the "green queens"—queens hatched from green clutches. Two Turns had done little for her height, but her eyes showed an age far greater than her twelve Turns. "It won't last," she said. "In half a Turn, at most, we'll be back in our own time."

She wore the light robe that was used as both towel and body covering by so many of the Weyr's beach worshippers—she'd been part of one of several parties speckled up and down the beach who'd mixed their rest with swimming and sunbathing. Now her gaze swept down the sands toward Mirressa, sitting in the shade, and a look of pain twisted her face for a fleeting moment.

Xhinna, who'd been watching, nudged Fiona. The Weyrwoman, rubbing where the blue rider had scored on her in the previous bout, nodded quietly.

Presently, Jirana turned her attention back to them. "How did your practice go?" she asked Fiona. She turned to Xhinna. "Have you managed to disarm her yet?"

"Bruise, yes; disarm, no," Xhinna replied easily.

"You fight like a girl," Jirana said, deadpan.

"Take a sword and you'll see how I fight," Xhinna challenged.

"I think I've seen how you can fight, blue rider," Jirana returned easily, eyes twinkling.

"Did you want to challenge *me*, then?" Fiona asked with a grin.

Surprised, Jirana gave her a shocked look and hastily shook her head. "I'd never do that, Weyrwoman."

A noise from above and a sudden darkening of the sky heralded the arrival of a dragon. The three craned their necks up as a bronze dragon overflew them and banked into a steep turn. K'dan and Lurenth.

"Maybe you should practice anyway," Fiona said, tossing her blade toward Jirana before racing off to the shaded awning.

Jirana caught the leather-wrapped hilt easily and deftly sliced the air with a brilliant show of skill before lowering the blade to the ground.

"You need to practice more," she said to Xhinna. "You've got to be able to disarm her."

"Wouldn't it just be easier if you'd tell me why?" Xhinna asked irritably. The whole set of exercises, the months of sword practice, had all been at Jirana's urging.

"It might not happen," Jirana said with the same resigned but wistful tone that Xhinna had come to associate with the youngster's visions of things yet to come.

Xhinna abruptly dropped her practice blade and grabbed the little queen rider by the shoulders, pulling her into a tight embrace.

Pushing back, she raised Jirana's head with a gentle hand to meet her eyes and said, "You've asked me to trust you, little one. Can't you do the same with me?"

Jirana jerked her head from Xhinna's grasp and looked down at the ground. In a low voice she explained, "If I tell you, that might make it happen."

Xhinna sighed; it had not been the first time the girl had said such to her.

"He's chiding for his mother, yes, he is," Mirressa said in her sing-song voice as she passed little Xelinan up to Xhinna a short time later.

Xhinna's nose twitched. "And he needs changing," she added ruefully.

"Only just," Mirressa said, rising awkwardly from the ground on which she'd sat for the last several hours. She searched the carisak that hung from her side, pulled out a diaper, and handed it over to Xhinna. "When you're done, would you rinse out the others before bringing them back?"

"If you'll watch him."

"Of course!" Mirressa loved babies, and even though she had two herself, she was more than willing to look after any others.

Xhinna smiled at her, laid Xelinan down on the changing towel, quickly unwrapped the soiled bundle, and cleaned him up with prac-ticed ease. As she did, Mirressa prattled on. "Taria's got R'ney watch-ing Tarena and Taralin. Don't you think it's nice that he's so helpful?"

"I do," Xhinna agreed with a slow smile. "But if you think after all these months that you'll get me to tell you who's the father, you're sadly mistaken."

Mirressa sighed. "It's just that it'd be a help, you know—"

Xhinna stopped her with a quickly raised hand, then just as quickly returned to her task.

"You've got the whole *island* guessing," Mirressa persisted.

"Good," Xhinna said, finishing with Xelinan's diaper and leaning down to plant a big kiss on his beaming face. "It makes a pleasant diversion and reminds everyone that we are all entitled to our secrets."

"I suppose," Mirressa allowed. A moment later, as she handed Xhinna the wet-bag, she added, "And is it a secret about tonight's meeting?"

"Meeting?" Xhinna frowned and shook her head, thrusting the dirty diaper in the wet-bag and closing it quickly. "Tonight?" She shrugged. "I expect it's for planning. I don't doubt that K'dan is going to be reorganizing the fighting wings."

"Is he going to start the greens chewing firestone?"

"I don't know, Mirressa, he hasn't told me."

"But you know *everything* that goes on!"

"No, I *knew* everything," Xhinna corrected her. "Since then, I've had a baby and am quite happy to let others handle the bigger problems."

Mirressa made an unhappy noise.

"Can you watch him while I make a diaper run?" Xhinna asked, lifting Xelinan into her arms while at the same time deftly shrugging the heavy wet-bag onto her shoulder.

"Of course," Mirressa agreed easily, moving to take the baby from her. "Didn't I just say I would?" She scrunched up her face. "Or does this mean you plan to make a run of the whole beach?"

"Of course," Xhinna allowed. "No point in not getting all the diapers I can."

"You're a good person, you know."

It was a messy, stinky job made both more difficult and easier by doing it in the salt water on the ebbing tide. The diapers, so rinsed, would be boiled and properly cleaned when Xhinna brought them back to the burnt plateau, now more often called Meeyu Plateau; rinsing and recycling were more crucial now than ever, now that cloth was in such short supply with the added need to provide diapers and baby clothing.

It was an unanticipated side effect of the widespread realization that here on the Western Isle and now, back in time before the Third Pass, was the best time for the young women who rode blues, greens, and queens to complete their families.

Xhinna was chasing down a diaper that had gotten away from her and was threatening to be carried out to sea when a shadow above her alerted her to the arrival of Taria on green Coranth.

A few moments later, the green rider helped her snag the errant cloth and passed it back to her. "Doing stinky duty again, I see!"

"Someone's got to do it."

"And you don't mind."

"I wouldn't go *that* far," Xhinna protested. "But as Mirressa was watching the baby, it seemed a fair trade."

"Fair trade" was a phrase borrowed from the traders who had grown in importance and meaning as the inhabitants had outgrown Sky Weyr and overflowed throughout the Western Isle. It was all the result of Xhinna's simple message, left nearly three Turns back at the Red Butte, by the grave of Tenniz, Jirana's father and the Seer who had glimpsed this strange island future. It seemed more than fitting to Fiona, Lorana, and Xhinna that the dragonriders saved by the vision of the trader be willing to borrow from his people's customs and his bequests—particularly the strange Sights that his daughter, Jirana, had provided.

"You're thinking about her again," Taria said suddenly. "She and her queen were back in the trees just now."

"Did she send you here?"

Taria's silence was answer enough. A moment later, she sighed. "Her queen will be old enough soon."

"*That* doesn't worry her," Xhinna said, recalling a recent conversation with Jirana. "She'll rise when we're ready," Jirana had assured her. Laspanth, the first of six "green queens" was still small for a gold and clearly growing, so perhaps there was no reason to doubt Jirana on this. That hadn't stopped Fiona from bringing the matter up with Xhinna, nor Xhinna from worrying about it.

"So what does?" Taria asked. Confidentially, she added, "She's always sending me to you when you get worried about her, you know."

"Trying to distract me?" Xhinna guessed.

"Hmph!" Taria said. "One, you're impossible to distract when you've your mind on something; and two, if I wanted to distract you, I wouldn't be talking about it."

Xhinna chuckled, rinsed another diaper, and placed it back into the bag. She motioned to Taria who, with a wrinkle of her nose, gamely pulled out a few diapers and joined in the cleansing.

The dark-haired rider was right on both counts: Xhinna would not let herself be distracted when she thought something was important; and regardless, no matter how important her thoughts, Taria could always distract her if she really desired.

In the past two Turns their relationship had grown both stronger and freer than Xhinna could possibly have imagined. They no longer needed to be in sight of each other or constantly touching; in fact, they now took joy in being able to recount separate adventures, to revel in the strength of their bonds rather than railing against them.

Xhinna could feel that special connection with Taria, that increased joy in her presence, the knowledge that they were free enough to go their separate ways without fear of hurting each other, and the greater joy that, when they could, they preferred each other's company above all others. Not that they were exclusive—they couldn't quite be, because of the nature of their bonds with their dragons. Taria was willing to cheer when Tazith outflew browns to catch other greens; Xhinna was willing to stand in honor as Coranth was caught by another blue. But Xhinna and Taria had learned to adjust and thrive in those situations. What mattered most was what *they* chose—not what dragon passion compelled.

As it was with them, so it was with the other greens and blues throughout the Western Isle.

"So what is it?" Taria asked, bringing Xhinna's focus back to the present—and to the pleasant surprise that, in her reverie, she'd finished rinsing the last of the diapers. Taria passed her back her handful and Xhinna put them into the wet-bag, gladly sealing it and trudging out of the surf to the dry shore.

"Something's bothering her," Xhinna said grumpily.

"Not her scar?"

"No," Xhinna said with a quick shake of her head. "You can hardly see that, and it's not as though she's worried about the looks she gets from the boys."

"I like scars," Taria said slyly, tracing the line of Xhinna's scar through the shirt on her back.

"Whatever it is," Xhinna said, accepting the oblique apology for the scar that J'keran's knife had left, and continuing single-mindedly on the question at hand, "it's not going to happen for a while."

"How can you say?"

"Because she's not that desperate," Xhinna said. "She'd be angry with me, fighting with me, if this were something coming soon."

"She could be wrong, you know," Taria said.

"Well, even if she is, it's getting me quite fit," Xhinna replied, grinning as she caught the look of pleasure that spread across her partner's face. Xhinna shook her head and trudged farther back up the sands. "I've got to drop these off and pick up Xelinan."

"I'll get Xelinan," Taria offered.

"Or you could take these," Xhinna countered.

"Oh, let's see—cute, adorable boy or bag of smelly diapers? What a hard choice!" Taria said, racing to leap upon Coranth's neck and urging the green skyward before Xhinna could utter another word. She waved down from above, a wicked grin spreading across her face.

Xhinna chuckled, shaking her head ruefully.

The Meeyu Plateau most clearly showed the industry that had occurred since Fiona, T'mar, and the others had come back in time to join Xhinna in response to the simple polyhedral marker she'd left at Red Butte, inscribed on all three upright sides with the same one word: *Come.*

She remembered the evening—nearly two Turns ago—when she got Fiona's description of the events that led them there:

"So, there's D'gan, all high and mighty right up until his Kaloth collapses from the injection of the dragon sickness cure, and then he starts bellowing and raging all over the place until we could calm him down and get him to his weyr," Fiona had said as she brought Xhinna up to date on the several days they'd spent back in Telgar Weyr. She shook her head trying to shake her anger out of it. "And then, that last night, acting like *he* was the Weyrleader . . ."

"Well, he was," Xhinna said.

"Half a Turn ago before he and all his dragons were lost *between*," Fiona agreed. "But not now."

"He has over three hundred riders who think otherwise," Lorana disagreed from where she sat nearby. "And they're planning on riding Fall with High Reaches today."

Fiona made a sour face. "You should have heard him go on about the new firestone," she said. "He practically accused me of sabotage for ordering the old stuff removed, and then one of his bronze riders nearly jumped out of his skin when one of our weyrlings dropped a rock in a bucket of water by accident." She brightened. "After that, he changed his tune, but he never said anything to me."

"He'd hoped to ignore us," Jeila said.

"He might still succeed," T'mar said. Fiona shot him an angry look and the bronze rider raised his hands defensively.

"He's got almost more dragons than all the other Weyrs put together," he pointed out. "We're all exhausted, and his riders are still in their prime, ready for anything. We really *can't* reject his aid."

"And the blues and greens we brought back would have needed a sevenday at least to learn to chew firestone," Fiona said in agreement. "So D'gan can ignore us, leave us out of the Fall, and we have nothing to do about it," she ended bitterly. She sighed and sat back dejectedly in her chair. Xhinna threw her a questioning look.

"And another thing," Fiona said, gesturing toward Shaneese, who sat nearby. "Remember how the weyrfolk were when we first arrived?"

Xhinna nodded, her stomach clenching in anger. The weyrfolk were used to D'gan: He demanded their instant respect and was not very caring when it came to women.

"Well, Shaneese's L'rat is now alive and well," Fiona said, her lips curled in anger, "and he believes that T'mar is a poacher." She shook her head. "He even told T'mar: 'As you've a woman already, I want mine back.'"

"Shaneese tried to deal with it diplomatically," Jeila said with a sour look, "but that didn't work."

"We were like a Weyr within a Weyr," Fiona said with an expression that was alarming both for its ferocity and its resignation. "When we found your first message, it was nothing to find enough volunteers—"

Xhinna coughed and gave the Weyrwoman a reproving look.

"Really it wasn't," T'mar added in agreement. He glanced around the strange plateau and the dragon-filled broom trees in the distance. "We hadn't quite realized what you'd been planning, I must admit."

"Well, once we found the second marker—wise of you to set them far apart—*we* realized just how much we wanted to see our children," Fiona said, reaching for Lorana, "and our bronzes' riders."

"Particularly K'dan," T'mar opined with a grin. Fiona started a hot retort, but then gave him a second, more probing look and just nodded.

"If only to relieve him of nonstop parental duties," she agreed. A moment later she returned to her story. "And then D'gan came up to us, saying that there was a Fall at High Reaches and wanting to know how many of our riders could haul firestone for *his* fighting dragons."

She changed her voice to a mocking imitation of the old Telgar Weyrleader: "'I don't allow shirkers in my Weyr.'"

"Uh oh!" Xhinna said.

"I told him: 'This is *my* Weyr, bronze rider' and he said, 'We've no need for impertinence' and then, can you believe it? He turned to T'mar and said, 'If you can't control your women—and you have far too many of them if you ask me—'"

"He didn't!" Xhinna and Taria exclaimed in unison.

Fiona nodded solemnly and then looked up at them, eyes blazing, but it was Jeila who, with awe in her voice, said, "And then she said, 'Enough. You will be silent now.'"

H'nez, Jeila, and T'mar all broke into laughter.

"I thought he was going to burst, the way his eyes bulged," Jeila continued. "Shards, I didn't think he could even speak, but just as he was about to, all three of our queens bellowed as one. The old queen called back, but she didn't sound like she was angry, only resigned." She glanced toward Fiona, continuing, "So the Weyrwoman said—"

" 'We're leaving. We'll be back when we're needed,' " Fiona said. "And then, would you believe, our old Mekiar comes along and says—" She turned to the old potter to let him speak.

"Well . . ." Mekiar, glad to be invited to participate, smiled as he said, "I merely said, 'Would you perhaps need a potter where you're going?' "

"But—" Xhinna gestured at all the riders from other Weyrs. All the young weyrlings who'd grown up with her and Tazith, Taria, and Coranth were arrayed there, including all four queens and all the bronzes.

"The story's not done yet," Fiona said. "So when we went to leave, D'gan tried to block us, but the queens put an end to *that*."

"He didn't give up, did he?" Taria asked. She'd known him from her childhood at Telgar Weyr.

"Oh, no!" Fiona exclaimed. "It wasn't until the others"—she waved a hand at the non-Telgar riders—"arrived that things were finally sorted." Her smile dimpled. "You see, I thought that if we were going to do this, we should be certain not to do it by halves."

"But what of the other Weyrs?" Taria objected. "Surely they didn't—"

"Ah, but they did!" Jeila said with a laugh. "In fact—" and she waved a hand for Fiona to finish the story.

"Lorana spoke with them," Fiona said. "You should have seen the look on D'gan's face when he saw them. And then I told him, 'The others are a parting gift, as it were.' "

"Others?" Xhinna asked.

"That's just what D'gan said!" Jeila laughed. "Because when he looked up he saw not only all our Eastern weyrlings and riders but—" and again she waved to Fiona to finish.

"Not only Tullea on her Minith, but Sonia of High Reaches on

Lyrinth, Cisca of Fort on Melirth, and Dalia of Ista on Bidenth all gliding in for a landing—and all looking as though they were going to have more than a few words with Telgar's old Weyrleader."

"And now we're here!" Jeila said in conclusion, smiling all around.

"Of course, there is one catch," T'mar said somberly.

Xhinna and the others of Sky Weyr had given him all their attention then, ready to hear what came next, but it was K'dan who spoke up instead: "We can't fail."

And they hadn't. There were enough dragons and more to repopulate all the Weyrs of Pern. In half a Turn or less, they'd be able to return home, triumphant, ready to fight Thread.

The hectic days of scouting, building, and struggling to establish all the extra dragons and riders across the Western Isle were over. The days of mating flight after mating flight—with the horrifying specter of battles between mating queens and mating greens—were nearly done, and besides, Xhinna and her riders had learned how to distract and separate amorous dragons safely.

Soon it would be all over, they'd go back, and Pern would be safe.

So why was it she was so worried? And if it was just that she felt things had gone too well for too long, then why was Jirana still acting so oddly?

SEVENTEEN
▼▼▼▼▼▼▼▼▼▼▼▼

Journey to Starlight

Zirenth says you should join them, Tazith told Xhinna as they wheeled around toward a landing.

Zirenth? *T'mar?*

He is in the stone, Tazith replied. Xhinna's lips twitched at her blue's title for the first housing that had been built on the reclaimed Meeyu Plateau. Bare rock, with a few smaller piles of sand, made the whole area look like a blight on the otherwise green plain that stretched out under the watch of the Sky Weyr's broom trees.

Scouring the plateau of all life and soil had been R'ney's solution to the problem of tunnel snakes, superceded by the brilliant plan of uniting Mrreows and dragon eggs to spot and counter any assaults on the unhatched dragonets. Almost as a sop to R'ney, two dragons had clutched on the sandpiles, but most preferred the comfort of the long, sandy beaches.

The upside of gouging the earth down to the rock and letting the torrential rains churn the ground into mud had been runoff that included a large amount of gold dust. The gold dust, in turn, had been used to surreptitiously purchase those items that could not be found or made on the Western Isle by the industrious riders and weyrfolk.

The bare rock, augmented by sands and stout iron, had been the primary home for the baby Meeyus and adult Mrreows that helped guard the defenseless dragon eggs from the depredations of the ever-hungry tunnel snakes. The Mrreows and the Meeyus preferred any of the six-limbed creatures of Pern as their prey, so enlisting them to protect the dragons had its drawbacks—particularly as the Mrreows grew older and less controllable by either human or dragon.

The solution had been to retire the intractable beasts to one of the many smaller islands that dotted the oceans surrounding the great Eastern and Western Isles of Pern. Xhinna's own Scruff had been one of the first to be so placed, and a pang of sorrow went through her even as she realized it was prompted by the sight and smell of the cages and the noise of the latest litter of little Meeyus.

Jirana and the other Green-queens—as the green queen riders had come to be known—were gathered around, chatting among themselves and instructing a group of younger helpers in the care and feeding of the cute but noisy beasts. Xhinna made a note to speak with Jirana about this—the beasts wouldn't be needed for guard duty once the last of the clutches had Hatched, and it would be an unkindness to break the hearts of yet another generation of youngsters who would have to leave the Mrreows behind when they finally abandoned the Western Isle.

T'mar? Xhinna wondered. What did he want? And what, she thought guiltily, did I do wrong?

He says to say that you did nothing wrong, Tazith said just then, as if the Southriver Weyrleader had been touching her mind just as easily as her blue dragon could.

To comfortably house and support all the dragons and riders, it had been decided in the first month after the arrival of Fiona and the other 126 dragons to spread out throughout the Western Isle. In addition to Sky Weyr—the name had stuck, despite all of Xhinna's protests—they created five additional Weyrs: Midriver, Southriver, Southern, Western, and Northern.

Fiona's desire to spend time with her children and K'dan had grown from inclination into permanence. While T'mar had taken the lead in everything, he was too good a leader not to involve everyone, and so it was mutually decided that H'nez and C'tov, as the next two most experienced wingleaders, would be the temporary Weyrleaders of the Northern and Southern Weyrs. X'lerin, ever tactful, offered to relinquish his leadership at Sky Weyr to K'dan and, as a consequence, was assigned to start Midriver Weyr—an assignment made permanent when his Kivith flew Indeera's queen Morurth when she rose. There was no established Weyrleader at the Western Weyr, which was ably run by the Weyrwoman, Garra, with T'mar aiding as needed in the leadership that W'vin and his brown Jorth provided to the adult riders.

Xhinna's wing was not, to her surprise, disbanded. In fact, both the queen and bronze weyrling riders insisted on staying with her at Sky Weyr in spite of the lure of better positions elsewhere. But at Xhinna's insistence and in defiance of Fiona—who had been delighted with the notion of a blue wingleader—the young bronze riders themselves had rotated through the leadership of the fledgling wing, able to lean on the assistance of both Xhinna and R'ney as wingseconds.

The queens and their riders, naturally, had become the business of Fiona as Weyrwoman, but with Taria's connivance, Xhinna had found herself compelled to take on much of that, as well, as Fiona had, in a very unconvincing tone, apologized for being too busy with her other duties.

So some things had changed—and many hadn't.

Danirry had been elevated to wingsecond, third in command of what was still known as Xhinna's wing, when the work had become too much for the combined efforts of Xhinna, R'ney, and whichever bronze rider had the position.

"Actually, you brought it on yourself," Jepara had remarked when Xhinna had once let the strain show. Jepara, like Danirry, was a secret source of pride for Xhinna: The young queen rider had matured a lot and was often found at the forefront of Weyr activity. When Xhinna had groaned at her, Jepara had laughed, quoting, " 'What's the reward for a job well done?' "

Xhinna's groan had become louder before she muttered, "I'll get you for that."

Xhinna was sorry that Jepara's Sarurth would probably not rise before they returned to the Northern Continent.

Now she pulled herself out of her musings as she heard voices in the first of the rooms of the Stone Hold. She nodded to those working under the wide awnings spread from each side of the stone building and made her way into the entrance, following T'mar's voice.

"You sent for me?" Xhinna asked as she entered the room that most often served as the Sky Weyr council room.

"I did," T'mar said, rising from his chair on the opposite side of the table that filled the center of the room and extending his hand toward her. Xhinna took it in a quick grasp. With his other hand, T'mar gestured her toward a seat.

Xhinna nodded to the others in the room, not surprised at the sight of X'lerin, H'nez, C'tov, K'dan, and Fiona. With T'mar present, she had expected nothing more than a full council of the Weyrleaders. They often met—that was no surprise. That they wanted her, however, was.

"I understand you've been thrashing the Weyrwoman again," T'mar began in a bantering tone.

"I'm only trying to keep her fit, Weyrleader," Xhinna had said in the same tone. "Far be it for me to say that she's getting out of shape—"

"Ha!" Fiona cried.

"No, indeed not," K'dan agreed blandly.

"And *who* was it stopped our bout today?" Fiona asked with no rancor in her tone.

The others chuckled, and then T'mar leaned forward in the manner that Xhinna had come to recognize as his "getting down to business" posture.

"Getting down to business," T'mar said, predictably, "we're wondering if we can add to your duties."

"Weyrleader?" she said, glancing toward K'dan. His dragon was only now starting to flame—at half a Turn under three, perhaps a bit too soon—but his authority as Weyrleader had been firmly established from the moment T'mar had first thrust it upon him. As T'mar had said at the time, "If ever there's a person able to lead *this* lot, it's you."

K'dan, to Xhinna's surprise, had seriously suggested her instead, but when she'd thrown her wholehearted support behind T'mar, the harper had smoothly bowed to the inevitable—which Xhinna had thought not only right but very diplomatic of him, given that Fiona would have added her voice to the argument if he hadn't. And no one resisted Fiona for long.

A flash of thought crossed Xhinna's mind—did Jirana want Xhinna to learn how to resist Fiona? She shook the thought away even as K'dan said, "Actually, it was my idea."

"And if we let the men keep talking, we'll all die before they get to it," Fiona said in exasperation. "What they're trying *not* to ask, is whether you'd be willing to start flying watch for us."

"Watch?"

"Thread's due soon," T'mar said. "We don't know when, and we don't know where—on these isles—it will fall."

"We need to establish the pattern, so we can predict the Falls," K'dan put in.

"And," H'nez added, clearly following an earlier conversation, "we don't know if the first Falls will be dust like they were for us back home."

"I see," Xhinna said. "But why me?"

"*That* is my fault," Fiona confessed, waving a hand at the Weyr-leaders. "I told them that you'd jump at the chance to go back to the Dawn Sisters." She leaned forward in her chair, her eyes never leaving Xhinna's face as she added triumphantly, "And I'm right, aren't I?"

"The Dawn Sisters?" Taria repeated that evening as they gathered their food and found a cool place amongst the eggs in which to eat.

"What about the Dawn Sisters?" Jepara demanded, following behind them with a plate of her own.

"Dawn Sisters?" Mirressa echoed as she joined the others.

"Wait a moment!" Jepara demanded, holding up a hand. "Let's get the whole wing here, and then you can talk."

"It's not our wing, Weyrwoman," Meeya declared sternly. "Fiona—"

"Gave us back to Xhinna," Jepara reminded her. "If you recall, she said—"

" 'You can learn a lot from her,' " Meeya quoted. Of all the riders, she had the best memory after Fiona. In fact, she had spent all her spare time with K'dan and Fiona learning Ballads and writing Records. She had a good voice and was often in demand, singing solo or duet with the harper.

"So," Jepara said, glancing around to assure herself that the whole extended wing was present, "teach."

"Wingleader?" Xhinna said.

"I'd like to know myself," M'gel, Turenth's rider, allowed. He was one of the youngest of the fourteen bronze riders who had Impressed the only eggs to survive the Great Clutch of Eastern Weyr, but he was neither apologetic about his age nor jealous of the temporary rank he'd assumed. That was why, when the bronze riders had all completed their two-month duties, he had been selected as the first to take another month-long round.

Xhinna held up a restraining hand to indicate that she was sorting out her thoughts, but Taria said, "Eat first, talk later!"

When Xhinna started to protest, Taria reminded her, "You've a feeding coming up, and who knows how soon."

Xhinna nodded and bent her head to her plate, chewing slowly after the first growled warning from Jepara and thinking while she swallowed.

What K'dan had said made sense. Of all the wings in Western, Xhinna's was the oldest and most familiar with the landmarks of the island. Xhinna herself had been to the Dawn Sisters nearly five Turns earlier when the Telgar riders had retraced Lorana's reasoning to discover the Great Isles.

From the position of the Dawn Sisters, it was thought, it should be possible to track the fall of Thread and give early warning if the Isles were threatened.

"Okay, now talk!" Jepara demanded as Xhinna cleared the last of her plate.

"She might want seconds," Taria muttered.

"I'll get them for her *after*," Jepara promised, leaning closer to Xhinna. "Just tell us."

Xhinna shared a quick look with Taria—the queen rider looked so much like one of the beaming-faced weyrchildren they'd minded so many Turns before—and then she began, "We need to look for Thread."

"Of course," Jepara said dismissively. "So what?"

"They want us all to go to the Dawn Sisters?" Meeya broke in.

Xhinna shook her head. "No, just us," she said, waving toward the other blue and green riders.

"What?" Jepara cried, glancing to her fellow queen riders for support. "Why not us?"

"Because we can lose greens and blues, not queens," Alimma replied. For all that she tried to sound bitter about it, Xhinna could hear the excitement in the young rider's voice.

"No! No, not by the Egg of Faranth!" Jepara cried. "We ride with you."

"You'll have to take that up with Fiona," Xhinna said.

Jepara shot her a startled look. "Didn't you ask her?"

Xhinna shook her head. "The matter didn't come up."

Jepara harrumphed and rose to her feet. "Well, then, I'll bring it up right now!"

As she stormed off, Taria and Alimma rose behind her, saying in chorus, "This I've got to see."

"Two Marks says she wins," Xhinna ventured calmly.

All eyes turned toward her. "Against Fiona?"

Xhinna nodded slowly. She glanced around at the remainder of the wing—about half had trailed after Jepara. She raised her plate and asked pleadingly, "Anyone going for more?"

M'gel offered, saying, as he scampered over to the cooking fires, "Call me when she comes back."

Fortunately, he was back and Xhinna had finished her seconds before they heard a triumphant shout and the sound of people racing back to their gathering.

"She won!" Taria said to Xhinna in amazement.

· Xhinna smiled, laid her plate to one side, and held out a hand, palm up. "Pay up."

▼ ▼ ▼

"The first Threadfall was over Benden Weyr and Bitra Hold on the first day of the new Turn," K'dan said as he, M'gel, R'ney, Danirry, Xhinna, and Fiona were clustered around the Council table in the stone hall early the next morning.

"So we've got about a bit under a month," Fiona said. Colfet had been called upon to use his navigational skills in reading the night sky to verify that they currently were in the seventh day of the last month of the Turn, the five hundred and seventh Turn since Landing.

"We know that Thread falls on a seventy-five day cycle," K'dan continued. "So if we can match the Fall here with a Fall back home, we'll be able to predict all the other Falls."

"Well, only after we've mapped the Falls here," Fiona corrected.

"True," K'dan agreed. "Which is why we decided that sending watchers up to the Dawn Sisters was the best idea."

"I don't understand," M'gel said.

"Are you saying, Weyrleader, that we use the location to spy Threadfalls and then use the difference in time to check for similar falls over the Great Isles?" R'ney asked.

"Yes," K'dan said, rewarding the brown rider with a grin.

"But because of the time difference, Thread falling over Benden could be matched by Thread falling here the day *before*!" Danirry exclaimed with a horrified look.

"Which is why we'll need to send our watchers up in pairs," Fiona said.

"Two pairs," Xhinna corrected.

The Weyrwoman motioned for her to explain, so Xhinna said, "We'll need one pair to watch on this side of Pern, another pair for the other side."

"Why pairs?" K'dan asked, his eyes narrowing.

"We're going to be up so high, we have to worry about our air," Xhinna said. "So we'll need—"

"We'll need more dragons," Danirry interrupted, her brows puckered in thought. Before anyone could respond, she held up a hand begging for attention. "We'll need to switch off quickly—say every ten minutes or so, and we'll need, as Xhinna said, two pairs of watchers. And we'll need a twenty-four-hour watch.

"Until we try," she continued, "we won't know how long we can keep sending up pairs before we have to rest them—"

"Certainly no more than six hours," K'dan said. "As long as a Fall."

"I'd say less than that," R'ney said. "We want the riders and dragons to be alert; we don't know if we can even spot Thread at that height—"

"And we can't time it to find out, either," Fiona interjected with a rueful look. "We're too near the knot in time for us to try."

The knot *between* had been created when Fiona and the others from the Eastern Isle had jumped forward in time—only to find themselves trapped with the old dragonriders of Telgar Weyr in a trap or "knot" of fear. Lorana had broken the knot but it still existed *between* at that point in time, as Xhinna had discovered when she'd tried to jump forward to Telgar Weyr nearly three turns past. X'lerin and the other riders had volunteered to take the risky jump *back* in time to aid Xhinna. They had succeeded and discovered that the trap only snared those jumping *forward* in time through the time when the original "knot" was formed.

Everyone agreed that the simplest way to avoid the "knot" was to wait until they were past the time when the knot had been formed.

And that meant that they still had to wait. There was a risk in going *between* at all—that they might choose to go exactly when the "knot" had formed—but that risk was much less when going *between* places than it was going *between* times.

"Let's start with one hour and see how things work then," Xhinna suggested. "I'd prefer to be more cautious than foolhardy."

"But with that, you'd want . . ." Danirry's eyes took on an abstracted look at she worked the numbers in her head. "Ninety-six," she said firmly.

K'dan glanced at Fiona. "We'll have to ask the other Weyrs, then."

"But the bronzes could—" M'gel began in protest.

Fiona raised a hand to cut him off. "I think I'd prefer to have your bronzes full-grown rather than half-frozen."

M'gel sat back in his chair, reluctant to press his position further.

"There will be plenty for us to do soon enough," K'dan said. "And in the meantime, the best we can do is pretty good."

K'dan's Lurenth was no older than M'gel's Turenth, and he imposed upon his dragon the same restrictions he'd imposed on all the others, following the advice of T'mar and the other more experienced riders in allowing the younger bronzes to mature as much as possible before beginning their strenuous training.

"If Thread falls here, Weyrleader, we may not have a choice," Danirry said.

"I know," K'dan agreed. "Which is why we're going to start drilling all the dragons who have two Turns or more with firestone."

"Firestone?" Xhinna exclaimed, thinking of Taria and her green.

"Yes," K'dan said. "We don't have as much as we'd like, so we'll be sparing, but T'mar has suggested that we'll want to be sure that each Weyr is able to defend itself. And for that we'll need more than the older dragons we have."

"Well, I suppose it's about time we had the greens chewing firestone," Fiona said. "Another set of mating flights and we couldn't find enough Candidates to match on all Pern."

Xhinna flicked her eyes away so that the Weyrwoman wouldn't guess her thoughts—for it was clear to her that Fiona was miffed that the greens had so outproduced the queens, going so far even as to produce six queens on their own. But there was no denying the truth in what Fiona had said—they were now at a point where another round of clutching would leave Western unable to support the increased dragon and human populations.

In addition to the original 128 older dragons, there were another 1,558 who had two or more Turns of age.

"We'll start with the oldest wings and work down to the young ones," K'dan said.

"So in addition to everything else, we'll be training with firestone?" M'gel asked.

"Yes," Fiona said. She turned to K'dan, who nodded in agreement to her unspoken question. A moment later a loud, long rustle of wings outside announced the arrival of a large number of dragons. K'dan and Fiona rose, heading to greet the newcomers, gesturing for the others to follow.

Outside were the rest of their wing.

"Can I have the bronzes over here?" K'dan said, indicating a spot to his right. Perplexed, the wing split, with the fourteen bronze riders moving to one side. K'dan waited until there was silence and then a moment longer, as though sad at what he was going to say. "I'm afraid we're going to have to break up this wing."

The hiss of surprise came from every mouth.

"It's time," Fiona said. She turned to Xhinna and smiled. "While we all know that blues aren't supposed to lead wings, we've seen too many bad examples of the results of following Tradition too closely." She looked toward M'gel as she added, "This is not to say that the current leadership is wanting in any way. But I'm sure it comes as no surprise to any of you when I say that the Weyrwoman and I were willing to let this wing continue in its present form because we recognized that most of its leadership came not from those riding bronzes but—"

"A blue!" Danirry cried exultantly, patting Xhinna's shoulder hard.

"Indeed," K'dan agreed, giving the wingsecond a quelling look.

"But you said last night that the queens—," M'gel protested, looking at Fiona.

"The queens can continue with Xhinna," K'dan said, cutting the bronze rider's protest short. He grinned at M'gel. "But we need you—" He waved a hand at the collected bronze riders. "— to take charge of your own wings."

"They need you to learn to flame," Xhinna said, raising her voice to carry over the growing sounds of protest.

"Flaming?" J'sarte asked, intrigued.

"Thread will come soon," K'dan said. "And we're going to need wings prepared to fight it."

"But . . . what about Xhinna?" M'gel asked, turning a troubled glance toward the blue rider.

"And R'ney, and Danirry!" J'sarte added.

"We've got a special task for them," K'dan said. "They'll be train-ing with firestone, too, but for the moment we're going to keep that much of the Sky wing intact." He smiled at Xhinna, R'ney, and Danirry before turning back to the bronzes. "In the meantime, wingleaders, perhaps you'd care to join me in council?"

"Except Xhinna, of course," Fiona said, as the bronze riders ea-gerly filed through the doorway after K'dan.

K'dan paused in the doorway and turned back, smiling. "Of course, *Wingleader* Xhinna will need to plan the details of her wing."

Xhinna opened her mouth to protest. She'd given up the position once already and had no desire to add to her duties, but Fiona caught her eye and waggled a finger at her.

"No good deed goes unrewarded," Danirry remarked in an aside to Xhinna.

"Don't think about trying to wiggle out of it," R'ney added just as firmly.

Xhinna nodded in resignation, but her eyes sought out Taria's. The green rider met them with her own dark eyes and held her gaze. for a long moment before her lips curved up in a smile.

Coranth says that Taria won't let you out of doing diapers, Tazith re-layed. Xhinna's blue eyes danced and she returned Taria's grin with a small smile.

Wingleader.

"You're going to be getting some help in this," Fiona said. Above them the sky darkened as a group of dragons burst overhead from *between.*

Xhinna glanced up in surprise to see Talenth, Fiona's queen. Lor-ana was astride her, and behind her were the six green queens as well as two distinct wings of blues, greens, and browns. The queens landed first, as was their right, and Jirana came bounding over, followed by the five other young girls who had Impressed the green queens. They were all fit and tan, as was to be expected from their days spent lying under the sun guarding the Hatching Grounds against tunnel snakes. The girls were all near Jirana's age—much younger than normal for a

Candidate—but they had all formed the strange connection with their queens *before* the Hatching. It was their ability to hear the unhatched queens that protected the sands from the depradations of tunnel snakes, aided by the growing population of Meeyus and older Mrre-ows.

"But what about the eggs?" Danirry asked as she noticed Jirana.

"We've got that covered," Jirana assured her.

Xhinna turned thoughtfully to Fiona. How had the Weyrwoman known how many were needed?

"You were talking with Terin, weren't you?" Xhinna asked.

"Danirry's not the only one good with sums," Fiona said, smiling in acknowledgment.

Lorana was trailed by someone whom Xhinna couldn't immediately identify and then—"Seban!"

"I thought having an old hand around to advise you wouldn't be amiss," Fiona said as the ex-dragonrider waved in reply.

"I know we've blues and greens to spare, but I'm still surprised that we don't have more browns or bronzes," said Avarra, the blue rider sent from X'lerin's Midriver Weyr, who was leading their twenty-four blues and greens.

"Well, as you say, we have them to spare," R'ney, one of the few brown riders in their wing, allowed a little smugly.

"I try never to argue with Weyrleaders," Xhinna said.

Jerilli, the blue leader of the Northern contingent sent by H'nez, nodded vigorously.

The three wingleaders and their nine wingseconds were all gathered under one of the outside awnings hung off the stone hall, the rest of the dragonriders having gone to the beach to help with the egg guard.

Jirana and the other young queen riders were seated cross-legged in a ring away from the table, while Lorana and the Sky queen riders were seated behind Xhinna.

"Anyway," Xhinna said, "what I think we should do first is set up the watch order. After that, we'll make a quick visit to the Dawn Sisters so that we can instruct the riders of our wings."

"I pity the wing that's got the night shift," Avarra said.

"Oh, let me guess," R'ney muttered under his breath even as Xhinna said, "That would be mine."

Danirry, who'd heard the brown rider's quiet words, smirked at him and shook her head, looking at her wingleader resignedly. "Like you could bet differently."

"That's all very nice, but what are *we* to do?" Jepara demanded.

"No one knows how long a dragon can stay up by the Dawn Sisters," Lorana said. "I've an idea, as Minith and I tried first, but we're not certain."

"I see," Jepara said, apparently unable to unleash her usually biting tongue on the older, revered ex-dragonrider.

"We're going to need you and your queens to keep an eye on us," Xhinna said.

"That's it?" Jepara exclaimed, clearly expecting more.

"And rescue us, if need be," Danirry added, looking glum.

"Rescue—" Jepara began, but she stopped as understanding blossomed on her face. She turned to Xhinna. "So this is dangerous?"

"Very," Lorana said. "We need the queens to keep watch, to guard the greens and blues on watch."

"It's like guarding the eggs, only harder," little Devon piped up. She was just a sevenday younger than Jirana—much to the other's disgust at losing her position as the youngest queen rider on Pern. Even so, she had been the first to be picked by Jirana when she and Xhinna had gone on Search for riders for the green queens. Now, nearly three Turns later, she and Jirana were nearing adolescence, while Kiminy, the eldest by two Turns, was beginning to giggle at the looks given her by the younger bronze riders.

Xhinna had had little chance to see any of them since their Impression, but they'd all seemed pleasant, sweet, and just a little different—marked, as it were, by their strange queens with whom they could communicate before they were Hatched.

"They don't have the Sight, too, do they?" Xhinna had asked

Jirana after the five had all Impressed exactly as the young trader girl had predicted.

"I don't think so," Jirana had said, giving the question her full attention and adding with a shrug, "They might."

Xhinna now turned to Jirana, saying, "I want you and the other young queens to be certain that you don't try to catch us. Leave that to the bigger queens."

Jirana nodded. Around her, the others nodded just as solemnly, except the older Kiminy, who winked at Xhinna.

"But we'll be able to go up to the Dawn Sisters, right?" dark-haired Elodie asked.

"Yes," Lorana said. "You need to be able to *see* where you're watching."

"Between you and Jepara's queens, we'll have to ask you to take two-hour watches—"

"But even with the green queens, that's only eleven of us!" Jepara objected. Before anyone could reply, another queen burst into the sky overhead and dropped with appalling speed to the ground below, her wings cupping at the very last moment. Her rider scrambled off and rushed over, crying, "Sorry I'm late, I had a broken arm to mend!"

"Bekka?" Jepara called in astonishment.

"Is that a problem?" the sturdy healer demanded, her eyes flashing.

"You'll take the dawn shift, then," Jepara declared, "seeing as you were late."

"I was—" Bekka's hot protest died as she caught a look from Lorana. "That's fine." A moment later she added, reflectively, "I'm usually up by then doing my rounds."

"You'll have your second do them," Jepara ordered. "You'll need your full attention for this."

"When did your queen rise?" Bekka demanded hotly. She and the other queen rider had locked horns on so many occasions that Xhinna had feared they would finally come to blows, but so far, their arguments had always dissipated just short of that. After a while, Xhinna decided that their bickering was just their way of being friendly to each other. She'd seen them stick up for each other's best interest countless times in the past two Turns, but it still seemed to her a strange way of expressing affection.

"Before yours, certainly!" Jepara snapped back.

"Enough," Xhinna growled, cutting her eyes to the horrified looks of the other blue and queen riders. "Bekka—that would be great. I think Jepara has just volunteered to precede you—"

"I did not!" Jepara snapped. Xhinna lowered her head toward her with raised brows and the queen rider sighed, saying to Bekka, "Don't expect any *klah*."

"You'd probably spit in it," Bekka shot back.

"I hadn't thought of that," Jepara said, smiling sweetly.

"Children," Xhinna said to the two of them, earning her a pair of dark looks—both of them were as near her age as made no difference.

"Are you sure you'd like them watching out for you?" Avarra asked in a choked voice.

"Absolutely," Xhinna said. "I'd trust them with my life."

"I can take the watch before Jepara," Jirana offered.

"No, take the watch with Bekka," Jepara said, turning toward the younger rider with an affectionate look. Her gaze fell on the other young queen riders and she added, "Maybe Devon will watch with me."

The youngest queen rider beamed in agreement.

In short order the watches were set, Lorana noting them down on a slate for K'dan's later confirmation.

"So, when can we go up?" Jepara asked when the last dispositions were made.

"Food first, then flying," Bekka said authoritatively.

"Then, let's eat!" Jepara said, springing to her feet.

Bekka coughed significantly and nodded toward Xhinna and Lorana. Jepara gave her a quizzical look and then blushed. "I mean, if that's all right with you?"

Xhinna had to force herself to school her expression as she replied, "Of course."

As the others filtered away, Lorana waited behind until only she and Xhinna were left. Then the ex-queenrider leaned over and said,

"When were you going to tell them that they'll have to wait until dawn?"

"After they've eaten and are feeling sleepy," Xhinna told her. Lorana's eyes widened in surprise and she gave the blue rider a wide smile. "I thought I'd have them practice afterward at altitude, to get their dragons used to holding air, the way you told me."

"I see," Lorana said approvingly.

"Would you like a ride to the High Kitchen?" Xhinna said, rising as she spied R'ney, Taria, and Danirry waiting patiently by their dragons.

"No, I think I'll stay here and have a word with Fiona," Lorana said, waving a hand at her. "You go on."

X̃hinna and Taria sat at the large table in what they'd come to call the High Kitchen. "Here they come," Taria murmured.

In the Turns since they'd come to Sky Weyr, they'd learned that while spring and summer were often mild and pleasant, fall and winter were not the nicest seasons for tree dwellers. Fortunately, they had learned the lesson early and had discovered that some broom trees were more accommodating than others. So the original kitchen area had been superceded by a much larger, fully enclosed area in X'lerin's broom tree—the one that the Weyrleader and his bronze Kivith had occupied. Softer pinus wood had been used to lay a floor and erect walls and ceilings for the large room. After that, several more rooms had been constructed in other broom trees, providing winter quarters that were later expanded to house most of the Weyr.

The High Kitchen provided sufficient seating for no more than a full wing at best, so Xhinna had arranged for the various wings to eat in shifts. Tonight she had invited the wingleaders, queen riders, and wingseconds to eat first, as they would immediately after be going up to the Dawn Sisters.

Taria had managed to insinuate herself into the group with accepting nods from both R'ney and Danirry, and then had insisted that Xhinna eat quickly, predicting that the other two female blue riders would seek her out.

Sure enough, both Jerilli and Avarra were already making their way toward Xhinna.

"May we sit with you?" Avarra asked.

"Of course," R'ney said, moving closer to Taria and elbowing her to make more room. "Danirry, move away from the wingleader—you get to see her every day."

Danirry favored him with a look that was a cross between a glare and a grin, but dutifully moved away.

Xhinna was just as unsurprised as Taria at their desire to sit with her—slightly more than half of all the new green riders and just a bit more than one in three blue riders were women, a tremendous break with Weyr tradition brought about mostly because of the dearth of able-bodied males of suitable Searching age.

Xhinna susupected that Nerra might have slightly "stacked the deck," as R'ney had once described it, assiduously succoring girls by getting them into her orphanage, but whether or not that was true, she doubted that the Lady Holder's discrimination would matter much in the long term. Able-bodied men and lads had been drafted first into the recovery after the Plague, and all too often women had been left to shift for themselves, with the tragic result that many young girls had been left homeless and starving.

Soon, rigid, inflexible old-timers like D'gan were going to be confronted with the new reality. Given both Fiona's and Nerra's harsh words, Xhinna was rather hoping she'd have the chance to see his reaction firsthand, although she was the first to bet against his "dying of apoplexy at the mere sight," as Fiona had so cheerfully predicted.

There was an equally vigorous discussion of the possible reaction of Weyrwoman Tullea to the new organizations. There, Xhinna was in agreement with Fiona's prediction that the tetchy Benden Weyrwoman would be at least secretly and maybe even openly ecstatic.

The betting was spread more evenly upon the reactions of various Lord Holders, Fiona covering all wagers against her father having a negative reaction. She seemed surprised to have no takers, but having played several games of chance with Fiona, Xhinna was reasonably sure that the blond Weyrwoman was bluffing.

Avarra pursed her lips in a thin line, glanced toward R'ney, and then said to Xhinna, "We were hoping to talk with you alone."

"No," Xhinna said, surprised to hear the word echoed by R'ney and Danirry. "I trust my wing."

Avarra's look grew darker and she cut her eyes toward Jerilli.

"We were hoping that you would talk with T'mar," Jerilli said finally, filling in the other's silence.

"About what?"

"About this assignment!" Avarra said angrily, tamping down her volume so only the first word carried throughout the room. She leaned closer toward Xhinna, continuing at just above a whisper. "Aren't you as mad about it as we are?"

"Mad?" Xhinna repeated in a normal tone of voice. "Why should I be?"

"It's beneath you, that's why!" Avarra said. "We should be part of a fighting wing, not sent off on some silly 'errand' like we were mere weyrlings."

Xhinna looked in surprise at the other woman and then glanced to Jerilli to see the same expression on her face.

"I'm sure if you really feel that way, you've only to tell X'lerin and he'll have you back in an instant," Danirry said. "In fact, why don't I have Kiarith tell him . . ."

"Danirry!" Xhinna snapped at the blue rider. She turned to Avarra and Jerilli. "Didn't H'nez send you here?"

"Yes," Jerilli said, the hurt in her voice obvious. "I'd hoped—"

"Excuse me, may I join you?" an older man's voice interjected.

"Seban!" Xhinna cried in delight as she identified him. "Certainly! You can sit opposite me." She motioned for Taria to make room.

Seban sat and nodded to Avarra and Jerilli before saying in a pleasant tone, "I'm afraid I couldn't help hearing some of what was said."

Both of the blue riders looked slightly green at this because they'd had several prior encounters with the ex-dragonrider, either as Weyrlingmaster or general troubleshooter and occasional rider of various dragons, most particularly Xhinna's own Tazith.

Seban had accepted Xhinna's request with mixed emotions, and she was certain that he'd never completely conquered them, but still he rode when she asked—and he did the same favor for many others, especially those who, like Xhinna, were too great with child to safely fly for a while. He'd even taken Tazith on a few mating flights that Xhinna had been unable to attend for one reason or another. He was admired, respected, and revered throughout the Western Isle.

"Seban," Avarra said in protest, "it's just not fair—"

"Fair doesn't enter into it," R'ney interrupted. Seban raised a calming hand, and with the added weight of a glare from Xhinna, the brown rider subsided, nodding an apology to the ex-dragonrider.

"It's not a question of fair, dragonrider," Seban said, "but it is a question of honor."

"Honor?" Jerilli repeated hopefully. "So you see—"

"The three wings chosen to protect Pern are all led by women," Seban continued.

"Protect?" Avarra protested, her eyebrows rising high, "how can you—"

"How many dragons are there here on the Western Isle, do you know?" Seban asked.

"Nearly two thousand," Jerilli said, glancing to Avarra for confirmation.

"And what would they eat if Thread destroys the island?" Seban asked.

Jerilli's brow puckered.

"This is very lush land," Xhinna said. "We don't know how quickly a burrow would spread, but we *do* know that, once established, there are no natural boundaries from one shore to the next."

"We had to fire several valleys at Southern Boll because of burrows," Seban reminded them.

"And they lost a valley at Bitra," Xhinna said, recalling Fiona's account of the Threadfall that was still in their future.

"That was after our time," Jerilli confessed. She, like all the other new riders on the Western Isle, had been rescued from the time between the last of the Plague and the start of the Third Pass. She glanced at Xhinna. "None of us have seen Threadfall, though—"

"I have," Xhinna interrupted. She glanced over to R'ney, her eyes burning with a sense of urgency, as she continued, "Back at Eastern—"

"When you brought us back in time to here," R'ney recalled, turning to Taria.

"That was near to this time," Taria said, eyes wide. She looked at Xhinna. "We should tell Fiona—"

"I already have," Xhinna said. She turned back to Avarra and Jerilli. "So, do you understand the need?"

"But up at the Dawn Sisters?" Avarra asked, still protesting.

"It's a good place to start," Xhinna said. She smiled at the other two blue riders. "Do you understand now that your Weyrleaders entrusted you—and your riders—with a great burden?"

Jerilli slowly nodded. "Sorry we were such fools."

"I know X'lerin pretty well," Xhinna reminded her. "After all, he was the first to make me wingleader."

Jerilli's mouth fell into an "O" of recollection. Xhinna turned to Avarra, adding, "And I know H'nez reasonably well. Certainly well enough to know that he'd never appoint a fool to lead a wing." She raised an eyebrow. "Do you still want to protest?"

"No," Jerilli said, going quite red. "I think I want to hide."

"Don't do that!" R'ney told her. She looked over at him. "Wingleaders are supposed to make mistakes," he continued, glancing toward Danirry as his face expanded into a grin, and the two continued in unison: "That's why they have wingseconds—"

Xhinna joined in: "—to correct them!"

EIGHTEEN
▼▼▼▼▼▼▼▼▼▼▼

A Fall Through Nothing

As expected, the riders were tired and a bit sleepy after their rich meal, so although they grumbled, they were rather relieved to learn that they wouldn't be expected to go all the way to the Dawn Sisters on their first flight.

"Remember, the Dawn Sisters are always following the dawn," Xhinna said to her riders as they gathered into their assigned pairs. "We'll start with the first watch at dawn over Eastern's farthest shore."

She held her arms above her head to quell the expected uproar.

"The first group will pass off the watch to the next group, and so on until we've followed the Dawn Sisters all the way around Pern," Xhinna continued.

"But we'll only see dawn, then!" Avarra said.

"Yes," Lorana said, moving to stand by Xhinna. "The group that gets dawn at Benden needs to pay special attention. The same for the Telgar group and the High Reaches group."

"Why High Reaches, why not Fort?"

"Because the Isles are more in line with High Reaches than with Fort," Xhinna explained. "What we'll do next is we'll keep coordinated watches over Benden, Telgar, and High Reaches—from our height, we're certain to spot any Threadfall that occurs during daylight."

"So the groups will let the Dawn Sisters pass out of sight?" Jerilli said.

"Yes, we'll set it up so that each of the three groups over the Northern Continent watches for eight hours—split into eight pairs each—and we'll set up a twenty-four-hour watch here, plus we'll have an all-day guard set at the easternmost tip of the Eastern Isle in case Thread comes at night."

"And if Thread *does* come at night?" someone asked. "We've no watch-whers here."

"T'mar and the other Weyrleaders are working on that," Lorana told them.

"Our mission is to find the Thread when it falls on the Northern Continent at the same time as it's falling here," Xhinna told them.

"Why can't we go up now?" Jirana asked, her question receiving enthusiastic murmurs.

"Because to go to the Dawn Sisters now would require us to time it," Xhinna told them. "And that we can no longer do."

"What?" came a stunned chorus.

"It's too dangerous," Xhinna said. "We're too near the time when D'gan and Fiona—"

"Oh!" Jirana exclaimed, her voice matched by sounds of understanding from the rest.

"We'd get trapped—"

"But Lorana would save us—"

"Only if she could find us," Danirry reminded them. "And she only barely found Fiona."

Her words prompted a thoughtful silence among the riders.

"Which is why it's vital to get good images from the riders already in place," Xhinna said. "In the meantime, I'd like us to practice going as high as we can—beyond where we can breathe."

"What?"

"It's been done before," Xhinna said, raising her voice to quell the protests. "Lorana did it when she went to the Dawn Sisters."

All heads turned to the ex-dragonrider. Lorana smiled.

"Minith and I took extra air with us," she said. Seeing the puzzled looks of the others, she explained, "When you go *between* your dragon brings a bubble of air around it."

"How will we know when we're out of air?" Avarra asked.

"Well, some of you might not know Weyrleader T'mar too well, but those of you who do will not be surprised to hear that he's come up with an experiment he'd like us to try," Xhinna told them. "It'll be important and it will fill the rest of our day—"

"Then the sooner you tell us, the sooner we can get on with it," Jepara interjected.

"We'll go up in our assigned pairs with the assigned queens keeping watch, but we'll each bring a sack of firestone—"

"Firestone!"

"Some of our dragons haven't chewed firestone yet!"

"Which is also part of T'mar's plan," Xhinna said, raising her voice once more to be heard. "We'll start low and get everyone flaming, then we'll go above the usual levels to see how well and long we can flame there, too. Slowly, we'll work our way up to the point where the stars come out—"

"The stars!" Jirana cried excitedly. "Xhinna, please, please, can we get up there, too?"

"Maybe at the end, little one, when we can have others watch for you—"

"What are we watching for?" Jerilli asked.

"We're watching for when we run out of breathable air," Xhinna said.

"It's not as easy as you might guess," Bekka chimed in before either Jepara or anyone else could object. "For some, it's rather like being drunk; for others it's quite different."

"Color starts to go from your sight and you get really sleepy," Lorana recalled. "That's the danger: not recognizing the signs in time."

"And that's why we go in pairs and we have a queen keeping tabs," Xhinna said. She glanced toward Avarra. "No matter what some may think, we haven't enough blues and greens to be losing any." She turned toward Seban and said to the ex-dragonrider, "Seban, I'd like you to ride with me on Tazith."

Seban's eyes brightened and he nodded.

"You could come with me, Daddy," Bekka offered shyly.

"I'd like that very much," Seban told her.

"Lady Lorana, would you care for a view from the back of a magnificent brown?" R'ney asked with a regal bow toward the ex-dragonrider. Lorana accepted with a polite nod.

"I've already arranged for us to draw firestone," Xhinna said. "We'll each take a sack." She gestured toward the other stone building at the far end of the Meeyu Plateau. "I've got a detail of weyrlings standing by."

"We get our firestone and then what?" Avarra asked.

"We'll meet on the beach, southside below the last clutch of eggs," Xhinna said. "K'dan has offered to help instruct in chewing and flaming before we take to the skies."

"Can we get *all* this done before dark?" Jerilli wondered.

"If not, we'll flame on through the dark," Xhinna replied. "In fact, T'mar has another experiment—"

"Why are we not surprised?" Avarra muttered, getting a laugh from the others.

"There's a notion that the good air, as it gets colder, gets lower to the ground—"

"Everyone knows that!" Avarra protested.

"—the question is *how* low," Xhinna continued, ignoring the interruption. "K'dan will start with the wingleaders and wingseconds, then we'll train the rest of the flight."

There were unhappy murmurs from the queen riders who would, by necessity, be excluded from teaching their queens to chew firestone lest they become sterile. Xhinna smiled at Lorana, who took her cue and told them, "While K'dan is teaching them to flame, brown rider R'ney and I will be teaching the queens how to use the agenothree throwers."

The queen's wing flew low, near the ground to catch any Thread that the higher-flying fighting wings might miss. Because queens couldn't chew firestone and remain fertile, the queen riders used agenothree throwers. The throwers were bulky back-mounted cylinders filled with the agenothree acid and rigged with nozzles that directed the acid spray to burn Thread out of the sky.

"Excellent!" Bekka and Jepara cried in unison.

▼ ▼ ▼

It took over an hour to get all the dragons in the three wings flaming efficiently. By then they'd consumed slightly more than a quarter of the sack of firestone they'd each been issued.

Xhinna, relaying through Tazith, had the wings separate into their working pairs. With the queens divvied up amongst the groups, they rose to the very highest levels at which dragons normally flew. Xhinna ordered them to confirm that their dragons could still flame and all had the chance to find out how difficult it was for their dragons to climb higher—R'ney's brown and all the larger queens found they could still climb feebly, but the blues and greens were at their limit.

Then, with Lorana relaying, they went *between* to emerge a thousand meters farther up, the dragons flapping their wings frantically.

Stop, Lorana's voice echoed calmly through the group. Slowly, one by one, the dragons stopped flapping—and discovered that they were falling no faster than when they had been flapping. *Flame.*

With some surprise, the dragons discovered that they could still flame, which calmed them.

Again they went *between* and up another thousand meters. When they'd climbed four thousand meters above their normal height— nearly seven thousand meters above the ground—the dragons found they couldn't flame and their riders complained of the cold.

Back! Lorana sent, accompanied by the image of the warm sands of the beach.

The blessed warmth engulfed them and Xhinna took a deep breath, only to let it out in a rush.

Where's Mirressa? Tazith, where's Valcanth?

I see her! Lorana's mental voice called, and before Xhinna could react, R'ney's brown Rowerth, Bekka's Pinorth, and Jepara's Sarurth were all arcing skyward heading toward—

—a small dark shape, limply plummeting from the sky above them.

The two queens and one brown were suddenly joined by a burst of brilliant bronze dragons moving toward them, forming a large canopy beneath the dot, which resolved into the shape of a small green with a rider flopping about—Xhinna was glad that she'd insisted on full fighting straps for everyone.

The queens and the brown edged under the falling shape and the bronzes made a stairway beneath them. The green was caught by the queens and the brown, then passed from one pair of bronzes to the next until finally the limp pair were reverently lowered to the soft sand.

Xhinna and Seban were off of Tazith's back and rushing across the sands to the limp green and her rider before anyone else could move.

"Mirressa! Mirressa!" Xhinna shouted. Oh, don't be dead! she cried to herself. Please don't be dead! She pulled her belt knife and started to hack at the straps that tied the motionless form onto her green's neck.

"She's not breathing!" Seban shouted. How could he know that? Xhinna wondered dimly even as she pulled the green rider off her mount—and then she realized: Seban was talking about green Valcanth.

Lorana! Fiona! Help Valcanth! Xhinna cried, knowing that Tazith would relay her plea without urging.

"I'm here!" a small voice piped up. It was Jirana, racing up to join them.

What could one little—Xhinna cut the thought off as she saw the cold, pale, blue skin of Mirressa. "No!"

She pulled Mirressa down and laid her on the ground.

"No time, now, Xhinna, you've got to breathe for her," someone else ordered. Taria. And suddenly she was beside her. "You know what to do." Taria turned over her shoulder to shout, "Someone get a board, something we can put under her!"

"I'm here."

Xhinna hardly heard Bekka's voice. She was already leaning forward, opening Mirressa's mouth, and ensuring that she hadn't swallowed her tongue. She leaned down and gave Mirressa two quick breaths as she'd been taught, then turned aside, gasping in breath for the both of them and listening to the air coming out of Mirressa's still body.

"Stand aside, we've got the board!" a strong male voice cried. Recognizing M'gel, Xhinna stood and moved back. A crowd had gathered. She turned to see Lorana and Jirana standing by Valcanth's head, their eyes closed, their bodies taut, expressions strained.

Tazith! Xhinna called. *Valcanth must breathe!* She reached out to the rest of her wing. *Help Valcanth breathe!*

She moved over to Lorana and stood behind her and Jirana. For one startled moment, she noticed that the two were breathing in unison and then she closed her eyes, reached out, and joined in. She felt others come join her, bound in by the will of their dragons, even as she felt Taria position herself with Mirressa.

And slowly, the cold, still shape of the dragon changed. A twitch, a judder, and then—

"She's breathing!" Jirana's cry was marked by sobs and a heaving chest. "She's breathing!"

"They're both breathing!" Taria exclaimed.

Xhinna opened her eyes just in time to see Lorana rushing toward the green's head. Valcanth's eyelids were fluttering.

You're fine, Lorana assured the dragon. *Mirressa is fine. You'll both do fine.*

Xhinna's attention returned to the small form in front of her: Jirana, shoulders shaking miserably, bawling quietly to herself. Xhinna moved around to kneel before the small queen rider.

Quietly she said, "You knew, didn't you?" She gestured toward Mirressa. "You knew that was going to happen."

Jirana's brown eyes opened and met Xhinna's dark blue ones. Xhinna pulled the girl tight against her. "It's over," she said soothingly, "you did it, it's over."

"You can't tell anyone," Jirana whispered into Xhinna's hair. "It's the Sight."

Xhinna stiffened as she heard the words. Jirana added, "It's not over. It's going to get worse."

Xhinna pulled back and, with all the tenderness of a big sister, kissed Jirana's tears away before hugging her once more and whispering back, "Thank you for trusting me."

Jirana sniffed and slowly got herself back under control. With one final grateful nod, she pulled away from Xhinna, saying, "I'm all right now."

Xhinna gave her a half-smile and stood up. "Of course you are."

▼ ▼ ▼

"Okay, now explain it again," Lorana said calmly to Mirressa after they'd fortified the green rider with warm *klah* and food.

"I was cold," Mirressa said. "And Valcanth was cold, too, and then—all of a sudden—I was toasty warm, all dreamy and nice. And we were falling, but it didn't matter because we were so warm—"

"Did your cheeks tingle?" Lorana asked.

Mirressa's brows puckered and her hands rose involuntarily to her face. "I don't know," she said. "Maybe."

"That's the danger," Bekka said, turning to face the rest of the gathered wings. "The danger is that this creeps up unnoticed and then—" She gestured to Mirressa.

"So the moment you feel the slightest bit strange," Lorana said, pointing a finger to the ground, "come back down."

"But—" Avarra started in protest.

"No matter what, come down," Lorana told her. "We can't afford to lose you."

"But what if coming down means missing Thread?" Avarra blurted.

"We can always send up replacements," Xhinna said. "We lose less time sending up a replacement early than trying to catch a falling dragon."

"Shards, that's too true!" Jepara murmured from where she sat next to Mirressa. Mirressa looked up at her and made a face, but Jepara, to Xhinna's surprise, merely shushed the green rider and stroked her hair while, on the other side of her, Meeya patted the green rider's shoulder.

"We should have seen it," Devon said with a frown. "We should have noticed—"

"We were all coming back," Xhinna said. "We only noticed when we started to count heads."

"Something you do instinctively," Lorana said, casting an approving look at her.

"I should have seen it," Danirry said in a very small voice. "I'm sorry, Mirressa, I should have noticed—"

"You were a dragonlength away, how could you?" Mirressa replied. "No, *I* should have realized—"

"The thing is, this will be different for everyone," Bekka said, cutting across the growing recriminations. She turned to Lorana and Xhinna. "What we really need to do is set it up so that *everyone* gets a chance to know what it feels like for them."

"You want to risk every one of us?" Avarra cried in surprise. She was backed by a tumult of agreeing murmurs.

"It's the only way to know for certain," Bekka retorted firmly. She gestured toward Mirressa. "Unless you want to hope we'll catch you when we're not even looking."

Jerilli protested, "How can we hope to take watch when—"

"I think we'll do what Bekka says," Xhinna said.

"If only we could do it without all the risk," Avarra said. "If only we could find out while still here on the ground."

"You can," Jirana piped up. "Just hold your breath."

"What?" several riders cried.

"No offense, little rider," Avarra said, careful to remain respectful of a queen rider, "but—"

"She's right," Bekka said. She held up a hand. "Oh, it won't be quite the same, but it would give you an idea, a starting point as it were."

"I wish we'd thought of it sooner," Lorana said. Then she shrugged. "They do say that the burnt hand learns best about fire."

She turned to Xhinna, passing the job on to her.

Xhinna smiled at her in acknowledgment, took a deep breath, and then said, "Here's what we'll do: We'll break into our pairs and each will hold their breath until they can't, while the other will count the time. We'll mark it and switch off." She turned to Mirressa. "You and Danirry will sit this out, I'll have you two recording—"

"But—" Danirry started in protest only to be cut off by Xhinna's look. "Very well."

It took close to an hour for everyone to complete the drill satisfactorily and mark the times. At Avarra's suggestion, they tried twice.

The longest anyone could hold their breath was just a bit more than a slow count of seventy—an honor split between R'ney and

Avarra. The young queen riders insisted·on being included and had the shortest times, being still in their growth, while the smaller riders, surprisingly, had mixed results. Xhinna was pleased with her count of sixty-seven and worried by Taria's count of fifty-three.

"Okay, now it's time to learn Lorana's trick," Xhinna said when she and the other two wingleaders were satisfied.

"I don't know if it's a trick, really," Lorana said. "It's easiest to try if we go up way high."

"So Lorana, if you can give us the right coordinates, the wingleaders and wingseconds will go up," Xhinna said. "And when you think we've been there too long, have us come back."

The other green, blue, brown, and queen riders could not hide their disappointment, so Xhinna told them, "While we're up, break into your groups, and when Lorana comes back we'll take turns bringing you up, as well."

The groans subsided. Xhinna glanced to Lorana, who gestured to R'ney, and the two mounted his brown Rowerth. As Xhinna clambered up onto Tazith, she motioned for Danirry to mount her blue Kiarith.

"May I come?" Seban asked. Xhinna thought for a moment and nodded. "Certainly!" To the others she said, "Don't forget to tighten your straps!"

In moments, the nine dragons were airborne, and then, taking the image from Lorana, they winked out, *between*.

Xhinna gasped at the sight that filled her eyes when they came out of *between*. Stars. Brilliant, glowing stars. She swiveled her head and saw in the distance a bright red orb: the Red Star.

Look down, Lorana told her, and she swiveled her head to look through the gap between her left arm and her left leg.

It's beautiful! Xhinna exclaimed as she saw the brown and green shades of the Great Isles so very far below. She looked to her right and thought she could spy a smudge on the horizon—High Reaches Tip or perhaps even Tillek, she wasn't sure. Blue, laced with thin, white streaky clouds, marked the ocean, which filled most of her view. She

was just beginning to try to make out the patch that would be Sky
Weyr's Meeyu Plateau when—

Come back! Lorana's voice was full and firm. There was no dis-
obeying it.

And then they were back in the sky above the beaches, warm and
pummeled by a chorus of voices—human and dragon.

After that Xhinna went aloft three more times, first with Taria,
then with a reluctant Mirressa and Danirry, and finally with Bekka
and Jirana, all while the other wings rotated wingseconds, wingleaders, and riders up to the starry height above beautiful Pern.

"I never thought it would be so beautiful," Jirana remarked when they
were once again on the ground. The sun was setting and it was getting very cold on the beach where they'd gathered. In the distance,
north of them, fires had been lit to warm the eggs against the cold and
light the night against tunnel snakes. She turned to her little queen
and absently rubbed the queen's eye ridges as she continued, "I've
only seen it when—"

"I know," Xhinna said. Quickly she corrected herself, "At least, I
can imagine."

Jirana seemed ready to argue, then shook her head, sighing.

"You've got friends, you know," Xhinna said. "We're sisters because of Fiona—"

"Losing friends is what's hard," Jirana said miserably.

"Little one," Xhinna replied, moving an open hand toward the
youngster, "there's no point in mourning them before they're gone."

Jirana raised a hand to meet Xhinna's, fingers touching fingers, as
she whispered, "You'll see."

Xhinna shivered.

"She's not your child—why don't you bring it up with Javissa?" Taria
said later that night as they were settling their babies into bed.

"Because I offered my support, not her mother's," Xhinna replied.

Taria turned from the small bed where she'd laid Tarena and gave

Xhinna a small smile. "Then, as you said, don't mourn before it's time."

"She must be awfully lonely . . ."

"How can she be? She's got the whole Weyr watching over her, five queen riders who positively adore her, and every Weyrleader hanging off her very words!" Taria shook her head. "It's a wonder she's not more spoiled than she is." Xhinna gave her a sharp look, but Taria just smiled. "And you, my dear, are among the worst!"

"Really?" Xhinna said, examining her feelings critically. She hadn't thought she'd doted on the youngster overmuch, but perhaps . . .

"And I'm next in line," Taria said, chuckling. She fluffed the final pillow, eyed the sleeping room carefully, turned the glow, and gestured for Xhinna to precede her. "Now," she said quietly as she moved along the thick branches that marked the hallway from one room to another, "we're going to need to sleep—you've got an early start, remember."

Taria's soft breathing was comfort enough to lull Xhinna quickly off to sleep. She had slept for several hours, she was certain, when she woke and spied a pair of small eyes peering from the entrance. Through long practice, she extended a hand from underneath the covers and beckoned the child to join them. Naturally, it was only a matter of moments before the bed was filled with cold, squiggly children. Taria surfaced long enough to roll an eye at Xhinna's lack of discipline, and then she was asleep once more, while Xhinna reveled in the squirmy warm bodies that were a small portion of *her* children.

"You've too many babies," Taria had said when Xhinna had broached the notion of getting pregnant again after Xelinan's birth. In reply to Xhinna's surprised look, Taria had explained, "Not only ours, but all the blues and greens."

There was truth in Taria's words, for the tight-knit group of blue and green riders that inhabited Sky Weyr, as well as many from the other Weyrs, had all asked Xhinna to stand in their place if, in the Turns to come, anything should happen to leave their babies without parents. Neither Xhinna nor Taria could deny these heartfelt requests, no more than could the others so honored. Xelinan had many fathers, including K'dan, T'mar, R'ney, X'lerin, Colfet, Seban, and all the bronze riders among the weyrlings that Xhinna had brought to the Sky Weyr more than two Turns before. The children played together and were watched together by various honorary parents and real parents, and it was a relief to know that, in the worst of cases, the children would all still have the love and support that they'd need.

It also meant that all the children were well-adjusted and cheerful, not so reliant on any one parent that the loss would be tragic to them.

It really was one of the greatest gifts Taria had given her—to be able to build and grow a family that was freely shared and fully loved.

Which was why, Xhinna thought as she tried to drift back to sleep, Jirana's sorrow so upset her. Not just for the strange green queen rider, but also for what it meant for her extended family.

It's going to get worse. Jirana had never been wrong.

NINETEEN
▼▼▼▼▼▼▼▼▼▼▼

A Flame in
the Void

"Xhinna."

The voice that woke her was quiet and male. J'riz. Xhinna's nose twitched as the scent of warm *klah* wafted her way.

"Shh," she said, nodding toward sleeping Taria and the bumps that were various children. She shooed him out of the room as she slipped out from under the covers in what she hoped was a deft and draft-free move.

"Ugh!" Taria muttered, accompanied by various anxious sounds from the babies. She popped open a bleary eye as Xhinna turned back toward her, her expression full of apology, and closed it again with an accepting nod.

Relieved, Xhinna crept out of their room, took the mug of *klah* from J'riz with a thankful nod, and sent him off on the rest of his morning rounds.

She dressed quickly and made her way over to the Healer's Quarters to find Mirressa already there, talking anxiously to Bekka.

"I *can't* watch after the babies *and* you both, Mirressa," Bekka was grumbling as Xhinna entered. "You'll have to get Aressil or Javissa—"

"But—" Mirressa protested.

"Actually," Xhinna interposed smoothly, "I've already arranged with Fiona."

Mirressa's eyebrows shot up in surprise and she started to protest, but Xhinna cut her off. "It's not as though she doesn't *owe* us, after all."

"But—"

"You, in particular," Xhinna cut across the green rider's incipient objection.

"She's right, and you know it," Bekka said. She smiled at the green rider, adding, "And why do you think she's used you so unmercifully to sit her brood if she didn't intend return payment?"

Mirressa's objections died on her lips as she digested Bekka's words.

"And it's not as if she won't pester my mother or Aressil or Colfet or any one of a dozen others to help at it," J'riz added with a grin.

"He's right," Xhinna said to the green rider. "Now, come on, we've got work to do."

"It's still dark out," Mirressa said.

"It's lightening, and we've got to catch the Dawn Sisters over Eastern, not here," Xhinna reminded her.

Mirressa sucked her lower lip worriedly.

"Go on!" Bekka said, shooing both of them out of her office. "There's firestone waiting at the top of the trees."

Xhinna looked at her in surprise.

"I made the boy get it," Bekka said, nodding toward J'riz, who tried his best to look put upon. With any other person, J'riz's brilliant green eyes and miserable look would have at least won an "Ahhh!" of sympathy, but Bekka merely swatted him on the arm. "Guide them up—I don't need their broken necks to deal with on top of everything else."

"As you say, Weyrwoman," J'riz returned with a low and overly obsequious bow. Bekka snarled at him and he took off like a wounded Meeyu, Xhinna and Mirressa trailing behind, neither of them taken in by the act.

At the top of the broom trees the weather was less forgiving and as the morning breeze picked up, moist with the threat of later rain, Xhinna was glad that she'd chosen her warmest riding gear.

She and Mirressa picked up their firestone sacks, waved farewell to J'riz, and called their dragons to them.

"We're going to Eastern first," Xhinna said just before they mounted. "We'll fly straight to the near coast to warm up, then *between* to Eastern's far coast. When we get there, we'll do a quick check with Lorana and then go up to the Dawn Sisters."

Mirressa nodded. Xhinna leaned forward to pat her on the arm. "Are you ready?"

Mirressa took a deep breath. "Yes."

The flight between the islands was a good thirty minutes and in that time the night brightened considerably.

As Xhinna had hoped, the dawn and the Dawn Sisters were still a short ways off the Eastern Isle's east coast when the two dragons emerged from *between*. Xhinna had them slowly circle to recover from the cold and then contacted Lorana, who arrived on Talenth and gave them the image of their destination. And then, each taking a deep gulp of air, Xhinna and Mirressa took their dragons *between*.

Eastern Isle lay far below. The gleaming shapes of the three brilliant spacefaring ships that so many Turns before had brought humankind to Pern floated nearby as silent sentinels to the dawn they followed.

Xhinna urged Tazith closer to Mirressa and her Valcanth, caught the green rider's attention, and received her assurance that she was all right. Satisfied, Xhinna turned first to peer at the nearest ship and then looked down at the beautiful blue-and-green orb that was their home.

Mirressa says she can see High Reaches Tip, Tazith relayed. Xhinna bent over the other side of his neck to crane down. Spotting the dark smudge that was the far tip of the Northern Continent—home—she waved back to Mirressa in agreement. Then she returned to the other side, studying the terrain below and glancing about for any sign of Thread.

It's time. Talenth's voice was clear, and Xhinna knew that all the dragonriders could hear it.

The next group? Xhinna asked. As if in answer, another pair of dragons—Alimma's blue Amanth and Aliyal's green Leyanth—popped into sight. They were surrounded by a thin nimbus—the air that Lorana had said they'd bring with them.

Alimma waved. Xhinna waved back, gestured to Mirressa, and then ordered Tazith to return.

Back once more above Eastern, Mirressa laughed and waved to Xhinna and Lorana both.

She says that wasn't too bad, Tazith relayed.

Tell her she can go back, Xhinna said. *I'm going to stay on.*

Mirressa waved in acknowledgment, and then she and her green Valcanth were gone *between*. Instinctively, Xhinna checked with Bekka to be sure that dragon and rider had returned safely.

She's making breakfast, came the relayed reply, devoid of any intonation from having passed through two different dragon minds. Xhinna smiled.

Cliova and J'valin appeared and dutifully relieved Alimma and Aliyal; just as quickly, they were relieved by R'ney and Taria, and so on until the entire wing had been up to the Dawn Sisters.

By then the dawn had moved back to the Western Isle, and Xhinna and Lorana had moved with it.

Avarra and her wing arrived in time to take up the sunward chase just as Jepara insisted that Lorana take a break. Xhinna could see the reluctance in the older woman's eyes, but Jepara wouldn't back down and at last Lorana relented.

"She's really quite dedicated," Xhinna said as she and Lorana made their way into the Kitchen Hall. Seeing the look in the older woman's eyes, she added with a chuckle, "And you're keeping an eye on things anyway."

"I was," Lorana admitted, placing a couple of warm rolls beside the redfruit on her plate. "She's got the images just right, so I'll not worry."

"That is, until the next queen takes over," Xhinna guessed. Lorana admitted as much with a twitch of her shoulders. Xhinna gestured toward the table where Mirressa and some others of her wing were seated. "Would you like to join us?"

Lorana acceded, and shortly they were joined by Weyrwoman Fiona and Weyrleader K'dan. The large table filled up as R'ney, Danirry, Cliova, Alimma, Aliyal, and the others all returned.

It was Mirressa who said it best, her shining eyes trained on Lorana: "Thank you! I have never seen anything so amazing!"

"It's nice to see what we're fighting for, isn't it?" Fiona commented.

The others were talking excitedly about all the features they'd seen, comparing notes on the colors and sights that the moving dawn had brought them.

"I think we should stay up longer next time," Danirry said during a lull in the conversation. Fiona glanced at Lorana and Xhinna.

"I think it's too early," Xhinna said. "Let's wait until we've got the full orbit done, then we'll see."

"I think you're right," Lorana agreed. She was about to say something more when Jirana rushed up, forcing open a spot between Xhinna and Taria.

"When can I go up?" the little queen rider demanded. "All the queens want to know!"

"Even Bekka?"

Jirana rolled her eyes. "Who do you think sent me?"

"Isn't J'riz going up now?" Xhinna asked, glancing toward Lorana, who nodded. J'riz was paired with J'valin, rider of blue Nerinath.

"Would there be any chance Bekka would take up another when she goes?" Seban asked.

"If she doesn't, I'll take you myself," Fiona said.

"Bekka's Pinorth is up to it," K'dan said. The queen had a tendency—in common with her rider—of over-exerting herself; K'dan made a point of keeping tabs on her.

"Well, then," K'dan said, gesturing to Jirana and Fiona. "When you're finished, with Lorana's agreement, we'll all take a look."

▼ ▼ ▼

They arrived near the Dawn Sisters when they were midway across the Western Isle, nearly over Midriver Weyr, although they couldn't make it out through the vast expanse of green growth and brown earth beneath them—more green than brown.

Xhinna waved to the surprised riders of Avarra's wing who had expected to be alone on this watch, while Lorana quickly relayed explanations for their intrusion. Xhinna caught snatches of conversations relayed to her by Tazith, but she was more interested in staring at the view below, trailing her eyes east and west to the extreme edges of the sun's light, trying to absorb the huge expanse of the vista.

Eight hours, Tazith said. When he caught Xhinna's surprise, the blue added, *K'dan says that we're seeing about eight hours of sunlight.*

All too soon it was time to return. Xhinna waved at the watch riders, and then they went *between* once more, and back to Sky Weyr.

At the start of the next watch, Xhinna and Mirressa got their image from the last pair of Jerilli's wing and went up to the Dawn Sisters. Each assured herself that the other was not suffering from oxygen starvation, and then they took quick scans of the new horizon until finally it was time for them to hand off to the next pair.

Three hours later, they repeated the effort, this time seeing a smudge on the western horizon that must have been Benden's shoreline.

When they went up again, they were right over the mountains that surrounded the Weyr itself.

They can't see us, can they? Mirressa relayed through her Valcanth to Xhinna.

The Dawn Sisters are bright lights in the sky, Xhinna relayed back by way of answer.

And then, once more, it was time to return earthward.

Back at Sky Weyr, the two dragonriders warmed themselves with *klah* before Xhinna checked in with her other riders and the two other wingleaders. The initial excitement was waning, but it had renewed at the sight of their home continent.

"We need to start keeping an eye out for Thread," Xhinna said to Avarra and Jerilli later as the watch riders took post with the dawn over Telgar Weyr.

"I thought we had a month at least," Avarra protested.

"We can't be certain," Xhinna said. "We know that there were dustfalls before the Fall over Benden, Bitra, and Tillek."

Jerilli furrowed her brows. "Thread fell at three different places?"

Xhinna shook her head. "The fall over Benden continued to Bitra. The fall over Tillek was separate."

Xhinna could tell that the blue rider was confused. "I've asked K'dan if he could draw us a map."

"Ah, so that's why he was up with us earlier!" Avarra exclaimed. She quickly explained that the Weyrleader had joined her watch for a while over Benden and was even now up with the Dawn Sisters over Telgar.

Lorana is with him, Tazith added in unbidden anticipation of Xhinna's thoughts.

Thank you! she replied warmly. Lorana and K'dan were both gifted at drawing, although the ex-queenrider seemed to have more flair than the new Weyrleader.

"So when we've followed the Dawn Sisters back here, what next?" Avarra asked.

"Then we start our proper watch," Xhinna told her. "We'll need a watch stationary over Benden from sunrise to sunset, the same for Telgar and High Reaches—"

"That should let us see everything there," Jerilli agreed.

"And we'll keep the same length of watch here over the Great Isles."

"We'll have fourteen hours over the Northern Continent, but only eleven over our own," Jerilli noted. When Avarra grunted in confusion, Jerilli explained, "We only get eight hours of sunlight in one place; there's six hours' difference between Benden and High Reaches, whereas we've only got three at best between the easternmost of Eastern and the westernmost of Western."

"Oh, I see," Avarra said a bit doubtfully. She glanced at Xhinna. "So how do we manage that?"

"I'm open for suggestions," Xhinna said, throwing her hands wide.

"No, you're not," Jerilli countered with a chuckle. "You've already got something in mind and you'd prefer us to come up with it on our own."

"You've been taking lessons from the Weyrwoman, haven't you?" Avarra asked.

"Actually, I think it's just general wingleader deviousness," Jerilli said. Avarra gave her a look, so she said, "Don't you do the same with your people?"

"I'm still pretty new at this," Avarra said diffidently. She turned to Xhinna. "So, you have a plan?"

"I think it's simple enough," Jerilli said. "We've got three hours of slack on this side, so we double or triple up."

"That's pretty much what I was thinking," Xhinna agreed. "I was also thinking that we should stay up longer—"

"How long?"

"How do you feel about five minutes?"

"Nervous," Avarra admitted.

"If we set it up right, we could have overlaps," Jerilli said. "That would give us more than one pair at any one moment, and the newer pair could ensure that the older pair was still safe."

"I'd prefer three minutes and do that as well," Avarra said.

"I think starting with three minutes makes sense," Xhinna said.

"Very well," Jerilli said, "we'll start with three minutes."

"The biggest problem is to keep everyone from getting bored," Xhinna said.

Jerilli gave her an astonished look. "What? Looking at home from so high up?"

"It's always the same!" Jerilli complained when they met in the evening six days later. "I'm practically *wishing* something would happen."

The three wings had performed brilliantly, picking up the new schedule without a hitch and sticking to it steadfastly, despite the difference in time zones and the stress of being up in the lifeless cold near the twinkling stars.

"Why don't we switch around, so people are looking at different places?" Avarra suggested.

"Because if we do that, we lose the advantage of having people trained to spot differences in the terrain they know so well," Xhinna replied.

Avarra pinched her lips together in disappointment.

"We can continue with flaming," Jerilli said.

"We've been doing that," Avarra snapped. She shot the other wingleader an apologetic look immediately, but her words hung in the air.

"I think we're doing all that we can," Xhinna said. She raised a hand as the other two started to protest. "I know that the work seems dull now—"

"And it'll be near a month before we first see Thread—" Jerilli interjected sourly.

"Actually, not true," Xhinna corrected, raising a hand to forestall Jerilli's protests. "We know that dustfall was seen over Fort two days before Turn's End—"

"Great, so we've only nineteen more days to—"

Thread! Thread! Thread falls over Bitra!

The three riders were out of the room and into the air in an instant, grateful for the sacks of firestone that were still tied to the neck of their dragons.

Tazith, tell K'dan that we're going to investigate, Xhinna told her dragon as they rose into the evening air. *Tell the wing to join me at the Dawn Sisters.* She paused for a moment. *Have you got the image?*

In response, Tazith took them *between.* They burst out in the early morning sky high over Benden, next to the watch riders who were still close to the Dawn Sisters.

Xhinna quickly found Bitra. There, dark smudges seemed to mar the landscape. She looked around, saw the rest of her wing form around her, and called to her blue, *Take us there!*

They came out in the sky high above Bitra. The air was cold, and the pocket of evening air that Tazith had brought with them from over Sky Weyr shone at its edges with small ice crystals frozen by the colder Bitra air.

Without urging, the blue turned his head to her and Xhinna found herself fumbling as she opened a firestone sack and fed him chunks. She knew, without looking, that behind her the rest of her wing was doing the same.

Far, far above Bitra, the dragons prepared for what they had been born and bred to do: flame and kill Thread.

No flame! Tazith cried as his first belch brought forth only the merest flicker of light.

Lower, lower! Fall with *it!* Danirry's Kiarith relayed.

Do it, Xhinna agreed.

They fell, twenty-five dragons in unison, following the small oblongs through the thin atmosphere.

R'ney is worried about our air, Tazith relayed after they'd fallen for thousands of meters.

Look! Look at the Thread! Coranth relayed.

Xhinna looked at the Thread, so tantalizingly close, deadly, threatening. The clumps were changing, glowing with a heat of their own and—extending, growing, streaming into—

Thread! Tazith bellowed, bursting forth with another belch of firestone—this time it lit and the streaming Thread in front of him caught fire, crisped, and charred into nothingness.

Behind her, Xhinna suddenly heard the triumphant bellows of the dragons, heard the roar of flame, and the fantastic sound of Thread charring, burning, turning into lifeless dust.

Avarra, Jerilli! Xhinna called. Where Tazith had found them was suddenly empty as they went *between* and Xhinna knew that the two other wings were en route to join them. And then, to her left she saw Jerilli, waving and crying with joy; to her right, Avarra was diving toward a clump of Thread and flaming at it even as it started to stream from a small ball into its normal, long, thread-like shape.

They flew until there was no more Thread, until there was only dust, until Xhinna and the others had exhausted their sacks of firestone.

Back, Xhinna called to the exhausted riders and dragons. *Back to the Weyr.*

Moments later, there was nothing over Bitra to indicate that the Sky Dragons had ever been present, except for small shards of ash that were presently borne upward and away by the morning breeze.

"**W**e caught it just as it was Threading!" Davissa exclaimed jubilantly, rushing to grab Xhinna in a bear hug. Xhinna had barely a moment to catch her breath before the two of them were engulfed in huge, strong arms and lifted off their feet.

"We did it, we did it!" R'ney's voice boomed in Xhinna's ears.

"Put us down, put us down!" she begged, banging on R'ney's arm ineffectually and laughing all the while. No sooner had the brown rider complied than Xhinna found herself embraced once more, this time by the two exuberant blue riders.

"You know what this means—," she said to them, only to hear K'dan reply, "It means that perhaps you should report to the Weyrleader."

Instantly the circle broke and Xhinna turned to meet the bronze rider's eyes.

"Oh, come on, it's not like it's necessary," Fiona said, moving by K'dan's side. "Danirry's Kiarith reported to everyone, and you knew that Xhinna and her—ahem—*consorts* were going to fight the Thread."

"It worked! It worked just like I thought it would!" Danirry crowed exultantly, causing everyone to turn toward her with wide eyes. "Flaming Thread!"

"Uh, dear . . . ," R'ney prompted.

At this, Danirry seemed to realize that she'd left a few important words out—a habit of hers that her fellow blues and greens had come to accept, but which was foreign to most others.

"I'm sorry, Weyrleader," Danirry said. "It's just that I was sure we could flame the Thread up high, just as it blossomed—"

"Blossomed?" Fiona cut in, her face going pale at the revolting image.

"Spooled, then, if you will," Danirry corrected with a quick shrug.

"Please explain, blue rider, and assume that we've never heard what you're talking about before," Fiona said.

"Because we haven't," R'ney added, reaching forward to poke the blue rider affectionately on the shoulder. "Once again, dear heart, you forget what you haven't told us."

"Oh," Danirry said, only slightly repentant. She collected herself, glanced in the direction of K'dan and Fiona, and then said, "Well, it's just that I thought that—well, Thread burns, right?"

K'dan nodded slowly.

"And it grows; it eats things," Danirry continued. "So it's something that lives and needs air." She glanced around, her eyes darting quickly toward K'dan and Fiona before coming to rest on Xhinna as she took a deep breath. "So I figure that it lives. And if it lives, then while it's in the cold of space it must be dead—"

"Dead?" K'dan repeated, his brows furrowed.

"Asleep, like a seed out of the ground," Danirry said. "Inert, if you will."

"I see," K'dan said.

"So when it falls, something has to wake it, as it were, or it would still be a seed when it hit the soil, wouldn't it?" Danirry said.

"We're with you," R'ney said encouragingly.

"So I figured that when it woke up would be when it was at its most vulnerable, when it would be smallest and easiest to destroy," Danirry continued. She looked K'dan full in the eyes as she concluded, "Just when it was spooling out into Thread. Just when there was enough air to slow it down, enough air that we could flame it into dust."

"By the First Egg!" Fiona swore in awe. She glanced to K'dan.

"It worked?" K'dan asked.

"Perfectly," Xhinna said, moving to Danirry's side and hugging the blue rider's shoulders. She glanced toward Avarra and Jerilli. "Not a dragon or rider injured, and no Thread reached the ground."

"We could kill it before it ever got near enough to threaten Pern," Fiona said, looking up hopefully to the Sky Weyrleader.

"Yes," K'dan said abstractedly.

"You're worried about the timing, aren't you, Weyrleader?" Danirry asked in the silence that fell.

"Thread fell over Bitra?" T'mar asked as he and the other Weyrleaders—along with Danirry, R'ney, and the three blue wingleaders—gathered later that evening in the stone hall of Sky Weyr. "So early?"

"What matters more is where will it fall next," Fiona said. She looked at K'dan.

"From what we've determined, this Fall is preceded by the Fall over Benden and Keroon," K'dan said. He laid out a map of the Northern Continent; it was marked with long, thin swaths running northeast to southwest. He pointed at one, then flicked his finger to another. "After which, there'll be a Fall over Nerat and Upper Crom, and then—"

"But our first Fall came over Benden and Igen, and not until the new Turn!" H'nez protested.

"There were three dustfalls before that," T'mar recalled. "One at Fort, one at High Reaches Tip, one at Southern Tillek."

"What if—" Danirry began. Then, realizing the august company surrounding her, she cut herself off abruptly.

"Please," K'dan said, gesturing for her to continue.

"I was just thinking, Weyrleaders," Danirry said, blushing lightly, "what if those dust Falls were because—well, because we'd flown them?"

"What?" "How?" "When?" The cries echoed around the stone room.

"And the other Falls?" T'mar asked. "If K'dan's right, there are . . ." He gestured for K'dan to fill in the number, but it was Fiona who said, "Five more Falls between now and that first dustfall." T'mar nodded his thanks, then continued, "Are you suggesting we flew them all ourselves?"

"Why not?" Avarra said, glancing toward H'nez before continuing, "We had no casualties, not so much as a dragon scratched. If we keep doing that, Thread has no chance against us!"

Outside, a chorus of bugles from the greens and blues of the three wings shook the air.

"You'll need the queens to catch you," a small voice spoke up from the doorway as silence fell. It was Jirana.

"I think that's an excellent idea!" Fiona said, nodding so fiercely at K'dan and the other Weyrleaders that they all, wisely, kept silent.

"We still will need to keep watch," K'dan said. "We don't know when Thread will fall *here,* after all."

"It would not be wise to trust both the watch *and* these Falls to just three wings," H'nez said.

"Well, we've got wings to spare," Terin spoke up, nodding at C'tov, the nominal Weyrleader of her Southern Weyr. She glanced expectantly at T'mar, who stood as Weyrleader of both the Southriver and Western Weyrs.

T'mar smiled. "Let me talk with Garra and Jassi," he said. "I'm pretty sure we'll be able to free a wing each."

"Keep the bronzes for catching," Jirana said. The others looked at her and she blushed. "I'm sorry, I meant to—"

"You meant to do *exactly* what you did," Fiona said, smiling and wagging a finger at the young queen rider. She turned to T'mar, who frowned at the girl before nodding to the Weyrwoman and saying resignedly, "She's right. It makes more sense to have the blues and greens up high, and the browns and bronzes down low to catch—"

"Because there's no way a blue can catch a bronze," C'tov said with a chuckle and an apologetic waggle of his eyebrows to the blue riders present.

Xhinna said to R'ney, "While I'd hate to lose your services fighting Thread, I can think of no one I'd prefer to have catching us if we were to fall."

R'ney frowned, then nodded. "Put that way, Wingleader, I accept."

"Flightleader?" Xhinna exclaimed when Fiona and K'dan sprang their latest surprise on her the next morning in the High Kitchen.

"Well, 'Weyrleader' seems perhaps a bit much," K'dan told her, barely able to keep the grin off his face.

"Although Flightleader is an insult, because you'll be in charge of *two* Flights," Fiona added. She turned to K'dan, suggesting, "Overleader?"

"No," Xhinna said, raising her hands in horror. She knew how persuasive Fiona could be, particularly with the Weyrleader. Well, actually, pretty much with *all* the Weyrleaders. It was absolutely necessary to nip this in the bud. "No, anything but that!"

"So, *Flightleader* it is," Fiona said triumphantly.

"Still," K'dan began, clearly enjoying himself, "it's not quite right, because you'll be in charge of six wings."

"*Flightleader* will do fine," Xhinna muttered. Shaking her head, she looked across the table at the two of them. Settling her gaze on Fiona, she accused, "You set me up for this."

"Well, of course," Fiona agreed easily. "Although far be it from me to suggest that perhaps you actually *earned* it—"

"No, that would be my job," K'dan inserted. He grinned at Xhinna. "You've got all the qualifications. And, you'll note, the other Weyrleaders all saw fit to send their best—"

"And not a bronze among them," Xhinna noted tartly.

"Well, that's not fair," Fiona said, her light tone evaporating. "Jirana makes too much sense with her notion of catching falling dragons—"

"If it's practical," Xhinna cut in.

"Well, it worked for you," Fiona said, forcing Xhinna to remember Turns back to when she and Tazith had made their abortive attempt to jump forward in time, only to be rescued by X'lerin and his wing. "And it worked for me," the Weyrwoman continued, "and it worked for T'mar. But, admittedly, we had a whole Weyr ready to help, so I think, all things considered, it really *is* better to stick with blues and greens on these Sky Wings—"

"Sky Wings?" Xhinna interrupted.

"Well, I don't think Space Wings makes much sense," Fiona continued, thoroughly enjoying herself, "as you're not really up in space for all that long, after all."

"Sky Wings," Xhinna repeated with a long sigh of resignation.

She was rewarded with chuckles from the Weyrwoman and Weyr-leader, which was what she'd intended.

"And we'll base them here, at Sky Weyr," K'dan said. When Xhinna shot him a startled look, he waved it aside. "T'mar agrees. That's partly because you've managed to convince so many queen riders to stay here—"

"Not that we're complaining," Fiona interrupted, another smile blossoming on her lips. "Even Talenth has decided to take it as a compliment."

"Anyway," K'dan continued, ignoring Fiona's outburst, "the extra queens make it that much easier to build catching wings—"

"Catching wings?" Xhinna repeated.

"I like the sound of that!" Fiona said.

"You're taking charge of them, aren't you?" Xhinna begged.

Fiona chuckled and waved away Xhinna's worry. "Of course," she said. "Although I'm not so foolish as to separate Jirana from the rest of her charges."

"But without the green queens, how—"

"How will we guard the Hatching Grounds?" Fiona guessed. "J'keran and his guard will do the bulk of the work, but Jirana has assured me that her queens are keeping constantly in touch with the eggs."

K'dan shook his head in renewed awe at the strange arrangement that existed between unhatched eggs and the green queens. It had been, over the past several Turns, the cause of many late-night conversations throughout the six Weyrs of the Western Isle.

Xhinna thought about the other queen riders and pursed her lips in a small frown. "You'll need—"

"To win over your Jepara?" Fiona guessed, smiling once again as she took in Xhinna's astonished look. Taking pity, she explained, "Well, it wasn't hard to guess that that would be your next consideration."

"I don't think there'll be any problem in that," K'dan said, nodding toward the distance. Xhinna turned to see Jepara making her way toward them, a tray in her hands. Xhinna smiled and waved at the queen rider, who smiled back and quickly joined them.

"We were just talking about you," Fiona said as Jepara sat. The gold rider nodded, unperturbed.

"I'd heard about the other wings," Jepara said, nodding toward Xhinna. "I gather we're going to be given more duties?"

"I'm going to form the queen's wing," Fiona said. "I'd like you to be my wingsecond."

"What about Jirana?"

"She'll be my other wingsecond, responsible for the green queens," Fiona said, ignoring the look of distate that flashed across Jepara's face. "But as your wing will have the larger dragons, I'm expecting you and the browns and bronzes—"

"Bronzes?" Jepara interrupted, her voice filled with anticipation.

"J'sarte and the others with dragons his age," Fiona said. She raised a hand to forestall Jepara, adding, "They'll have their normal duties, but in an emergency, I'm expecting you to incorporate them into any 'catching' we may have to perform."

"We're also assigning some of the younger greens and blues— those old enough to fly for short periods—to your exercises," K'dan added. "They'll be attached to the various wings, so the bronzes will be able to direct them as you need."

"Need?"

"Well, you've got to practice catching," Fiona said. "So I figured we could have them stand in. It'd be good exercise for them, as well."

Jepara nodded, her expression thoughtful. Xhinna wanted to stay, but she'd finished her breakfast and she could feel the looks of R'ney, Danirry, and the rest of her wing on her. Rising, she nodded to Fiona and K'dan, and smiled at Jepara. "I must go."

"Fly safe," K'dan said. Fiona echoed him, but Jepara merely waved dismissively, and Xhinna suppressed a chuckle, delighted by the ease with which Fiona had ensnared the difficult queen rider's attention.

"Catching wings," Fiona murmured approvingly and then, with a cry that startled everyone she shouted, "Sky wings! Skyleader!"

Xhinna raced out before Fiona could formally pin the appellation on her.

▼ ▼ ▼

Xhinna was glad she did not make assignments of the new wings until she'd met with their leaders. She had a quick talk with them, outlining their duties and the problems of high sky flight before inviting Avarra and Jerilli to join them for a more in-depth conversation.

Reflecting on the numerous times she and Jirana had ridden in Search, she knew that the odds were more than even that any blue or green rider would be female. The older riders, in a distinct but revered minority, found the change both difficult and pleasing.

"At least I don't have to look at your old scarred face all the time!" was a common refrain among some of them. Several had been skeptical initially, believing that women wouldn't be up to the rigors of riding a fighting dragon, but Xhinna had been at the forefront of dismantling that concern. Still, she found herself having to fight the fear that these new wingleaders and their wings had been assigned to her because they weren't considered good enough to fight in "proper" wings.

When she thought about it, though, she realized that if fighting Thread at the heights worked as well as it had the first time, it would be *these* six wings that would bear the brunt of fighting Thread for the foreseeable future—not the "proper" wings flying in the thicker, warmer air near the ground. So it would be up to Xhinna to be sure that these wings could meet the challenge.

All the faces were familiar to her. They looked at her expectantly and almost with awe. She'd Searched them; she'd assured them as young girls and women that they *could* become dragonriders, that there was a hope for them far beyond the dank confines of their dying cotholds and fallow fields. She, Jirana, Taria, and a few others had been the ones to warn them for the first time about *between*, to bring them forward in time from the end of the Plague years to the lush Western Isle where they had begun new lives.

Warmed by this realization, Xhinna smiled at them.

"I don't know what you've been told, but we're here to save Pern," she said, plunging into a recounting of the past several days leading up to the high-altitude battle with Thread.

"So we find the Thread, fall with it until it streams, and burn it out of the sky?" Maleena, the Southriver wingleader, summarized when Xhinna had finished.

"Precisely," Xhinna said emphatically.

"But—up that high, how do we breathe?" Kalee of Southern Weyr asked.

"*That* is the problem and why we're only flying blues and greens up high," Xhinna said. "The blues and greens are the only ones small enough that the others can safely catch them if they run out of air."

"I've got two browns for wingseconds," Torra of Western Weyr said. "They're good flyers; I hate to lose them."

"You won't," Xhinna told her firmly. "One of my wingseconds flies a brown, too."

"So what does he do?"

"Well, this last Threadfall he flew with us," Xhinna admitted. "But now, we'll have the browns form up with the queens and bronzes as catchers."

"Queens and bronzes?" someone asked, the exact moment someone else echoed, "Catchers?"

"We're going to start your wings the way we started the others," Xhinna said as she told Tazith to send in Avarra and Jerilli. "We'll start by training you on flying higher, then on flying up to the Dawn Sisters—"

"When do we get to fight Thread?" Maleena asked. "We'd started firestone training, but—"

"You won't stop," Xhinna told her. "In fact, we've accelerated it—" She paused as Avarra and Jerilli entered. "—and we're working on new tactics." She waved for the other two wingleaders to take seats and was pleased when they chose to sit supportively on either side of her. Xhinna introduced them briefly and then continued, "I was just saying how we're going to accelerate our firestone training—"

"I've got a plan here," Avarra said, tapping a slate protruding from the carisak hanging off her shoulder. Xhinna started to say something, but the other interrupted, adding, "And before you ask, I worked it through with Danirry and R'ney already."

Xhinna nodded. "I was thinking that we could pair each new wing with one of the older wings—"

"That's inefficient," Avarra said. "It makes more sense if you take your wing and train them." She glanced to Jerilli, who nodded. "We can continue the space watch while you're training them, and then we can start rotating their wings up through the space watch while training with the resting wings."

Xhinna raised an eyebrow and turned to Jerilli, who nodded.

"Well," Xhinna said a bit bemusedly, "it appears we've got everything all figured out!"

"Not quite," Avarra said. Xhinna turned to her. "Apparently Jepara and Jirana want to be involved in the altitude training." She glanced at the other wingleader and rose to her feet, gesturing for Jerilli to precede her. "So, while we're working ourselves to the bone, we'll leave you to handle that little thing!"

The three new wingleaders laughed at the dismayed expression on Xhinna's face.

In the end, it was not as much a "little thing" as Avarra had so blithely surmised, nor was it as big a thing as Xhinna had feared. Partly that was because R'ney and Danirry had already discussed the situation and had several solutions in mind, and partly because, for all her prickliness, Jepara was too eager to be doing something useful to be difficult for long.

Jirana was a different matter, and by the end of the day Xhinna found herself exasperated at the way the girl shadowed her throughout all the exercises.

When they finally returned for the evening meal, Xhinna was ready to tear strips out of the youngster and bore down on her at the High Kitchen with just that intent.

"Jirana," she began sternly as she seated herself opposite the young queen rider—and then she stopped. The other five green queen riders were all at the same table, all chewing slowly and looking not just tired, but subdued. When she noticed that while they cast nervous glances toward her, they reserved their most worried looks for

Jirana, she changed her tone and her words in a heartbeat. "What is it, little one?"

"Nothing," Jirana replied morosely. Xhinna made a derisive noise and the dark-haired, dark-eyed trader girl looked up at her, shaking her head. "Nothing you can change."

Instead of returning to her dinner, Jirana kept her eyes on Xhinna, tracing every line in her face, scrutinizing her as though trying to drink a permanent image through her eyes to store in her brain—an image to keep when the original was lost.

Xhinna was stunned by the implications. She reached forward to touch Jirana's hand, but the girl jerked it back as if stung—or touched by a cold spirit.

Xhinna realized that she could think of nothing to say to someone who had seen her death somewhere in the future. She looked away, her lips going tight, then looked down at her plate. In the distance she heard some babies cry and thought of her Xelinan, and then of Taria, of Tarena, of Taralin, of all the babies that she wouldn't—

"No," she said firmly, bringing her eyes back up to meet Jirana's. The queen rider looked back at her in mild surprise. Commandingly, Xhinna said to her, "Finish your dinner."

Jirana's eyes flashed for a moment, but she complied, eating quickly and silently.

"Done?" Xhinna asked when Jirana put down her fork. The girl nodded and Xhinna rose. "Come on, then."

The other young queen riders looked at Jirana, afraid to offer support, desperate to help.

"I'm going to talk to her alone," Xhinna told them, trying to make her tone light. They didn't seem very relieved at her words; Xhinna sighed and gestured for Jirana to follow her.

Outside, she led the girl up to the tops of the broom trees. In the dead of winter, cold breezes blew that cut through the warmth of wher-hide jackets and scarves built to withstand the cold of *between*, but the air was fresh, brisk—alive.

Xhinna found a spot that still had thick leaves and sat cross-legged. She beckoned Jirana to sit in front of her and the youngster complied, scooting her back against Xhinna's chest tightly for both warmth and contact. Xhinna reached up and ran her splayed fingers through the girl's fine, dark hair. Jirana leaned back contentedly.

It had been a special thing that had grown up between them in the past couple of Turns: that Xhinna and Jirana would trade turns combing knots out of each other's hair although, in truth, as Jirana had the longer hair it was more Xhinna who did the combing and Jirana who did the luxuriating. But for Xhinna it was like really having the little sister she'd always wished for—a relationship entirely different from the one she had with Taria. There was a strange comfort in it, the warmth of a shared ritual, a hidden joke, a chance to love and be loving in the way that only sisters could.

"I'm going to die," Xhinna said, leaning forward so that her soft words carried to Jirana's ear.

The girl jerked and then leaned back again as Xhinna continued stroking her hair.

"Yes." The word was whipped away by the evening winds, but not before Xhinna heard it.

"You're going to die," Xhinna said, her lips close to Jirana's left ear.

"Someday," Jirana agreed.

"I'm not dead yet," Xhinna said. Jirana jerked out of her hands and turned to stare at her. Xhinna smiled. "Don't kill me ahead of time."

With a sob, Jirana turned around and thrust herself against Xhinna, wrapping her arms tightly around her and crying uncontrollably.

"I wish it were me!" she said when she finally found enough air to speak.

"And *I* wish it weren't," Xhinna replied firmly.

Jirana's brows came together in confusion.

"I'd love to live to see you old. I'd love to see your children, your loves, to see your queen's clutches," Xhinna said. "But I'd much rather *not* see all that than have *you* miss it."

"I want you with me," Jirana said. She bit her lip and beat against Xhinna's chest feebly with her fists. "It's not fair! It's not fair! It's not fair!"

She collapsed against Xhinna again, muttering into her chest, "And it hurts so much."

"Would it hurt less if you could share it with someone?" Xhinna asked, cupping her arms around the young rider's back and rocking slowly back and forth.

"It'd just hurt them, too," Jirana muttered despairingly.

"If anything happens to me, you talk to Seban," Xhinna said. Jirana looked up at her. "He's been through so much—he'll hear you. You can share with him."

"I'd much prefer to talk to you," Jirana insisted.

"And I, you," Xhinna agreed. "And so, now, is there anything else you'd like to tell me?"

"I could be wrong," Jirana said in a small voice. "I hope I'm wrong."

Xhinna wasn't sure how much credence to put in the young Seer's hopes. Thus far, she'd been right about everything.

In the end, Xhinna decided to take her own advice and said nothing about the incident to Taria or anyone else. From the looks of the five young green-queen riders, she guessed that they suspected something of what was up but did not know for certain.

K'dan, however, approached her late the next day, looking troubled.

"I'd like you to double the watch," he told her without preamble. He explained that he and Fiona had been arguing over the frequency of the Falls. Given that no Thread had fallen on the Northern Continent until the dustfalls first seen at the start of the next Turn, there might be nothing to worry about. Then he added, "But . . ."

"'Better safe than sorry,'" Xhinna quoted, grinning at him and raising a hand in a salute. "As you wish, Weyrleader."

And so she'd reorganized the watch, so that her wing flew midmorning over Benden and mid-evening over the Eastern Isle. Maleena, Kalee, and Torra were disappointed with the changes but Xhinna felt that they could easily be left in Jepara's extremely capable hands.

"By the end of this week, at the most, you'll be ready to join us," Xhinna had promised them. Only one of their riders had succumbed to the lack of air the way Mirressa had, and the blue and his rider had been quickly recovered by R'ney, Jepara, and the other queens—much to their satisfaction. The promise mollified them all, except for Torra, who seemed to have greater empathy than most and had noticed the worried way Jirana had been following Xhinna with her eyes.

"You'll be careful, won't you?" Torra had asked in a moment when she'd managed to get Xhinna out of earshot. "Jirana's really worried about you."

"I know," Xhinna had replied. "I'll be careful. I've lots to live for."

Torra opened her mouth, but could find nothing more to say.

Xhinna was just getting ready to return from her position in the evening sky over Benden Weyr when she spotted it—a dark smudge, spots . . .

Thread! she cried. Tazith bellowed, turning his head toward her even as she loosened the opening of the nearest firestone sack. Feeding him chunks of firestone, she commanded him to fall upon the Thread, ordering the rest of her wing and the wings of Jerilli and Avarra to join her.

They fell from the dark nothing of space through the freezing cold of the thin, unbreathable air until they were approaching the smudges of Thread and then—

Tazith flamed. In an instant, flames erupted to her left and right and suddenly the sky was full of flaming dragons.

Thread! Thread falls over Eastern!

Who? Xhinna thought in surprise, and then her face crumpled into horror as she thought of the unguarded Eastern Isle, lush and—

Tazith, go! she shouted. *Rouse the Weyrs!*

In an instant they were *between*, and then Xhinna was in the air over the Eastern Isle, searching frantically for Thread. She found it, and Tazith started flaming unthinkingly. They dived, rose, dived again, always keeping to the highest heights, the great blue's lungs laboring to heave in enough air to breathe, Xhinna gasping with him, unable to tell if it were her need or her sympathetic imitation of his need and—

Maleena, Torra, to me! Xhinna called, adding, *Tazith, tell Avarra to lead the Fall over Benden.*

I have, Tazith relayed as he turned to her for more firestone. *Lurenth says that the Weyrs are flying over Eastern.*

Xhinna had a sudden memory of flashing light in the distance the day she had brought K'dan and the other weyrlings back in time from the Eastern Isle to Western—that had been today! The lights had been dragons flaming!

She shook the thought from her mind as Tazith relayed Avarra's answer to her, and she led her wing in the assault against the fresh-streaming Thread.

She lost all track of time. Suddenly she and Tazith were hovering in the high, thin air, and Xhinna realized that she was shivering uncontrollably.

Come down! A voice called to them and Xhinna found herself obeying, returning to the Sky Weyr. She smiled as she made out the shape of a little girl standing at the top of the Kitchen Hall's broom tree: Jirana.

"Drink this up, put this on," Jirana said, peremptorily handing Xhinna a mug of hot *klah* and a blanket the moment the blue rider hit the top branches of the broom tree. "And when you're done, I've warm mash for Tazith." She waved a hand at the blue commandingly, shouting, "And you're to eat it all, no excuses!"

Tazith rumbled in reluctant compliance. Jirana, seeing that Xhinna was taking care of herself, hefted a steaming bucket and hauled it over to the blue's muzzle. "Eat it all! You're practically frozen!"

Xhinna found herself shivering in the blanket and sank to her haunches, then sat cross-legged, twitching the blanket more tightly around her as she sipped the marvelously warm liquid.

"The others?" she asked when her teeth stopped chattering. The sound of wings and riders landing half-answered her question, with Jirana saying, "You were the worst; they're being taken care of."

Xhinna looked around. Aside from her wing they were alone. "Where's Fiona?"

Jirana paced back to Tazith and stood in front of Xhinna, considering her words.

"Where is everyone?"

"There were burrows," Jirana told her simply. "They've lost a quarter of Eastern Isle. They're building a fire-break."

"What?" Xhinna said, starting to rise only to be waved back down.

"They'll have it under control," Jirana said. "It was worse than they'd thought. The burrows spread quicker than they normally do—the soil here is too rich."

"And Avarra? Jerilli? The others?"

"They're coming back now," Jirana said as another figure joined them: Taria. Xhinna patted the ground beside her, and the weary green rider collapsed, leaning against her and murmuring gratefully when Xhinna spread the blanket inclusively over her shoulders.

Xhinna recalled her duties and checked in with Tazith. *Have R'ney and Danirry report in.*

Even as she thought that, she recalled the frantic moments that had just passed and—

"Danirry?" Xhinna said.

"We couldn't catch her," Jirana said, the tremble in her voice suddenly loud in Xhinna's ears. Why hadn't she heard it before? Why hadn't she noticed that the girl was crying?

"We tried," Jirana said, lowering herself to her knees in front of Xhinna. "We tried. Laspanth and I almost caught her but—but we couldn't—she slid off and we—"

"We lost her," another voice added from the darkness in stone-cold tones. It was Jepara. She came up through the passage from the High Kitchen and sat next to Jirana, looking at Xhinna, her eyes spangled with tears. "I'm sorry, Xhinna, we tried but—we weren't enough, we weren't fast enough and—"

"Where is she?" Xhinna asked softly, trying to concentrate beyond the sound of Taria's crying.

"She fell into the sea," Jirana said. "We couldn't find her." She turned to Jepara. "They dived into the water, but they couldn't find her." She was silent for a moment and then offered in solace, "I don't think they felt any pain. They were out of air—they'd fainted and they didn't even know what had happened."

Xhinna wrapped a hand around Taria's and clasped it tight. The green rider clenched her hand in return.

Xhinna looked at Jirana, saw the red-rimmed eyes in the dim evening light, saw the darker look in them, and realized—Jirana had known.

Worse, in the young queen rider's eyes she could plainly see the future. Without words, Jirana's sad, miserable expression told her: You're next.

TWENTY
▼▼▼▼▼▼▼▼▼▼▼▼

Farewell to a Dreamer

"Now we know the worst," T'mar said as the Weyrleaders gathered in the Council Room of Sky Weyr's stone hall early the next morning.

"True," K'dan agreed, "but we also can now plot our Falls, and there's good news in that."

"Good news?" H'nez echoed skeptically. He gestured eastward. "One burrow and we nearly lost a whole island! What happens if a burrow strikes here?"

"We'll have to be certain that none does," T'mar said with a wave of his hand. He nodded to K'dan. "Your Sky wings worked admirably. Why can't *we* use them?"

"We could," K'dan agreed. "But the dangers of fighting Thread so high were amply demonstrated—"

"One rider is not a great loss," H'nez said.

"One experienced rider," K'dan countered. "In two Falls, we've lost one—"

"That's much better than we've seen in any Fall on the Northern Continent," C'tov reminded him. He waved a hand at K'dan in sympathy. "Any loss is hard, and by all accounts, your Danirry was a marvelous and talented person but—"

"I know," K'dan said. He shook himself and continued, "But now that we know when the Falls will come here, perhaps we don't need the Sky wings anymore."

"What?" C'tov said.

"We were lucky," K'dan said.

"I'm not sure I could say that after fighting that burrow in Eastern," H'nez replied.

"It took nearly three full Weyrs to even start to control that mess," X'lerin said, shaking his head in awe.

"If we'd caught it sooner, it wouldn't have been so much trouble," K'dan said.

"I don't know," T'mar replied. "That burrow was faster and rooted in deeper than we've ever seen them—we were lucky to lose only as much as we did."

"And that was nearly a quarter of the whole island," H'nez said. He was still amazed. "It was *so* fast!"

"We were hampered by nightfall, by not knowing what was happening," K'dan countered. "But now that we know, we'll be better prepared—"

"Better yet, if we can use the Skies," C'tov observed.

"K'dan, you said we were lucky?" T'mar said, redirecting the conversation.

"Yes," K'dan said, tapping a parchment in front of him. The tanners of the Weyrs weren't quite as good at the craft of making skins usable for writing as others back on the Northern Continent, but it sufficed for simple drawings. "From what we recall, with these two Falls we can predict that we'll have another Fall—this time over the southern end of both islands, twenty-six days from now."

"That long?"

"That accurate?"

"Actually, the Fall should come at about three in the morning, our time," K'dan said. "It will match the Falls over Benden Weyr, Bitra, and Igen Weyr—the first Fall that was flown by Benden and Telgar."

"So we have time to plan and prepare," T'mar said, nodding thoughtfully. The others looked relieved.

"And then?" H'nez prompted. "When's our next Fall?"

"Nine days and nine hours later, we'll have a Fall that brushes the southern end of our Eastern Isle," K'dan said. "That's the same time as the Fall over Igen and Ista's tip."

"How long?"

"It starts, if we're right, just about halfway over the Southern bay and peters out over the sea far to the west."

"Thread falls from northeast to southwest," T'mar reminded them. He glanced at K'dan. "So, not a full Fall, then?"

K'dan nodded. "Probably two or three hours at most."

"Better than six," H'nez muttered approvingly. He cocked an eye at K'dan. "And then?"

"We've a break for fifteen days and fifteen hours, and then we'll have the same Fall we just fought all over again," K'dan said, pursing his lips tightly.

"Nine and nine, fifteen and fifteen?" C'tov asked.

"Each Fall comes three days and three hours after the last one," K'dan said. "These islands are so small that more Falls miss than hit."

"But back home?" T'mar asked. No matter that they'd been on the Western Isle nearly three Turns, the Northern Continent was still home to all.

K'dan frowned, trying to think. "After Benden and Keroon, it would be Nerat and Upper Crom—but it didn't happen."

H'nez gave him a questioning look and the Sky Weyrleader explained, "The first signs of Thread were the dustfalls over Fort, High Reaches Tip, and Southern Tillek—there was no mention of dustfall over Nerat or Crom." He shrugged. "Probably the dustfall was dispersed by high winds, so no one noticed it. It's winter; the weather is usually too cold for Thread—colder up on high, as we now know."

"So, the Sky wings—you think we should disband them?" H'nez asked K'dan.

"Two queens couldn't catch one blue," K'dan said. "Six wings are now completely demoralized, their riders shaken." He pursed his lips and shook his head. "They've learned a lot about flying high and the dangers of thin air. Let them go back to their Weyrs, split them up so that they can spread the knowledge and forget the pain."

H'nez shook his head doubtfully. "Dragons and riders will die, K'dan, no matter how much we wish otherwise."

"I know," K'dan said. "But to have them freeze to death or die by asphyxiation?" He shook his head. "That's not honorable."

F*iona says you're to sleep,* Tazith said as soon as Xhinna's eyelids fluttered open. *You're to rest until you're cranky, she said.*

Xhinna's lips twitched: It sounded like her blue was quoting the Weyrwoman directly.

She was surrounded by warmth. Taria was there and smaller bodies and—

Xhinna jumped out of the bed with an angry bellow. She threw on robes and cinched them tight against the cold morning air before racing out of their quarters, leaving a bewildered Taria behind.

Where's R'ney? Xhinna demanded of her blue. Tazith replied equitably with an image, and Xhinna stalked off. She found the brown rider sleeping in an alcove of the walled dormitory. When she moved slowly over to him, she noticed small eyes looking up at her and heard a thin gasp, almost a mew of despair.

Xhinna slipped under the covers, slid up tight next to R'ney, and pulled little Davinna between them, cuddling and shushing the distraught baby.

"She wanted her mother," R'ney murmured, awakened by the shifting of bodies. "I think she wants milk." In a very small voice he added, "I can't give her any."

Xhinna shushed him softly and pulled the baby to her. She'd been ready to wean Xelinan, but she'd held off and was grateful now that she could ease the baby's discomfort.

Davinna was fussy, but soon enough she fell back asleep, content at the warmth of Xhinna's body and the sound of R'ney's gentle breathing.

R'ney surfaced again long enough to ask, "What are you doing here?"

"I promised," Xhinna said. "I promised her I'd look after hers and her heart's."

"You're a good one, the best," R'ney said, reaching a hand to brush her cheek.

"Sleep," she ordered, moving his hand back to his chest. R'ney, exhausted by grief and the hard fight the day before, needed no more urging.

Hours later, Xhinna was surprised by a muffled noise of surprise and woke to see Mirressa looking down at her.

"I came for the baby," the green rider said. "I figured—"

"I only had a little," Xhinna said, grabbing little Davinna and passing her out from under the covers to Mirressa's waiting hands. "She'll probably want more."

"She's got a whole wing," Mirressa said, biting her lips to keep back her tears. And then, forcefully, she said, "You know it: She's got a whole wing!"

"'Always and forever,'" Xhinna said, quoting the vow she'd given Danirry on the birth of Davinna.

Mirressa gulped in agreement and rushed off before her grief erupted over the fussy child in her arms.

"Where's the baby?" R'ney asked a few moments later.

"Mirressa has her," Xhinna replied. She was surprised when R'ney kept moving, trying to force himself past her. "She's okay, don't worry."

"I'm not worried, I need to get up, there's work to be done," R'ney said. He gave her a quizzical look. "Why aren't you up?"

"Fiona told us to rest," Xhinna said.

"'Rest when you're dead,'" R'ney said, quoting the old dragonriders jest. "If you're not going to get up, let me pass so I can get up."

Xhinna thought for a moment and then got up. She cocked an eyebrow at her remaining wingsecond and said, "Are you going to be all right?"

"As soon as I get some breakfast," R'ney allowed. "What about you?"

"I'm going to check on Taria and the babies," Xhinna said. She nodded back toward his bunk. "I want you sleeping in our quarters from now on." She caught the mulish look on his face and corrected herself. "I at least want you to consider it home and leave Davinna with us. We've got enough little ones that one more won't matter."

"She matters to me," R'ney said feelingly.

"Of course," Xhinna told him. "And you know I didn't mean it that way." She met his eyes. "But if you could, I think it'd be best if you stayed with me and Taria."

R'ney squinted. "What aren't you telling me?"

"I'd take it as a personal favor," Xhinna told him honestly.

R'ney held her gaze for a moment longer before reluctantly yielding in the contest of wills. "I'll think about it."

Xhinna's wing gathered slowly at one table in the High Kitchen, late for breakfast. Mirressa and Taria came together, Mirressa giving R'ney a brief smile before assuring him, "Javissa's watching the babies. Fiona's with her."

"And the baby?"

Mirressa smiled. "She's asleep." Mirressa cast a wistful eye on the food spread on the table and R'ney busied himself making sure that the nursing mother had her fill. Xhinna was also hungrier than usual, filling her plate three times before settling back, content.

R'ney picked at his food until J'valin and Mirressa chided him, and then, to stop their nagging, the brown rider emptied his plate twice before announcing loudly that he was full.

A silence descended on the group and Xhinna tried to think what to say to relieve it. Finally, in irritation, she rose from the table and strode out of the hall.

She and Tazith flew out far beyond the usual bounds of the Weyr and landed in a field and she searched it, looking for something to mark the blue rider's passing but found nothing and, in disgust, flew back to the Meeyu Plateau. When she saw R'ney's Rowerth down in the slight valley below, she told Tazith to land beside him.

She found R'ney near the sluiceway that he and Danirry had built. She stood there for several moments, mute, trying to think of something to say. Finally, "She saved Pern, you know."

R'ney turned to her, silent.

"You did, too," Xhinna said. She gestured to the sluiceway. "The gold helped save us. We used it to rebuild where nothing else would work."

R'ney nodded silently. It was a discovery Turns old now, the realization that the gold dust could be used to finance the rebuilding that would be needed to support the return of the Western dragons to the Northern Continent. It wasn't enough to have two thousand dragons—they had to be fed, too. Without the gold to encourage the growth of herds, there would be too few herdbeasts for the dragons' needs. And the gold had already helped those desperate to rebuild and recover from the Plague that had killed so many. That it had gone more to Crom, Igen, Keroon, and Telgar had as much to do with who had been sending it as with where it was needed.

"And she saved us again last night," Xhinna continued. It had been Danirry who had warned about the Thread falling over the Eastern Isle—her warning had been her last words.

"I know," R'ney said, the words coming raw out of his throat.

"More people will die to save Pern," Xhinna told him.

Again, R'ney nodded. At last he turned to her. "Your little one, the trader girl, she told you, didn't she?"

"No," Xhinna said. "But I think she knew."

"And she thinks you're next, doesn't she?"

Xhinna said nothing, but prodded by the look in his eyes, she nodded once, curtly.

"Must be hard."

"No, not really."

"Not you," R'ney said. "Jirana. Bearing all that weight on her own."

They stood together, silent, their eyes darting around the clearing until finally, R'ney said, "You know, she doesn't need anything."

Xhinna looked over at him, surprised.

"Danirry," R'ney said to clarify. He nodded at the sluice and the mud and then pointed to the Meeyu Plateau. "We can't forget her, not even if we try."

"I'll miss her," Xhinna confessed. She remembered the young, painfully thin girl she had first met at Crom Hold, and recalled how strong that girl had grown in the Turns since. She had saved Pern— twice. Surely that was worth more than any memorial.

"I'll miss you," R'ney said, meeting her eyes and then looking away into the distance.

"As I told Jirana," Xhinna replied testily, "I'm not gone yet."

Xhinna's hope to make Danirry's remembrance a simple affair for her wing only didn't survive its first encounter with Jepara and, judging by the raised eyebrows from Fiona later, wouldn't have lasted any longer if the obstreperous queen rider hadn't been the first to find Xhinna.

"No, no, no—you can't!" Jepara insisted, her voice rising with each word.

"It's the wing's affair," Xhinna said, taken aback.

"Did she not belong to the Weyr, too?" Jepara demanded, pressing on before Xhinna could reply to ask, "And wasn't she one of the first new riders to Impress? And didn't she suggest sluicing for gold?" Xhinna was given just enough time to nod before Jepara stormed on, "And shouldn't we all have the chance to thank and honor her for all she's done for us?"

"She wouldn't want a big fuss," Xhinna protested.

"*She's* not here!" Jepara said. "Her wishes don't count!"

Xhinna stared at her in surprise, and Jepara moved closer, holding her hands out entreatingly. "It's our chance to say good-bye to her." Jepara closed her eyes tightly and when she opened them again, the corners were wet with the tears that she'd only half-suppressed. "We're going to lose more before this Pass is over, Xhinna. Do you really want to start this way?"

"What do you suggest?" Xhinna asked, coming as close as she could to admitting how little energy she had after the strain of the past several days.

Jepara leaned down to look deep into Xhinna's eyes and then, reaching a hand to touch her wrist, said quietly, "How about you let me organize this? As one of her Weyrwomen?"

Xhinna nodded silently.

▼ ▼ ▼

And so now, as the sun matched the point at which Danirry's final lifesaving cry had been uttered, the six Weyrs were all gathered, their wings arrayed in Flights and the Flights stacked on top of each other as the queens of all flew out to sea, their path lit by the dragons of all five Weyrleaders.

In the center of the V formation a single bright light—a torch to mark the lost rider and dragon—was seen, falling to the sea and sizzling out as it hit the water.

Then, in a brilliant burst of light, all the oldest dragons breathed fire into the air.

And then it was dark, quiet, and cold.

Weyr by Weyr they departed for their homes, until only the Sky wings remained stubbornly behind.

Rest well, blue rider, Xhinna thought, knowing her words would be echoed by Tazith to all the dragons surrounding them. *You've earned it.*

TWENTY-ONE
▼▼▼▼▼▼▼▼▼▼▼▼

Feast for the Fallen

"K'dan approved it," J'keran said as he greeted the returning Sky riders with a cask of special brew. Fiona had told Xhinna to have them land on the Meeyu Plateau, and Xhinna was surprised to see their path illuminated by a huge bonfire that had not been there when they'd left. J'keran waved at the cask, adding, "Guaranteed to do the job and no more."

Xhinna nodded gratefully to the brown rider.

K'dan moved forward, his prized gitar hung over his shoulder. "Tonight I am here as harper." He nodded into the distance, and Xhinna was surprised to see X'lerin step out of the shadows.

She felt a hand on her shoulder and raised her opposite hand to cover it—from the angle, she knew it was R'ney's hand. Taria moved in to her other side and wrapped an arm around Xhinna's waist.

"Weyrleader," Xhinna said, nodding to X'lerin. "Will you drink with us?"

"My pleasure," X'lerin said. He nodded to J'keran to do the honors, and in moments the cask was broached and mugs filled. X'lerin took a quick sip, choked, and passed the mug to Xhinna. "Wingleader."

Xhinna took a quick sip and was surprised as fire roared down to her belly. She passed the cup up to R'ney, who took his sip, then coughed, "It's smooth!" before passing it over to Taria.

"The children—" Taria started to protest.

"Tonight, the Weyr looks after its children," K'dan called out loudly. "Isn't that so, Weyrleader?"

"It is," X'lerin replied with a firm nod and a gesture to J'keran, who was steadily filling up more mugs and passing them around. "And harper, have you a proper song for the occasion?"

"I think I do," K'dan said, looking mournfully at J'keran, who laughed and said, "Never let it be said Sky Weyr would parch its harper!" He passed a full mug to K'dan, who took a quick gulp, coughed, and looked at the mug with eyes wide, before setting it down carefully beside him and bringing his gitar around to his front.

"*Drummer, beat,*" he began in a loud, clear voice. He looked around the group waiting with a hand ready for the next chord.

"*Piper, blow,*" Taria responded in clear rich tones.

"*Harper, strike,*" K'dan sang out. He eyed the crowd.

"*And soldier, go,*" R'ney's tearful voice rang out.

Xhinna felt all eyes on her and she stepped forward and nodded to K'dan. It took her two tries to get the words past her heart-stopped throat:

"*Free the flame and sear the grasses.*"

And then the entire plateau shook as all the riders sang out:

"*Till the dawning Red Star passes.*"

Xhinna reached for the next mug and drained it in one gulp. K'dan waited a moment before launching into a rollicking tune that had all of them singing and laughing and stepping together.

After that, Xhinna lost all track of time.

She awoke in a strange place and it took her a long while to realize that it was one of the stone hall rooms, filled with soft mattresses, pillows, quilts, and snoring riders. She tried to move, but a small arm pushed her back.

"You did not—" Xhinna began loudly as she recognized the arm and then, as the protest from her ears registered achingly on her brain, she reduced her voice to a whisper. "You did not spend the night here."

"Shh," Jirana told her muzzily, shaking her head in a motion that could either have been negation or irritation.

The young queen rider's advice was easy to take, as Xhinna's head told her that whatever K'dan had decided, J'keran's drink was far, far stronger than any she'd ever tasted.

I'm bringing klah. The voice seemed to speak quietly in her head. Xhinna looked around and then turned as a path of light split the dark of the room and someone entered. Lorana.

Jirana slowly got to her knees and then helped Xhinna up. Together the two of them made their way to Lorana and out into the morning light. Xhinna was just about to drop the curtain back when a hand intercepted it and Jepara, her eyes beaming, joined them.

Lorana led them to another interior room, the Council Room, also thankfully darkened.

Xhinna smelled not only hot *klah* but warm rolls and fresh butter. Her stomach flipped briefly, but then settled down again, eager for sustenance.

They sat around the table, eating and drinking quietly until Xhinna felt well enough to question Jirana. She did so with a single raised eyebrow and a demanding look.

"I had one sip," Jirana said defensively. She made a sour face. "Yuck! I don't know why anyone would drink that stuff."

"And your mother knows?" Xhinna demanded.

"Lorana does," Jirana said. "And I'm old enough—"

"You've only—"

"I've nearly thirteen Turns," Jirana cut across. "Not that I intend to drink myself silly like J'keran or—" She glanced significantly at Xhinna and then over to Jepara, but said nothing.

"Children drink wine mixed with water just after they're weaned," Jepara said on Jirana's behalf.

"That was *not* wine," Xhinna said.

"You're ignoring the point," Jirana said, grabbing another roll and applying a very liberal amount of butter before tearing into it. After she swallowed, she said, "I'd permission, I was responsible, and—"

"You appointed yourself my keeper," Xhinna said.

Jirana, to her surprise, grinned. "Actually, I was in charge of your drink."

Xhinna's eyes went wide and she turned to Jepara who tried, quite unsuccessfully, to look innocent. "And you were the shoulder to lean on?"

"I was one of your carcass bearers," Jepara said, smiling sweetly. She nodded to Jirana. "Her orders were to be certain that your cup was never empty." The older queen rider smirked in positive delight as she added, "She was quite dutiful."

"R'ney?"

"K'dan," Jepara said.

"Taria?"

"Me," Lorana said.

"A queen or bronze for every member of your wing," Jepara told her. "Of course, we had to double up some, but it was not as hard as you'd think."

"And our duties?" Xhinna asked.

"Completed where necessary, or deferred," Lorana said. She leaned forward. "After all you've done, it was only fitting."

"We won't be doing this for every fallen rider?"

"I don't know, it certainly seems like a good idea," Jepara said, her eyes dancing mischievously.

Xhinna was speechless. Jirana refilled her mug and passed it back to her. "More *klah*?"

It took the wing the better part of the day to recover from the evening's revelry, and when they did, their mood was dour.

In summer and spring, the broom trees provided a marvelous shelter and home. In the midst of winter, they were not so accommodating, and only the large wooden walls carefully attached to the many platforms that had been built below the treetops provided the needed shelter. Building the walls and setting them up took time and effort, so winter shelter was necessarily very confining and scarce.

The stone hall on the burnt plateau—Meeyu Plateau—provided

relief, but it was actually easier to expand the platforms beneath the broom trees than to carefully construct or expand the fitted stone hall.

"How much longer until we can return?" Alimma asked querulously as the wing gathered at one long table for dinner in the High Kitchen.

"We've yet to mark Turn's end," R'ney said, "so we've got eight months—nearly nine here yet."

"We're still so far back in time that Lorana hasn't yet discovered the cure," Mirressa added. "We can't possibly go back until after that at the earliest."

"That's when D'gan and Telgar were lost *between*," Taria said. She pursed her lips. "Will we hear that again, here?"

"I don't know," Xhinna said, making a note to bring it up with K'dan when she could.

"That's when Lorana lost her queen, isn't it?" Jirana spoke up unexpectedly beside them. R'ney raised an eyebrow at the young gold rider, but moved down the bench, motioning for her to join them.

"And Seban will lose his blue Serth," Xhinna added, glancing around for the blue rider and wondering why she hadn't seen him recently.

"And so many others," Taria agreed sadly. Her eyes took on a distant look and she grew so quiet that Xhinna shot her a troubled look. Taria noticed it and said apologetically, "It's just that I remember when D'gan went. His son, D'lin, went for help and . . . no one ever found him."

"Was he lost *between*?" R'ney wondered. The others shrugged. "Wasn't he found when D'gan was rescued?"

"No," Taria said. The others looked at her, so she explained, "I asked Lorana." She made a sad face. "He was a nice lad; I'd hoped he'd been saved."

"Must have been hard on D'gan," R'ney said.

Xhinna found herself nodding. It was a moment before she realized that silence had descended around her and still another before a cough alerted her to the arrival of a newcomer.

It was Jepara. Xhinna looked up at her.

"So what's the plan, Sky leader?" Jepara asked, nodding toward Jirana. "My small ears have gone quiet."

Xhinna gave her a blank look. To her surprise, Jepara scooped up Jirana, took her seat, and placed the younger rider in her lap before leaning forward conspiratorially.

"I've seen the charts," Jepara told them.

"And?"

"And Thread should fall at Nerat and Upper Crom tomorrow morning," Jepara said. R'ney, Taria, and the others all glanced questioningly at Xhinna, who nodded reluctantly.

"But K'dan says that no Fall, not even dust, was reported," Xhinna said.

"Would it hurt to be certain?" Taria asked. Xhinna felt a tense agreement from the rest of the riders.

"It would be better if we had Lorana—" Xhinna broke off as she caught a jerky movement opposite the table. She eyed Jirana and Jepara both very carefully. "We'd need someone to give us a good image."

"That can be arranged," Jepara said with a wave of her hand.

"And firestone," Xhinna added.

"That you can get on your own just for the asking," Jepara said. "Especially if you make it clear that you'll be practicing with bronzes and browns."

"And queens?" Xhinna asked, raising an eyebrow suggestively.

"Well, at least two," Jepara agreed. "Although I'd heard that Meeya is getting antsy to do more flying, and perhaps Hannah, Karrina, and Latara."

"Just look?" Xhinna asked, trying to match Jepara's innocent tone.

"And where's the harm in that?" Jepara wondered.

"I can't see any," Taria replied, turning to R'ney and asking, "Can you?"

"It'd do us some good," R'ney replied. He raised an eyebrow at Xhinna. "What do you think?"

▼ ▼ ▼

Xhinna couldn't figure out why Taria acted so smug later that night, or why Jirana seemed so unworried when they gathered in the morning until Jepara said, "You're staying here, of course."

The queen rider cut off her outburst with a hand. "You must know that K'dan will be keeping his eye on you."

"And he won't notice that you and all the rest of the wing are missing?"

"Of course not!"

Xhinna gave her a skeptical look.

"Most of us will be here, training with you, practicing flaming just as he'd want," R'ney said, taking pity on his wingleader.

"And the missing ones will be dropping practice Thread?" Xhinna guessed.

"Exactly," Taria said. "It's just that some of the Thread droppers will need to gather the long willow leaves we use, and others will be up high, and in all that—"

"No one will notice a pair of missing dragons," Jirana said, smiling happily up at Xhinna.

"Well," Xhinna said, glancing warningly toward R'ney, "it's said that a wise wingleader leaves the hard work to her seconds."

"And we all know you're wise," Jepara said in a tone that was just shy of taunting.

Xhinna frowned, then looked around. "We're a wingsecond short—"

"Ah," R'ney said, shifting his stance in a way that showed his discomfort with the topic.

Xhinna hated pressing the issue, but felt she had to. "Under the circumstances, it'd be better if we were at our full strength." She turned her head toward J'valin, rider of blue Nerinath. His dragon was half a Turn younger than R'ney's brown Rowerth, but he was well grown.

"I was wondering," interjected a tenor voice as a figure emerged from the knot of riders, "if perhaps you'd be willing to let me . . ." It was J'keran.

"He's got experience," Jepara said, moving close to pitch her words for Xhinna's ears only.

Certainly he had experience—he'd fought Thread for nearly half a Turn, had nearly killed Xhinna in a drunken rage, and had taken Taria and her Coranth off to live as outlaws even to the point of trying to steal Candidates for Coranth's clutch.

His life was forfeit to her and she'd given it to the Weyr and, more specifically, to Jirana, whose Mrreow-claw injuries had nearly killed her. Since then, J'keran had slowly transformed from the young girl's guard to the guard of all the Hatching Grounds for all six Weyrs—and he took his duty very seriously. Since that day when Jirana had touched her queen Laspanth still in the shell and guided the dragon-riders to destroy all the ravaging tunnel snakes, not a single egg had been lost. Much—perhaps most—due to J'keran.

Xhinna could sense R'ney's outrage and Taria's . . . challenge—it was not contempt—as clearly as though both were dragons. She understood R'ney's feelings and spent a few moments coming to grips with Taria's odd emotions before nodding to the man who stood before her, projecting strength, honesty, and—unless she missed her guess—pure, unadulterated terror.

"Your duty's done," Xhinna told him. "You have earned back your honor and your life." Her eyes strayed to Jirana, who was bouncing on her feet, her throat moving with unspoken words, her eyes silently urging Xhinna on. "If the Weyrwoman is satisfied—"

"More than satisfied!" Jirana cried jubilantly.

"Then, with the Weyrleader's permission," Xhinna told J'keran, "I'd be honored to have you fly with us."

Xhinna felt Taria's fingers clasp around hers. Xhinna reached around and hugged her, then stood away, watching J'keran's reaction. She saw his eyes widen and then she nodded to him.

J'keran's brown Perinth was a fine mount, well grown, well loved, well trained, and proven in countless Falls and mating flights. Xhinna accepted that Perinth might outfly her blue Tazith, that Taria might smile once more at his attention, but she wasn't upset. Her bonds with Taria, born in youth and first love, were too strong now after Turns together for anyone to sever them.

"We'll need your Perinth to train with Sarurth, Laspanth, and Rowerth," Xhinna told him. J'keran nodded, encouraged by the beaming smile from Jirana. "But what about your guard duties?"

"I'll retain them, if I may," J'keran said. He raised a hand as he added, "There's only the one last Hatching, and that will be in a matter of weeks." He gave her a sad, wistful look that she understood too well—the greens had all chewed firestone and never again could he or Xhinna hope that there might be weyrlings sired by their dragons. "Besides," he added, nodding toward Jirana, "we've arranged a good watch."

"Very well," Xhinna said, "you'll train with the catchers. J'valin and Cliova will take first watch, followed by—"

"If it pleases you, Wingleader," R'ney cut across her words with a diffident look, "we've got that figured out already. What's needed now is to get on with the flaming before someone starts asking awkward questions."

Xhinna responded with a flurry of orders and a dismissive wave at the group of catchers.

In short order, she and Tazith were airborne over Eastern Isle, not far from the abandoned camp she'd fled nearly three Turns before.

Lorana says they're on station, Tazith relayed as Xhinna and three others waited for any sign of the green willow practice Thread they were supposed to be flaming.

Ten minutes later, she was bored and switched, having Tazith climb high to take on a round of practice-Thread flinging. They had just reached their position and were settling on an even path when—

Thread! Thread falls at Nerat! Mirressa's green Valcanth cried as the image from high in the dark blue sky came to Xhinna.

Tell them to follow it, Xhinna said, *then have the catchers move into position and have the wing—*

Lorana says we need to stay with the catchers, Tazith interrupted.

With a stubborn cry, Xhinna ordered Tazith to close up with the queens and the browns who flew as catchers.

They came out from *between* just as the other dragons bugled in distress and bunched close together.

Mirressa! Xhinna cried, seeing her and her green dragon tumbling toward them. Xhinna had just an instant to wonder who was trailing the Thread when the answer came to her and she cried: *Go, Tazith!*

Between again and back, high, high over the eastern edge of the Nerat peninsula—still lush and green even in midwinter.

Find it! Xhinna urged her blue as she strained her eyes for the telltale smudge of Thread. Her teeth were chattering, and she shivered from the multiple trips *between* and multiple returns to the high cold, airless spaces way above where dragons normally flew and flamed.

And then she saw it—a line of what looked like large pebbles or stones but dirtier. Tazith rumbled in agreement and turned his head for more firestone. Even as the small balls started to glow and spread into the long, thin wisps that were Thread, she and Tazith were diving on it, flaming. *Tell the others!*

They come, Tazith said. A moment later, he and Xhinna were surprised when he opened his huge jaws and no flame burst forth. *Warm,* the blue said to her.

Xhinna blinked in surprise. Her teeth weren't chattering anymore. She was warm, as if she were resting in a hot tub after a long day's flying and flaming. Idly she wondered why the air was so warm. And why didn't Tazith's flame burst around the Thread?

It was getting dark, too. The colors were going gray and darkness was closing around from behind her. But she was warm, Tazith was warm. It was nice being warm.

And then the darkness closed in.

TWENTY-TWO
▼▼▼▼▼▼▼▼▼▼▼▼

The Kiss of Hope

Someone was crying. They'd been crying a long time because they were in that awful, horrible heaving stage where they could barely breathe and when they did, all they could do was sob once more.

It was cold. The ground was cold. She was freezing.

Someone was kissing her.

"Breathe!" she heard someone beg. "Breathe, please breathe!"

Whoever was kissing her was doing a poor job. Xhinna tried to respond and then—

"Ewwww! Yuk!" another voice cried and the lips were gone as the voice spat, "*Ptah*, yuk! She tried to kiss me!"

"Move *away*!" another voice, the one that had ordered her to breathe, said irritably, and then there were lips on hers once more, lips that she knew, and suddenly Xhinna realized that she was alive, lying on cold, hard stone, and that the first kisser had been—

"Lift me up," she whispered as she broke the kiss and met Taria's tear-stained eyes. She reached for and found Taria's hand and Taria clenched it tightly. She saw resistance rise in Taria's eyes, but shook her head just enough to communicate her need. The green rider nodded just as lightly, then tightened her grip on Xhinna's arm and helped her to sit up, moving quickly to come around behind her, propping her back up with her knees.

"Ptah, ptui, ptui!" Jepara said, still trying disgustedly to remove the last vestiges of her life-giving kiss from her lips. She eyed Xhinna and said darkly, "Don't ever expect me to do that again!"

Xhinna heard a gasp and looked up to see Jirana launching herself at her.

"You're alive, you're alive, you're alive!" Jirana cried at the top of her lungs, grabbing Xhinna tightly around the middle and kissing her madly with relief. Jirana pulled back, her face crumpling as she said, "You were blue, you were dead. I saw it."

"And now you've seen me breathing the life back into her," Jepara said sourly. She looked down at Xhinna and ordered, "Don't *ever* make me have to do that again!"

"Thread?" Xhinna asked, finding it hard to breathe and even harder to speak.

Jirana shook her head in exasperation, then threw herself back to her feet and started dancing around once more, crying, "She's alive, she's alive, she's alive!"

"The Thread's gone," Taria said. "The rest of the wing managed it."

"We caught you just after Mirressa," J'keran's deep voice said from the distance.

"Mirressa?"

"She's well," Lorana said, moving into Xhinna's line of vision and smiling down at her. "She recovered quickly once we got her on the ground."

"Which we'd no sooner done than Jirana was screaming about you and how you were dead—" R'ney called from the distance. Xhinna guessed that he was tending to Mirressa.

"And you were," Jirana said, moving back into view, no longer dancing. She knelt down before Xhinna and grabbed her hand. "I saw it. You were dead."

"Well, not anymore," Jepara said briskly, moving to stand behind the younger queen rider. "And from now on, a little more telling and a little less dwelling, young lady!"

Jirana leaned her head back to rest against Jepara's stomach and met the eyes of the Weyrwoman looking sternly down at her.

"But I can't!" Jirana complained. She lowered her head and looked to Xhinna, then Lorana. "I can't break time."

"No," Jepara said, "but that doesn't mean you have to suffer in silence." The gold rider dropped down behind Jirana and wrapped her arms around her, leaning in close but speaking clearly enough for everyone to hear. "A burden shared is a burden lessened."

"Are you part of Sky?" Taria chimed in. Jirana looked her way and nodded once, firmly. "Then you talk to us."

"But—"

"We'll keep your secrets, little one," Xhinna said, annoyed that her voice was still so wispy. Jirana's eyes strayed to hers. A spark of understanding passed between them, and Xhinna's lips quirked. She raised a finger and beckoned the trader girl close enough to whisper, "If it worries you, try me first."

EPILOGUE
▼▼▼▼▼▼▼▼▼▼▼▼▼

Eight Months Later

Xhinna looked down at the sight arrayed below her. The sky was full of dragons. All six Western Weyrs had gathered here at Sky Weyr for the last time.

A white line on the sleeve of her wher-hide jacket distracted her and she moved her arm so she could, once again, count the twenty white lines—well, only ten on that arm; there were another ten on the other sleeve—that each marked a Fall flown by her and the Sky dragons.

Twenty Falls. Two casualties. And *no* burrows.

Cliova had joined Danirry in the Sky Weyr roll of honor after she and her green Bemorth had succumbed to the altitude sickness at a moment when the catchers had been busy elsewhere. Like Danirry before her, tragically, her absence had not been noted until it was too late. Her death had caused Xhinna to change her tactics—much to her personal annoyance even though to the relief of others—and now the wingleaders *all* flew with the catcher dragons, maintaining constant alert. Since then there had been no other losses.

Cliova's Bemorth had had a clutch on the sands, and her eighteen hatchlings were among the ninety-six others greeted fervently at the last Hatching of Sky Weyr.

The hatchlings and their weyrlings were all gone now, having been transported to Igen Weyr for eventual distribution to their "proper" Weyrs.

Even so, Xhinna was in the presence of over two thousand dragons, more than half of whom were ready and able, and blooded in the fight against Thread.

Jirana says: "You did it," Tazith relayed to her.

Xhinna shook her head firmly. She sought out and found the queen and her rider, nestled proudly in the great wings of the queen dragons that were arrayed below her.

Tell her, WE did it.

K'dan says for you to give the signal, Tazith relayed as he bugled triumphantly.

Me?

Lorana has given us the image, the blue dragon added, sensing the growing rebellion in his rider. *Are we ready?*

Behind her, Seban chuckled, having observed her and been the recipient of her dragon's thoughts. "He's twitting you and he's right," the ex-dragonrider shouted in her ear. He waved a hand down at the thousands of dragons below them. "It's your right—you've earned it, dragonrider."

Xhinna groaned, then joined in the ex-dragonrider's bellow of laughter.

You'd think, Xhinna mused, that by now I'd learn to give in gracefully.

Never, Tazith replied.

Very well, Xhinna said, taking one last, long, wistful look at the broom trees and the Weyr that had given them life. *Let's go.*

As one, on her command, the dragons of the Western Isle blinked out *between* to return, triumphant, to the fight to save Pern.

CHRONOLOGY OF THE
SECOND INTERVAL/THIRD PASS

DATE (AL)	EVENT	BOOK
492.4	Marriage: Terregar and Silstra	*Dragon's Kin*
493.10	Kisk Hatches	*Dragons' Kin*
494.1	Kindan to Harper Hall	*Dragon's Kin*
495.8	C'tov Impresses Sereth	*Dragon's Fire*
496.8	Plague Starts	*Dragonharper*
497.5	Plague Ends	*Dragonharper*
498.7.2	Fort Weyr riders arrive back in time at Igen Weyr	*Dragonsblood, Dragonheart*
501.3.18	Fort Weyr riders return from Igen Weyr	*Dragonheart*
507.11.17	Fiona Impresses Talenth	*Dragonheart*
507.12.20	Lorana Impresses Arith	*Dragonsblood*
508.1.7	Start of Third Pass	*Dragonsblood, Dragonheart*
508.1.19	Arith goes *between*	*Dragonsblood, Dragonheart*
508.1.27	Fort Weyr riders time it back ten Turns to Igen Weyr	*Dragonsblood, Dragonheart*
508.2.2	Fort Weyr riders return from Igen Weyr	*Dragonsblood, Dragonheart*
508.2.8	Telgar Weyr jumps to nowhere Fiona, T'mar, H'nez to Telgar Weyr Kindan, Fiona to Telgar Weyr	*Dragongirl*

On Pernese time:

The Pernese date their time from their arrival on Pern, referring to each Turn as "After Landing" (AL).

The Pernese calendar is composed of 13 months, each of 28 days (four weeks, or sevendays) with a special "Turnover" day at the end of each Turn for a total of 365 days.

ABOUT THE AUTHORS

ANNE MCCAFFREY wrote the very first Pern novel, *Dragon-flight,* more than forty years ago. She received a plethora of awards, including the Grand Master Nebula Award, and was inducted into the Science Fiction Hall of Fame.

She passed away in November 2011, leaving an immense following of dedicated fans worldwide.

TODD MCCAFFREY is Anne McCaffrey's middle child and has written three solo books on Pern as well as five collaborations with his mother, of which *Sky Dragons* is the last.

He and his sister, Georgeanne Kennedy, are the only two people designated by Anne McCaffrey to write in the Pern universe.

pernhome.com

ABOUT THE TYPE

This book is set in Palatino, designed by Hermann Zapf for the Stempel foundry in 1950. It is one of the most widely used typefaces in the world today. Classical Italian Renaissance letterforms blend with the crispness of line needed for twentieth-century printing processes, and Palatino's generous width aids readability at small sizes. Although Zapf originally intended it to be a display face, the graceful and highly legible Palatino is a frequent choice for setting text.